PRAISE FOR KAREN REDMAN

"Karen Redman's debut novel, *Flawed Judgment*, will thrill you with one plot twist after another."

DiAnn Mills, Bestselling Author of
DEADLY ENCOUNTER

FLAWED JUDGMENT

A Shana Doyle Mystery

KAREN REDMAN

Schuyler and Pfister Publishing

Publisher: Schuyler and Pfister Publishing

ISBN: 978-1-7377599-2-8

Cover design by Hannah Linder Designs

To my wonderful husband, who has been there every step of the way. Words cannot express how much his constant support has meant to me during this process. His encouragement, ideas, and most of all, his patience helped make this book a reality.

All my love.

CHAPTER 1

May 28th, 1999, Friday

SHE HAD MADE A MESS of her life, but tonight, it would all change. Adam had promised to meet her at his warehouse office to go to dinner to celebrate their twentieth wedding anniversary. She planned to surprise him with her one-week sobriety chip, to show him all his efforts over the years to get her into AA hadn't gone in vain.

Her favorite sundress lay on the bed. The navy-blue one that Adam had said made her look thin. She opened her bureau drawer and pulled out a set of underwear. A full bottle of Crown Royal revealed itself, as though taunting her. She closed the drawer, letting the bottle stay as a reminder of what was...not what was going to be.

The card she picked out was still in the Hallmark bag. She pulled it out and placed the chip inside. Unable to find a pen in her nightstand, she checked Adam's. As she opened his drawer an envelope with an attorney's name caught her eye. She cautiously opened it. All the excitement about the evening flew out of her body. She collapsed onto the bed. Divorce papers. How could she face him tonight? With tears in her eyes, she turned and stared at her bureau.

She woke chilled, sprawled out on a cold floor. Her mouth hung open and saliva dripped out. She licked her lips. The air was thick with the powerful scent of rubber. She slowly opened her eyes and snapped them shut to stop the whirling images of the flickering fluorescent lights high above. How had she gotten to Adam's warehouse?

An ache pierced the back of her head, radiating down her neck, and a fiery pain spread over her face, much like a wicked hangover, but worse. She turned on her side and moaned.

Through cloudy vision, she saw automobile tires stacked floor to ceiling. A forklift parked by the entrance. The large wall clock above the corner offices seemed to dance in circles. She squeezed her eyes and looked at the clock again—7:35. What happened tonight? She remembered leaving the house around 5:00 to meet Adam, but everything after that was a blur.

Where was Adam? He never broke a promise. Then it rushed back to her. The divorce papers. The Crown Royal. Her throat tightened as her eyes welled. Had Adam seen her drunk and left? How could she save her marriage now?

She blinked the tears away to focus. Light streamed from the corner office next to Adam's. Pieces of her memory returned. Two men were talking in there earlier. A shadowy figure paced back and forth. Fear clutched her chest. Something didn't feel right. An urgency to get away surged through her.

Crawling to a steel pole, her hand brushed through a sticky, gel-like substance. Ignoring it, she reached the pole and struggled to pull herself up. Her head pounded. She touched the back of her head and flinched. Blood stained her fingertips.

The screech of rusty hinges weighed heavily in the air. A door slammed, echoing metal against metal. Shoes thudded on the concrete. She painfully squinted in the sound's direction. Oh, Adam, let it be you.

The footsteps grew closer.

A blurry, tall figure approached her.

She tried to clear her vision.

It wasn't Adam.

Without warning, a closed fist smacked her hard. Her face burned and the taste of blood swirled through her mouth. She let go of the pole and crumbled to the concrete. Barely conscious, she kept perfectly still, daring not to move.

A door opened from the direction of the office. Rubber soles squeaked, racing toward her. A high-pitched voice called out. "Stop hitting her."

"Relax. She's out cold," a deep voice said. "What do you want me to do with her?"

Where had she heard that voice?

"I found her car keys," the high-pitched voice said.

"I'll get someone to come for it."

If her car was gone, Adam would never know she came to meet him.

The high-pitched voice cracked. "We need to keep her out of circulation for a while."

Out of circulation? What did he mean? Who were these men?

"Limo's out back," the deep voice said. "I left bleach by the door. Clean up any sign of blood."

She wanted to run, but how could she without them stopping her? Keeping up the pretense of being unconscious, she kept her body still.

Clammy hands slipped under her armpits and tugged on her sundress. Goosebumps tingled her flesh.

The man with the deep voice sniffed. "Whoa! Do you smell that?" His fruity, warm breath sprayed on her face. "What the hell is on her? It's sickening."

"Never mind. Let's get her out of here." The other man grabbed her ankles. His voice strained. "Damn, she's heavy."

The jarring caused a painful clawing at the back of her eyes. She bit her lip to prevent making a sound. Within seconds, the screech of hinges and the warm night air bathed her face. The metal door banged from behind and she flinched, hoping the men carrying her hadn't noticed.

The deep-voiced man's breathing became sporadic. "Put...her down."

"You okay? What's wrong?"

"I'm fine. Just put her down."

The gravel scratched her bare arms. A click met her ears. They flung her onto a hard surface, and she couldn't help but groan. Feeling the prickly carpet beneath her—it must be a trunk of a car. The latch connected, and the light faded. Their voices grew faint outside her confined space.

"She's awake," the high-pitched voice said.

Footsteps crunched and a car door opened.

"I'll take care of her," the deep voice said, and the car door closed.

Lying in the blackness, she banged on the roof of the trunk, hoping to plead with the remaining man. "Please let me out!"

The engine started. Frantically, she banged again—screaming. "Can you hear me? Help me...please."

The muffled sound of a heavy metal rock song blared and cut the roar of the motor coming through the tailpipe. She stopped banging. What was the use?

She massaged her hands and jerked her head away from the offensive odor. The disgusting slime she picked up from the warehouse floor clung to her hand. She gagged and swallowed hard to fight back the urge to vomit. The acid from the whiskey burned the back of her throat.

The car sped up and swerved from side to side, tossing her against the spare tire. She sucked in a deep breath, but the stale air pinched her throat and she coughed. Beads of sweat dripped down her temples.

The music ended. Traveling along a straight stretch of road, a sudden dread jolted her. Had those men done something to Adam? She sobbed, praying for his safety. Tears poured from the corners of her swollen eyes, fearing she might never see him again.

The song played again, only louder, and the speakers vibrated. The driver's off-key voice sang along, drowning out the lyrics. With a sharp turn and a sudden stop, her body thrust forward. She winced. The engine died, ending the music, the song still ringing in her ears. A car door opened and slammed. Seconds later, a key scratched the lock. Her heart beat so fast it felt like it would explode.

The trunk lid rose. She lifted her head and tried to adjust her eyesight to the light.

"You stupid bitch," he said. "If only you had stayed unconscious."

She struggled to breathe. "Please…please let me go. I won't say anything."

"What do you take me for? You already heard too much."

"Please—"

"It's way past that now. You know who I am."

She blinked to make out the man glaring down at her. "I know you? No, I—"

His face. It all rushed back to her now.

CHAPTER 2

Five Days Later
June 2nd, Wednesday

DETECTIVE SHANA DOYLE stood in the kitchen of her Rittenhouse Square third floor walk-up in Philadelphia, wearing her workout shorts and worn Penn State T-shirt, ready for her ritual after she closed a murder case. A brisk two-mile walk, followed by solving one of her cryptograms, always cleared her mind. But this time, it might take a longer walk and more than one of her crypts to do the trick. The image of her latest case, the murder of an eight-year-old abused girl, had haunted her all week. She couldn't get it out of her mind. The little girl lying on her kitchen floor, her long golden hair sucking up a pool of her blood, while her mother screamed in tears.

The smell of freshly brewed coffee crept into her nostrils and diverted her attention. She poured a cup and shook her head to wipe out the visual. She hadn't gotten a good night's sleep since the case started, and her body felt it. Handling murders of adults was one thing, but a child? Her eyes grew moist, and she blinked to clear them.

One year as a patrol officer and five as a homicide detective was long enough to see just about everything. She considered herself strong, from what she had to endure with a terrible marriage and raising two girls with their absentee father after the divorce. But now, at forty-seven, a murder of a child crushed her. It was cases like this recent one when she wondered if she made the right decision to change careers to join law enforcement six years ago. Everyone thought she was nuts and at times she could agree with them. But then bringing a murderer, like this little girl's father, to justice made it all worthwhile.

She took a sip of coffee before she made her way to the living room. While she sat at her antique desk, inherited from her favorite aunt, she leafed through the mail from the week. The blinking red light on the answering machine caught her eye. She hadn't noticed it last night, drained from the murdered girl's case, she'd gone straight to bed. She pressed the play button.

Hey, Shana. Getting the gang together Friday night at PJ's. We've missed you. Hope you can make it this time. It's been too long. Please try.

Jules's message wasn't the first one and probably wouldn't be the last. Shana thought of the gang. Her close friends since high school: Madeline, Ros, Jules, and their husbands. All whom she'd distanced herself from over the last several months, for reasons only she and her shrink knew.

She glanced at the silver bifold frame at the corner of her desk. Her two grown daughters were on one side. On the other, her parents' photo taken before their horrific car accident. She used that term loosely in her mind—accident.

The desk clock displayed 7:10 a.m. Still weary from lack of sleep…maybe the walk could wait. She pulled open the desk drawer. The rubber-banded stack of cryptograms she'd accumulated from the Sunday *Messenger* was in its usual spot. She picked up the stack. Beneath it lay a manilla file with information on her parents' accident. It had curled edges, smudges of coffee stains, and had grown thicker since their deaths almost seven months ago. She stared at the file for several seconds and recalled what the shrink had told her. Out of sight. Out of mind. Why hadn't she listened?

Her cell vibrated on the desk, which she'd left that way from last night, hoping to isolate herself this morning. She ignored the call, and it finally stopped, but then the vibration started again. Placing the crypts on the desk, she flipped open her cell and recognized the number. "Damn it!" She groaned, knowing she had to take the call.

"They found a body in an alley off Snyder," the dispatcher said.

Shana sat back hard. "Is anyone else available?"

"All the guys are out on cases."

Her posture sagged, and she wrote down the address dispatch gave her. "I'll get there as soon as I can."

CHAPTER 3

June 2nd, Wednesday

DRIVING TO THE CRIME SCENE, Shana cranked the air at full blast and turned up the volume on the radio talk show. "Hottest morning since 1995. Heat index 105," the voice said. "Special report coming up next. Y2K fears—will your data be safe when computers turn from the year 1999 to 2000. Stay tuned."

"Oh my God. Enough already with the Y2K." She silenced the radio and shook her head, wondering why programmers only allowed two digits for a year. Like the year 2000 would never come?

Twenty minutes later, Shana passed South Philadelphia High School and arrived at the scene. She parked behind forensics' blue SUV, a patrol car, and the coroner's white van. Stepping out of her car, she cursed the homicide dress code when the oppressive heat slapped her in the face. She slipped on her jacket and reached for a barrette from the inside pocket. Shortly after she became a detective, she had pockets sewn inside all her on-the-job jackets to hold personal items to avoid carrying a purse while working.

Only a few spectators milled about. Logan McIntyre approached. The *Messenger's* crime reporter and her friend Jules's husband. His groomed sandy hair and sharp features caused him to resemble a young Robert Redford, except for the receding hairline that now glistened from perspiration.

"First on the scene, I see." Shana clipped her hair up behind her head. "Bloodhound on the scent?"

"Woof-Woof," he said, giving her the once over. "Did you do something different with your hair? It's lighter."

The only time she saw him now was at a crime scene.

"I had blonde streaks added last week," she said.

His pen and pad in hand, ready to write. "So, what's going on?"

"I have a scene to process."

He put his pad in his shirt pocket. "I'll be here."

"Of course you will."

She headed toward the trash truck backed in the alley and scrunched her nose from the sickening stench of an odor, like raw chicken beyond its expiration date, that hung heavy in the air. Undoubtedly worsened with the humidity at an all-time high. She cupped her hand over her nose as she stepped her black sneakers over unrecognizable dark, furry clumps and around puddles of unknown origins.

A young officer wearing a surgical mask stepped close. Shana flashed her badge, and he handed her a mask.

"Got these from the coroner, ma'am," he said. "It's rancid back there."

When did she become a ma'am? "What happened?" She placed on the mask and slipped on latex gloves from her side jacket pocket.

"Two trashmen found a naked female body in a dumpster."

Shana slipped on shoe booties, adjusting her slacks over them, and followed the officer. They ducked under the crime scene tape and walked between the building and the trash truck. Overhead, a rusted light hung above a rear entrance at one of the restaurants and crackled as it flickered on and off. Tall brick buildings blocked the sunlight, giving some relief from the heated morning, but denied any hope of a breeze. They reached an open area behind the truck. The air felt stifling, like sliding into a heated car that had sat in the hot sun for hours. Beads of sweat formed on her forehead.

The forensic team was busy working the scene. Men wearing white jumpsuits and surgical masks scurried about taking pictures.

"The coroner's on the other side of the truck." The officer pointed to the two trashmen near the dumpster. "They're the ones that found the victim. The older man claims he smelled something odd on the body."

Shana cocked her head. "Are you kidding me? How odd?"

"He didn't say."

She studied the men and turned to the officer. "I'll question them later."

"I got contact information from the spectators and the trashmen." The officer handed her a page from his notepad. "None of the spectators saw anything."

"Any surveillance cameras in the alley?"

"No. There weren't any in the surrounding areas either."

Sergeant Frank Ellis, a tight figure of a man in his mid-forties wearing his uniformed short-sleeve whites, stepped around the truck. He carefully tip-toed with his shoe booties over the clumps of trash as the officer passed him and handed him a mask.

"What are you doing here, Sarge?" Shana said.

"Whew. This stench is horrible." He slipped on the mask. "A little shorthanded. I'm here until I can assign you another detective."

In between partners at the moment, she hoped whoever he assigned would not be her old partner, Russell Fits.

Sarge snapped on gloves. "Give me an update, Doyle."

"Female naked body, no witnesses, except for the two

trashmen." She pointed in their direction. "One claims he smelled something odd on the body."

"Really?" He looked over at the men. "Let's see what Mac has for us first."

The chief medical examiner, Dr. Malcolm Boyd, stood over the body wearing his black coroner jumpsuit. He'd only been in his position six months and insisted everyone be on a first-name basis. A fresh change from the previous chief. Sweat dripped down the sides of his face from his white wavy hair into his trimmed salt and pepper beard.

He stopped writing and moved his mask below his chin. "Hey, Frank. Good, you have a mask. Garbage smell…tough."

Sarge chuckled. "Plus, the dead body odor."

Mac peered over his reading glasses and smiled. "Morning Shana."

She dismissed the familiar look, one he'd given her before, and nodded back. "Morning Mac. Did you find any unusual odors?"

"If you're referring to what the trashman said, nothing other than the typical body stench and garbage."

Sarge glanced down at the body. "What else do you have?"

Mac clipped his pen to the top of the clipboard and held it to his side. "Someone wanted to hide this woman's identity, that's for sure. All her teeth were extracted. Cleanly, I might add. Fingernails cut to the skin. Numerous bruises and cuts showed she'd been badly beaten. There was a contusion at the back of her head. Based on the blowfly larvae, her liver temperature, and the decomposition of the body, I would say the time of death was about four days ago. We're done here if you want to take a look."

Shana squatted and inspected the heavy-set woman. Her large breasts leaned to each side. Dried blood-stained hair stuck to the side of her face, partially hiding the open wounds. Blood foam leaked from her mouth and nose. Her lips were sunken in.

Nails were clipped to the stub. Dried blood by her nail roots and black burnt marks on each fingertip. No wedding ring.

"You're right," Shana said. "Someone definitely wanted to hide her identity." She shook her head and continued to scan the body. "Another senseless death. Strange, she ended up here. Any distinguishing marks?"

"Two toes are missing on the right foot," Mac said. "Old wounds."

Mac's assistant Jonesy, a scrawny young man, lifted the bottom of the body bag that had draped the victim's feet.

Shana eased the victim's hair away from her face.

"Any questions?" Mac said.

She shifted her gaze from the woman's face to her feet. A sudden sadness crept over her. Could it be—

"Doyle...questions?" Sarge said.

"Oh, sorry. What did you say?"

"Do you have questions?"

"Ah...no." She blew out a slow breath and stood. "I think I know who she is."

CHAPTER 4

June 2nd, Wednesday

SHANA RUBBED THE DAMP nape of her neck and fixated on Jonesy, zipping up the body bag.

"Doyle. So, who's the victim?" Sarge said.

"Oh…I think she might be a high school classmate of mine, Eileen Detweiler."

"You think? Didn't you recognize her?"

"Not the way she looks now." Shana remembered Eileen's figure thirty years ago in high school. Petite, big-breasted, a popular item with the boys. "Last time I saw her or her husband was at their wedding twenty years ago. A couple of days before the ceremony, she dropped a knife, severing two toes on her right foot."

"No ID?" Sarge said.

Mac shook his head. "None that we could find."

"Then she's a Jane Doe."

Mac packed up his satchel and removed his reading glasses, placing them in his chest pocket. "Hate these Jane Doe cases."

The sweat trickled through Shana's scalp like little ants running through her hair. As Mac and Jonesy struggled to carry the full body bag between the truck and the building, she felt somewhat numb, wondering if her suspicion was correct.

Sarge wiped the sweat from his forehead with the back of his wrist. "Let's question the trashmen."

They passed the forensic team, still busy sifting through the garbage, and reached the men near the dumpster, who weren't shielding anything over their nose or mouth. One of them visibly older than the other. Both were about the same height, dressed in navy blue overalls with the city's emblem. Their faces were shiny from sweat. Shana felt sympathy for them in their heavy uniforms in the oppressive heat. But they didn't seem to mind. She introduced herself and Sarge.

Shana pulled her tape recorder from her jacket pocket and proceeded with her standard process of recording her interviews, which helped her transcribe more detailed case notes. Voice inflections were something she couldn't put on paper.

She faced the men and talked through her mask. "I'm going to record this, okay?"

"No problem," the older man said.

She pressed record. "Please state your names and how you found the body."

The older man stepped forward. "I'm Bill Roberts." He pointed to the other man. "And this is my partner, Timmy Finley. He doesn't like to talk much, so ask me your questions."

The shy younger man nodded.

Knowing witnesses at crime scenes could be unreliable, suspecting the victim could be her classmate, Shana hoped the older man would detail his recollection.

"Mr. Roberts, tell us what happened, and *please* be specific."

"Did the cop tell you I smelled a weird odor?"

"Yes. Can you describe it?"

"A strong skunk-like sulfur smell. But not exactly. I've seen and smelled a lot of things collecting trash in the last thirty-five years. Smelled nothing like it before, even when I found a couple of dead bodies."

Shana pulled her sweaty mask down away from her face, airing it out. She took a breath and rested it back.

The younger trashman leaned over and whispered in Mr. Roberts's ear.

"Does he have something to say about what you found?" Shana said.

"It's nothing."

"Let me decide if it's nothing."

Mr. Roberts rolled his eyes. "All right...Timmy said you're a real looker."

His partner blushed and lowered his head.

What an odd comment to make at a crime scene, but Shana took it as a compliment and gave a slight smile. "Let's continue, Mr. Roberts. Could you identify the odor if you smelled it again?"

"You betcha. Heaven knows this is not the time to brag, but my nickname is the 'nose' at the company. They have contests trying to stump me. To most people, trash smells like trash, but if you dump a pile of trash in front of me, I can tell what's in it."

His partner nodded again.

Shana turned her attention to Mr. Roberts. "What else can you tell us?"

"Well, there was this one time, I smelled the difference between a rotten banana and rotten cucumber—"

"No." Shana grinned. "What I mean is about the crime scene."

"Oh. Timmy and me always get to the 6th Street dumpster at about 5:30 on Monday, Wednesday, and Friday mornings. We were late today cos there was a traffic jam on 5th Street."

"What time did you get here?"

Mr. Roberts checked his watch. "Boy, is my wife gonna be pissed. I was supposed to take her to breakfast. It's almost 9:00. Anyway, got here around 6:30. We backed up the truck like we always do. I got out and walked around to the dumpster. That's how we do it. Timmy drives and I direct his backup. Then I started the lever for the lift."

"The lift?"

"The two arms that fit into the dumpster. When the lift was in place, Timmy came out to help me and stood on the runner on the other side of the truck. Sometimes trash falls out and we have poles to jam it into the back of the truck. The dumpster was full. Didn't collect trash this past Monday cos of the holiday. It was halfway in the air, and when the lid opened, I saw an arm. I yelled for Timmy to stop, but he couldn't hear me with the lift running. The dumpster was upside down when he finally saw me."

"Yep." The younger man finally spoke.

Mr. Roberts eyed his watch again. "I should call my wife. How much longer is this going to take? We need to finish our route."

Shana moved her recorder to her other hand. "Not too much longer. What happened next?"

"After we dumped most of the trash, the woman's arm waved in front of my face. That's when I noticed the odor, and then the body fell out and hit the ground. I called the cops."

Shana turned to Sarge. "Any questions?"

"No. You covered it all."

"Let me know if you want me to do a smell test," Mr. Roberts said.

Shana held back a smile, thinking about the prospect. "We'll be in touch if we have any more questions." She stopped the recorder and handed Mr. Roberts her card. "You guys are free to go."

On the way out of the alley, Sarge gave the go-ahead for forensics to leave. He and Shana removed their masks, gloves, and shoe booties and handed them to the officer while Sarge instructed him to secure the scene. Shana licked the salty sweat from her upper lip, still wondering if the victim could be Eileen. Reporters hustled over. The officer rushed over and yelled for them to step back. Questions rang out.

Logan pushed through the other reporters and called out. "What's going on, Sergeant Ellis?"

Sarge stepped closer to the crowd. "A woman's body was found in a dumpster. We need to wait for the coroner's report."

Logan pressed on. "Who was the victim?"

"No further comment," Sarge said and walked back to Shana.

The other reporters shouted more questions. Shana flashed a hand stop and followed Sarge to his car out of earshot of others.

Sarge faced Shana and folded his arms. "Doyle, how confident are you that this body is your classmate?"

"Too much of a coincidence about the missing toes."

"Check with Missing Persons. See if they have any recent reports that fit the description of the victim. Let's cover all the bases."

Sweat trickled down the sides of Shana's face and she brushed it away. "Damn heat! Sarge, what do you think about Mr. Roberts? He was pretty detailed. Sounded convincing about the odor."

Sarge rubbed his military-style buzz cut in his thinking mode and quickly stopped. He looked at the dampness on his hand and wiped it on his black trousers. "I've seen and heard a lot of things in my over twenty years on the force, but this takes the cake. We're in an alley filled with garbage. A dead body that's who knows how old. Hot as hell out here and this guy mentions a weird odor. Go to the morgue and see what Mac comes up with."

Witnessing an autopsy wasn't high on Shana's list of things she liked about her job, but believing this victim could be Eileen, she almost looked forward to it.

CHAPTER 5

June 2nd, Wednesday

TREVOR RICHMOND TOOK the elevator from the garage level to the fifth floor of the Mellon Independence Center on Market Street, known as the MIC building. He carried a box of donuts and entered the small two-office suite he shared with his wife Madeline while she campaigned for state senate in Pennsylvania's District 7.

He said good morning to their secretary Iris, a round figure of a woman, whom Madeline brought with her from the marketing firm when she left.

Iris stared at the donut box as Trevor handed it to her.

"Thank you, Mr. Richmond. Did they have any chocolate croissants?"

"They only had one. It's on top."

She lifted the lid. The chocolate and freshly made donut scent drifted out. She grabbed a croissant and handed him his messages.

He glanced at the first one. "Adam Detweiler called?"

Iris took a bite and moved the croissant to the side of her mouth. "Yes. He said he wanted to come in this afternoon to see you, but I didn't know your schedule." She swallowed. "He asked that you call him at home."

Trevor studied the rest of his messages as he entered

Madeline's office. She stood from behind her walnut desk bordered by a deep burgundy and hunter-green mosaic rug.

"Hi, honey," she said. "Things are going great with the campaign. I have a good feeling about the election."

He envied her enthusiasm, even in the face of a difficult situation like running against a seasoned politician. "I'm glad you're optimistic."

She made her way toward him and stood close, meeting him eye to eye. "Oh hon…Don't be so serious all the time." She gave him a peck on the lips.

After all these years, Trevor still admired her beauty. Her blonde bob never had a hair out of place, her makeup impeccably applied. The tasteful gold jewelry and Ralph Lauren clothes complimented her trim body but hurt his wallet. They sat on the microfiber cream couch, under the large signed lithograph of LeRoy Neiman's painting of *Tavern on the Green*.

"I handed over my last case at the law firm," Trevor said. "I'm all yours now."

"That's great. This must've been hard to take that sabbatical. I hope this doesn't hurt your business."

"Don't be silly. This is a great opportunity for you. I'm so proud of you for taking this on. And don't worry about the law firm. Being the owner has its perks."

"That reminds me. We leased this center city office space because it was down the street from your firm. Since the campaign is taking off, we should look into larger spaces. We're going to need more room for volunteers."

He smiled. "You took the words right out of my mouth. We should get some space in your district. I'm thinking Chestnut Hill, near home. Get Iris to look into it. You didn't say anything about my haircut."

She stared at him. "Oh. It looks great. With your hair slicked back like that, makes it look a much deeper black."

"You better *love* it for those prices. It was your idea."

Trevor would do anything for Madeline, right down to changing his hairstyle.

He pointed to his head. "This isn't exactly a haircut when only a fraction of my hair was on the salon's floor." Trevor sniffed. "New perfume?"

"Do you like it?"

His nostrils flared. "Smells earthy, like that oil you used to wear. Patchouli, wasn't it?" He glared at her. "So how much did this new perfume cost?"

"Not too much. Only $45.00 an ounce."

"What! Shit, Maddie. You can't keep spending like this. And while we're talking about it, this haircut," he gestured air quotes, "is out of our price range. With you leaving the marketing firm and my sabbatical, our savings won't last long. We've already gone through most of the money I got from my old firm for that lawsuit settlement."

Her features tightened taking on a more serious tone. "What about the fundraiser last month?

"Remember that was almost a break-even."

"How about your law firm?"

"Sorry, Maddie. Any profits won't be distributed until after the first quarter of next year."

She raised her eyebrows. "And your companies?"

Little did she know, TR Tires is in the red, and RedChem showed barely a profit. "I can't take out money from a corporation for a political campaign. Let's see how much the next fundraiser will net us."

Madeline crossed her legs. "I've been doing some reading on a new campaign fundraising process. Getting donations through the internet. I think that would work for us."

"Sounds like a good idea, but we'd have to hire a tech person which we can't afford. Adam wanted to meet me this afternoon.

Maybe he'll have some ideas?"

"Why is he coming in?"

"Don't know. He wants me to call him at home."

She rested her arm on the back of the couch. "Still pisses me off Jenkins is going to run again."

Senator Curt Jenkins has been the senator in District 7 for sixteen years. He announced his retirement last year but withdrew it after Madeline entered the race.

"From what I hear," she said, "if I weren't a woman, he would've retired."

"Ignore the rumors."

Madeline shook her head. "Hard to do. That man hasn't made any changes in his district since his first year and he's over seventy. It's time for him to move on."

"We've gone over this before, Maddie. Let's focus on the fundraiser coming up."

She faced him. "There's something from last month's fundraiser I wanted to talk to you about. I don't know why I didn't think of it until now."

Trevor leafed through his pink message slips, half listening. "Yeah. What's that?"

"Eileen tried to warn me about something."

He clenched the slips tight. Pain flared in his upper stomach. "Warn you about what?"

"We were in the ladies' lounge. Her speech was slurred, but I'm positive I heard her right."

He stared at the pink slips, not registering any names or numbers.

Madeline patted his leg. "You need to listen. I'm sure she said my campaign is in trouble. I asked her what she meant, and she said I'd have to wait and see. Something about the way she said it concerned me. I tried to talk to her later, but Adam had already gotten her out of there."

Trevor hid a slow, deep breath and stopped focusing on the messages. "Maddie, it was probably nothing. She was drunk. Have you heard from the kids?"

She stared at the floor.

"Maddie. Did you hear me? Any word from the kids?"

"Oh…yes." She faced him. "Exciting news. Both of them will be home in August. Can't wait to see them."

"Me too."

Madeline gave Trevor an intense stare. "I can't shake the feeling about what Eileen may have wanted to tell me."

He kissed her cheek. "Let's focus on your fundraiser at the end of this month."

In his office across the hall, Trevor threw the message slips in his trash can, knowing if any were important, they'd call back. He dropped into his leather desk chair and swiveled around facing the oil painting of a river scene, from an unknown artist that covered the wall safe left from the previous tenant. His stomach burned, visualizing inside the safe. Could Adam have gotten a call from the blackmailers too? Could that be why Adam wanted to meet him today?

Trevor massaged below his rib cage and reached into his pocket for the roll of lemon-flavored Tums and popped two. He chewed quickly to minimize the citrus taste at the back of his mouth. The last time the blackmailers contacted him was the Friday before Memorial Day. The deep raspy voice on the phone had told him to wait for instructions, but they never came.

CHAPTER 6

June 2nd, Wednesday

WHEELS ROLLED INTO the wall and the metal door clicked shut on drawer H15, ending the final chapter of the life of Shana's latest victim, Jane Doe. It was almost noon when the autopsy on the woman had ended. Even with no positive ID, Shana's gut told her it was Eileen, and her gut was usually right. The sound of voices from the other pathologists and clanking instruments echoed in the adjoining room. She removed her mask, stepped to the sink, pulled a paper towel from the wall dispenser, and wiped the Vicks from under her nose.

When she entered Mac's office down the hall to wait for the written report, the smell of burnt coffee drifted out. The burner on top of the filing cabinet was still on, and the glass pot had turned almost black. Shana turned it off and sunk in the worn couch. She pulled out her recorder, switched out the interview tape of Mr. Roberts to a blank one. Recording her thoughts and transcribing them onto what she called her notes disk helped her to be more effective in analyzing an ongoing investigation. She dictated.

"*Note to myself: There was something about the trashman. Check on him with his company. Could he have smelled a unique odor? Did it exist? Odor not found in the autopsy. No official ID of the victim. Missing toes…It must be Eileen.*"

She stopped recording and made her way to the large double glass door bookcase behind Mac's desk filled with numerous anatomy books. New items had been added. A dark wooden frame with a group photo of him and, most likely, his wife with their four children. Next to it, a small photo of a little boy in a simple silver frame engraved grandchild. Her eyes widened. "Grandchild?" She had thought there would be an age difference between them, but a grandchild?

Another frame held a photo of a much younger Mac in Army fatigues. On the wall to the right of the bookshelf hung a plaque. She studied it. Special citation, dated 1990, for exemplary service awarded to Dr. Malcolm Boyd, Forensic Pathologist, City of Philadelphia.

Mac entered, and she turned to face him.

He sniffed and glanced at the coffee pot. "Was that thing on?"

"Yes. I turned it off."

"Thanks."

He stepped nearer and stood a full head taller than her, about six-foot-two or three. "I see you were reading my award." He placed a file on his desk. "Just got around to getting my personal items unpacked."

"I didn't know you worked here before. What was the award?"

He looked at the plaque. "Frank and I worked on a project together and we both earned that citation."

"Sarge doesn't have his plaque hanging in his office."

"He's a bare-bones kinda guy."

"Tell me about the project?"

"We were assigned to help with the closure of the mental institution, Byberry, in Northeast Philadelphia. The conditions were horrible. It reminded me of some war zones in Vietnam. I was part of the medical team to move the patients to a nearby reputable facility. Frank was a detective then. He helped with the background on some patients and discovered a teenage boy who had a seizure and never regained his memory. The boy fit the age progression of a ten-year-old, who went missing nine years prior on one of Frank's unsolved cases."

"That's sad. But good he found the boy."

"Frank became a sergeant after that and I accepted an offer for the chief medical examiner in Baltimore."

"So why come back to Philly?"

He turned to the family group photo, face void of expression. "My wife Faye died almost four years ago from breast cancer."

"How horrible…I'm sorry."

"Thanks. My kids live near the city now. So, when the chief here retired, I applied."

She turned to the photos again. "You have a grandchild?"

"Yes. A grandson." A grin spread across his face. "Wondering how old I am? Don't let the color of my hair fool you. I started turning gray in high school. In case you're wondering, I'm forty-eight."

It was as if he read her mind. "Wasn't wondering, but thanks for the info. Tell me about your grandson."

Mac beamed. "What a spitfire. He just turned two. Lots of energy." His smile faded. "Sorry to say my wife Faye will never meet him."

That look. She felt his sadness, remembering her father in the hospital before he died, with tubes coming out of every part of his body. She knew only too well how those feelings can stay with you.

Mac handed her the autopsy file. She read the condensed version at the top portion of the report. Blood type O, height 5'2", weight 180 pounds. Based on her bones, estimated age to be between 45-47.

Her age. Another clue the woman could be Eileen. Shana faced Mac. "Date of death, May 28th. The time is missing."

"I suspect late on that date, but I can't be sure. The amount of alcohol in her system made it difficult to determine."

She turned the page. "You have here the preliminary cause of death as alcohol poisoning."

"The tox won't be back for a while, but I don't think my findings will change. Even factoring in the ethanol levels that would increase postmortem, her BAC was dangerously high enough to cause her death. Her liver showed signs of cirrhosis. The needle puncture I found in the fold of her elbow had traces of alcohol. An injection of alcohol would explain her high levels. What's puzzling is the puncture hole also had traces of insulin, but no evidence the victim had diabetes."

"Could the contusion at the back of her head have anything to do with her death?"

"She had a slight concussion, possibly from a fall. With her alcohol levels, it might have contributed. I sent the small fiber I found under her left nail bed out for further analysis, but I suspect it's from a carpet of some kind."

"And the fingerprints burnt off?"

"No substance found around her fingers."

Shana closed the file. "What's your thoughts about the odor Mr. Roberts claimed he smelled? Do you think any of those unidentified substances you found on the body could've caused the odor he described?"

"I'm not sure. In my experience, based on where she was found, the items could be anything from animal feces to human urine. Who knows what she picked up from either the trash or the alley when she fell? Forensics is working on the analysis and will contact us if anything is out of the ordinary. Do you think the victim could be your classmate?"

"I'm leaning that way."

"Not that I want the victim to be your classmate, but it would be one less Jane Doe. I sent over a copy of the report to Frank. It's officially a homicide."

CHAPTER 7

June 2nd, Wednesday

SHANA DROVE INTO the parking lot of police headquarters off Race Street, known as the roundhouse, a concrete structure shaped like a set of handcuffs. The building design was groundbreaking back in the '60s and a staple topic at the academy. In the elevator heading for homicide, she tried to push the autopsy out of her mind, as best she could. But suspecting the victim might be Eileen, the sound of her ribs being cut had sent a chill through her that still lingered.

The doors slid open on the fourth floor. Dylan Holden from IT, a tall lanky young man with thick-rimmed glasses, entered as Shana stepped out.

"All checked out Detective Doyle." He pushed his glasses up the bridge of his nose. "Diagnostics were successful."

"Glad to hear it."

She wasn't sure what diagnostics meant but guessed it had something to do with the year 2000 scare.

The cubicles in homicide were small, grouped in sets of two, and void of personal items. Privacy was non-existent with detectives moving about, but Shana could zone them out when she worked on a case. A benefit she gained in raising two girls. A black ribbon, with the words rest in peace, hung on the empty cubicle wall next to hers. The practical joke started when her first partner, Russell Fits, left her after he told his buddies he wanted to be re-assigned to a man. Now waiting for her fourth partner, she learned to ignore the ribbons.

She plopped onto her mesh support chair, slipped on headphones, and transcribed key highlights from Mr. Roberts's interview. After she saved the document in the folder named Murder Case date code 06021999 to the hard drive, she placed a printed copy in the case book. When she returned to her desk, a file lay on top with large black lettering—Missing Persons Division. Of all the times she wanted her gut to be wrong, it was now. She opened it slowly. Her stomach knotted when she saw the name Eileen Detweiler printed at the top of the report. On the second line under distinguishing marks, missing fourth and fifth toes on the right foot. She took a heavy sigh. No doubt in her mind now, the Jane Doe was Eileen.

The filing date of May 31st caught Shana's eye. Based on the date of death of May 28th, Eileen was already dead. The photo in the back of the file, of a heavyset woman with graying hair, looked older than her forty-seven years. No wonder Shana didn't recognize her.

A clerk from dispatch approached and handed Shana two pink message slips. She read them. They were both from Adam Detweiler, Eileen's husband.

"Hold on." Shana stopped the clerk from leaving. "There's no message, no number. Did he say anything?"

"Only that he would call you back, which you can see he did."

"Why didn't you call me?" She scolded.

The clerk backed off. "I asked him if I should contact you and he said he would call you."

He left and Shana stared at the messages. Time-stamped one at 8:00 this morning and the other an hour later. Why would Adam call her after twenty years and why today?

Her phone rang. She stared at it fearing it might be Adam. What would she say? She cautiously answered.

"I'm not asking for a statement about this morning," Logan said.

Relieved it wasn't Adam, she let out a quiet sigh. "Then why are you calling?"

"I found out the woman in the dumpster had two missing toes on her right foot."

She gritted her teeth. "Who gave you that information?"

"Never mind. It's Eileen Detweiler, isn't it?"

"What makes you say that?"

"Because Adam called me two days ago, frantic that Eileen had been missing, and it wasn't like her usual disappearance. With the missing toes, it has to be her."

Logan received a call too. She glanced at her desk calendar. Two days ago, would be the 31st. The day Adam filed a report with Missing Persons. Her curiosity peeked. "What do you mean by usual disappearance?"

"Oh, that's right. We haven't seen you in a while, so you wouldn't have known. Adam confided in me on our fishing trip two months ago that Eileen had a drinking and gambling problem. She took those bus trips to the casinos in Atlantic City. Sometimes she would be missing for a day or two, but on the call, he said this time it was longer."

"How long has this been going on?"

"Adam didn't say, but I got the impression it's been building up over time. He blamed himself for the long hours he put in at TR Tires and he said things got worse when he accepted to work with Madeline on her campaign."

"He worked with Madeline?"

"Another thing you missed. He started about a few months ago as a liaison between the unions and her campaign."

Logan getting his digs in about her not seeing the gang lately cut to the bone. She couldn't seem to stop immersing herself in her murder cases, leaving little time to herself, let alone her close friends. Transference neurosis is what her shrink called it. Obsessed with solving crimes, if she couldn't solve the reason for her parents' supposed accident.

She ignored Logan's comment about what she missed and focused on his call with Adam. "What else did Adam say?"

"When I asked him what he wanted me to do, he hesitated. It seemed he wanted to tell me something, but then he quickly ended the call. After what I found out from my contact at the morgue, I almost called Adam, but thought I should talk to you first."

"Good call. Please don't call him."

"Then it is Eileen," he blurted.

"Let me do my job."

He lowered his voice. "Exclusive...please."

His tone was serious. Unlike other times when he would make a joke out of it.

"I need to go," she said.

Although Logan gave her good information, Shana would want to hear it firsthand from Adam. She grabbed both files and her tape and headed for Sarge's office. A wooden L-shaped desk, two padded metal trimmed chairs, and a four-drawer metal filing cabinet in the corner. Orderly, like his military background. The ginger and fresh lemon scent from his protein drink filled his office, which he drank after his workouts. He stopped sipping on his clear plastic thermos and locked her recording of Mr. Roberts in his filing cabinet, as he did with all her interview tapes.

They discussed the autopsy report, and she handed him the Missing Person's file. "This confirms my suspicions. Jane Doe is Eileen Detweiler. She'd been missing since Friday, May 28th, which ties in with what Mac determined is the date of death.

What's strange is, her husband called me twice this morning, but I never connected with him."

"You said you hadn't seen or heard from them for twenty years. Why do you suppose the husband called you now?"

"I'll find out when I visit him."

Sarge opened the Missing Person's file. "Says here the husband reported her missing on May 31st. Find out why he waited so long." He rested back and closed the file. "Take Fits with you."

Her eyes popped. "What! Are you kidding me?" Remembering his open office door, she lowered her voice. "You promised I wouldn't have to work with him again."

"You've had three partners in the last three years."

She blew out a breath. "I knew when I joined homicide, I would have my work cut out for me, being the token female. But I didn't realize the amount of male chauvinism that still existed. My record should speak for itself. Damn it! These guys should realize by now I'd have their backs."

"Doyle, I know it hasn't been easy, but you made it work with Fits before, so he's your partner again. What happened was four years ago."

Still careful to keep her voice low. "The years don't matter to me. I can't afford to have Fits mess up another one of my cases. Rules are rules and Fits didn't follow protocol. What about Detective Briggs? He's competent."

"No. It's Fits." Sarge's stern voice told her the decision had been made. "You're the lead." He handed the files back to her. "Take the photo from the Missing Person's file and canvas the area after you talk to the husband."

Working with Fits again was something she didn't expect or welcome and hoped he would be on his best behavior, whatever that was.

CHAPTER 8

PHILIP ANDERSON STOOD in his office doorway on the sixth floor of the *Messenger* building on Broad Street. The morning edition had already been released, but activity still buzzed from the vast sea of paper-stacked cubicles working on the evening edition. The frenzy about the year 2000, if computers could handle the digit change from 1999, dominated the news. That overshadowed the heated campaigns for the state senate race between the incumbent, Senator Curt Jenkins, and Philip's friend Madeline Richmond. Ringing phones and clicking computer keyboards hovered over the room. The sounds spurred his memory of when he first became an investigative reporter. Not that he regretted the promotion to managing editor, but he missed the adrenaline rush from a hot lead.

On his credenza under his framed Pulitzer Plaque, were piles of reporters' drafts for his review, which meant he would miss another dinner again with Ros. Sitting at his desk, waiting for his computer to boot up, he stared at the family photo of his wife, and their three children in a simple wooden frame. Ros's nervous habit had returned, twirling her hair on top of her head. She hadn't done that since she had postpartum depression after their daughter Kelsey's birth fourteen years ago. She'd told Philip last night it returned because of Kelsey's demanding singing career.

But Ros's habit started again so suddenly, and Kelsey's career had been going on since she was ten. Could there be another reason? He shook off his concerns when the screen flashed and he keyed in his VPN password.

A little while later, Logan McIntyre entered, wearing his worn jeans and white button-down collar shirt with the sleeves rolled up. His hands full with two cups of coffee, he kicked the office door closed behind him.

"I figured we could talk over coffee," Logan rested the cups on Philip's desk and pulled a chair close.

Philip reached for a cup. "I read your draft on Madeline's profile story. It's good as usual."

"Thanks. Didn't get your hair cut, I see."

"I canceled." Philip tucked his hair behind his ears. "Not ready to get rid of it."

"That's okay with me." Logan grinned. "I won $50.00 that you would *not* get it cut."

"Glad I could be of service," Philip smirked as he popped the lid off the Styrofoam cup. The steam rose and the strong coffee aroma filled his nostril. "Smells good. Thanks. What's going on?" He slowly took a sip.

Logan picked up his cup and blew on it. "I believe the cops found Eileen Detweiler's body in a dumpster early this morning."

Philip spit his coffee back in the cup. "What!"

"My source in the coroner's office told me they ruled her a Jane Doe, but the victim was our age and there were two missing toes on her right foot. Don't you remember Eileen had that accident a couple of days before her wedding when she dropped a knife? We joked she might fall over at the altar."

Philip brushed away the coffee from around his mouth. "Don't say we. That was all you. Do you really think it's her?"

"Yes. I do. I received a call from Adam two days ago. He was really upset. Remember I told you Eileen had disappearing acts? Well, Adam told me she went missing again, but this time she'd been gone longer than usual. I told Shana about it and she told me to back off. She wouldn't confirm it was Eileen, but she didn't deny it either. Maybe I should call Adam."

"Hey. Don't do that. Wait until you get confirmation from Shana."

"All right." Logan took a sip of coffee. "I also wanted to talk to you about my interview with Madeline, and something I left out of my draft. When I asked about her campaign finances, she told me they had a starter fund. She said Trevor received $100,000 from his old law firm, Denver and Brown, for a lawsuit settlement. And get this, the funds came in only a week after Madeline announced her candidacy for state senator last year. Sounded suspicious." Logan gestured in air quotes. "Lawsuit settlement, just when they need the money."

Philip placed his cup to the side of his desk after taking a sip. "Maybe it's a coincidence."

Logan cocked his head. "Coincidence, my ass. So, I investigated further. Nothing's posted in the records in Philadelphia or the surrounding counties about a lawsuit settlement involving that firm around those dates. I went back over two years. I'll call Denver and Brown and try to get a statement. If it's not a valid case settlement, then it could be a plant to look like a campaign contribution violation from a corporation."

Philip chuckled. "There you go with your conspiracy theories. Why don't you let me look into the law firm? I'll see what my source at the IRS has to say. You need to finish the profile stories on Madeline and Senator Jenkins for Sunday's edition."

"Not going to happen. I could only get an appointment on Monday with the senator. I tried to see him yesterday at his office across the street, but his secretary nixed it."

"Then let's do a puff piece on both Madeline and Jenkins for the evening edition." Philip eyed the desk clock. "You have time."

"I'd love for us to endorse Madeline."

Philip's postured stiffened. "Why would you bring that up now? We *never* endorse a candidate, even a friend."

"I don't trust the senator. When his wife died, she left him deep in debt, and his mansion needs a lot of upkeep. I did some checking. My source at his bank told me he's getting $8,000 a month cash deposited into his account in addition to his senator's salary. He's getting money from someone. Maybe the unions."

"If you think he's getting kickbacks, we need proof. Mind if I tag along on your Monday interview since Senator Jenkins is high profile?"

Logan agreed and stood, took his last sip of coffee, and tossed his cup in the trash can in the corner. "Score."

"Remember, honor Shana's wishes. Wait until she updates you on the case."

"Sure. Let me know what you find out about Denver and Brown." Logan closed the door behind him.

Two thoughts went through Philip's mind as if each fighting for space in his head. He worried about Ros and how she might take the news if the Jane Doe was proven to be Eileen. Ros was the only one who stayed in contact with Eileen since her and Adam's wedding. His mind shifted to his friend Trevor and the $100,000 payment. Timing too close to Madeline's announcement. It sounded questionable. Friend or no friend, Logan would dig deeper regardless of what Philip told him, unless Philip got in front of it first.

Philip logged onto his computer and created a new document on Trevor Richmond, in his Follow Up folder, naming it TR. A habit he formed years ago to keep his own notes on stories the reporters were investigating, especially sensitive ones. He finished typing what Logan had found, saved the document, and placed a call to his friend at the IRS.

CHAPTER 9

June 2nd, Wednesday

SHANA WASN'T SURE what made her angrier, that she had to work with her ex-partner Detective Russell Fits again, or the male detectives didn't trust a woman to have their backs. She waited in her car at the front of the roundhouse and took her last bite of a turkey sandwich she'd picked up from a vendor on the street. At nearly 2:00 p.m., Fits headed her way, wearing his usual gray suit with a navy-blue tie. His tall stature and weathered tan skin gave him a rugged outdoorsman appearance. But with his middle-aged spare tire hanging over his belt, outdoor activities were not in his wheelhouse. Although he wasn't Shana's type, he was handsome in his own right, with a full head of dark hair and hazel eyes. He climbed into her car. A fresh scent of Irish Spring soap, masked by some heavy musky cologne, filled the car.

"Still overdoing it in the cologne department, I see," Shana said. "What's with the wet hair?"

"Took a quick shower." His chest thrust out. "Just got back from the gym."

She did a double-take. "Did you say gym?"

"I'm trying to get in shape."

Shana snickered as she drove off. "Shape? Since when?"

"Since my physical last month. Sarge said you were sure this Jane Doe was a high school classmate of yours?"

Shana told him about the Missing Person's report and the severed toes she remembered from Eileen's wedding. When a smart remark about the missing toes didn't surface, she was sure Sarge told him to behave.

Fits fiddled with his seatbelt. "Sarge said your classmate's husband called you today?"

"Yes. Not sure why he called me after twenty years, or if he knew about his wife's death. He didn't leave a message or a number."

She hated informing anyone of their loved one's death, but telling Adam about Eileen made her insides churn.

"Since we're partners again," Fits said, "I moved my stuff to the cubicle next to yours."

Shana raised an eyebrow. "Did you remove the rest-in-peace ribbon?"

"Should we keep it for the next one?"

"You guys get a big kick out of that, don't you?" She scoffed.

Fits rested his arm on the car door. "For the record, the rest in peace thing wasn't my idea."

She headed out of town on the Schuylkill Expressway toward Perkasie. Fits rambled on about the woman he'd slept with the night before. Shana cringed, picturing him in bed with anyone. She tuned him out, as she'd done in the past, although his rambling made the hour-long ride seem faster.

Shana turned at the elementary school onto West Street. They drove past the dead-end sign and parked on the street in front of Adam and Eileen's small vintage cape cod house. She and Fits walked up the brick path to the front door, and she noticed a few scraps of what looked like vinyl siding and roofing material in the flower beds. She rang the doorbell. No answer. She rang again.

Fits stepped to the side of the house. "Doyle! There's smoke coming from the back."

They raced to the detached garage. Smoke flowed from

underneath the garage door. Shana banged her fists while Fits searched for another entrance.

"Anyone in there?" she shouted.

A car engine hummed. She yanked on the handle hard until her arms ached. Unable to lift the door, she hammered her fists again. "Hey! Can anyone hear me?"

Fits belted out. "Doyle, over here!"

Shana ran to the side of the garage. Fits fired his gun at the lock. Sparks flew, and he kicked in the side door. Exhaust fumes drifted out. She took a deep breath and cupped her arm over her mouth before rushing in. Fits followed. She banged on the opener on the wall and the front garage door rose. They ran out, coughing. Shana turned to see if anyone was in the car. The smoke cleared. "Fits, call 911."

Shana hurried back into the garage and opened the car door. Adam fell into her arms. She felt his neck for a pulse. None.

Fits rushed to her side. "They're on their way."

They dragged the body into the driveway. Shana knelt and gave Adam CPR until she was certain she couldn't revive him. She felt his pulse again. Still none. She slumped back and brushed away the sweat from her forehead with the back of her hand. Staring at Adam's lifeless body, an overwhelming sadness ran through her. Her eyes teared, and she blinked to clear them. She thought back to his phone message. If only she—

"Looks like suicide," Fits said. "Maybe he heard about his wife?"

Shana dabbed her eyes with the heel of her hands. "How could he? That's why we're here." Shana stood.

"You okay Doyle? You look upset. I thought you said you hadn't seen or heard from these people for twenty years? Were you close?"

She remembered how much she and Adam enjoyed challenging each other with their self-developed cryptograms.

Sad it ended shortly before he got married. Eileen never understood their mutual passion and gave Adam such a hard time that he stopped contacting Shana.

"Closer more with the husband than my classmate." She squatted and examined Adam's body again. "His hair's wet." She noticed his light blue dress shirt. "His collar on his shirt is damp."

"It's stinking hot." Fits wiped his perspired forehead. "In that garage, in a closed car, he could have sweated a lot."

"But something doesn't feel right. Why weren't his armpits wet?"

Fits looked down at the body. "I see your point."

Shana clipped her hair up behind her head.

"Do they have any kids?" Fits said.

"No. Thank God. It would be heart-wrenching to lose two parents so suddenly."

How well she understood that tragedy.

The paramedics arrived and Shana directed them to Adam's body. She stepped close to Fits. "Stay here with the paramedics. I think we have probable cause to inspect the house. The condition of the body looks suspicious. I'll check the house for a suicide note. If there isn't one, then we need *our* team here, so don't let the paramedics do anything but check his vitals to confirm he's dead."

Shana walked up the three concrete steps and slipped on her usual crime scene gear. She entered the unlocked back door and the air-conditioning cooled her. If Adam had left a suicide note, her experience told her it would be in plain sight. Shana inspected the kitchen, careful not to disrupt anything. Walking through the living room, she stopped for a moment. A large silver frame of Adam and Eileen's wedding photo was on the end table. Her eyes drew her to the cast on Eileen's right foot, peeking out from under her gown. Next to it was a brass frame with a photo of Eileen that matched the one in the Missing Person's file.

Upstairs, the first bedroom on the right was set up as an

office. Nothing seemed to be out of order. She entered the hall bath. Clean. Towels doubled folded over the towel racks. The soap dish had an undisturbed bar of soap.

She entered what appeared to be Eileen and Adam's bedroom. The bed was unmade. So far, no note.

In the master bathroom, a drip pattered on the tub drain. Small puddles of water were on the floor. She bent down and noticed a red spot on the rim of the club foot tub. Shana inspected it closer. She dabbed it and rubbed it between her gloved fingers. It was still fresh. She flipped open her cell.

"Sarge, we're at Adam Detweiler's. He's dead. It's a crime scene."

CHAPTER 10

NOW A DOUBLE HOMICIDE, Shana and Fits stood near Adam's body with the paramedics when a local patrol car pulled in front of the house. A young female officer and a much older male officer exited.

As they approached, Shana flashed her badge and introduced herself and Fits.

The male officer said, "Your sergeant gave our captain all the details, and we were told to cooperate any way we can."

"Thanks," Shana said. "The search warrant and our team are on their way."

Fits extended his hand to the female officer with a sheepish grin. "Hello. My name is Russell."

The woman reached for his hand and smiled back.

Shana pulled Fits away and whispered. "Really? We're at a crime scene."

"All right. But did you see the way she looked at me?"

"Stay focused on the case." Shana shook her head.

The bushes rustled between the driveway and the house next door.

A woman's voice came through the hedge. "Detective I have some information."

Shana stepped close, unable to see. "Who's there?"

"I'm the Detweilers' neighbor."

"Stay there. I'll come to you."

Shana motioned for Fits to step away from the female officer. "I'll question the neighbor. When our team gets here, tell the paramedics they can leave. Keep an eye on those locals, and I mean professionally. If they want to observe the investigation, make sure they wear gloves."

She sighed as she walked to the end of the driveway regretting what she'd just said. Fits plucked her nerves, but she didn't want to relish in his blunder about messing up evidence when he neglected to wear gloves on the murder case involving the Assistant District Attorney. Shana walked around the hedge and found a similar cape cod-style house with dormers. A short, older woman who appeared to be in her mid to late seventies, waited by the hedge. Her gray hair in a bun reminded Shana of an elementary school teacher she had many years ago.

Shana stepped through the tall grass full of dandelions and reached the woman. "I'm Detective Doyle."

"I heard your name through the hedge. I'm Victoria Gardner. I've been Eileen and Adam's neighbor for the past ten years. Did Adam commit suicide?"

"Still investigating. You mentioned having information."

"I've noticed strange happenings over there recently." The woman swatted a bee away. "Why don't we go inside my house?"

They walked through the high grass to the front of the cape cod. As Shana entered, the cool air washed over her. She tugged her blouse away from her body.

"Hot out there, isn't it, Detective?"

"That's an understatement."

Shana followed the woman down a long hardwood floor hallway and sniffed when she passed the kitchen. The scent of apples and cinnamon snuck into Shana's nostrils.

"I made an apple pie," the woman said. "Care for some?"

"No, thanks."

In the living room, the sun shone through tall windows flanking both sides of the stone fireplace. Shana observed how sparse the house was of personal items.

"Have a seat, Detective."

Shana nestled into a sun-stained floral wing-backed chair next to the fireplace. "Is it Miss or Mrs. Gardner?"

"It's Ms. Gardner. I don't believe in women's lib, but I like the sound of Ms. That's what I liked to be called at school. I'm a retired schoolteacher from Perkasie Elementary. It's the one on the corner."

"That's convenient. You live here alone?"

"Yes."

The woman raised her hand and pushed the wispy hairs to straighten them into her bun. She reached for a white teacup from the end table. The distinct scent of Earl Grey tea floated in the air.

"Oh, forgive me, Detective. Do you want any tea?"

"No, that's okay. I'm good."

Shana pulled her recorder from her pocket. "Do you mind if I tape this?"

The woman stared at Shana for a few seconds before she spoke. "I…guess it's okay."

"Make sure you talk clearly and take your time." Shana pressed record.

"Okay. Last month, early in the morning, a black limousine brought Eileen home."

"Last month? I thought you would discuss what just happened next door."

"Oh…I thought you wanted to know when strange things started."

It wasn't what Shana expected, but she would play along, hoping the woman would talk about today's events before long. "Go on Ms. Gardner. When was this?"

"It was around 4:00 in the morning on May 18th."

"You sure about the date?"

"Yes. I had trouble sleeping because the night before I met a friend for dinner and I had a glass of wine, which made me restless, so I came downstairs to get some warm milk."

The woman took a sip of her tea. "When I was heating my glass of milk, I noticed the headlights coming down the street. A man got out of the limousine and opened the door for Eileen."

"Wait a minute. How could you see over the hedge?"

The woman placed the cup back on the end table. "Come here, I'll show you a little secret."

Shana paused the recorder and followed the woman to a large window in the dining room. The woman pointed to a dead spot in the hedge facing Eileen and Adam's house. The spot was large enough to see an unobstructed view to their back door and the street in front. Shana pressed record again and dictated what the woman showed her.

"Not many cars, let alone limousines, come down this dead-end street," Ms. Gardner said. "Especially at 4:00 in the morning."

As they made their way back to the living room, Shana continued her questioning. "By any chance did you get a license plate number of the limo?"

"No."

"Can you describe the man who got out of it?"

They took their seats and Ms. Gardner put a finger to her lips. "Let me think. He was tall and muscular. Had on a tight, dark T-shirt. You know, those men who have their shirts too tight to show off their muscles. I never saw him before."

"What happened after that?"

"Eileen entered her house."

Shana had to get this woman to talk about today. "Since you could see through to the Detweilers' back door, did you notice anything earlier today?"

"I was napping, and the sirens woke me up. My bedroom is upstairs, on the other side of the house. When I came downstairs, I noticed the commotion."

"Anything else, Ms. Gardner?"

"Eileen came home in the middle of the night two nights ago?"

Knowing Eileen's time of death was now five days ago, Shana thought the woman must be confused. "Two nights ago, are you sure?"

"Yes. Another night I couldn't sleep. Eileen came home in a car I didn't recognize. It pulled up to the front of the house and she got out and ran inside. It's not unusual. Eileen coming home late or early in the morning. She did that a lot."

"Anything else you can remember?"

"There is one thing. They had a new roof and siding put on their house about two weeks ago. In my few conversations with Eileen, she always complained about money, so I don't know how they could've afforded that. And speaking of Eileen, where is she? I didn't see her today."

"We're still trying to contact her. Do you have anything else?"

"No. I think that's it."

Shana stopped the recorder. "Is there anyone else in the neighborhood we can talk to?"

"No. There're only three houses on this street. The house next door to me is for sale and has been vacant for months."

While Shana handed the woman her card, she wondered what else this woman may have seen with her unusual sleep patterns.

CHAPTER 11

June 2nd, Wednesday

SHANA LEFT MS. GARDNER and walked up the driveway of Eileen and Adam's house. Philadelphia's forensic team and Mac had already arrived. Jonesy was placing a black body bag next to Adam. Shana greeted him and headed to meet Mac in the garage. Fumes still lingered from the exhaust and she coughed.

Mac peered over the top of his reading glasses. "Seeing you twice in one day. Not good."

"Wish it were under better circumstances."

"I gave Russell the search warrant. Frank said our Jane Doe is this guy's wife."

"Yes, the Missing Person's file confirmed the Jane Doe is Eileen Detweiler." Shana motioned at the body on the driveway and blew out a deep breath. "And…that's her husband, Adam."

"My records still have her as a Jane Doe. Haven't had a formal ID yet."

Notifying the parents came to Shana's mind and how hard it would be on them. "I'll get you a formal ID after I talk to both sets of parents. Tell me what you found."

Mac held his clipboard to his side. "Based on the liver temperature, the body has been dead only a couple of hours."

"A couple hours?" Her throat tightened. She wondered if she and Fits arrived sooner, could this have been prevented? She glanced back at Adam's body. Her eyes welled.

"Were you close?"

She thought about their cryptogram passion. "At one time."

"I'm so sorry." Mac stood next to the open car door and pointed to the wet stains on the driver's headrest. "Did you notice this?"

"Yes. Adam's hair was wet and his shirt collar damp. Mac, if he was alive in this hot garage when he started the engine, wouldn't sweat marks be under his armpits?"

"Not if he was already dead."

"You just confirmed my suspicions. The master bathroom had water on the floor under the tub. I'll make sure the forensic team gets a sample of water from the house. Anything else?"

"There was a contusion at the back of his head."

"That would explain the blood I found on the rim of the tub. Whoever tried to clean it up missed a spot. I'll be in the house."

Shana passed Jonesy wheeling the gurney up the driveway. Adam's body was already in the body bag. A sadness consumed her knowing his next stop would be the morgue where his wife lay in the same state. She entered the air-conditioned house and fanned herself. A slight smile came to her when Fits lectured the local officers about wearing gloves. The forensic team was busy taking pictures, fingerprints, and bagging evidence.

Shana snapped on gloves and told Fits about Mac's estimated time of death.

"We must have just missed the doer," he said.

"What did you search so far?"

"Only the kitchen. There was one message on the answering machine from May 28th." He pressed play. It was Adam's voice.

Eileen, you there? Pick up....Eileen....change of plans. Pick up.... Then a click.

Shana choked up hearing his voice after twenty years. She cleared her throat. "I wonder what change of plans meant? Was there a time stamp on the tape?"

"Yes. 5:05 p.m. What did the neighbor say? Anything interesting?"

"I'll tell you later. May have to question her again." Shana faced the local officers. "Do you know the next-door neighbor, Victoria Gardner?"

"No, sorry," the male officer said. "We were just assigned to this area."

Shana faced Fits. "I'll take the upstairs."

The phone on the kitchen counter rang. Fits reached to answer it.

"Let it ring," Shana said.

The answering machine clicked, and the call ended. No message.

CHAPTER 12

June 2nd, Wednesday

TREVOR RICHMOND ENDED the second call to Adam's house without leaving a message, knowing they were notorious for not retrieving them. Iris entered, handed Trevor the evening edition of the *Messenger* and the *Daily Telecast,* and left. He read them every day to keep up with the news from both sides of the aisle. To get his mind off his troubles, he unfolded the *Daily Telecast* first and smelled the fresh published paper and ink. An unflattering side view image of Senator Jenkins was on the front page, stressing his protruded belly. The headlines read—Senator Curt Jenkins, the best choice for Pennsylvania State Senate District 7.

He tossed the *Daily Telecast* into the trash can and unfolded the *Messenger.* Head shots of Senator Jenkins and Madeline were on the front page. General information on both with no endorsement. Just affiliation, age, background, views. Good to see the *Messenger* stayed true to its nature.

Madeline entered his office and checked her Rolex. "Hey, hon. It's almost 5:00. Did you get in touch with Adam?"

"No. I called him twice. No answer."

She tilted her head. "I can't seem to let go of Eileen's comment."

Trevor unraveled the roll of Tums. "Please, Maddie. Stop

thinking about her. She was drunk." He popped two in his mouth.

She rested on the edge of one of the barrel chairs in front of his desk. "You need to do something about that indigestion. Look at you. It's getting worse, isn't it?"

How could he even tell her the reason for the flare-ups? "I don't think so."

"All right." Madeline leaned back in the chair. "But please promise you'll go back to the doctor."

He thought about his last physical when the doctor told him to get rid of stress, like that could happen anytime soon. He'd agreed to appease her. "I'll make an appointment."

She lowered her brow. "Trevor, is there anything you aren't telling me?"

He hid his fear about the blackmailer and pulled a file from the side of his desk. How could he have been so stupid to fall for a phone call tip on the senator? "I need to go over the financials of my companies."

"You're worried about them, aren't you? How are they doing?"

Trevor knew this was a courtesy question. Madeline never took an interest in his family businesses. That was Trevor's responsibility. Another item to add to the stress list.

"You don't want to know." Trevor took a deep breath and blew it out slowly, rubbing his upper stomach again. He opened the file.

"If there's a problem, why don't you sell one of the companies?"

"I can't."

"Trevor, keeping your promise to your father is admirable, but I'm sure if he were still alive, he would tell you the same thing."

Should he tell her? He wasn't sure she'd believe him or

understand. "Maddie."

"Yes? What is it? I should get working on my speech."

Her focus on her speech wouldn't allow the attention needed to discuss the blackmail. "Oh…it's nothing…just that I love you."

"Awe. I love you too, honey. Go to the doctor, please."

After she left, Trevor rested his head back. He ached inside, remembering the promise he'd made to his father while the man lay dying of pancreatic cancer. To keep the legacy going. No matter what.

Iris stood in his doorway. "Mr. Richmond, line one is for you. It's Philip Anderson."

"Thanks." He picked up the phone.

"Do you have any time to meet me tonight?" Philip said.

"Is this about the profile article on Madeline?"

"Ah…sure. PJ's around 7:00?"

Trevor agreed and stared at the financials. Maybe Maddie's right. He should sell one of the companies.

CHAPTER 13

June 2nd, Wednesday

IN THE MASTER BATHROOM on the second floor of Adam and Eileen's house, Shana instructed a young man from forensic to get samples of the blood from the rim of the tub and of the water. She adjusted her gloves and headed into the bedroom. When she opened the third drawer down in the bureau, the female undergarments had a scent of lilacs. She moved them aside and found a half-empty bottle of Crown Royal. Eileen's drinking problem did exist.

A man's wallet and watch were set on top of the nightstand to the right of the bed, which didn't line up the same as the nightstand on the other side. The leg imprints in the carpet were deep, where it must have rested before. She pulled open the top drawer. A cream-colored envelope with Bailey and Bailey, Esq. printed in calligraphy was inside. She unfolded it. At the top of the document, Detweiler versus Detweiler, Petition of Divorce. Underneath the divorce papers was an unsigned card with the caption 'I'm sorry' in capital letters. It contained a one-week sobriety chip from AA. Could Eileen have stopped drinking?

After inspecting the other contents, she tried to slide the drawer back, but it jammed. She pulled the drawer out and discovered something taped to the top of the inside. She reached in, carefully pulled it out, and unfolded a piece of paper, noting

RedChem's letterhead. The pattern of the letters was familiar to her. Like a cryptogram, she and Adam developed years ago to challenge each other.

In the next bedroom, she opened a large desk drawer and found several files. One had about six months of bank statements with canceled checks. After inspecting the entire second floor she carried what she found downstairs and handed them to Fits. He placed them in a larger evidence bag.

"Where are the locals?" Shana said.

"They got a call and left. By the way, she gave me her number."

"Really?" Shana rolled her eyes. "Couldn't help yourself, could you?"

Shana stepped out of the earshot of others and pulled her recorder from her side jacket pocket. After she switched Ms. Gardner's interview tape for her notes tape, she dictated:

"Note to myself: A cryptic note found. Looks familiar, like a cryptogram. Why was it on RedChem's letterhead? Why did Adam call me this morning and not leave a message? Could he have wanted to tell me about the cryptic note? Sobriety chip and divorce papers were found in the nightstand. What did Adam's message change of plans mean? Check out the divorce papers and their finances. The neighbor Ms. Gardner...could she be reliable? Did Eileen come home on May 18th in a limo? Who was the man that brought her home?"

She stopped recording and walked back to Fits.

"Still doing your notes on tape, I see," he said.

"Sure am."

The forensic team announced they had finished and headed out the back door.

Shana faced Fits. "Lock up here. I'll see if Mac is done."

She left the house and made her way to the garage as Mac was packing up. "When are you doing the autopsy?"

He slid his reading glasses into his chest pocket. "Tomorrow morning. I put Jane Doe's ahead of other cases, so I'm a little behind." He picked up his satchel. "You going to be there or Fits?"

"Probably me."

Mac helped Jonesy push the gurney into the coroner's van. Shana watched until the van drove out of sight. Fits met her at the end of the driveway.

"Strange we didn't see any reporters," Shana said. "They usually circle like vultures."

"I wondered that as well. The local officer told me dispatch wouldn't get notified of a suicide. So, nothing went out on the wire."

"I'm glad the press wasn't here. One less thing to deal with. Did you secure the house?"

"Give me some credit. I locked every door, including both locks on the back door. Crime scene tape in place."

As long as Fits was going to be her partner, she needed to give him some amount of trust. "Sorry. Good job."

They reached the car. Shana opened her driver's side door and talked over the top. "Hey. The comment before about wearing gloves—"

"That's okay. I get it." Fits opened the passenger side door. "It's probably on everyone's mind in homicide, anyway." He avoided eye contact and lowered his head. "You're the only one with the guts to say anything to my face."

Shana thought of the guys in homicide, and how they would've never said one of their own messed up a crime scene.

She felt his avoidance and peered at the gloomy clouds forming in the distance. "Looks like rain. I'll inform the parents. It might be better coming from someone they know. You can canvas the area around Eileen's crime scene and update Sarge with what we found here. Start on reviewing those bank statements too." Shana looked at her watch. "It might be too late to contact the law firm about the divorce papers, but you can try. Not clear from the documents who initiated it."

Fits stood at attention. "Anything else, El Capitan?"

They got into the car.

"I want to make sure this doesn't turn into a cold case," Shana said.

"Cold case? That's a laugh." He shrugged. "You afraid this will ruin your perfect record?"

Fits back to his arrogance, she gritted her teeth.

Shana started the engine. "The victims were friends. That's all."

"If you say so."

"Make a copy of that note. I think it might be a cryptogram. I want to see if I can decipher it."

"I almost forgot you had a thing for cryptograms." Fits buckled his seatbelt. "Crank up the air. Tell me about the neighbor."

After Shana dropped Fits off, she headed to the parents to deliver the sad news. She informed Eileen's parents first. It was heartbreaking how they were in denial about their daughter's death. When she walked up the slate-paved sidewalk to the front door of Adam's parents' house, her stomach churned dreading going through the notification process again. The door opened and a tall thin gray-haired man greeted her. It almost took her breath away how much Adam resembled his father. "Mr. Detweiler, do you mind if I come in? I have some sad news…"

Later that evening in her apartment she replayed, in her mind, the parents' reaction to the news. She cringed at the thought of going through questioning them tomorrow at the morgue.

At her desk, she inserted a blank three-and-a-half-inch disk into her laptop and opened a new Word document. After she transcribed her thoughts from Eileen's and Adam's crime scenes onto her notes disk, her mind couldn't shake the regret that she hadn't talked to Adam this morning. Could she have prevented his death?

She saved the document in a folder named Detweiler Case and erased the tape leaving it clear for the next day. The question still circled in her mind. Why would Adam leave the note on RedChem's letterhead, Trevor's company?

CHAPTER 14

June 2ⁿᵈ, Wednesday

TREVOR ARRIVED AT PJ'S a little before 7:00 p.m. The special on the board by the door, pot roast, gravy, and mashed potatoes caused Trevor's mouth to water. He sat at a booth in the back, eager to meet Philip about Madeline's profile story, knowing it would showcase her accomplishments. Vice President of Grange Marketing Firm, one of the largest in Pennsylvania. On the board of several charitable organizations, volunteer work at soup kitchens, getting her master's degree at age 32, mother and wife. The list could go on and on.

He thought back to five years ago when he introduced Madeline to a friend of his at a cocktail party, who'd just been elected as one of the incoming state senators for New Jersey. Almost the entire evening Madeline had talked to him about local politics. The glow on her face then was the same look Madeline had last year when she'd told Trevor about running for the Pennsylvania state senate.

After Senator Curt Jenkins withdrew his retirement, Trevor knew it would be a tough race, especially with the senator in his fourth term, but he hoped with the advertising, the profile story in the paper, and campaigning hard, Madeline would have a fighting chance.

Before long, Philip arrived. He hung his raincoat on the

hook by the booth and slid in. "Hi Trevor. You been waiting long?"

"No, not long."

"How's the campaign going?"

"A little tight on the funds, but going well."

The waitress served glasses of water, took their orders for coffee, and left. They passed pleasantries about their children's experiences in college. Philip took several sips of water throughout their conversation. Why wasn't Philip asking about information for Madeline's profile story? It was as if he was stalling.

Trevor gave Philip a quizzical stare. "You didn't ask me here to talk about the kids. What about Madeline's story?"

Philip pushed his dark brown wavy hair behind his ears and took a deep breath. "I'm not here about the profile story."

"Then why did you want to meet?"

"Something came up earlier today from Logan that could be some concern for you and Madeline."

Philip stopped when the waitress served their coffee.

"Can I get you anything else," she said.

"In a few minutes." Philip waited until she left before he continued. "In Logan's interview with Madeline, he asked her about campaign contributions. She told him initially she would use funds you received from your previous firm, Denver and Brown, on an old lawsuit settlement. When Madeline mentioned when you received it last year, Logan got suspicious."

"Suspicious about what?"

Philip's brown eyes stared at him unblinking. "Don't you find it odd, that you received $100,000 only a short time after Madeline's announcement and after the senator re-entered the race?"

"No. I don't. The senior partner told me it was from an old lawsuit that finally settled."

"You know Logan and his bloodhound instincts. He investigated Philadelphia and the surrounding counties. He couldn't find any lawsuit settlement registered anywhere under Denver and Brown. Frankly, Trevor, I find it suspicious too, so I contacted a friend at the IRS."

Trevor's stomach burned. "The IRS!"

"I wanted to find out about the firm. They reported a significant loss last year. And per their returns, there weren't any large sources of income to warrant payment to you of $100,000 or any expenses in that amount."

"This is crazy." Trevor leaned forward and peered at Philip. "What are you implying?"

"Look Trevor. Besides being my friend, I owe you after you got that trumped-up plagiarism charge against me dismissed. I wanted to give you a chance to check out the funds before Logan digs deeper. This $100,000 could be construed as a campaign contribution. I don't have to tell you how illegal it is to accept this large sum from a corporation."

Trevor shook his head. "I can't believe Denver and Brown would get involved with anything underhanded. It's such a small firm in Ottsville."

"Exactly. Too small to notice. If Logan uncovers something illegal, he would feel compelled to report on it, friend or no friend. And, as the managing editor, I couldn't stop the story."

"What can you do about Logan?"

Philip reached for his cup. "Oh, it's cold now. Don't worry about Logan."

The waitress looked their way.

"I'm not hungry," Trevor said. "I want to get back to the office and look into this."

"I don't think I want anything either." Philip left money on the table. "I'll walk you out."

Trevor slid out of the booth and grabbed his umbrella. Outside, he stood under the awning and watched Philip push his coat collar up and dash through the pouring rain to his car. If he hadn't bailed Philip out years ago, would this kind of information hit the newsstand before he found out more? Could it be a plant? But why? Could Philip keep Logan under control?

CHAPTER 15

June 2nd, Wednesday

IN THE PARKING GARAGE under the MIC building, Trevor stared at the windshield wipers swishing back and forth until they screeched. He cut the engine and rested his head against the steering wheel. Philip's conversation repeated in his head, like a warning flash on the TV screen of nasty weather approaching. *Logan investigated the $100,000 lawsuit. No evidence of a lawsuit settled anywhere.*

In the elevator heading to his office floor, he recalled the meeting last year with Karl Denver, the senior partner at Denver and Brown. Karl had suggested using the settlement check for Madeline's campaign.

Trevor fumed at himself that he hadn't verified the settlement. He feared Philip's suspicions could be right. It was too coincidental. Acid burned in his upper stomach.

When he entered the outer office, Madeline called out. "Trevor is that you?"

"Yes." He walked slowly into her office. A Stage Deli brown paper bag rested on the side of her desk. He could smell the Russian dressing. Must be their famous Reuben.

"Iris told me before she left, you met with Philip? Was that about my profile story?" She pulled the sandwich out of the bag. "Hon, did you eat? You can have half."

He couldn't tell her about what Philip suspected until he knew more. Food was the last thing his stomach needed. "I had something at PJ's. Philip wanted more information to round out the profile story."

"Oh. What more did he need?"

"Just some information on me and the kids. I'll be across the hall."

He hurried out and rushed to his office, closing the door behind him. On top of waiting to hear from the blackmailers, now he had to worry about a potential bogus lawsuit settlement. He sat behind his desk and took the plastic bottle of Tums from the drawer, which had now replaced the roll. He popped two and pressed in the number of his friend, the junior partner at the firm, tapping his hand on his desk. "Oh, please be there."

After several rings, the man answered, "Walter Brown here."

"This is Trevor."

"How are you? I haven't heard from you in ages. Why are you calling me on my cell?"

Trevor cleared his throat. "I need to talk to you about something sensitive. Can you talk?"

"Let me close my door." In a few seconds, Walter came back on the line. "Okay. What's up?"

"Do you remember that old class-action lawsuit against that pharmaceutical company?"

"Geez Trevor that was years ago. Way before you left."

They haven't spoken since Trevor left Denver and Brown to start his own firm twelve years ago. But could he trust Walter to look into this? Trevor took the chance and told Walter his suspicions.

Silence fell on the other end. "This is a serious accusation," Walter finally said.

"Can you please check it out…discreetly?"

More silence. Trevor was sure Walter was weighing his

options carefully and wouldn't blame him if he declined.

"Give me some time to get back to you," Walter said. "But I can't imagine the firm would be involved with planting a phony contribution."

Now more waiting.

CHAPTER 16

June 3rd, Thursday

PHILIP SAT AT HIS DESK at the *Messenger* the next morning and turned on his computer. He opened the TR Word document to recap his conversation with Trevor from last night and what he found out from his friend at the IRS on Denver and Brown. After he saved the document, he received a non-descript call from Grant Harriman the chief managing editor, and close friend, to come up to his office. Philip retrieved his copy of the penthouse key from his desk drawer and within minutes he arrived on the fourteenth floor.

A faint buzzing sound caught his attention. A camera near the ceiling moved toward him and the doors to Grant's office swung open. Philip took a few steps into his office and jerked when the doors closed behind him. "There's already a security key access to your floor. Why do you need this door sensor and the camera?"

"I saw this on a TV show. It's a way to monitor visitors. I have it tied to security downstairs, and I have total control over who comes into my office."

The sprinkles of gray around Grant's temples made him look distinguished. When he stepped out from behind his desk, Philip couldn't help but compare his creaseless khakis to Grant's tan tailored slacks. Glimpsing at the Pulitzer Plaque hanging above Grant's credenza, the ceremony quickly ran through Philip's mind. It was the first for Philip, and the paper, receiving such a high honor on the coverage of the Jeffrey Dahmer copycat murderer. Philip sat on the curved couch facing the floor-to-ceiling windows and glanced at the city skyline over Billy Penn.

Grant sat on the other end of the couch. "Great view, isn't it? Sometimes it's all I need to keep my perspective on things."

The faint scent of new construction caused Philip to look beyond the office into the adjoining room. "Looks like the new bedroom suite is done."

The paper had been in Grant's wife's family for over three generations. After she died two years ago, she'd left Grant an enormous fortune, which he continues to pour into the paper whenever there's a shortfall. But building living quarters at the *Messenger* was a little over the top.

"You shouldn't stay here all the time," Philip said. "It's not healthy."

"I sold my condo in Old City."

"Why? You loved that place."

"Not now. Too lonely. I thought for sure you'd get your hair cut. I heard Logan won the bet."

"Yeah, he did." Philip pushed his hair behind his ears.

Grant rested his arm on the back of the couch. "Good front page on Senator Jenkins and Madeline Richmond. How are Logan's profile stories coming?"

"Still working on them. You know Logan. He wants to be thorough."

"I was thinking. We should endorse Madeline—"

"What!" Philip cocked his head, recalling Logan saying the same thing yesterday. "We've *never* endorsed a candidate for any election."

"Maybe it's time we change."

Philip thought of the funds Trevor received from his old law firm. If it turned out to be something illegal, it would be disastrous for the paper to endorse Madeline. "I don't agree with that. The election is still over a year away. Anything can happen."

"True. But I wonder about Jenkins. He doesn't make enough from his senator's position to support the upkeep of his mansion. You should look into his finances."

Logan's research echoed in Philip's mind about the senator's lifestyle. Grant had been out of the day-to-day operation for some time now, and he didn't have the heart to let Grant know his idea wasn't new. "Good idea, Grant. We'll print the stories on Madeline and the senator at the same time. Let the public make their own decision."

"When will the stories be ready?"

"Logan and I are meeting with Jenkins on Monday. So, we should be able to get both in next Sunday's edition."

"You're going with Logan?"

"Absolutely. High profile." Philip leaned forward. "Grant. We've been friends for a long time. I'm worried about you being here twenty-four-seven. Why don't you start dating? It's been two years."

"At fifty-seven, I'm too old to venture into the single bar scene. Not my style. I thought of one of those dating services but then decided against it. With no heirs, I don't want a young chick after my money."

"You should at least try."

"We'll see. Now to why I wanted to see you. I'm considering posting stories on the internet. It will be the year 2000 soon. We need to get with the times. There's been a growing amount of news posted on the internet, causing our newspaper subscriptions and advertising contacts to decline. It's putting a strain on the *Messenger* finances."

"Who did you have in mind to head this?"

"Dylan Holden is an IT consultant for us. I thought I would make him a permanent employee."

Philip stood. "Sounds like a good idea. Anything else?"

"No. Just a reminder, don't forget to check on Jenkins's finances."

CHAPTER 17

June 3rd, Thursday

WHEN SHANA ARRIVED early morning in homicide, Fits greeted her and handed her a copy of the cryptic note. She placed it on the top of her desk. "I thought you would be at the gym,"

"Maybe I'll go on a diet instead. Physical exercise is not for me."

Shana shook her head. "Any luck on canvassing the area yesterday?"

"Nope. Not a shock though. You know how people don't like to get involved. How'd notifying the parents go?"

"As expected, heartbreaking." She eased into her chair. "Didn't get much out of them last night. I'm going to question them more today when they ID the bodies. Did you check out Ms. Gardner?"

"Yeah. Perkasie Elementary confirmed she retired two years ago, and she's lived at that address for ten years."

"How about the divorce attorney?"

"He said Adam started the divorce, but it wasn't formal."

"Not formal? What's that supposed to mean?"

"Got me." Fits shrugged. "I tried to find out more, but he cited attorney-client privilege. I printed off Eileen and Adam's credit report and compared it to the bank statements. Let me show you."

Shana stepped over to Fits's cubicle and he pointed to an inch-thick stack of papers in the middle of his desk.

"This is all from their credit?" she said. "Did you check for duplicates? In my experience, that happens sometimes when reports are not merged with other agencies."

"No duplicates." Fits flipped through the pages. "Their outstanding credit card debt totaled around $15,000. Their bank statements showed basic checks for electric bills, phone bills, things like that." He turned the pages. "There were direct deposits each week from TR Tires. Appears to be Adam's paycheck. However, I found a large deposit of $50,000 deposited on May 20th." Fits pointed to a highlighted line.

Shana examined it. "Any indication of what that is?"

"No. And there's a $10,000 check written to a company, Roofsrus on May 24th."

"That explains the new roof and siding."

Fits continued. "I cross-referenced other check withdrawals against the credit report and found they matched the payoffs of their charge accounts."

"Contact the bank. See if that large deposit was in cash."

"Already did. I got a warrant and spoke to the bank manager. He remembered it was cash because Adam brought it in a tan briefcase. And Adam had the same briefcase with him when he withdrew $25,000 in cash on June 1st. The balance is around $500.00 now. I updated the Sarge on all of this."

"Good job, Fits." She was pleased to see he was back to his old self. "Type up notes on what you found and put them in the case book."

She sat at her desk, stared at the cryptic note, and examined the letters, TFUEBJL MWDT NKHL FXHXX. There appeared to be an address on the bottom right corner—790 Center Edge Pine Hollow Road. She turned on her computer, pulled the keyboard close, and typed in the address in a Yahoo search. No such address existed in Philadelphia or any of the surrounding areas.

In the bottom left corner of the note were the words Rubik's Cube followed by numbers 7, 6, 5, 4, 3, 2, 1. With nothing on the note triggering a clue, she moved it to the side. She slid in her notes disk, which she now carried with her, and typed.

Where did Adam get $50,000 and what was the $25,000 withdrawal on June 1st? Address on the cryptic note—nothing in the area. No record in a Yahoo Search. Could it even be an address? Divorce not formal. Adam started the paperwork but didn't follow through. Why?

After she transcribed Ms. Gardner's interview, she saved the document to the Murder Case 06021999 folder on her hard drive and put a printed copy in the case book. She looked at her watch and handed the tape to Fits. "Give this to Sarge. I'm going to the coroner's office."

A couple of hours later the autopsy on Adam had finished, and Shana waited in Mac's office for the written report. The Vicks scent stuck in her nostrils, but somehow the smell of brewed coffee snuck past it and she poured herself a cup. The next unpleasant task on her agenda—questioning the parents.

Mac entered and handed the file to her. "With the contusion on the back of Adam Detweiler's head and the water in his lungs, I'm officially ruling this a homicide. The speck of blood found on the tub matched his. The time of death, between 2:00 and 3:00 yesterday afternoon. I sent over a copy of the report to homicide."

Shana swallowed hard. "If only Fits and I had arrived an hour sooner, Adam would still be alive."

"You don't know that."

"Perhaps you're right. Why would someone kill him and move him to the garage in broad daylight? Whoever it was would've risked being seen."

"That's a good question."

"Mac, I'm wondering if there's a link between the two

murders. Maybe the cryptic note I found will provide a clue."

"Cryptic note?"

"I found a note in Adam's nightstand and I think it's a cryptogram. He and I had this mutual passion for solving them and we used to stump each other with our own crypts. The letters in the note looked familiar and I'm going to try to decipher it."

Jonesy stood in the doorway and cleared his throat. "Should I get the bodies ready for viewing?"

"Yes," Mac said. "I'll call you when we're ready."

Shana faced Mac after Jonesy left. "It seems heartless to question the parents after they ID their loved ones. They were so upset last night. I'm hoping they can tell me more today."

"I understand how you must feel." His soft voice had a tone of compassion. "I can tell you my thoughts on the subject."

"Please do." She took a sip of coffee.

"When a loved one identifies the deceased, they remember things. Events, conversations they may have otherwise forgotten. Perhaps it's fear or regret to face what they may have blocked out. Finding the killer will be justified revenge for them. They'll expect you to be their heroine. In their eyes, you will be the one who can deliver."

"I intend to do everything I can to give them that."

"I know you will." He stepped closer to her. "Shana, it never seems to be the right time, but I was wondering if you would like to have dinner sometime."

The way he looked at her at crime scenes always seemed to be more than passing pleasantries. Now she knew for sure. No one feature made him handsome, although his crystal blue eyes came close. She hadn't had a date in almost a year, and she was attracted to him. But red flags plagued her, like the look on his face when he talked about his deceased wife.

"Shana…How about it? You free tomorrow?"

She took another sip of her coffee. So many reasons to say no ran through her head. Dating a co-worker, not to mention the teasing from the guys in homicide dating the chief medical examiner. A harmless dinner wouldn't hurt, but she must keep this casual. "How about if I meet you at PJ's in Conshohocken tomorrow night at 8:00?"

Although she hadn't been at PJ's in months, she still thought of it as her haven. It wasn't too far from where she used to live. Fond memories of her gang rushed through her mind, making her miss being around them. PJ's was the place where they tried to lift her spirits while going through a divorce and where they consoled her when her parents died.

"Great. I'll be there," he said.

She left her cup in his office and followed him to the newly built viewing room, donated by a wealthy oilman after he had to identify his wife in the morgue. Shana wished they had this room when she had to identify her mother after the accident, or what was left of her. She could still see the death certificate in her mind. Cause of death. Decapitation.

Mac opened the door and gestured her inside. The room had a soft touch, a lit lamp on an end table, a camel color cloth couch, and a side chair to match, sort of a welcoming feel. Although with a viewing monitor in front of the couch, it snapped the reality of the real reason for the room.

The wall phone rang. Mac answered and turned to Shana. "Adam's parents are here."

CHAPTER 18

June 3rd, Thursday

MAC ESCORTED ADAM'S parents into the viewing room. The man's tall and lean frame towered over his wife's petite height and weight. His Old Spice cologne scent reminded Shana of her college criminology professor.

Lines of sadness spread over the man's face. "Sorry, we weren't much help last night."

"You don't have to explain," Shana said. "Again, sorry for your loss."

The couple sat on the couch and Shana eased onto the chair facing them. Mac explained the viewing process to prepare them. The comforting softness in Mac's voice seemed to calm them. They both nodded as if they understood, but Shana was sure they had no idea what they were about to see.

Mac pressed the intercom box on the wall and buzzed Jonesy. Within seconds, Mac turned on the viewing screen. A white sheet covered Adam's body on a metal examining table.

Shana's heart ached for his parents. They must be hoping the body under the sheet wasn't Adam. She would be hoping too if the body was one of her children.

Through their hugs, tears, and sobs, they identified the body. Mac turned off the viewing screen.

Shana softened her voice, dreading what she was about to

say. "I'm so sorry I have to tell you this. We believe Adam was murdered."

"Murdered!" Mrs. Detweiler gasped, covered her mouth, and wept.

Mr. Detweiler raised his voice. "Oh my God. You said last night it looked like suicide."

Shana's eyes watered seeing them so upset. She handed Mrs. Detweiler a box of tissues.

"We weren't sure until this morning." Shana pulled out her recorder. "I know this is hard, but are you up to answering some questions?"

The gray-haired man took a heavy sigh and nodded, as his wife dried her tears.

Shana pressed record. "Do you know anyone who would want to harm Adam?"

The man took a moment before speaking. Shana assumed he tried to find his voice the way men do when they're working to hold back emotion.

"Everyone loved Adam," he said.

Mrs. Detweiler blinked her tears away. "Adam was a wonderful son." The woman smiled like mothers do when remembering a tender moment about their child, but then tears trickled down her cheeks.

Shana remembered Logan's conversation. "I understand besides his job at TR Tires, Adam worked on Madeline Richmond's campaign as a liaison with the unions."

"That's right," Mr. Detweiler said.

"Did Adam mention any work issues?"

"Not that I can recall."

"What can you tell us about their marriage?" Shana said.

"Things weren't the same after the second miscarriage," Mrs. Detweiler said.

"I had no idea. I'm so sorry."

"It was years ago. They kept it pretty quiet. Unfortunately, Eileen never got over not having a child and started drinking."

Mr. Detweiler faced Shana. "They were having money problems too. Eileen would take these bus trips to Atlantic City to gamble. Sometimes she wouldn't return for a day or two. Adam followed her one time after several thousands of dollars appeared on their credit card. That caused a financial strain on an already fragile marriage." He turned to his wife. "I told him we would help with their debt, but you know how stubborn he is…was."

The man's eyes welled, and he paused before he continued. "Adam told me he blamed himself for working so much. After his attempts to get Eileen into AA failed, he took one last effort to get her to stop drinking."

His wife glared at him. "What do you mean?"

"He had divorce papers drawn up."

"Divorce?" Mrs. Detweiler arched her back. "What are you saying?"

"He wasn't going to go through with it. He just wanted to scare her into stop drinking."

So that's what the attorney meant by not formal.

The woman reached for her husband's hand and tears streamed down her cheeks. "If we only had helped Adam."

He wrapped his arms around his wife as she sobbed.

Shana switched her recorder to her other hand. "We found the divorce papers in a nightstand drawer…along with a one-week sobriety chip."

"Oh my God!" Mrs. Detweiler tried to speak through her tears. "She was…turning her life around."

Her husband cupped his hands over hers. "Hon, take deep breaths."

Mac stepped over to the small refrigerator in the corner and returned with bottles of water.

Mr. Detweiler unscrewed the cap, handed the bottle to his wife, and turned to Shana. "Adam did act strange these last weeks after he had a meeting at RedChem in New Jersey."

"Why did he go there?"

"He said the meeting had something to do with TR Tires."

"When was this?"

"May 17th. Everything seemed to change after that."

"Changed how?"

"He called us really upset, I think around 2:30 the next morning. He said he couldn't sleep, and that Eileen hadn't been home since the 16th. We went over to calm him down." Mr. Detweiler lowered his brow appearing to ponder his thoughts. "Now that I think about it, when we got there Adam seemed more nervous about his meeting at RedChem than Eileen's disappearance."

"Why do you say that?"

"His demeanor differed from other times Eileen went missing."

"When did Eileen come home?"

"Shortly after we got there. We heard a car out front and went outside. Eileen got out of a black limousine. She could hardly walk she was so drunk. Adam had to help her into the house."

"What time was that?"

"I think about 3:30 or 4:00."

"Did you recognize the limo or get a license plate number?"

"No. We were focused on Eileen. When we went into the house, Adam asked her where she'd been. She said, 'I was forced to do it' and begged Adam to understand. Then she passed out. The next day, Eileen didn't remember anything. At least that's what she told Adam."

Shana thought about Ms. Gardner's interview. "Did you see anyone else get out of the limo?"

Mr. Detweiler shook his head. "It took off after Eileen got out, so we didn't see who was driving."

"Could anyone else have seen the limo, maybe a neighbor?"

Mrs. Detweiler seemed to get her composure. "The only neighbor they have is Victoria Gardner. She's a real busy body, but I don't think even she would've seen the limousine that early in the morning."

"Do you remember anything else significant about that night?" Shana said.

Mr. Detweiler studied his wife. "Remember, the briefcase on the front lawn?"

"That's right," she said. "Eileen had it with her. Adam brought it into the house."

Shana thought about the briefcase Adam had at the bank. "Can you describe the briefcase?"

The man took a sip of water. "Tan, a little worn."

"Did Adam open it?"

"No. At least not with us there."

Suspicious if there was money in the briefcase, Shana said, "Tell me more about their financial situation."

"Things seemed to turn around recently," Mr. Detweiler said. "Adam told me he got a bonus from TR Tries for assisting a settlement between the unions and management and they were able to make improvements to the house."

Shana avoided pursuing the $50,000 cash deposit, doubting it could have been a bonus. It wasn't the time to dispute what their son had told them. "A couple more questions. When Eileen went missing on May 28th, why did Adam wait until May 31st to file a missing person's report?"

"I guess because she always would turn up," Mr. Detweiler said. "Adam was afraid something happened to her this time...and he was right."

"There was a message on their answering machine, left on the 28th from Adam. He called out Eileen's name to pick up, but he did say...change of plans. Do you know what he meant?"

Mr. Detweiler shook his head. "No. Strange. That was their wedding anniversary. Don't know why Adam would leave any message though. They never listened to them."

"We also found a half-empty bottle of Crown Royal in Eileen's bureau."

"Oh no," Mrs. Detweiler said. "If Adam saw the sobriety chip and the bottle, he must have been devastated."

Her husband patted his wife's hand. "We don't know that."

"Could Eileen have seen the divorce papers?" Shana said.

"Maybe," Mr. Detweiler said.

Shana leaned forward. "Would Eileen drive if she was drunk?"

"She'd been known to do that."

"What was the make and model of Eileen's car? I'll put an APB out on it."

"A red Chevy Camaro. I think it's a 1995. I don't know the license number."

"I'll find out."

The wall phone rang and Mac answered the call. "Have them wait in the lobby. I'll be right down."

He turned to Shana. "Eileen's parents, the Connors are here. I'll meet them downstairs." The door closed behind him.

"Shana," Mrs. Detweiler said. "Please be patient with Eileen's mother. She has Alzheimer's."

Mrs. Detweiler stared at the blank viewing screen with her red-rimmed eyes. "This is a horrible way to see your child." The woman lowered her head. "Despite Eileen's troubles, we loved her."

Shana stopped the recorder and walked with the Detweilers to the elevator.

The doors slid open, they entered and turned to face Shana. Sadness clouded Mr. Detweiler's features. "Please find whoever did this to our son."

His request plucked at Shana's heart. "I will."

The other elevator arrived, and Mac escorted a short plump gray-haired woman and an equally short gray-haired thin man out into the hall.

The woman had that same spacy look that Shana remembered last night when she informed them of Eileen's murder. Shana greeted them and gently cupped the man's hand in hers. "As I said last night, I'm so sorry for your loss."

"Loss?" The woman turned to her husband. "What is she talking about?"

Mac stood behind them shaking his head. Shana followed Eileen's parents and Mac down the hall to the viewing room.

"Please, have a seat in there," Mac said to the Connors as he gently took Shana's arm and held her back before closing the door. "I suspect Mrs. Connor has Alzheimer's. I went over the process with them in the lobby, and all she did was talk about how Eileen would be home from school soon."

"I noticed something odd about her last night when I informed them of Eileen's death. And Adam's mother confirmed Mrs. Connor's problem after you left."

"I'm not sure you'll get anything from these people."

And Mac was right. Eileen's mother thought she viewed a TV show, and the actress resembled Eileen. Mr. Connor through welled-up eyes identified his daughter's body. Neither one could contribute anything to the events before Adam's or Eileen's deaths, other than confirming Eileen had a drinking problem. When the couple left the viewing room, Shana watched them shuffle down the hall, Mr. Connor guiding his wife.

Shana turned to Mac. "It's so sad, isn't it? Eileen's mother will probably never know what happened to her daughter."

"Maybe that's a good thing."

"Mac, with Eileen being an alcoholic, why would an injection kill her?"

"An alcoholic would have a certain level of alcohol already in their system. If someone knew about her addiction, they'd know her tolerance would be high and an alcohol injection would be the easiest way to kill her."

Shana felt an adrenaline rush. "This could be a lead, Mac. The killer may have known Eileen or at least her habits."

CHAPTER 19

June 3rd, Thursday

DRIVING BACK TO THE roundhouse, Shana couldn't shake the parents' interviews. Her heart ached at seeing them in such a grievous state and recalling what Adam's parents told her. Could Shana have at least saved Adam if she'd gotten his calls in time? A tear wound its way down her cheek and she wiped it away.

In homicide Shana dropped into her desk chair, emotionally drained.

Fits leaned over the cubicle. "There's pizza in the kitchen."

"Not hungry. What happened to the diet?"

"Not working for me. Interview with the parents…rough?"

"Yeah. Real rough." She sat straight. "Anything from forensics on the cryptic note?"

"Adam's fingerprints were the only ones on it. Read the autopsy report on Adam." Fits pressed his lips together. "The doer can't be too smart. An autopsy would reveal water in the lungs. If it weren't for us being on the scene, I bet those two local blues would have written it up as a suicide."

"You're probably right. Give me some time to transcribe the parents' interviews before I update you and Sarge."

Through several starts and stops, in between catching her breath hearing the parents again, Shana finished transcribing highlights from the interview and saved the document to the 06021999 folder on her hard drive. After she put her printed copy in the case book, while still fresh in her mind, she pulled her notes disk from her inside jacket pocket, slid it in, and typed.

Eileen did come home in a limo the morning of May 18th. Who owns the limo? Where was Eileen the night of the 16th and 17th? Why did she stop drinking? If she didn't remember where she was, then why did she say she was forced to do it? Do what? Per the parents, no one else got out of the limo. Why did Ms. Gardner claim a tall muscular man was there? Could the briefcase Adam had at the bank on the 20th be the same one Eileen had on the 18th? What was in it? Is that where Adam got $50,000? Unlikely a bonus. Why was Adam upset after his visit to RedChem on May 17th and who did he meet there? Did the divorce papers take Eileen over the edge? Where did Eileen go on May 28th?

She saved the disk, put it back in her jacket, and she and Fits went to see Sarge. As they entered Sarge's office, he stopped sipping on the clear plastic thermos of the light green ginger and lemon concoction. Shana told them how she and Adam had a mutual passion for cryptograms, and that she started to try to decipher the cryptic note with no results.

Shana handed Sarge the interview tape. "I'd like to work on the note some more."

Sarge stood and locked the tape in his filing cabinet. "You can try. But I sent a copy of the note to a friend at the FBI in the Cryptanalysis and Racketeering Records Unit. See what they can come up with. Shana, did you learn anything from the parents?" Sarge sat back behind his desk.

"The Connors, Eileen's parents...nothing. Her mother has Alzheimer's. Adam's parents had some interesting information." Shana recapped their interview.

"Sounds like Eileen Detweiler had a lot of issues," Sarge said. "A black limo could belong to anyone."

"So, Adam wasn't going through with the divorce," Fits said. "That must be what the attorney meant by not formal."

Shana nodded. "Looks like it."

"What about that briefcase Eileen had with her on May 18th?" Sarge said.

"I'm thinking cash was in it. That would explain the deposit Adam made of $50,000 on May 20th. And as the bank manager said, Adam came in with a tan briefcase. It would have to be the same one. According to Adam's parents, Eileen and Adam were deep in debt, so where else could Adam have gotten that kind of money? I didn't mention the amount of the deposit to his parents, but I find it highly unlikely it was a bonus as his father claimed."

"Where did that money come from? And why was the briefcase with Eileen, and where is it now? Could you have missed it when you searched the house?"

She shook her head. "I don't remember seeing one. But we weren't looking for it either."

"Go back to the house. See if the briefcase is there, and question the neighbor again." Sarge slurped the last of his drink. "Get her to clarify the dates when she saw Eileen last and why she claims a tall muscular man brought Eileen home when the parents didn't see anyone get out of the limo. What's with the connection between TR Tires and RedChem?"

"They're both owned by Trevor Richmond," Shana said.

"We need to find out what he knows about Adam's visit to RedChem on the 17th. And since Adam worked on Madeline Richmond's campaign, we should question her as well."

"For the record..." Shana fumbled to find the words. "The Richmonds are friends of mine."

Sarge gave her a cautious stare. "Can you be objective?"

She thought about how she hadn't been around them in months and now she would have to see them on a professional level. "Of course. Not a problem."

"Don't worry, Sarge," Fits said. "I'll go with Doyle and make sure we're covered."

His arrogance returned. Anger tramped through her and she jerked her head at Fits. "What the hell is that supposed to mean?"

Fits raised his hands. "Hey. I'm just saying. Since they're your friends, I'll make sure the interview isn't compromised."

She glared at him. "I don't need your supervision."

Sarge held a hand stop at Fits. "If Doyle says it's not a problem, then it's not. Besides, since they're Doyle's friends, we may have the advantage to gather specific information to help the investigation."

Minutes later, Shana stormed out of the roundhouse and sprinted over puddles from the earlier rain on her way to the parking lot.

Fits ran after her. "Wait up, Doyle."

When they reached the car, Shana pointed her clenched fist at him. Her expression stiffened. "How dare you make a comment like that to Sarge?"

"Damn it, Doyle. I was trying to help."

Shana opened the driver's side door, slid in, and slammed it hard.

Fits got in on the passenger side. "Forget it!" He grabbed his door and shut it. "That's the last time I'll help you out."

Shana backed out of the parking space and hit the gas pedal, swerving on the wet roads. The tires squealed.

"Shit, Doyle." Fits grabbed the handle on the car door. "Take it easy."

She sped going fifty in a twenty-five mile an hour zone. Reality hit her and she slowed, tightening her grip around the steering wheel. "You of all people know what it's like being questioned about your integrity."

"That's a low blow, Doyle."

CHAPTER 20

AFTER AN HOUR of driving in silence, Shana pulled into Adam and Eileen's driveway. Her role meant giving Fits orders, but if it were up to her words wouldn't be spoken until they completed their tasks. "Let's question Ms. Gardner first."

They treaded through the ankle-height wet grass, full of drooped dandelions, to Victoria Gardner's front door. The air smelled fresh from the summer thunderstorm earlier. Shana introduced Fits to the gray-haired woman and requested to question her again. They stomped their wet feet on the front mat and followed the woman to her living room.

Ms. Gardner sunk into the couch. "Please sit. I've made a nice pot of tea. Would you care for any?"

They declined and sat in faded wing-backed chairs flanking the fireplace. Shana pulled out her tape recorder. The woman scooted close to the coffee table and poured the steaming liquid into a white cup. A familiar scent of Earl Grey filled Shana's nostrils.

"Ms. Gardner, I'd like to record some clarifications from our previous interview."

"Sure. Anything I can do to help."

Shana pressed record. "You told me you saw Eileen about two nights ago, coming home early in the morning."

The woman blew on her tea. "Too hot." She rested the cup on the coffee table. "I'm not sure now whether it was two nights or longer. After you left yesterday, I noticed my notes on my calendar in the kitchen. I was in center city doing volunteer work at the library on May 28th and stayed at my friend's house for the weekend. I came home on May 30th. You can check with her. Anyway, I may have been mistaken when I saw Eileen last."

"So, are you sure about the limousine last month?"

"Oh. Yes. I'm sure about that."

"You described a tall muscular man who got out of the limo with Eileen. Did you see him help her into the house?"

"I'm not sure now. Let me get you my friend's number."

The woman stood and left the living room.

Fits motioned for Shana to stop the recording and whispered. "This lady is senile. Are we going to take her seriously?"

Shana raised her finger to her mouth. "Shh."

Ms. Gardner returned with a piece of paper and handed it to Shana. "My friend's name is Flora McGenley. Here's her number."

"Thanks." Shana pressed record again and faced the woman. "Can you give more details about the man in the limousine, other than he was tall and muscular?"

"I don't remember anything else about him. Detective Doyle, did I tell you he was bald?"

"No. You didn't."

"Oh, I didn't? Sorry."

"If there's nothing else, I guess we're finished." Shana reached for the tape recorder.

"There is something," Ms. Gardner said. "A police car pulled in front of their house this morning. I was standing in the kitchen cleaning my dishes and I saw a man get out."

"Could you tell us anything about him or if it was a local

patrol car?" Fits said.

"Sorry. I didn't get a good look." Ms. Gardner sipped on her tea. "The car was only there for about fifteen minutes."

Shana turned off the recorder and put it in her jacket pocket. "Thanks for your time."

While walking back to Eileen and Adam's house, Fits said, "Looks like the hedge lady may be confused."

Shana ignored his comment, not giving Fits satisfaction she found his nickname for Ms. Gardner amusing.

"Doyle, I want to apologize for the comment I made about questioning Trevor Richmond."

An apology rarely came from Fits. She couldn't figure him out, although she had tried. He was a good detective, at least years ago. But somewhere along the line without warning—bam, he would go off the rails, so to speak. She often wondered if her rejection of his affection made him derail.

Shana gave him an icy stare. "It's the way you said it in front of Sarge."

"Again sorry. Can we talk about the case?"

Gradually the lines of anger in her brow softened, knowing the case should come ahead of her resentment toward him. "Okay."

"So, what do you think about a patrol car at the house? Ms. Gardner isn't able to describe the man getting out of it, but she could describe a man who dropped Eileen off weeks ago, who according to Adam's parents wasn't there. And what's with her remembering now the man was bald?"

"She's not reliable. Maybe there wasn't a patrol car here earlier. Let's check out the house."

When they walked up the three concrete steps to Eileen and Adam's backdoor, Fits examined the crime scene tape. "I swore I put this tape on differently yesterday."

He slid the key into the doorknob and turned, the door opened.

Fits turned to Shana. "I swear I locked the deadbolt yesterday."

"Are you sure?"

"Doyle, I know you think I mess up, but believe me I locked both."

"Then someone *was* here."

CHAPTER 21

June 3rd, Thursday

LATER THAT DAY, Shana and Fits talked in Sarge's office, about the next steps in the case. The commissioner's press conference on the Detweiler murders finished earlier with his typical release. Dates, times, and both murders were still under investigation. Forensics had gone back to Eileen and Adam's house—no new fingerprints.

"If someone was at their house this morning," Shana said. "Not sure what they might've taken or been after. Nothing was disrupted, that I could see. And no sign of a briefcase."

"Maybe it was the doer who came back to the house," Sarge said, "looking for the briefcase, assuming it was even there."

"But Ms. Gardner claimed it was a police car."

"Check with Perkasie police. They could have sent over a car. Doyle, did you make an appointment to question the Richmonds?"

Shana expected a facial expression from Fits, but there was none. "Yes. Tomorrow morning. I also want to question the trashman, Mr. Roberts again."

Sarge lowered his brow. "Why? Mac didn't find anything in the autopsy, and forensics found nothing in the trash from the dumpster that would relate to the odor described by Mr. Roberts."

"But he was so convinced he smelled something on Eileen's body. Need to get more details from him. If the smell is for real, then the trashman is the only one who can identify it."

Fits rolled his eyes and grunted. "Odor from a trashman?"

Annoyed, Shana glared at him. "We've seen and heard stranger things."

"Doyle, you may have something," Sarge said. "Get Mr. Roberts down here for more questions and include Mac."

Back at her desk, after Shana transcribed Ms. Gardner's second interview and saved it to her hard drive, she called Ms. Gardner's friend Flora, who confirmed they were together from May 28th to May 30th. Shana then slid in her notes disk and typed.

Why did Ms. Gardner just remember the man she claimed brought Eileen home on May 18th was bald? More details about a man the parents said wasn't there. What was a patrol car doing at Eileen and Adam's house this morning? Ms. Gardner couldn't identify the man? Who was it? What was he after? Again—Ms. Gardner not reliable.

She saved her disk and slipped it into her inside jacket pocket. After she gave Ms. Gardner's interview tape to Sarge and placed a hard copy in the case book, she made calls to Mr. Roberts and Mac. Her final call to the motor pool.

Fits peered over the cubical wall as Shana ended her last call. "What did the motor pool have to say?"

"All unmarked and patrol cars were properly accounted for that day."

"I just called Perkasie Police. They didn't send anybody back to the scene. Ms. Gardner seemed to fumble about your additional questions, so maybe she's mistaken about the patrol car."

"Maybe she was mistaken about a lot of things. Remember she couldn't even describe the person. Anyway, Mr. Roberts and Mac agreed to a meeting. They'll be here at 6:00."

"I still think this meeting is crazy."

"For your information, I checked with the trash company's HR department. It's noted in Mr. Roberts's file, he's the only one who has been on the job as long as he has and hasn't lost his sense of smell. You need to be open-minded."

"Whatever. I'm getting some coffee. Want any?"

He'd better be on his best behavior. "No thanks."

Her phone rang, and before she could say hello, Logan blurted out. "I told you it was Eileen. And Adam! Oh my God! Now I'm sure Adam had something important to tell me. If only he'd told me whatever was bothering him. Maybe his death could've been prevented."

"You can't think that way, Logan." But how could she convince him when she had the same thoughts?

"Can you tell me any other details about the murders?"

"I don't have anything else to tell you other than the write-up you received from the press conference?"

Logan pressed on. "Is there a link between the two murders?"

Fits returned with coffee and sat at his cubicle.

Shana cradled the receiver on her shoulder. "Logan, if I could tell you more, I would."

His voice cracked on the other end. "Can you keep me posted? Not so much for an exclusive, but I feel I owe Adam."

Shana heard his grief. "I understand. Talk later."

Fits leaned on the cubicle wall. "Your buddy Logan wanting an exclusive I bet?"

"You know reporters."

Her thoughts went to the phone calls she and Logan received from Adam. What did Adam want to tell them?

CHAPTER 22

June 3rd, Thursday

SHANA AND FITS WAITED in the conference room for Mr. Roberts's interview. Within minutes Mac arrived. Seeing him made her heart flutter. She almost felt like a schoolgirl. Ever since he'd asked her out, it was as if she'd noticed him for the first time.

She fought back a smile, careful to be professional, and shook Mac's hand. "Thanks for coming."

"Hey doc," Fits said.

Mac sat next to Shana. "Russell. I told you it's okay to call me Mac."

Fits shrugged. "I like doc."

"Okay. Suit yourself."

Promptly at 6:00 p.m., an officer escorted a medium-built man, clean-shaven, with thinning hair, into the conference room. She almost didn't recognize him as the trashman from the crime scene.

Shana made introductions.

Mr. Roberts scanned the room and pulled out the heavy high-back chair near Fits at the head of the twelve-foot-long mahogany table. "Wow, what a layout. So, this is where my tax dollars go."

Shana smiled. "We appreciate you making time for us, Mr. Roberts. I'm recording this conversation. Any objections?"

"Nope. I heard on the news they identified the woman. Glad she's not a Jane Doe."

"We are too," Mac said.

"Sad about her husband."

Shana dictated the date, time, and those present.

Mac opened a file and clicked his pen. "Mr. Roberts, we want to ask you some questions about the odor you claimed you smelled on the body. We didn't find any traces of an unexplained odor in the autopsy or from items analyzed by forensics. Can you relate the smell to *anything* familiar?"

"As I said in the alley when the dead woman's hand brushed by my face, I smelled a skunk-like, strong sulfur odor. Real fowl. I never smelled anything like that before, even from dead bodies, but that smell almost made me barf."

Mac jotted down notes.

Fits rested his chair back on its hind legs. "What makes you think you could smell something other than trash? You're a trashman."

Shana turned to Fits, hiding her glare.

Mr. Roberts snapped at Fits. "Just cos I collect trash doesn't mean I don't have a good sense of smell. Check with my company's HR."

"We did," Shana said.

Mr. Roberts sat erect. "Then you know I still have my sense of smell after thirty-five years with the company. And per Human Resources, the title is," he used air quotes and scowled at Fits, "sanitation engineer. I can tell you just had pizza from the garlic smell."

Fits rocked his chair back and forth. "What makes you think I didn't have pasta with garlic?"

Mr. Roberts smirked. "I worked in a restaurant in my younger years, and I know the difference between pizza sauce with garlic and pasta sauce with garlic."

"We have a regular Sherlock Holmes here." Fits dropped his

chair forward.

Once again Shana hid her glare at Fits.

Mac rested his arms on the table and faced Mr. Roberts. "Did you see anything on the victim's hand?"

"No. It happened so fast."

Mac continued to make notes. "Mr. Roberts, the dumpster where she was found is in an area with rental apartments and restaurants. Ever smell anything like that odor before or even close to it in that area?"

"Nope."

Shana faced Mac. "Any other questions?"

"I think I have enough."

Mr. Roberts stood. "I'd be glad to put my nose in action with a smell test. But don't wait too long, I can feel a cold coming on." He gave a hardy laugh. "Just kidding."

Shana and Mac smiled while Fits rolled his eyes.

She turned off the recorder. "Mr. Roberts. Thanks for coming down."

The man left and Shana faced Mac. "If there was an odor on her body Mr. Roberts didn't recognize, then it could mean Eileen might've been killed somewhere else."

Fits smirked. "Finding this odor's going to be like finding a needle in a haystack."

Mac peered at Fits. "We need to check *every* angle." He grabbed his file and left the room without saying goodbye.

"A little touchy, isn't he?" Fits said.

"Touchy!" Shana slapped the file closed. "You were condescending to Mr. Roberts."

Fits charged for the door and pushed it hard against the wall as he stormed out. As much as she didn't want to agree with Fits, she had to admit Mac's actions were a little strange. On her way back to her cubicle, Fits had gathered with his male buddies. They whispered and snickered. She ignored them and set the file and tape recorder on her desk.

"Hey, Doyle," Detective Briggs called from across the room. "Fits tells us you have a sniffer to investigate." The other detectives burst into laughter.

It surprised her Briggs had joined in. She thought he would be above this, but then again, he was Fits's partner years before Shana. Loyalty ran deep, at least between her male counterparts.

She glared at them. "Why don't you worry about your own investigations. I'm sure you need to."

Sarge stepped out of his office, and the room grew silent. "Doyle, I'd like a word."

Shana walked across the room, ignoring the stares from the other detectives, and entered Sarge's office.

He motioned for her to sit. "How'd the interview go with Mr. Roberts?"

Shana told him their theory that Eileen most likely was killed elsewhere.

"Makes sense." Sarge lowered his voice. "I received a call from Mayor Gaffney. Seems he's taking an interest in the Detweiler case. He wants to see us tomorrow afternoon."

"Why both of us?"

"Not sure. Keep this between us."

"From Fits too?"

Sarge peered out of his office in Fits's direction. "Let me worry about him. I have a budget meeting with the lieutenant tomorrow. The mayor wants to see us in his office at 2:00. I'll meet you there."

Even with her recent dealings with Fits's arrogance, as her partner, she didn't like keeping this from him. But she trusted Sarge and knew he must have his reasons.

Back at her desk, after she finished transcribing Mr. Roberts's interview, she slid in her disk and typed another note. *Where was Eileen killed?*

CHAPTER 23

June 3rd, Thursday

MADELINE RICHMOND STORMED into Trevor's office, waving the newspaper in her hand. "Did you see the *Messenger*'s evening edition?"

"Not yet."

She slapped the paper on his desk. "Look at the front page. Our pictures are next to Adam and Eileen. Logan's article mentioned Adam's involvement with my campaign. Perhaps I'm paranoid, but it looks like we had something to do with their deaths. We can't have something like this hanging over our heads during the campaign."

Trevor tried to ignore her ranting. His pulse quickened, speculating if Adam received a call from the blackmailers too. Could he have been killed because he refused to cooperate?

Madeline shoved the *Messenger* closer to him and tapped the paper with her freshly polished nails. "Read this." Her new perfume floated near his nose, reminding him of her extravagance.

He skimmed the first paragraph of the article. "Calm down, Maddie. Logan correctly reported our statement. It's still under investigation, which is typical."

She paced his office. "Why would both of them be murdered? It's so disturbing."

Trevor rubbed his stomach. "I know."

"What if what Eileen wanted to tell me at the last fundraiser was a warning? Could it be she knew something that put her and Adam in danger?"

Dear God, she's back wondering about Eileen's conversation. Trevor hid his clenched fist at his side. "Stop the speculations, Maddie. Let the cops finish their investigation."

Tears formed in her eyes. Trevor put a box of tissues from his bottom drawer on the top of his desk. She stopped pacing and pulled one out, dabbing the watermarks under her eyes, careful not to smear her make-up. "What are we going to do without Adam? He was crucial to my stance on the unions."

"We'll get through this." He reached into his top desk drawer for the bottle of Tums.

"Honey. Look at you. You're worried too. Did you make an appointment with the doctor?"

"I told you I would. I'm fine. It's just my indigestion."

Madeline eased into the chair. "I can't stop wondering what Eileen wanted to tell me. What do you think she meant?"

"Please…let it go."

She sighed. "I guess you're right." She stood and threw the tissue in the trash can. "I'll be in my office."

After Madeline left, Trevor moved to his window. Rain clouds loomed in the distance. On the street below, a cab pulled up in front of the building and dropped off his fare.

His thoughts went to the cab ride he took to meet Madeline at the Bon Auberge restaurant last year when she'd told him she wanted to run for Senator Jenkins's seat. It was great timing for him, to help her with her campaign. He had needed a break after defending a twelve-year-old boy of murdering his abusive father.

He stepped back to his desk and switched gears to rehearse anticipated questions from Shana tomorrow like he did so many times in his career of questioning witnesses on the stand. But this time, he would be the one being questioned.

CHAPTER 24

June 3rd, Thursday

PHILIP DREADED WHAT MIGHT wait for him at home, not knowing what to expect after he talked to Ros earlier about the deaths of Adam and Eileen. It was the first time in months he was home in time for dinner. Comforting Ros became foremost in his mind. She would probably have out the medical journal looking for a new health remedy for him to prevent any illness, which she typically did after a death no matter what the cause.

He pulled into the driveway of his split-level home in Conshohocken where he lived with his wife and three children for the past fourteen years. When he entered through the inside door from the garage, the aroma of oregano, garlic, and tomatoes filled the house.

Ros called out. "Is that you, Philip?"

"Yes."

He followed Ros's voice to the laundry room. She stood on her tiptoes, reaching into the bottom of the washing machine.

After she put the wet clothes into the dryer, she faced him. "When are you getting your hair cut? You keep putting it off. You promised."

"Never mind that." He pulled her close, her head resting on his shoulders as he stroked her curly hair. "We should talk about

Adam and Eileen."

She pulled away and picked up the laundry basket full of clothes.

"Ros. Everything okay?"

"I'm fine."

He followed her through the family room and up the steps into the kitchen. A large pot simmered on top of the stove.

She placed the basket on the chair by the pantry. "I'm making a fresh batch of gravy."

Even though you couldn't mistake Ros's Irish heritage from her mother's side with her pale complexion and auburn hair, she prided herself in being half Italian and used the term gravy for pasta sauce.

As she was smothering a plate full of spaghetti with her gravy, Philip looked around for the medical journal. Nowhere in sight. Good sign.

She set the plate on the table. "I can warm up some garlic bread. Kelsey's at her friend's house in the Poconos for the weekend. It's an in-service day at school tomorrow. The boys called from college. Said they are excited about coming home in August."

"I'm looking forward to seeing them."

She perused inside the refrigerator and moved containers around on the shelf. "Philip, your health drink is still in here."

"Who cares about that stupid spinach drink?" He nudged her away from the refrigerator and closed the door. "You need to sit down."

He sat at the table and noticed a paid receipt for $100.00 on the lazy susan. He picked it up, read it, and waved it at her. "What's this. You went to Madame X again?"

She snatched it from Philip's hand. "She helps me."

He gritted his teeth. "That psychic can't tell a Tarot Card from a regular playing card. All she wanted was your money after your father died. What a joke. Claiming she could speak to the dead."

Her voice rose. "She spoke to my father."

"Please Ros, promise me you won't go back to her? I'm worried about you. You're acting as nothing happened. Adam and Eileen were murdered."

She settled into a chair at the table and twirled her hair on the top of her head between her fingers. "I'm fine. Stop worrying about me."

"How can I when you started that hair-twirling habit again?"

She squinted her eyes at him. "I told you before, it's Kelsey's schedule."

"Ros, don't you have questions about Adam and Eileen?"

"No." She yawned. "I'm exhausted. I think I'll go to bed."

Philip looked at the wall clock. "It's only a little after 8:30."

Ros stood, stepped over to the stove, and turned it off. "You need anything else?"

"I'm good." He watched as she poured the hot gravy into a glass container and put it into the refrigerator. "You sure you don't want to talk?"

"I just need a good night's rest." She shuffled out of the kitchen and climbed the stairs.

Philip forked his spaghetti as he stared at the receipt. Why would she be seeing Madame X again? And why didn't Ros ask questions about Adam's and Eileen's deaths? That's not like her. He had a hard time believing Ros's excuse for the twirling hair habit returned because of Kelsey's schedule. Although it had become more hectic with the *Annie* production. He finished his dinner and convinced himself she would be fine after a good night's sleep.

He grabbed a can of beer from the refrigerator and headed to his makeshift home office upstairs next to their bedroom. As he waited for the computer to boot up, he sipped on the beer. Within a few seconds, he typed in his password for the VPN and reviewed several reporters' stories.

Shortly after 10:00 p.m., he'd finished his beer and shut down his computer. He made his way to the bedroom and found Ros fast asleep. In the bathroom, Philip opened the medicine cabinet and a pill bottle dropped into the sink. He picked it up and read the prescription. Valium 5-30-99. Why did she get this filled? Could Kelsey's career be getting to her more than he thought, or was it the visit to Madame X…or something else?

CHAPTER 25

THE NEXT MORNING, SHANA and Fits arrived at the MIC building for their interview with Trevor and Madeline Richmond. While riding in the elevator from the parking garage, Fits started right in on his date last night with the young female officer he met at Adam's crime scene. "She's really into me."

Shana rolled her eyes. "Can you hold off telling me about your escapades for once? Let's focus on the case."

"Jealous Doyle?"

She smirked. "Don't flatter yourself."

"Any luck deciphering the note?"

"Still working on it. I thought part of the note was an address, but nothing turned up in a search."

They arrived on the fifth floor. The doors slid open and Shana faced Fits. "Let me do the talking."

He raised his hands, palms out. "You got it."

As they stepped off the elevate, Shana's eyes were drawn to Fits's shirt hanging over his belt, and the dark spot to the right of his tie. "What the hell's on your shirt?"

He lowered his arms and pushed his tie to the side. "Oh. Grape jam from breakfast."

Shana shook her head as he licked his fingers and tried to wipe it off.

They entered the reception area. Madeline rushed to embrace Shana, clutching her tight. Her sweet, earthy perfume snuck into Shana's nostrils.

"Oh darling, we can't believe it." Madeline released the hold. "We're sick about Adam and Eileen. How horrible, Eileen found in a dumpster. And Adam—"

"Yes. It is sad." Shana said as she and Fits followed Madeline into Trevor's office.

Shana hugged Trevor and smelled his freshly starched shirt. She introduced Fits.

Trevor gestured for them to sit as he made his way behind his desk and sat. "Shana. Your daughter is doing a great job as our IT Manager at TR Tires."

"Thanks. I'll let Cateline know. We need to ask you some questions about Eileen and Adam." Shana pulled out her recorder as she and Fits sat in the barrel chairs in front of his desk. "Okay if I tape this?"

"Of course," Trevor said. "We're here to help. Do you have any leads?"

"Still investigating." Shana pressed record. "Madeline, I understand Adam was working with you on your campaign."

"Yes. We needed to get a clear perspective about the unions and Trevor recommended him."

"I'm not up on political etiquette, but wouldn't that be a conflict of interest to have him work as the union representative at TR Tires and for your campaign?"

Trevor shook his head. "Actually no. Adam had a proven track record when he worked as a union rep at my other company RedChem. His insight was valuable."

"We're trying to retrace the steps of Adam and Eileen up to the time of their murders. When was the last time either of you saw Adam?"

"I think about a week ago," Trevor said. "But the morning of his…death, he called and left a message with our secretary. He wanted me to call him at home to schedule a meeting. I tried to reach him, but we never connected."

"Never connected?"

"Adam or Eileen never listened to their messages, so I called their home twice that day. I couldn't reach him." Trevor sighed. "If only I…talked to him. Oh, this makes me sick." Trevor sucked in a deep breath.

Shana thought of the call that came into Adam and Eileen's house the day of his death. It must've been Trevor.

"It's so upsetting." Madeline's eyes welled. "To think we wondered where Adam was…and he was already dead."

Trevor handed her a tissue, and she carefully dabbed the corners of her eyes.

Shana faced Trevor. "Why did Adam want to meet you?"

"I suspected it had something to do with the unions."

"Is there any relationship between your two companies, TR Tires and RedChem?"

"RedChem researches any chemical improvements to the tires."

"Trevor, is RedChem working on anything special for TR Tires?"

"Not that I know of."

Shana switched her recorder to her other hand. "Adam had a meeting at RedChem on May 17th. Do you know anything about that?"

"No. I don't know why he would've gone there. Nick Vega is my plant manager at TR Tires and he's the one who coordinates any changes RedChem recommends."

"Who would Nick Vega contact there?"

"Paul Edwards is in charge of research and handles the day-to-day business."

"Is there anything you can tell us about Eileen?"

Madeline spoke up. "Logan told us at one of our dinners,

that Adam confided in him a couple of months ago about Eileen's drinking and gambling problem. Sorry you weren't at the dinner, Shana."

Shana gave a slight smile as Madeline continued.

"We were concerned it might cause issues with Adam working on my campaign, but when we talked to him about it, he said he would keep it under control. But I don't think that happened."

"Maddie." Trevor glared wide-eyed at his wife. "No need to tell Shana."

"Let me be the judge of that." Shana turned to Madeline. "What are you talking about?"

"At my last fundraiser, Eileen said something strange to me."

Trevor jumped in to answer. "I told Maddie that Eileen was drunk. It meant nothing."

Shana faced Madeline. "Tell me what she said."

"She told me I would be sorry, and my campaign was in trouble. I passed it off blaming what she said on the booze, but now I'm not sure."

"Do you have any idea what she meant?"

Madeline shrugged. "Not a clue. But we worried she may be a liability if she came to any future events and we told Adam that. He seemed to understand."

"When was the fundraiser?" Shana said.

"May 19th."

"So that's the last time you both saw her?"

They responded in unison. "Yes."

"Do you have access to a limousine?"

Trevor lowered his brow. "No. Why?"

"Someone spotted a black limousine bringing Eileen home the morning of May 18th. Did Adam mention anything to either of you about that?"

"He didn't say anything to me." Trevor looked at Madeline.

"Did he say anything to you?"

Madeline shook her head. "First I heard this."

Shana recited the dates and times of death for Adam and Eileen and asked them to confirm their whereabouts.

Madeline arched her back. "You can't believe we're suspects."

"It's routine, Maddie." Trevor pulled his calendar close. "The 2nd we were here. As I said I was waiting to get in touch with Adam. Our secretary can vouch for that. She should be here soon." He flipped the pages. "On the 28th we were at the caterer's all-day planning for the campaign dinner later this month."

"I will need your contact there," Shana said.

He jotted a note and handed it to her.

"Anyone come to mind who might want to harm Adam?"

Trevor glanced at Madeline and back at Shana. "No, we don't. We can't even imagine anyone wanting ill-will toward Adam."

"What about Eileen?"

He winced and rubbed his upper stomach. Shana caught a glimpse of Fits tilting his head her way, knowing he noticed it too.

"Anything wrong, Trevor?" Shana said.

"Ah. No. We have no idea who might want to harm her." He studied his watch.

"We keeping you from something?"

"I have a meeting with the board at RedChem. Wanted to prepare for it. Do you have any more questions?"

"I guess we're done here." Shana turned off her recorder and stood. "We'll be in touch if we have any more questions."

Trevor's hug to Shana was rigid, much different from when he greeted her. Shana and Fits followed Madeline out of Trevor's office to where their secretary was now at her desk.

Madeline introduced Shana and Fits. "Iris. Can you tell these detectives where we were on June 2nd?"

"Of course. I'll never forget it. That was the day I received a call from Mr. Detweiler. He wanted to see Mr. Richmond, but he never called back." She lowered her head. "Sad to say, we now know why. We were all here in the office all day."

Madeline held the door for them to exit, grabbed Shana, and held her tight. "Darling, please try to make the gang's next dinner? We miss you."

Shana pulled away. "Sorry. It's the job."

Another reminder she had ignored her friends.

At the elevator, Fits pushed the down button. "Doyle, I have to apologize."

"Another apology? About getting back to your old ways with the guys after Mr. Roberts left?"

"Well, that too. I was way off base on how you'd handle questioning friends. You were objective. Don't know if I would've been that way with a friend of mine."

She smiled. "Thanks."

"So, your reporter friend Logan is friends with the Richmonds too?"

"We've all been friends since high school."

"I can feel my stomach telling me it's time to eat."

Shana checked her watch. "Right on time. It's almost noon."

"How about if I treat you to a cheesesteak at Jim's?"

"Apology and a free lunch. Is this a dream or a nightmare?"

"Very funny. Trying to make amends."

Knowing she had to meet Sarge at Mayor Gaffney's office later, she asked for a raincheck. "I want to get back to homicide and transcribe this interview. You can arrange a meeting with Vega and check out Trevor and Madeline's alibi with the caterer."

In the elevator, Fits turned to Shana. "RedChem. That's the name on the letterhead on the note you found at the Detweiler house, and one of Trevor's companies. He acted nervous when you asked if anyone wanted to harm Eileen. And again, when Madeline wanted to tell us what Eileen said at the fundraiser. Something doesn't seem right."

Her stomach tightened. "I noticed it too."

Of all times for Fits to pay attention to his craft. She hated to think of Trevor as a suspect.

Back at homicide, she transcribed her interview with Madeline and Trevor. As she replayed it, Trevor's voice did change with the mention of Eileen's name.

CHAPTER 26

WHILE WAITING FOR SARGE in the lobby at City Hall, Shana munched on a bag of barbeque potato chips. She hadn't had time to add notes to her disk in homicide, so she pulled out her recorder and quietly dictated in between chews.

"Note to myself: What did Eileen want to tell Madeline on the 19th? Was it related to when she came home on May 18th in the limo? Need to find out more about RedChem from Nick Vega. Why did Trevor seem nervous with the mention of Eileen's name? Could there be a connection between Trevor's two companies and Adam's note?"

She stopped recording when Sarge stepped out of the revolving doors into the lobby and approached her. After she updated him on the interview with Madeline and Trevor, Sarge asked about Fits.

"He actually complimented me on how I handled the Richmond interview."

"Glad to hear it. What are your plans to visit that chemical company, RedChem, and the TR manager, Nick Vega?"

"Fits is arranging a visit with Vega. Trevor mentioned talking to Paul Edwards at RedChem, but I want to wait to hear who Vega suggests." Shana crumbled the chips bag and tossed it in the trash can as they made their way to the stairs. "Sarge, do you have any idea why Mayor Gaffney wants to see us?"

"I can't remember the last time the mayor even cared about *any* case, and now he wants to get involved in this one. He's friends with Senator Jenkins, and this case involves someone who worked for the senator's opponent. It sounds suspicious. I only brought the file with the autopsy report and basic facts."

"Is there anything in the file about Mr. Roberts?"

"No. I left that out since we kept it out of the news. I'm also putting the case book under lock and key, just in case the mayor gets any bright ideas. After you transcribe your interviews, give me the hard copies."

"What about Fits?"

"Tell him I'm locking them up because of political reasons. He doesn't have to know about our meeting with the mayor."

They entered Mayor Raymond Gaffney's office on the second floor. Shana hugged the mayor's secretary Betty Leonard, a petite woman in her late fifties with short tightly cropped hair, wearing a polyester black suit.

Shana broke away and faced Sarge. "Betty and I worked on the Child Abuse Foundation with the mayor's late wife."

Sarge nodded.

"Shana, we miss you at the fundraiser meetings for the foundation," Betty said.

"Sorry. It's tough with my work schedule. Is the mayor here?"

"He went to get lunch and should be back soon. Why don't you have a seat? Do either of you want coffee?"

Before they could answer, the mayor waddled down the hall carrying a grease-stained white paper bag. Shana recognized the bag, Jim's on South Street. His disheveled suit pants rose in between his legs as he shuffled into the reception area. A strong aroma of onions, Italian meats, and oregano floated in. The hoagie's smell made Shana's mouth water after giving up a free lunch at Jim's with Fits.

The mayor extended his hand. "Detective Doyle and Sergeant Ellis, thank you for coming."

She noted the bruise on the mayor's knuckles. It looked like one of those bruises she remembered her father had from his heart condition after taking a blood thinner. It would take weeks to fade. If at all.

The mayor glanced at the file in Sarge's hand. "Come into my office. Betty, hold my calls."

After they entered, the mayor closed the door and motioned for them to sit in the leather chairs, while he walked behind his desk. The mayor placed the white bag on the corner of his desk and pulled out a handkerchief from his back pocket. He wiped his sweaty forehead as he squeezed his plump body between the arms of his chair. "I want to talk to you about the Detweiler case."

"Mayor, why the interest?" Sarge said.

"A union matter. With Adam Detweiler as a union representative for TR Tires, I want to make sure the investigation is going smoothly."

"Here's a preliminary report." Sarge handed the file to the mayor.

"Why don't you wait in the reception area while I read this?"

That made little sense to Shana, but she took Sarge's lead, and they stepped out of the office.

Betty stood. "Would you care for coffee now?"

"Sure," Shana said.

Sarge shook his head.

Standing near Betty's desk, Shana noticed the two lines on the phone, one was lit. Who had the mayor called? She reached for the cup of coffee Betty poured. "How is fundraising going for the Child Abuse Foundation?"

Betty sighed. "Not so good."

"I read they were on target for beating their donation goals. What happened?" Shana took a sip of coffee.

"Long story."

The light went out on the phone, and the mayor's voice sounded over the intercom. "Betty?"

She pressed the button. "Yes, Mayor Gaffney."

"Have the detective and sergeant come in."

Shana put her coffee cup on Betty's desk.

Betty raised a brow. "I guess you heard that? You can go right in."

As they entered the office, Shana blinked repeatedly to clear the overwhelming odor of onions that filled the air. They took their same seats.

The mayor rested back in his chair. "We need to talk."

Lettuce was sprawled on his desk from his half-eaten hoagie. Perspiration dripped from the mayor's temples. He pointed to the file in front of him and glared at Sarge. "This is nothing more than what the commissioner said at his press conference. There must be more."

"I told you on the phone this would be a preliminary report. We're still investigating."

The mayor slammed his fist on the file. "Sergeant Ellis, this could be damaging to the unions, if Adam Detweiler's murder has anything to do with Madeline Richmond's no-strike clause in union contracts."

"So, you're telling me this is political?"

The mayor's tie brushed the mayonnaise piled on the top of the hoagie. He pushed the sandwich aside and buzzed for Betty without saying a word. She entered with a rag. Shana suspected a common occurrence. Betty wiped up the mess on his desk while the mayor brushed off the mayonnaise from his tie.

After she left, the mayor folded his hands and calmed his voice. "We need to work together on this. I'd like to help if I can."

Sarge shifted in his chair. "Mayor Gaffney I assure you we're doing what we can and will inform you of the facts as they unfold."

"The facts!" The mayor slammed his fist again. His face reddened. He snuck a finger in between his tight shirt color and his bulging neck. "You must have more information." He took rapid, quick breaths as he pushed his heavy body from the snug-fitting armchair. He swaggered around and stood between Shana and Sarge. "This could be a very sensitive case with a union rep murdered. You need to keep me informed."

Shana cringed as his powerful onion breath shot her way.

On their way out, Sarge and Shana shook the mayor's sweaty hand. As they left the office, Betty pulled out two packets of hand wipes from her desk drawer.

Shana opened the packet. "Happen often?"

Betty raised her eyebrows. "More than you could imagine."

Sarge wiped his hands. "Let's get out of here."

Outside of the office, Shana turned to Sarge. "Do you ever wonder how the mayor got elected? He's such a slob. Not political material, if you ask me."

"Word is Senator Jenkins helped him get elected. They've been close since college."

As they headed for the stairs, Shana said, "Do you buy that he's concerned about Adam being a union rep as his interest in the Detweiler case?"

"Not particularly. Although, maybe he's concerned because Madeline Richmond's campaign promise about the union no-strike clause contradicts Senator Jenkins's view."

The mayor's outer office door opened and Betty called out. "Shana. Do you have a minute to talk about the foundation?"

"Go ahead," Sarge said. "I'll meet you back at the roundhouse."

Shana walked back to the mayor's office.

"It's not about the foundation," Betty whispered. "I have some information about Adam Detweiler and I don't want Sergeant Ellis to know until you hear what I have to say. I'll call you when I can."

Shana agreed and left City Hall.

When she arrived back in homicide, Fits stood by her cubicle. "We have a meeting with Nick Vega on Monday afternoon at 3:00. Couldn't get in there before then. He seemed pretty nervous when I told him we wanted to ask questions about the murders."

"What about the Richmonds' alibi?"

"All checked out. Want any coffee?"

"No. I'm good."

She sat at her desk and inserted her disk into the computer. After she transcribed her recent notes to herself, she typed new ones.

Why is the mayor so interested in the Detweiler case? His concern as a union matter seems a stretch. What did Betty want to tell me? Who did the mayor call while Sarge and I waited in the reception area?

CHAPTER 27

June 4th, Friday

THE MUFFLED SOUND of the Channel 6 News helicopter circled outside his window. He watched it angle between the towering buildings. Directly across window washers lowered their scaffolding down the side of the building. How annoying their presence must be to the inhabitants of the offices as they drifted by. Their pale gray uniforms made them almost invisible against the color of the building walls.

The phone rang, and he answered.

"It's me," Mayor Gaffney said on the other end.

"Why are you calling me here? And twice today."

"Detective Doyle and Sergeant Ellis just left. I don't think they're telling me everything."

"What do you mean?" he said.

"Detective Doyle has an impeccable close rate on her cases. Smart chick." The mayor raised his voice. "What if she finds out what's going on?"

He clenched the receiver tighter. "Gaffney, call your mole. See what you can find out." His voice rose. "And stop calling me on mundane things you should handle. Contact me if it's important and *only* if it's important."

He slammed the receiver down and watched the window washers descend their scaffolding to the lower floors. One side was lower than the other from the heavyset man. It reminded him of the mayor. That fat pompous idiot was becoming a liability and could ruin his plans.

CHAPTER 28

IN HER APARTMENT, SHANA was getting ready for her date with Mac. A sundress and sandals would be a pleasant change from her business attire; dress slacks, button-down blouse, and jacket. She dabbed a little Estee Lauder behind her ears and grabbed a purse from her bedroom closet. Carrying a purse seemed almost foreign to her when she never did on the job. She put her gun and badge in it and left her building. The maintenance men were busy working on the front entrance installing a new keypad security system. She got annoyed when they asked her to test it, fearing she would be late for her date.

On her way to PJ's, her enthusiasm to see Mac waned after she recalled her previous conversation with him and seeing his mannerisms change when he talked about his deceased wife. Could he be ready for a relationship? But what a treat it would be to date someone who understands the interruptions when called to a crime scene. She scolded herself for thinking that far ahead.

She entered PJ's and Mac waved from a corner table. He stood and pulled out the chair for her. Such a gentleman. The waiter came over and they ordered glasses of Merlot.

"I'm glad you agreed to have dinner with me," Mac said.

"I have to be honest." She unfolded the napkin and placed it on her lap. "I almost didn't accept. The guys in homicide would have a field day if they knew I went out with you." She recalled the taunting when she dated a fellow officer shortly after she joined the force. "I like to keep my personal life to myself. Away from my co-workers."

"I can be discreet."

She had a strong feeling he would be.

The waiter served their drinks, and Mac raised his glass for a toast. "Here's to a good evening."

They clicked and sipped their wine.

Mac rested his glass on the table and twirled the stem. "I wanted to apologize about the way I left after we questioned Mr. Roberts yesterday. I kinda jumped at Russell."

"Hey. You don't have to apologize for getting testy with Fits. It's easy to do."

"But I wanted to explain." Mac put a napkin on his lap. "Even though we identified the victim as Eileen Detweiler, she was originally a Jane Doe. My wife Faye's sister had drug problems and disappeared. Through the help of a private detective, they located her, in an unmarked county grave."

"Oh, how horrible."

His face turned solemn. "Before Faye died, I promised her I would focus on unidentified bodies to help them find their way home."

There's that look again. She needed to be careful. "I commend you for being passionate to identify the lost ones."

"An excellent word for it. Lost ones. But I have something else on my mind. The University of Pennsylvania recently tried to recruit me to teach forensic science. I've always wanted to teach, but I'm conflicted, because of my promise to my wife."

"Mac, could there be another solution? Perhaps the coroner's office would allow you to consult on unidentified bodies. Or you could contact the university to see if they would allow you to teach at night? If you enjoyed one more than the other, then you have your answer. Kind of ease into the change."

"I hadn't thought about that. Thanks for the idea. Enough about me. Tell me about you. I heard you're divorced." He drank some wine.

"Yes. It's been almost thirteen years now." Hearing her say the words, she couldn't believe it had been that long.

"Any thoughts of getting married again someday?"

Shana thought about the two guys who tried to get close to her over the last six years. They stopped calling when almost every date was interrupted by a call to a crime scene. "With my work schedule and my profession. It's almost impossible to have a relationship."

"Do you have children?"

"Yes. Two daughters. They're grown now and have places of their own."

"Must have been difficult being a single parent. Do they see their father much? Oh, I'm sorry. Am I getting too personal?"

She was almost embarrassed to say how her ex-husband never played a part in her daughters' lives when he'd only lived fifteen minutes away. Too busy with his new young wife. "I don't mind you asking. He didn't see them much."

"I couldn't do that. Not see my children."

"That's what separates the men from the boys." Shana took a sip of wine. "My parents helped me a lot after the divorce."

"Are you close with your parents?"

An older man walked by their table wearing a black cap and disrupted her thoughts. His stature and gait reminded her of her father. A slight smile came to her face. Mac was easy to talk to and for a moment she thought about telling him her suspicions her parents' accident was meant for her…but too soon to talk about her demons.

Shana stared at her glass of wine. "They were killed in a car accident six months ago this past March."

"I'm so sorry."

The waiter approached and Mac slipped on his reading glasses. They opened the menus and ordered their meals.

He removed his glasses. "Frank told me before you joined the force, you were in banking."

"So, you talked to Sarge about me?"

"Like I said I was interested in you. I don't think you have to worry about Frank. He knows how to be discreet. Why the interest in police work?"

"It's a long story."

"We have time." He sipped his wine.

Before when her dates asked about why she entered law enforcement, after her long explanation, they lost interest. Something told her, Mac wouldn't be like that.

"My interest started when I was in college. I attended a seminar on criminology. The speaker was one of Penn State's professors who was a retired Philadelphia homicide detective. I found it fascinating. Putting the pieces of a puzzle together. Like solving a cryptogram that my father got me hooked on when I was in high school. I took more courses on criminology and even thought about joining the force after I graduated, hoping to become a homicide detective."

"So, what happened?"

She recalled her ex-husband's comment while they dated in college. *A woman could never become a detective. That's a man's job.* She basked in the glory she proved him wrong.

"I met my ex in college," she continued. "And we planned on getting married after graduation. Women weren't in homicide back then, so I majored in business and minored in criminology."

"You don't strike me as the type of person who would have stopped pursuing a career because there weren't women in a profession."

Too soon to open up with Mac about her ex-husband's manipulative ways. Shana gave a half-smile. "It's funny how things happen. I backed off joining the force because of the lack of women, and here I am the first and still the only female in the city's homicide division. I guess things haven't changed much." She took a sip of wine. "I told you it was a long story."

"I'm still interested. Go on."

"Okay. After I worked in banking for a while, I applied for a vice president's position in the mortgage division, which I was well qualified for, but the board of directors gave it to a man. He not only didn't have any experience in that field but to add more salt to the wound, the president of the bank asked me to train him. Shortly after that, a local mortgage banking firm recruited me and under the circumstances, I jumped at it. They didn't have that stodgy male mentality."

"What caused you to leave your previous career and join the police force?"

"My desire for criminology reared its head when about six months before my youngest graduated from high school, I witnessed a mugging one night at the mortgage firm. I helped the victim recall events about the crime and gave details to a sketch artist that helped apprehend the perp. Soon after, my daughters were out of the house and were in college. In my early forties, I wasn't sure if I wanted to pursue changing careers so dramatically. So, I investigated my options and decided to go for it. Before I knew it, I sold my house in Conshohocken, left my friends, and moved into the apartment I have now in Rittenhouse Square."

The waiter served their meals. The smell of charcoal steak floated into her nostrils. Shana cut the filet and took a bite. "This is good."

Mac spooned sour cream onto his baked potato. "Frank said you have an excellent record. I don't know many detectives who have achieved such notoriety."

She chewed quickly and swallowed. "It's all in the details. I record my thoughts on a case and transcribe them onto a disk, which I analyze throughout an investigation. It helps me put the pieces of the puzzle together, so to speak. A habit I carried over from my previous career where there were tons of follow-up. I had a lot on my plate back then, juggling raising two girls, my job, and maintaining a house I got in the divorce. I had to keep it all straight."

Mac stared at her and smiled. "I'm in awe of how you handle things."

Her face warmed as she forked broccoli on her plate.

"Shana, I wanted to ask you out ever since I first met you. I tried to flirt a little when I saw you, but I always got the impression you weren't interested…all business."

She laughed. "Flirt at a crime scene?"

"Yeah." Mac chuckled. "I guess that sounded pretty stupid. I'm out of practice about dating. Hadn't thought about impressing a woman in almost twenty-five years."

The corners of her mouth curled. "Well for your information, I noticed. I guess I didn't think of you as someone to date. But I'm glad you finally asked me out."

The night slipped by and the waiter cleared the table. For once her brain followed her heart, and she managed to talk about everything else but the case. Mac had a calming effect on her she hadn't experienced with any other man.

"Shana, let's do this again. What do you think?"

She lowered her head and wondered if her obsession with engulfing herself in her cases would allow her time to start a relationship when she didn't even have time for her daughters or her best friends of over thirty years.

"Did I say something wrong?" Mac said. "I thought perhaps you were feeling the same way."

She searched for words without revealing her fixation. "I'm concerned about dating someone in my field. What if it doesn't work out? It would be uncomfortable for us both."

Mac reached for her hand and held it. "Why don't we see where this goes?"

She stared into his eyes and felt the warmth of his hand. How could she *not* give this a chance? "Okay. But promise me we'll be honest with each other if our relationship becomes a problem."

"Agreed."

"I need a fresh start in the morning. We better leave."

Mac paid the check, and they left the restaurant. He walked her to her car and reached for the handle to open the door. His body was close to hers. She raised her head. He bent to kiss her. It was a tender kiss at first and grew deeper when he wrapped his arms around her pulling her body into his. His embrace felt comforting and safe. Her heart fluttered. Their lips fit perfectly together. A sexual rush swept through her body, like nothing she'd ever felt before. Could she be getting involved too fast?

CHAPTER 29

June 5th, Saturday

HOW FITTING, for this morning to be such a dreary day for a funeral. The muggy air hung heavy after a brief rain shower. The steam on the roads from the heated blacktop hovered like a low, hazy fog.

Walking through the parking lot at the Perkasie Funeral Home, Shana thought about last night with Mac. She couldn't believe how comfortable she felt talking with him, as if they had been dating for years. And that kiss still etched in her mind brought a smile to her face. Under normal circumstances, she would've been excited telling her girlfriends about her date. But their friendship hadn't been normal for some time, and telling them now at a funeral would not be the time to rekindle their relationship. If that was even possible.

She entered the parlor and the powerful scent of nondescript flowers filled the air. Several wreaths on stands lined up at least ten feet before and after the position of the caskets. Each had black ribbons with the words rest in peace. Ironic, like the ones the guys had placed in her adjacent cubicle. She signed the condolence book and stood at the end of the receiving line, taking a deep breath, pumping in confidence.

You can do this.

She peeked around the crowd. The two closed caskets were

next to each other, just like her parents. Her stomach churned and her hands started to sweat. The air seemed to close in on her, and she blew out several long breaths. Right before she reached the coffins, she eyed the picture posters of Eileen and Adam and their family and friends, noticing Eileen with Ros, Jules, Madeline, and herself in their cap and gown at their high school graduation. She paid her respects and hurried from the line, tearing up feeling conflicting emotions for her parents, and Adam and Eileen.

Shana made her way to the foyer by the front entrance where her two girlfriends were. Jules, tall, impeccably dressed with everything matching, shoes, purse, jewelry. Next to her stood a much shorter Ros wearing her black funeral dress.

They all hugged each other through tears.

"This must've been difficult for you." Jules gently touched Shana's arm. "Double closed casket."

Shana let out a long exhale, blinking away tears, and nodded.

"Oh. I'm sorry, Shana," Jules said. "I shouldn't have brought it up."

"It's okay."

"We missed you last night, Shana. Did you get my message?"

"Yes. I got your message. I told you both when I became a detective, my time wouldn't be my own."

Shana had never told them about the psychiatrist visits and his transference diagnosis. She didn't want to get into that now and diverted the conversation.

"Jules, how do you like working for a vet?"

"Working there part-time is right up my alley. Satisfies my feelings after losing Sadie. Logan and I keep arguing about whether to get another hunting dog or a lap dog. I think I'm losing the fight since he likes to hunt so much."

Shana looked around. "Where's Philip and Logan?"

"Logan was one of the first ones here and had to leave," Jules said. "He's working on a story, as usual."

"Philip was here earlier too," Ros said.

Jules faced Shana. "Did you catch how Eileen's mom was? Talked about Eileen as if she were home in bed."

Shana peeked around the corner to Eileen's parents sitting in front of the coffin and turned back, recalling how Eileen's mother acted when they came to identify the body. "It may be a blessing, not realizing her daughter is dead."

"It's a shame Eileen had a drinking problem," Jules said and faced Ros. "We saw it first-hand."

Ros nodded.

"What do you mean?" Shana said.

"At Madeline's fundraiser last month." Jules stared at Shana. Her eyes narrowed. "You know the one you couldn't make."

Shana ignored the smart comment and smiled.

Ros twirled her hair on top of her head. Shana noted a worried look on Ros's face, one that seemed to form new lines around her eyes.

Jules continued. "Eileen was drunk and Adam got her out of there before she did any damage."

Shana faced Ros wondering if she knew about Eileen's miscarriages. "Ros, you were the one who kept in touch with Eileen after their wedding. Did you know why she started drinking?"

Ros's facial expression froze, and she stopped twirling her hair. "No. I need to get some air." She headed outside.

Shana grabbed Jules's arm, stopping her from following Ros. "That nervous habit is back. Has Ros been doing that long?"

"Now that you mention it, I noticed her doing that last night at dinner. Speaking of which, we are planning another dinner soon. Please try to make it this time."

"Let's go talk to Ros."

Outside in the drizzling rain, a man with a blue hooded parka positioned magnet funeral flags on the cars. Jules and

Shana approached Ros standing under the carport.

Shana stepped close to Ros. "Is everything okay?"

"Why?"

"Because your nervous habit is back."

Ros shrugged. "Oh...it's Kelsey's schedule. It's this production of *Annie* that's wearing me down a little. I'm okay."

Shana thought how odd. Ros has been dealing with her daughter's singing career for years and seemed to love every minute of it. Why now has it gotten to Ros?

"How is that show going?" Jules said.

"Rehearsals are almost done. Are you guys going to Madeline's campaign event later this month?"

"We are." Jules faced Shana. "I assume you'll be there?"

"I'm waiting to see if I'm on duty."

Jules pressed her lips together. "This is an important night for Madeline. We all need to be there."

"I'll try. Were Madeline and Trevor here?"

"Yes. Earlier. They couldn't stay. Something about speaking engagements. The gravesite is private, but are either of you staying for the service?"

Shana checked her watch. "Sorry. I have to get back to headquarters."

Ros pulled her keys from her purse. "I need to pick up Kelsey from her singing lessons."

Jules raised her arms in the air. "Well, I'll represent us and stay."

Shana hugged Ros then Jules and left. She dashed to her car to avoid the rain that started. When she slid in, she thought how nice it was to connect with her friends, if only for a little while. Although there were enough jabs that she hadn't been around them much. Seeing the way Ros acted with her nervous habit, Shana felt like a distant relative who'd been kept out of the loop about a sick aunt. She couldn't shake the suspicion something was wrong with Ros and it wasn't Kelsey's career.

CHAPTER 30

IN HIS OFFICE, TREVOR pulled the oil painting away from the wall and opened his safe. He rested the Denver and Brown large manilla envelope on top of the white envelope that held his other stress issue. As he closed the safe, the pain in his upper stomach intensified. How much more could he stand. Bogus lawsuit settlement, blackmailer looming out there somewhere, and TR Tires in financial trouble. He sat behind his desk and rested his head back. When will this all end?

He placed a call to Philip, who answered on the second ring.

"I met with the junior partner of my old firm, Walter Brown. Damn it, Philip. He told me Logan tried to contact him. I instructed Walter not to call him back."

"Trevor, I should tell Logan what's going on. He's a bloodhound through and through. I can't stop him from investigating."

"You can't tell him. Not yet."

Philip sighed. "Okay for now, but it might come to that. What did the junior partner tell you?"

"You were right. It's looking like a plant for an illegal campaign contribution. The senior partner, Karl Denver, deposited a check for $100,000 into his firm's account in November 1998. According to Walter, Karl instructed the accounting department to not record it since a check would go out immediately. The next day the firm issued a check for $100,000 made payable to me, and Karl told accounting to mark it as services rendered."

"So the lawsuit settlement wasn't true."

Trevor closed his eyes for a second. "I should have checked this out, especially when it came out of the blue and shortly after Madeline entered the race. The lawsuit Karl Denver told me settled is still open. But here's an interesting part to this. The check given to the firm was drawn on an account from Fork Bank in California under...Senator Jenkins's name."

"The Senator! Holy shit, Trevor. How much do you trust this Walter guy?"

"I don't think he would jeopardize the firm with an accusation like that if it weren't true."

"This sounds like a setup."

Trevor raised his voice. "Don't you think I know that?"

"What about the senior partner?"

"As soon as Walter inquired about the funds, Karl disappeared. Thank God Walter gave me copies of everything. I'm keeping them in my safe. Ever since you told me about this, I rehashed Karl's conversation when he gave me the check. He insisted I use the money for the campaign. This entire thing is a mess. Philip, what are you going to do with this information? You can't report on this. It would be disastrous for Madeline's campaign."

"But you have to let me tell Logan. He's not going to let go of his suspicions. I'll make sure he doesn't write about it. If he knows the situation, he'll stop digging."

"Give me some time to think this through. I'll let you know when you can tell Logan. I want to return the money, but we spent half of it on advertising. The fundraiser later this month should be more than enough to pay it back. I'll keep you posted."

Trevor's acid indigestion erupted. He would have to tell Madeline soon about the funds.

CHAPTER 31

June 5th, Saturday

THE FUNERAL HAD SPURRED all sorts of emotions for Shana. Missing her parents and distancing herself from lifelong friends and her daughters, suddenly became a regret she couldn't shake. You would've thought there would be a pill to control this transference neurosis, but as her shrink explained many times, therapy would be the best medicine. She needed to get back to see him. Melancholy set in and she made a call to her daughters, thankful they agreed to meet her for lunch at such short notice.

After she called Fits, telling him she would be in later, she arrived at PJ's and waited for her daughters at the hostess station. The area by the bar was set up for their special lunch buffet. A cook wheeled a table with a side of beef past her. The smell of slow-roasted prime rib hovered, and her mouth watered.

From the padded bench by the door, Shana noticed a young man, about in his mid-thirties or so, sitting in a nearby booth with whom she suspected were his two young daughters by the way he fussed over them cutting their food. It brought to mind an incident after her divorce when her daughters were not much older than those little girls. She recalled how her heart ached as she had watched her daughters sitting on the stairs at home, waiting for their father holding his birthday present. He never showed.

Her daughters entered the restaurant, diverting her thoughts about that day. Shana stood to greet them. Cateline, tall and lean dressed in tight jeans and a flowing white silk blouse stepped over and hugged Shana. Kim equally as thin, but at least a half-head shorter than her younger sister, dressed in a dark business suit, did the same. Seeing them made Shana realize how much she missed their frequent luncheons together.

"I have a meeting later," Kim said. "So, I can't stay long, Mom. But I'm glad you called." She sat on the bench and flared her square nose. "Something smells good. How long is the wait?"

"The hostess is checking for a table now," Shana said as she sat.

Cateline squeezed in between her sister and Shana. "I'm starving."

Within minutes the hostess escorted them to a table and a tall man impeccably dressed headed their way.

"Hi, Shana," the man said.

"Oh. Grant?" She almost didn't recognize him. "It's been a while."

"Yes, it has."

Shana made introductions. "Grant owns the *Messenger*. He's Philip's boss."

He smiled at Shana's daughters. "The last time I saw you both, you were just little girls. You've grown into beautiful women." He faced Shana and winked. "Just like your mom. Nice seeing you all again." Grant touched Shana's arm. "Hope to see you again soon."

Shana and her daughters followed the hostess to a corner table, and they all sat. A sheepish grin spread over Kim's lightly freckled rounded face. "What was that all about?"

"Have no idea," Shana said.

Kim hung her purse strap on the back of her chair. "He was flirting with you, Mom."

Shana chuckled. "Flirting! I don't think so." But inside, she wondered.

The waitress served complimentary mimosas and left.

Kim took a sip from the champagne glass and turned to Shana. "So...not that I'm complaining Mom, but why did you contact us today. We haven't seen you in months."

Shana could always count on Kim to cut right to the chase.

Cateline joined in. "We've been staying away giving you space so you could sort through whatever you're dealing with."

"Thanks for that. I had to attend a double casket funeral today for Adam and Eileen Detweiler. The caskets were...closed. I got a little sentimental about your grandparents."

"We miss Mom Mom and Pop Pop too," Kim said. "But it's been over six months. Mom, have you thought about talking with someone about it? I mean a therapist."

She never told her daughters she was seeing a shrink, the diagnosis, or her obsession wondering if their grandparents' deaths were not an accident. If they knew, they would want all the details, and she wasn't ready for that. "I'm working through it."

A compassionate gaze fell over Cateline's oval face. "The funeral must have been difficult."

"It was, and I'm glad it's over. I'm sorry I haven't been seeing you both. Let's get back to meeting more often."

Cateline picked up her mimosa. "We'd like that." After she took a sip, she faced Shana. "I didn't have much contact with Adam at TR Tires being in the IT department, but I did run into him when I was leaving work the Friday before Memorial Day. I was in such a rush to leave for the shore and I bumped into him in the parking lot. He was heading for the employee entrance and I knocked his briefcase out of his hand. He seemed to panic and caught the briefcase before it hit the ground. The way he acted I thought he would be angry, but he wasn't."

"That would've been the 28th?"

"Yes. The company closed early, but I stayed to finish up some paperwork. I'd hoped to get on the road by 4:00 to beat traffic, but that didn't happen. I didn't get out of there until 5:00. Right during rush hour."

"You said a briefcase? Was it tan, a little worn?"

"I wasn't paying attention. I was in such a hurry. Why?"

To camouflage the reason for the question, Shana said, "Oh, Adam, and I had this thing years ago about stumping each other with our cryptograms and when we would meet, he always had that briefcase with him."

"That's funny, Mom. Because he asked about you and if you were still into cryptograms. I didn't think he knew who I was."

The note. Shana's mind jumped to the case. It *was* meant for her to find.

"Interesting he asked about me. I hadn't seen him since his wedding twenty years ago." To avoid any additional questions, Shana faced Kim. "How's work?"

"Great. I'm the top sales rep for the third straight month."

"Fantastic."

"I still get people asking about you, Mom. They can't believe I'm in the mortgage business too, and you're now a detective."

"Nice to know I left an impression." She had fond memories of her mortgage banking days and the comradery she enjoyed.

Shana faced Cateline. "I ran into Trevor Richmond the other day." Holding back where she saw him. "He said you were doing a great job."

"Maybe now he'll review my proposal that's been on his desk for months. With the Y2K transition, we need a new system."

Kim took a sip of the mimosa and rested her arms on the table. "Sis, I talked to my friends who have similar positions as yours. Based on what you've told me, you're making several thousand dollars less."

Cateline pressed her lips together. "Money isn't everything."

"But—"

"Let it go, Kim," Shana said in her motherly authoritative voice.

Kim raised her hands. "All right."

Cateline gave Kim a sheepish grin, leaned over, and hugged her tight. "Thanks, sis, for caring."

Shana's heart warmed, remembering how years ago to settle disagreements, the girls would wrestle on the floor and Kim would laugh so hard that Cateline won by default. Sometimes Shana wished she could escape to those simpler times.

"For your information," Cateline said. "I overheard a conversation in the board room that there's going to be improvements to the tires, which should increase revenues for the company. I'm sure I'll benefit in my bonus."

Shana stopped drinking. The detective in her took hold. "Who was there?"

"Nick Vega, he's the TR Tires plant manager. And I think someone from RedChem. They do chemical research on how to improve the tires. Why do you want to know?"

Shana realized how she must sound. "If word got out, TR Tires may lose business to a competitor."

"Didn't think about that. Let's eat. I'm starved."

A little while later they returned to the table from the buffet.

Shana placed the napkin on her lap. "By the way. I had a date last night. His name is Mac."

Kim was about to put a forkful of the quiche in her mouth and stopped. "It's about time."

"I agree," Cateline said. "What does he do for a living? Where'd you meet him?"

"I met him on the job." Shana picked up her fork. "He's the chief medical examiner."

Kim closed her eyes and shivered. "You've got to be kidding! I can't even imagine the dinner conversation."

"We had a normal conversation."

Cateline glanced at her mother. "I'm glad, you're dating."

"Me too," Kim said.

Like a distant spectator, Shana listened as her daughters made plans to get together for drinks with their men. She felt warm inside that they were close. They finished their meals and Shana picked up the check.

Cateline stood. "When can we do this again? We miss you, Mom."

Kim nodded. "Let's not wait so long."

"Let me get through solving the Detweiler case. We'll do this more often. I promise."

On their way out of PJ's, they hugged each other and Shana reminded Cateline to keep the conversation she heard at TR Tires to herself.

Before Shana started the engine, she pulled her recorder out.

"*Note to myself: More questions for Nick Vega on what Cateline overheard. Cateline saw Adam at TR Tires at around 5:00 on the 28th with a briefcase and knocked it out of his hand. Why did Adam panic when it fell? Was it the same one Eileen brought home on May 18th? Who was Adam going to see? Adam asked Cateline about me and cryptograms. He must have left that note for me. Why?*"

CHAPTER 32

June 5th, Saturday

SHANA CALLED FITS after she had lunch with her daughters. No hits on the APB on Eileen's car and nothing new had surfaced on the case. Fits said he'd call if anything came up, so she decided to stay home and focus on reviewing her notes. She sat at her desk, flipped open her laptop, and slid in her notes disk. After she added what she dictated earlier, she became anxious for Vega's meeting on Monday hoping it would fill in some gaps. She stretched her arms and yawned. Must have been the mimosa. She grabbed a Pepsi from the refrigerator.

Back at her desk, she gulped down most of the soda and stared at her parents' photo in the bi-fold frame. A satisfied smile spread over her face for getting through the double casket funeral today without totally falling apart. She continued to review her notes.

An hour had passed and nothing revealed a direct path to a prime suspect. She pulled open her desk drawer and reached for the stack of cryptograms where she'd placed the copy of Adam's note. Her parents' file caught her eye. There was a time, after their accident, when she examined the contents daily searching for clues if the accident was meant for her. Although the urge struck her to review it again, she'd obeyed her shrink's orders and hadn't opened it in almost two months. Perhaps it was time to move it out of sight as he'd suggested. She put it on the top shelf of her bedroom closet.

The home phone rang, and she hurried to answer it.

"Shana, it's Grant."

She stared at the floor, searching for words. Why had he called?

"Shana…you there?"

"Ah…how did you get my number?"

"How about having dinner sometime?"

And there it was. The reason for the call. Her mind jumped to thoughts of Mac. "Well…I'm kind of seeing someone right now."

"Oh, do you mean the chief medical examiner?"

That caught her off guard. "How did you know?"

"So how about it?"

Turning down strangers was hard enough, but someone she knew made her uncomfortable.

"Grant, I appreciate the invitation, but I don't think so. I need to go."

How strange he knew who Mac was, and how did he get her unlisted home number? She shook off the call and pulled Adam's note from the stack of cryptograms. What appeared to be an address at the bottom puzzled her, after her previous search didn't reveal a valid address in the area. She stared at it for a while. No clues jumped out at her, so she placed it to the side. Maybe solving one of her crypts would stimulate her technique to help with Adam's note. She went to pull one from the stack when her cell phone pinged. She hesitated, fearing it might be Grant calling, and let it ring several times before she cautiously flipped it open.

"Oh, Betty…I was wondering when I would hear from you."

"I'm sorry. I should have called earlier, but I've been having second thoughts if I want to get involved. If the mayor finds out I'm talking to you—"

"If it's about the Detweiler case, you need to tell me."

Betty sighed. "Okay. Meet me tonight before I lose my nerve."

Shana agreed to the time and location. She put Adam's note back in the stack of crypts and placed them in the desk drawer. After changing into jeans and a loose-fitting shirt, she grabbed her 9mm and badge from her nightstand safe, and a purse from the closet. Heading for the door, she picked up her recorder from the desk and went to close the living room plantation shutters. The dark apartment directly across from hers had blinds raised halfway on an angle. It looked vacant. Strange, she knew the Canadian couple that lived in that apartment and hadn't heard they were moving out.

After she closed the shutters, she headed for the door and hesitated. She returned and retrieved her disk from her desk and put it in her purse along with her recorder. If it wasn't too late, after she met Betty, she'd go to the roundhouse to compare her notes disk to the transcribed interview notes on her office computer. Maybe something would jump out at her.

An hour later, in the parking lot behind the Main Street Newsstand in Manayunk, Betty got out of her dark blue Ford Taurus and slid her petite frame into Shana's passenger side. She must have worked today, dressed in her black polyester suit.

Betty stared out the front window. "I shouldn't have come. I'm not used to this kind of thing."

"Do you mind if I tape this?"

"Please no." Betty wrung her hands. "That makes me nervous."

"Okay. What did you want to tell me? Take your time."

Betty took a deep breath. "Adam Detweiler came to see Mayor Gaffney on June 1st and he seemed nervous."

Shana thought back to the timeline. June 1st was the date Adam withdrew $25,000 and the day before they found his body.

"Why did he come to see the mayor?"

"The mayor told me Mr. Detweiler wanted some statistics on the unions, but I think he only said that for my benefit."

"Did you hear any of the conversation?"

"Only muffled voices. With the mayor's paranoid tendencies, he had his office soundproofed last year when something he'd said was taken out of context."

"How long was Adam at his office?"

"Only about fifteen or twenty minutes. When the office door opened, I heard the word 'sorry.' I don't know if Mr. Detweiler said sorry for something or 'you'll be sorry.' Then he stormed out. When Mr. Detweiler arrived, he had a tan briefcase with a large stain. But he didn't have it when he left."

The mysterious briefcase again.

"What kind of stain?" Shana said.

"Like someone spilled oil on the outside."

"Does the mayor still have it?"

"I didn't see it the next day, so I thought Mr. Detweiler came back after I left." Betty stared at Shana. "My reputation has always been as a private and trustworthy secretary. This is difficult for me."

"You realize if what you've told me has anything to do with Adam's death, you may need to testify."

"I hope it doesn't come to that." Betty hesitated. "There's something else. After you and Sergeant Ellis left the mayor's office the other day, he called someone on his private line."

Shana nodded. "I noticed a light lit on a line when I was by your desk waiting for the mayor to read our report."

"I'm not sure who he talked to, but when he finished, he told me to get his Prozac refilled at the pharmacy. He claimed it helped his stress ever since his heart attack. Here's the number he called." Betty handed a piece of paper to Shana. "I got it from his private phone records."

"Why are you coming forward now, Betty?"

"Let's just say I don't like Mayor Gaffney's tactics." She lowered her head. "For one thing, he imposed new restrictions on the Child Abuse Foundation. With all their sub-committees, it would take months, if not a year for them to comply."

"Whoa." Shana jerked her head. "What restrictions?"

"There are three sub-committees now under the foundation's umbrella that support not just abused children but the family members as well. The mayor wanted a full audit of each one and stipulated support would stop until it's completed. If you can think of anything to help the foundation, please do so."

Shana gritted her teeth. "Bet the mayor's wife is turning over in her grave."

"I bet she is. That foundation was her life. She always had compassion for children not being able to have any of her own."

"Thanks for telling me." Shana blew out her frustration. "I still have connections, so I'll see what I can do. You said for one thing. Was there something else?"

Betty reached for the door handle. "Nothing you need to know."

It was a little before 9:00 p.m. when Betty drove off. Shana pulled out her cell and punched in the number Betty gave her. No one answered.

Exhausted by the day's events, Shana headed for home instead of the roundhouse. On the way, she dictated her thoughts.

"*Note to myself: Why did Adam meet with the mayor on June 1st? Does that tie in with Adam's $25,000 cash withdrawal on that date? Adam had a briefcase with him and left without it. It had a stain. Is it the same briefcase Eileen had? Where is the briefcase now?*"

She stopped the recorder and wondered what was the other thing Betty knew about the mayor?

CHAPTER 33

June 5th, Saturday

WEARINESS SETTLED into Shana as she climbed the three flights to her apartment. She yawned and reached into her purse for her keys. When she turned on the top floor landing, she saw her front door cracked open. Adrenaline darted through her. Instincts took over, and she dropped her purse, pulled her 9mm from the holster, and crept toward the door. As she pushed it open with the barrel of her gun, the faint odor of beer and wine drifted out. Her eyes were drawn to her desk on its side, the drawers broken in pieces tossed around the room, couch cushions torn to shreds. With the gun pointing outward, she shouted, "I'm the police." She stepped lightly across the hardwood floors leading to the kitchen.

The open refrigerator looked like a twister had swept over the shelves. Broken bottles of soda, wine, beer, and a spilled container of milk littered the floor. She inspected every room, confirmed all clear, and called dispatch.

After retrieving her purse from the hallway, she closed the door and took stock of the apartment. The contents of her desk were scattered everywhere. She lifted the glass coffee table, still in one piece, and placed it upright. The rubber-banded stack of cryptograms stuck out from under the pile of papers. She picked it up. The copy of Adam's note was the second from the top where she placed it before she went out. Could someone be after the note? Did they know it existed?

She placed the stack on the coffee table and propped up her desk chair. On the floor by her feet lay the shattered bi-fold picture frame of her daughters and parents. She picked it up and gently pulled out the broken glass making sure not to ruin the photos and rested it on the coffee table.

Within twenty minutes, sirens blared in the distance and grew closer. She let two officers into the building, one to stand at the front door. Back in her apartment, Shana sat on her desk chair and gave the other officer information. The forensic team arrived and dusted for fingerprints.

About an hour later Sergeant Ellis arrived and stepped over the broken desk drawer pieces. "What a mess, Doyle."

She slammed her fists on her thighs. "Look at this place!" Her nostrils flared. "Damn it. I can't believe this happened. What are you doing here?"

"I heard about the break-in from dispatch."

Shana motioned for Sarge to follow her into the kitchen.

"We're done in here," one of the forensic team said as he packed up and left the kitchen.

Sarge carefully stepped around the liquids on the floor and leaned against the counter. "Anything missing?"

"Not that I can tell. I went to meet Betty, the mayor's secretary, earlier. When I got home, I found the place like this."

She relayed what Betty had told her about Adam's visit to the mayor on June 1st.

"Interesting," Sarge said. "It can't be a coincidence that Adam withdrew cash on June 1st and then he shows up at the mayor's office...with a briefcase? And then he left the briefcase with the mayor? Adam's visit might explain why the mayor is anxious about the Detweiler case."

"Betty said the briefcase had a stain. There was no mention

from Adam's parents of a stain on the one Eileen had with her when she came home in the limo?"

Sarge rubbed his buzz and stopped. "Maybe it isn't the same. What was the mayor up to? We need to question him."

"Wait. If you question him, he's going to want to know how we found out about Adam's visit, which could get Betty into trouble."

He raised one hand. "I'll handle the mayor."

She told Sarge how Cateline ran into Adam, his briefcase, and what she overheard at TR Tires.

"That's right. Your daughter worked there. So, Adam had a briefcase on May 28th when your daughter saw him. Why would Adam panic when the briefcase dropped? Did she describe the briefcase to you? Did she say it had a stain?"

Shana picked up some of the broken bottles on the floor. "She didn't recall what it looked like."

"And a big announcement at TR Tires? You have a meeting to question Nick Vega on Monday, right?"

She placed the broken glass in the trash can. "Yes. Knowing Adam asked my daughter if I was still into cryptograms, makes me sure Adam left that note for me. And if he did, maybe it's a clue to his murder."

Hearing her speak those words aloud caused her to feel nauseous, and her gaze floated around the kitchen, not settling on one object.

"Shana, are you sure you're all right?"

Sarge hadn't called her by her first name since she joined homicide.

"I'll be fine. It's a little unnerving."

"Why don't you take off tomorrow and get things in order here. Fits will call you if anything comes up with the case."

A day off? She couldn't remember the last time that happened. "Thanks. I might take you up on that."

"What do you suppose the intruder was after?"

"I had time to think about it before the team arrived. The living room was the heaviest hit, particularly my desk. Before I went out, I transcribed my recorded notes onto my disk and erased the tape, like always. Then I put the disk in my desk."

"You think they were after your disk?"

"But I had it with me. Another thought was they were after Adam's note, but it was still in the stack of cryptograms where I left it. So, it couldn't have been that."

"What about your laptop?"

"I checked it earlier. Entered my password. Nothing seemed disturbed."

"Doyle, if your notes disk was what they were after, you need to make me a copy as a backup. I'll lock it up in homicide."

As they left the kitchen, Sarge motioned to the officer to help prop up her desk and said, "Any idea on how the intruder got in?"

Shana shrugged. "There were no scratches on the deadbolt. I checked it earlier. The owner of the building installed a new security keypad system on the outside yesterday. Whoever broke in must have seen me enter my code when I tested it with the installation man. High-powered binoculars would do the trick. It's the only explanation that makes sense."

"Anyone else in the building?"

"The other two tenants haven't been home for weeks."

Shana sat at her desk and made a copy of her notes disk for Sarge.

As she handed it to him, he said, "I'll stick around until forensics finishes. You going to be all right here tonight?"

"Yes. At least my bedroom is still in one piece."

"To be on the safe side, I'll have an officer staked outside."

"I don't think that's necessary."

"Precaution."

Almost an hour had passed. The forensic team completed

their sweep, and the officers and Sarge left. As she closed the door behind them, anger swept through her that someone invaded her space. But then her mind jumped to the case, and she pondered why her notes disk would be so important if that's what the intruder was after. A call from Mac interrupted her thoughts.

"I want to firm up our next date," he said.

"Can I call you tomorrow? Ah...someone broke into my apartment and—"

"What! You all right?"

"Yes, I'm fine." She viewed the disarray of her apartment. Was she really fine? "I wasn't here. Sarge put an officer across the street to keep an eye on me."

"Thank God you weren't home. I can come over."

His concern oozed through the phone.

"No. I'll be fine. I'll talk to you tomorrow."

After Mac's call, she thought at another time, she would've called her friends for comfort. But even if their relationship was back to before her parents were killed, she probably would've dealt with it herself rather than worry them. She made her way to her front window and opened the shutters to scan the neighborhood. The patrol car was parked on the other side a couple of car lengths away. Her eyes were drawn to the window on the third floor in the building directly across from hers. The blinds were down. They were closed halfway before she went to meet Betty. It was the apartment where the Canadian couple moved out. A chill went through her as if a cold winter wind had circled. Someone must have watched her from that apartment. With the other tenants in her building away, she felt alone. She closed the shutters.

CHAPTER 34

MINUTES LATER SHANA tried to wipe out the eerie feeling that someone had been in her apartment. She attempted to get her desk in some order, putting the frame of her daughters and parents in its usual spot. After picking up most of the papers from the floor, she sat and found herself emersed in Adam's note. She stared at the letters noticing spaces separating the groupings. TFUEBJL MWDT NKHL FXHXX. Could the reference to Rubik's Cube followed by numbers 7, 6, 5, 4, 3, 2, 1 in the corner be a clue on how to decipher the note?

"What's a Rubik's Cube but a hard puzzle to solve," she whispered.

She pulled out a notepad and worked the letters as she did on cryptograms. The Sunday *Messenger* would always have a letter clue, but there were none in the note. Two F's, three X's, two T's. No pattern emerged. What if the numbers at the end of the words Rubik's Cube, were a clue by itself? Maybe the descending numbers meant the letters should be reversed.

Shana recalled sending the self-developed cryptograms to Adam. She'd reverse letters that stumped him. Each time she would put a little twist on it. With that thought, she arranged the letters in reverse—LJBEUFT TDWM LHKN XXHXF—and stared at them. Her gaze shifted to the numbers in the corner.

Could they be a code as to what letters to use in the alphabet? She wrote down the alphabet and numbered each letter. But with only seven numbers in the note, it didn't make any sense.

A shower might clear her mind. After she checked her front door lock, she made her way to the bathroom. The steam from the hot shower circled in the air and fogged the mirror. As she wiped it clean, the reverse image of the wall clock caused her to turn. Could it be after 11:30 already?

She adjusted the water temperature, stepped in, and stood motionless allowing the warm water to spray her face, trying to wash away the creepy feeling someone had watched her. The lavender-scented body wash that claimed to help calm emotional stress, wasn't working. Suds from the shampoo poured down her face. The mirror image of the clock hit her again. She opened her eyes and washed the soap sting away. "Should the numbers be reversed?"

She turned off the shower. Wrapping a towel around her, she made her way to her desk. She reached for her notepad again and referred to the original first grouping of letters—TFUEBJL. What if the numbers reversed tie in with the letters of the alphabet? She remembered a similar method she used on one of her crypts to stump Adam and began to use that formula.

T is 1 letter past S

F is 2 letters past D

U is 3 letters past R

After she worked on all the groupings, it revealed— SDRAWDE LUAP MIEH EVETS. She leaned back in her chair. Her wet hair had almost dried. She fixated on the groupings and reversed them. SDRAWDE became Edwards. The next—Paul. The name Trevor told her was the operations manager at RedChem. Excited, she arranged the next group. Steve Heim. Adam had taken Shana's technique and applied it to his note. You outdid yourself, Adam, she thought. Saddened he wasn't there to receive the compliment.

Her pulse raced believing she may have solved the message, she flipped open the laptop, keyed in her password, and typed in the first name. Paul Edwards. The Yahoo search confirmed his position, operations manager of RedChem's Research Department. She searched the company's website and typed in Steve Heim in their site's search bar. His name appeared as a research chemist there.

She applied the same pattern to what appeared to be an address in the lower right corner of the note. Nothing made sense. Adam must have developed another type of code.

The intercom buzzed by the door and Mac's voice sounded from the speaker. "Shana, can I come up?"

She stood almost frozen. If she let him in, the officer down the street would see and who knows what rumors would fly around homicide. She didn't need to hear any teasing from her male counterparts—not now. But as she scanned her apartment in ruins, she felt an overwhelming desire to have him to lean on.

Shana looked down at the towel wrapped around her and pressed the intercom button. "Give me five."

She slipped on some lounging shorts, one of her worn T-shirts, and clipped her hair behind her head. Soon Mac stood in the doorway wearing his khakis and a baby blue polo that matched his eyes. His smile made her realize how much she needed his support. He entered, embraced her, and tenderly held her tight. Her body seemed to melt into his arms.

His voice was soft in her ear. "Shana, how are you?"

Her guard dropped like a fifty-pound weight. The reality of the break-in hit. Tears streamed down her cheeks. She sobbed into his chest.

He found a tissue box on the floor, pulled one out, and handed it to her. "I'm here for you."

She slowly pulled away getting her composure, angry at herself for letting her guard down like that.

She wiped the tears away. "Why did you come over?"

"I heard something in your voice on the phone that concerned me. I just felt I needed to be here."

"There's an officer down the street, and—"

"Don't worry." He touched her arm. "I took care of it."

"What do you mean?"

"I know how you are concerned about keeping your personal life private, so I told him I was the department's doctor and needed to check on you. I flashed my badge so fast he couldn't have seen I'm from the coroner's office."

She let out a sigh of relief. "Clever."

"Besides, your safety is more important and I don't care about rumors."

As she eased into the desk chair she gestured around the room. "As you can see, I don't have any place for you to sit."

Mac stepped toward her and picked up the picture frame from the desk. "Are these your daughters on the left side?"

"Yes, Taken last year."

"They're beautiful. Nice smiles." He glanced back at the frame. "And the other side is your parents?"

"Yes. Taken a month before their accident."

Mac placed the frame back on the desk, pulled the coffee table close to her, and sat on it. "You said your parents died in a car crash? If you don't mind me asking, how did it happen?"

Her mind flooded with thoughts of that night, her shrink's diagnosis, and her suspicions the accident was meant for her. Not the right time to discuss all that.

She stared at the frame. "They were on their way to the airport, heading back to Florida and they hit a tractor-trailer. I regret not being with them when they died."

"I lost both my parents too." Mac lowered his head. "My mother died a couple of years ago. I was with her when she passed. But my father died while I was at a conference."

"Oh. I'm sorry Mac."

"I've learned to deal with it. So, I can imagine how you felt not being with your parents when they died. Tell me about your daughters."

She knew Mac was trying to divert her attention from the break-in and welcomed it.

"My eldest, Kim is married. She entered the mortgage industry shortly after I left. That's where she met her husband. My other daughter, Cateline, works at TR Tires and has a nice boyfriend whom she lives with."

"TR Tires?"

"Yes. Ironic, isn't it?" She stared at the floor, her mind focused back on the case, diverting her thoughts from the events of the evening. "I had lunch with my daughters after Eileen and Adam's funeral, and Cateline told me she overheard a conversation at TR Tires that sounded suspicious to me."

"So, you want to talk about the case?"

"Sorry, I can't help it. You're a good sounding board. Besides, it takes my mind off the break-in."

She told Mac what Cateline overheard, who was present, and the relationship between TR Tires and RedChem. "We're going to question Nick Vega on Monday. Someone went to a lot of trouble to hide Eileen's identity. With Adam killed, and now I suspect someone is after my notes disk, there's a connection, I know it."

Mac placed his hand on hers. "Please be careful. A break-in with you not here is one thing, but the next time it may be more dangerous."

His concern came through with his touch.

Her mind switched again thinking about Adam's note and

she told Mac what it contained and how she solved most of it. "The address wasn't an address. At least I couldn't find it in a Yahoo search. The note was written on RedChem letterhead, and since it revealed two chemists' names who work there, that company must be involved. They do chemical research and TR Tires is one of their clients."

"I have a friend, Oliver Pendelton. He's a professor at the University of Pennsylvania and a top chemist in his field. If the note has something to do with chemicals, he may be able to help."

"Great idea. Can you arrange a meeting? Perhaps he can recognize something on the note I missed."

She became excited with the possibility that solving the entire note might bring closure to the case. "I'll give him a call tomorrow morning."

She surveyed the room. The reality of the break-in took hold again, and she shivered.

Mac stood and caressed her shoulders. "You're cold. Might be an aftershock."

He looked around and grabbed a blanket from under the mound of stuffing from the cushions. When he wrapped it around her, she sighed.

"There. Is that better?" he said.

His gentleness wrapped her inner self like the blanket he just wrapped around her.

She snugged the blanket up to her chin. "Thanks."

Mac helped her get the apartment in somewhat of an orderly fashion. They piled up the broken pieces from her antique desk drawers, mopped up the stench and stickiness from her kitchen floor, vacuumed the glass from the picture frame embedded in her area rug, and packed the stuffing from the couch pillows into a large garbage bag.

A couple of hours later, Shana sat in the desk chair and

yawned.

"I guess I'd better go," Mac said.

"I am tired." She yawned again. "Thanks so much for being here."

She walked him to the door, and they both reached for the knob at the same time. His body close to hers, she gazed up into his eyes. His warm breath swept over her face and he pulled her body close to his. She so wanted him to kiss her again recalling their last encounter. Their lips met. His whiskers brushed against her chin, but she didn't mind. She felt the same sensuous rush after his kiss the night at PJ's. It wouldn't be the right time to let this go any further, not with her frame of mind tonight.

It took everything in her power to push him away. "You better leave."

"I understand." He kissed her forehead and left.

After Mac's kiss, she found a new sense of energy. She sat at her desk and opened her laptop to review her notes disk. Something must be here the intruder wanted. She stared at the laptop screen, but her thoughts went to Mac. How could she feel this way after only one date and two kisses? Focus Shana. You have a crime to solve.

After she transcribed her recordings on what Betty told her, she reviewed all her notes on the Word document and created an up-to-date recap.

Trashman: His company confirmed his sensitive nose. Did a unique odor on Eileen's body exist? Not found in autopsy.

Briefcase: Who's the owner? Eileen had it on May 18th. Was money in it? Adam had it when he deposited $50,000 cash on May 20th. Adam had it on May 28th. Why did Adam panic when Cateline knocked it out of his hand? Adam had a briefcase with him on June 1st at Mayor Gaffney's office. It had a stain. He left it with the mayor.

RedChem: Who did Adam meet on May 17th. Upset after the visit? One of Trevor's companies. Were they doing special research for TR Tires? Could what Cateline heard be a windfall for TR Tires? What did Trevor know?

Eileen's death: Killed elsewhere? Why? Where was she on the night of May 16th and 17th? Who brought her home the morning of May 18th? What happened to make her stop drinking? What did Eileen want to tell Madeline on May 19th at her fundraiser? Message left for Eileen by Adam at 5:05 May 28th, change of plans. What did that mean? Where did Eileen go on May 28th? Why was Trevor nervous when questioned about Eileen?

Adam's death: Why was he killed? What did he know? Was it something RedChem was working on? Was it something related to Madeline's campaign? Adam at TR Tires May 28th at around 5:00. Who did Adam go to see? Adam withdrew $25,000 June 1st. Does this tie into his meeting with the mayor?

Ms. Gardner: Not reliable. Claims a tall, bald, muscular man brought Eileen home May 18th, but parents dispute the man existed. Did she see a patrol car at the house the day after Adam was found? Didn't see who got out. What else did she see through that hedge?

Limo: Who brought Eileen home on May 18th?

Cryptic Note: Why would Adam leave the note for me? What was he trying to tell me? Partially deciphered and revealed chemists from RedChem. What appears to be an address—is not. Can Mac's friend Oliver help solve the rest of the note?

Chemists: Paul Edwards and Steve Heim. What do they know? Could what Mr. Roberts smelled be a chemical? Could what Cateline heard at TR Tires have something to do with this?

Break-in: Could someone be after Adam's note? Did they know the note existed? If it's my notes disk they wanted, what was on it that was so important?

Mayor: *What is the real reason he is so interested in the Detweiler case? Who did the mayor call on his private line? Why did Adam meet with him on June 1st? What does the mayor know?*

She saved her disk, sat back, and yawned. The evening's events circled in her mind. The clock showed almost 2:00 a.m. After making sure her locks were secure, she made her way to the bedroom. Passing the trash bags of debris and her couch without cushions, made her uneasy that someone had violated her space.

CHAPTER 35

June 6th, Sunday

SHANA BOLTED up in bed. The glow of the alarm clock on the nightstand showed 3:12 a.m. Cold sweat dripped down her neck into her chest, and she fought to get her bearings with the break-in raging in her mind. She threw the pale green comforter off and sat on the edge of the bed holding her head in her hands. Horrified, the nightmare about her parents had returned. The funeral and the break-in must have triggered it. She carried on a conversation in her head as if she were sitting across from her shrink.

"Come on, Doc. It's been almost seven months," Shana would say.

The doctor would nod. "Need to get rid of the guilt."

Shana turned on the light. Doing the math in her head, it would be after 1:00 a.m. in Colorado, but she punched her brother's number into her cell phone, anyway.

A groggy voice answered after several rings.

"Ward, it's me."

He cleared his throat. "Oh my God, sis. Do you know what time it is?"

"I just wanted to talk."

"Hold on," he whispered. "Let me get out of the bedroom." Seconds later he said, "You've had one of those nightmares haven't you?"

She hesitated. "Yes."

"I thought they stopped a few months ago. Was it the same one?"

"Kind of…but this time the woman was running toward me with her arms outstretched. The snow had stopped, and the air cleared when I saw her. Blood was everywhere. It was Mom, and…she was headless. Ward, if only they hadn't flown up here for my birthday. If only they hadn't driven my car to the airport. Mom's conversation that Dad was uncomfortable driving in the storm, keeps playing over in my head. If only I had—"

"Stop, Shana. Mom and Dad's accident was just that. An accident on an icy night. You did everything you could to find out what happened. Your motor pool inspected your car and found nothing wrong. You aren't still harboring some notion that someone was after you?"

She thought of the many times she'd reviewed her parents' file with no clues the horrible tragedy was anything other than an accident, but she still wondered. Why did she put her job before her parents that night and let them use her car? "But if I'd only drove them. Then I would know for sure."

"Your shrink told you to let go of the guilt."

"But you weren't the one who had to identify Mom."

His heavy sigh told her he didn't want to rehash this again. "We've gone over this. I wish I had been there with you. Do you have any more of that anxiety medicine?"

"I don't want to take it."

"Well, you need to do something. You haven't had one of those nightmares in a long time. Why now?"

She avoided telling him about the break-in, fearing she would get a safety lecture. "I attended a double funeral yesterday. And the caskets were…closed."

"Shana. Why did you even go?"

In barely a whisper she said, "It's regarding a case I'm working on."

"As usual, the case comes first. I'm no doctor, but because of the closed caskets, it must have triggered your memories of Mom and Dad. You need meds."

She let out a sigh. "Solving this case would be my medication. Sorry I called."

"Hey," he said softly. "As much as I don't like being awakened in the middle of the night, you can call anytime."

"Thanks. I'll talk to you soon. Give my love to the family."

Her head pounded. In the bathroom, she stared at herself in the mirror. Her blue bloodshot eyes stared back at her. "Hey, girl. Get a grip."

She splashed water on her face and opened her medicine cabinet. The prescription bottle of Xanax sat on the bottom shelf. She reached for it. Printed on the label—take one when needed. The last time she took one of those pills, she couldn't focus, sleepy. She didn't need that type of distraction while working on this case and put the bottle back. She reached for the Tylenol.

CHAPTER 36

June 6th, Sunday

THE ALARM CLOCK BUZZED later that morning. Groggy, Shana fumbled for the off button and pressed it hard. Head under the pillow she peeked out at the digital clock—8:05. She nestled her head back, pulled the sheets and comforter over the back of her head trying to wipe out the images of the nightmare. What if they're returning? What if she can't control them again?

Without warning, her headache returned from last night. She struggled to get out of bed and staggered to her bathroom where she downed two more Tylenol. As she passed the bedroom doorway heading back to her bed, she caught sight of the trash bags by the front door bringing back the memory of the break-in.

Mac showing up last night was something she hadn't expected but was pleased he did. Recalling how he comforted her. His gentle ways. His patience. She realized she had approached a point of no return, falling for him and hard. But then doubt snuck in. What about his dead wife? Could he be ready to move on? For a moment she forgot about the nightmare and the break-in. Mac occupied her mind. Maybe he's the key to helping her forget about her parents' deaths.

While dressing, she mentally forced herself to run a checklist of what needed to be done today. Her cell pinged, she stepped to the nightstand and flipped it open.

"Sarge told me about the break-in," Fits said. "Are you okay? If you need anything, I'm here for you."

Support from Fits? Strange, but it felt nice. "Thanks. I'm fine. I focused on the case last night to get my mind off the break-in, and I was able to decipher some of the note. It revealed two names, and after I checked them out on the internet, they ironically work at RedChem. I'll call tomorrow and get appointments—"

"Wait. Why don't you let me do that?"

"No! I want to follow this through."

"All right. Sarge asked me to check out the building across from yours last night."

Her pulse quickened. "When did you do that?"

"After Sarge left."

Relieved Mac showed up much later. "What did you find out?"

"Landlady said the tenants on the third floor moved out Friday."

Shana recalled the vacant apartment directly across from hers. "Did she tell you why they left?"

"No. The landlady didn't have any other pertinent information. Sarge filled me in on what you found out from the mayor's secretary, and what your daughter overheard at TR Tires."

Shana glanced around her apartment. "I have a lot to do today. I'll be in tomorrow."

"I'll call if anything comes up. Take care of your apartment... and you."

Fits's concern was like his old self, but would it last?

It was early evening when the antique dealer had finished repairing the desk drawers, the maintenance man programmed a new security code, and the locksmith had completed installing two deadbolts. Thankfully, they'd agreed to come on a Sunday.

After they left, she stood in the kitchen doorway and surveyed her living room. Several emotions took hold. The one thing that struck hard was the feeling of vulnerability.

It reminded her of how her ex-husband's mental manipulation had made her feel shortly after they were married. He had found a small tear on the seam of a shirt he was wearing. She'd told him she would sew it, but his rage kicked in and he ripped the shirt from his body. It wasn't until he moved out that her friends had told her she was a different person married to him.

After the divorce, it sunk in how withdrawn she had become. It took almost a year to get back to her normal self. Normal. She wondered what that was?

She stood by her desk retracing her steps last night and turned to face the front window. The angle she'd been sitting before she left to meet Betty, blocked the view of her right desk drawer where she kept her crypts. The watcher wouldn't have seen her put Adam's note in the stack.

Doubting the note was what they were after, she stepped to the front window to open the shutters to let in the morning sunshine. Directly across the street was the vacant apartment she noticed last night. The blinds were still closed. Her eyes widened. "That's it."

She'd retrieved her disk *after* she closed the shutters last night. Whoever watched her must not have seen her go back for the disk before she left. That's why her desk was torn apart. They must have thought it was still there. It was the disk they were after.

Her phone rang, and she hurried to answer it. Philip's voice caught her by surprise.

"Ah...what's up?" she said.

"You still consider Ros one of your best friends...right?"

"Just because I haven't seen you guys in a while, doesn't

mean that has changed."

"Glad to hear it. Because I need a favor from you? Ros's nervous habit is back."

"Jules and I saw her do it at the funeral."

"She told me it's returned because of Kelsey's hectic schedule. I don't buy it. She only started this about a week ago and Kelsey's schedule has been going on for years. Each time I asked her why she started this now, we got into an argument."

Interesting, Philip doesn't think Kelsey's schedule is the reason either.

Shana sat at her desk. "So, what's the favor?"

"I was wondering if you and Jules could get Ros away someplace and talk to her. Find out what's really going on. I think she'll open up to you two."

"Not so sure, Philip. I haven't been around much. Are you sure she would be receptive to me calling?"

"I'm sure she will. Please? She's seeing Madame X again."

Shana squinted. "That charlatan. I thought we convinced Ros years ago the woman was only after money. Hated she preyed on Ros after her father died."

"That's not all. She didn't even ask any questions about Adam's and Eileen's deaths."

Shana raised her brow. Ros's inquisitive mind would want to know everything about their deaths. No matter what. "No questions? Okay, I'll get something scheduled. By any chance did you give Grant Harriman my unlisted home phone number?"

"No, why?"

"He called and asked me out."

"I've learned a long time ago not to question how Grant finds out things. Sorry. I guess this is my fault. Lately, he seemed so lonely. He sold his condo in Old City and built a bedroom suite in the *Messenger* building. I just don't think that's healthy to live where you work, so I told him he should start dating. I didn't think he would be after you. What did you say?"

"I declined. I'm kinda dating the chief medical examiner."

"Really? The medical examiner? Hope you don't talk shop. You'll call Ros?"

Shana agreed and knew now, there was something more wrong with Ros besides Kelsey's schedule. She made a quick call to Jules telling her about Philip's conversation and asked her to arrange a get-together.

"So now you have time to meet up with us?" Jules said.

Regret came over Shana, but she managed to change the subject. "How was the funeral service?"

"Heart-wrenching, like any other funeral."

"We need to find out what's going on with Ros. Can you please make the arrangements with her? Tell her whatever you like."

Shana ended the call promising to see her friends more often. But deep down, those were only words. She'd been obsessed with occupying her time with murder cases for so long, dealing with this transference thing, she wondered if she could stop. Had it become a habit? She read somewhere a habit formed within sixty-six days. Her judgment was usually spot on, but now, with this, not so sure.

CHAPTER 37

AFTER A GOOD NIGHT'S SLEEP without any hint of a nightmare, Shana arrived the next morning in homicide well rested ready to dive into the case again. It was around 9:00 a.m. Fits hadn't arrived yet. Sarge's office was empty. Not like Sarge to arrive after 7:00. Now that she deciphered some of the note revealing the two chemists, one of which Trevor mentioned, no need to wait for their interview with Vega to find out the contacts at RedChem.

She cradled the receiver on her shoulder, and munched on a protein bar from the vending machine, waiting for the receptionist at RedChem to get back on the line. "I'm sorry," the woman said. "Mr. Heim and Mr. Edwards are both at a convention and won't be back in the office until Wednesday. Have a nice day."

A click met her ears. She slammed the receiver back. After taking another bite of the stale bar, she stuck her tongue out at the taste and threw the rest into the trash can. Within minutes she heard Sarge greeting some officers. He approached her cubical and motioned her to follow him to his office.

Sarge sat behind his desk. "How are you handling the break-in?"

"It's a little freaky knowing someone watched me. I got a lot done yesterday. Cleaned up the apartment, and I deciphered part of Adam's note."

"Yes. Fits told me."

She told him how she figured out the code that revealed the two chemists at RedChem, and why she couldn't see them until Wednesday.

"You got farther along on the note than the FBI. Heard from them earlier. They haven't even started to decipher the note. Other cases ahead of ours."

"But I can't figure out what the address is at the bottom of the note. If it even is an address. RedChem does chemical research, so I was thinking maybe it's related to a chemical. Mac mentioned his friend, Oliver Pendelton, might be able to help."

"Oliver's your man. Mac enlists his help sometimes when the forensic team gets stumped. They get their feathers ruffled if we get outside help, so Mac and I agreed some time ago to keep Oliver a secret. Did you ever find out what the phone number was the mayor's secretary gave you?"

"No. After I tried the number myself a few times and didn't get an answer, I contacted a friend at the phone company and she said it has some type of privacy flag on it, untraceable. She told me those numbers are like Fort Knox and said a warrant wouldn't do any good. But she did tell me, the mayor called that number several times over the past weeks."

Sarge rubbed his chin. "Untraceable, huh?" He motioned for her to close the door.

Shana obliged. "What's going on?"

"I met with HR this morning. It pains me to say I had to put Fits on desk duty."

"Why?"

Sarge folded his arms. "I asked him to investigate the apartment building across the street from you."

"He called yesterday and told me the landlady had nothing significant to say. Only that the tenants moved out."

"Well, he messed up."

"How?"

"It seemed strange to me the couple moved out so unexpectedly. I asked Fits if anyone inquired about the apartment. He said no. Something didn't feel right, so I questioned the landlady myself. She said Fits never asked."

Her insides churned that Fits messed up again.

Sarge unfolded his arms. "According to the landlady, the tenants were having financial problems, and she waved rent for two months until they could get back on their feet. She was surprised they went back to Canada and didn't leave a forwarding address? But here's the kicker. The landlady told me after the Canadian couple left, a man inquired about their apartment. And he was tall, bald, and muscular."

Her eyes widened. "That's the description of the man Ms. Gardner claimed she saw bring Eileen home on May 18th. But I didn't think he existed, according to Adam's parents."

"The landlady told me something else. The man perspired a lot and his left eye seemed to look away from her. Like a glass eye."

"A glass eye, huh?"

"I told Fits all the details of your break-in." Sarge scowled. "He knew the vacant apartment was across from yours, but he didn't inspect it. I did though. Someone had tampered with the lock. I could tell immediately the bedroom had a direct view of your living room. I figured someone must've paid those tenants to move out, so they could monitor you. I had the place dusted for prints, but it was clean."

A chill ran through her as she scrambled trying to make sense of it. "Then someone *was* watching me from across the street."

Her thoughts went to Fits and how his mess up four years ago was more egregious than not questioning the landlady properly.

"Sarge, why didn't you put Fits on desk duty when evidence from the ADA's secretary's murder case almost got thrown out of court because of Fits?"

"I thought you would ask. I felt I owed him back then. When I joined homicide twenty years ago, I was Fits's partner, and he took me under his wing."

"I didn't know you had him as a partner."

"Not too many people do. He had been a detective for almost ten years then and had reached top detective status. With his experience, I was thankful he gave me some pointers. The brass had wanted to promote him to sergeant, but he declined. Said he enjoyed being on the street more. I gave him a lot of credit for making that decision. I can still remember what he said at my first homicide scene. Ignore what's in front of you—"

They recited in unison. "And go with your gut."

Sarge smiled. "I see he told you the same thing."

"Why did he change?"

"Not sure. Doyle, when you came on board, you were so by the book and thorough. I thought having you as his partner would shape him up, but it didn't. When he messed up on the ADA case, he pleaded with me not to put him on desk duty. You know the way the good old boy network works. So, I gave him a warning. That's why I insisted he become your partner again on this case. Hoping your attention to detail would rub off on him and he would snap out of his slump. But this time, I couldn't let it go."

She always thought Fits's arrogance and lack of thoroughness on his cases was him lashing out because of her rejections to his affections. Now she wondered what else had gone on in his life before she became his partner years ago.

Sarge rested his arms on the desk. "There's something else. I think there may be a leak from inside homicide."

She raised her brows. "What?"

"Late last night, I unlocked my desk drawer to add notes from my interview with the landlady. The copy of your disk you gave me and the printed case notes weren't in the order I'd placed them. After close inspection, there were scratches on the drawer lock. I checked the disk. It all seemed to be in order, but you may want to check it."

He unlocked his drawer and slid the disk into his computer. Shana viewed her notes. "All seems fine."

"I think someone may have taken a copy of the disk and the case notes."

"Sarge, what about—"

She glanced at the filing cabinet. Sarge did the same. They quickly stepped to the cabinet and Sarge unlocked it. Shana pulled out her recorder and placed in the first tape of Mr. Roberts's interview at the crime scene. It was still there. Then another and another until she was sure all the recordings were intact.

"Sarge, I reviewed my notes disk after the break-in and there didn't seem to be anything on it someone would be after."

"Unless someone thought there would be something on it. I'm suspicious about Mayor Gaffney. I think maybe he has someone spying for him. I haven't heard from him since we met with him. He'd been calling me daily about the Detweiler case and now silence. I tried to get in touch with him to question him about what his secretary told you, but he hasn't returned my calls. We need to keep this mole business quiet until we find out who it is."

CHAPTER 38

June 7th, Monday

PHILIP CONTACTED HIS FRIEND at the IRS to inquire about the senator after what Trevor told him. He learned of an investigation into Senator Jenkins on suspicion he embezzled state funds. They also confirmed what Trevor found out that an account exists in California at the Fork Bank in the senator's name, and the $8,000 monthly deposits Logan found out about. The right question posed the right way might reveal something from the senator today without jeopardizing the IRS investigation and Philip's promise to Trevor. He updated his Word document, saved it to the TR folder, and left his office.

Philip rushed out the *Messenger's* front entrance and almost tripped on the ropes hanging from above. He looked up. Two window washers were pulling the ropes to steady themselves on the steel scaffolding. Philip shouted at the men.

"Sorry, sir," one of them said. "We'll fix that."

The heavy-set man pulled on the rope. Philip jumped over it, dashed to the street, and climbed into Logan's silver Thunderbird double-parked in front.

"I told those guys earlier to take care of those ropes," Logan said. "The same thing happened to me across the street when I tried to see Senator Jenkins in his office."

Philip buckled the frayed seat belt. "Which reminds me.

Why are we going to interview the senator at his house?"

Logan pulled out into traffic. "Not sure. His secretary made the request. Guess he wants to show off his estate. It's not like he worked hard for that mansion. He inherited it from his rich uncle, who didn't have any other relatives."

"I thought you'd get rid of this car. You've had it since high school." Philip sniffed. "Smells like burnt hot dogs and beer."

"Can't seem to part with it," Logan smirked. "Kind of like your hair."

"Funny."

Logan stopped the car at a red light and turned to Philip. "Why don't you join me next time I go fishing? You'd think with having two boys and a girl, one of them would take up fishing or hunting. No such luck. Now that Adam's gone, I could use the company." Logan's face saddened. "I wish I would have done something when he called me the end of May."

"There wasn't anything you could've done."

"I guess." Logan peered out of the windshield at the traffic light. "So how about it?"

"Fishing's not my thing. But I'll go fishing with you if you'll join me for golf."

The green light flashed and Logan took off. "Golf isn't my thing. So, I guess we should just stick to what we know." Logan turned onto the Schuylkill Expressway heading out of the city. "I want to find out who's giving the senator that $8,000 each month."

"Be careful how you ask about that. We don't have any proof where that comes from."

"Got it. I have a strange feeling the senator knows something about this $100,000 given to Trevor. Who better than the senator to plant something that may end up discrediting Madeline?"

If Logan only knew how close his theory was. Philip recognized the look on Logan's face. He had the scent of his prey. "I can almost see your fangs popping out. We can't ask the senator about the lawsuit settlement payment to Trevor without proof. Why don't you ask him about his career? He's so self-absorbed. It might catch him off guard for you to dive into the money angle. Ease into the interview. Remember slow tortoise wins the race."

"He's talked about his career enough on talk shows. I haven't had you with me on a story in years. Why now?"

Philip rested his arm on the car door searching for words. "Like I said before. Prominent figure."

Within the hour, Logan pulled up to the large, black iron gates attached to the ten-foot-high stone walls surrounding Senator Curt Jenkins's property in Chestnut Hill. He pushed the button on the security box and flashed his press badge. The camera zoomed down at their car and in seconds the gates slowly opened. As they drove, the shadows from the sun shining through the tall walnut trees flickered on the winding driveway.

Philip gaped out the front window when the house came into view. "Look at this place. The pictures in the *Philadelphia Magazine* don't do it justice." They exited the car, and Philip gazed at the cathedral-like roof lines. "This is like something out of a gothic tale."

On the front entrance, a hand-carved dragon covered the entire wooden door.

"The handles are huge. Like his ego." Logan pointed to the middle of the door. "This is different. A doorbell on the dragon's nose." He rang it.

A tall, thin, older man wearing a black tux, opened the door. He requested their names and asked them to wait. Philip and Logan slipped into the foyer while the man walked toward the closed double doors on the left side of the winding staircase. Large gold-framed oil paintings of what Philip suspected were of the French countryside, covered the wall ascending the stairs.

Logan scanned the paintings. "You think these are

originals?"

Philip shrugged. "Remember take it slow."

The man returned. "Right this way, gentlemen. Senator Jenkins will see you in his drawing room."

Logan rolled his eyes and mouthed to Philip, "drawing room."

They followed the butler across a white marble floor. He opened the double doors, and the stale scent of old books hovered. Shelves containing worn leather-bound books with gold embossed titles covered two of the far walls, floor to ceiling. The senator sat on a walnut brown leather tufted chair behind a massive wooden desk. His short sandy red hair blended with his rosy complexion and gave him a bald appearance. When he stood, his belt cinched tight below his protruded belly, and his buttons were bursting on his starched pin-striped shirt.

The senator greeted them as they entered and he dismissed his butler. The diamond cufflinks caught Philip's eye as they shook hands. When the senator turned to make his way behind his desk, Philip noted from the back the senator's thin legs weren't proportionate to his large belly. "Thank you for taking the time, Senator. This will complete our profile story on you."

"Looking forward to reading it." Jenkins pointed to two large wing-back leather chairs in front of his desk. "Please have a seat. I'm always receptive to an interview, especially by the *Messenger*." He took a sip from a short glass containing a golden liquid. "Would either of you care for a soda? Water?" He held his glass up. "Something stronger?"

A little early to be drinking, Philip thought. He and Logan declined and eased into the chairs.

The senator took a sip of his drink. "Send Grant my regards."

Philip smiled. "I'll tell him." He would let Logan take the lead and wait for the right time to ask about Denver and Brown.

Logan pulled out his notepad. "Senator, how did you get

into politics."

Jenkins leaned his head back and swirled his palms around his potbelly in a clockwise motion. "I was fifteen when I realized I had a talent for negotiations, which has been instrumental in politics."

After a while, Philip discreetly checked his watch. Fifteen minutes had passed, and Jenkins still rambled on about what he called his superior negotiation tactics.

Jenkins tapped his hand on the arm of the chair and talked about outwitting Grant's wife's father, the owner of the *Messenger* at that time. "I started out asking for five cents. The paper cost fifteen cents. Five cents would have been unheard of to pay a delivery boy."

"Excuse me, Senator Jenkins," Logan said. "We heard the story from your telecast on Channel 6."

Jenkins rested his arms on his desk. "Oh, sorry. Of course. What questions do you have for my profile story?"

If Philip was to find out anything about Trevor's bogus lawsuit, he needed to jump in before Logan put his bloodhound instincts into action. He focused on the senator's expression. "Did you know years ago your opponent's husband used to work for a law firm, Denver and Brown in Ottsville?"

Confusion spread over Jenkins's round face. "No, I didn't. What does this have to do with my profile story?"

Philip couldn't press the issue further, in fear of divulging too much. "Logan why don't you continue."

Logan switched his gaze from Philip to the senator. "I'm sure you heard about the murders of Adam Detweiler and his wife. Did you know Adam worked for Trevor Richmond at TR Tires and Madeline's campaign?"

"Of course. I met Adam once. Never met his wife." Jenkins arched his back. "I have no information about the murders if that's what you're asking. Wouldn't that be a question from the police, not you?"

Logan jotted down some notes. "We're just trying to get a full picture of how well you know your opponent."

"I'm aware of Madeline Richmond's staff. Look if you don't have any questions for my profile story, then we need to end this interview."

"Okay…Senator, why did you decide to get back in the race? If you don't mind me saying so, I thought you would like to enjoy retirement. What plans do you have for the future, if you are re-elected?"

"What do you mean, *if* I'm re-elected? I'm sure the polls speak for themselves. I'm ahead by ten points."

Logan raised his eyebrows. "With all due respect, Senator. I received the latest poll yesterday, and Madeline Richmond is the one ahead by ten points."

He glared at Logan. "A woman would never win this election."

"Moving along. This house must need a lot of upkeep. Do you receive any other funds besides your political position? My readers will want to know how you can afford this lavish lifestyle."

Jenkins snapped. "My income stream has nothing to do with how successful I am as a senator."

Logan pressed on. "Aren't you receiving $8,000 a month in cash from another source and how would you handle the unions?"

Jenkins put both hands on his desk and abruptly stood, pushing his chair back against the wall. "This interview is over. I have work to do."

He pressed a button to the right of his phone. In seconds, the butler entered and escorted Philip and Logan out the front door. The heavy door shut behind them like a bank vault.

Once in the car, Philip said, "You hit a nerve about his finances. I didn't think you would've brought up Adam and

Eileen."

Logan started the engine and tilted his head at Philip. "And I didn't think you would've brought up about Denver and Brown and Trevor working for them."

Philip grasped for an excuse. "Without proof, there was a lawsuit settlement, the only way to test your theory about a planted contribution, was to find out how the senator would react to the name of the firm. It didn't look like it phased him."

Logan drove down the winding driveway to the main road. "I should have thought of that."

"That's why we make a good team. He didn't seem to know anything about the murders, but then again, he's a politician, master at diverting questions."

"I feel he's hiding something." Logan turned onto the main road. "I don't buy it that the senator didn't know Trevor worked for Denver and Brown. He would know everything about his opponent. I ah…tried to get in touch with a partner from Trevor's old firm, no luck."

"I told you I would find out about the firm from my source at the IRS."

Philip couldn't tell Logan he already knew he contacted the firm without divulging the conversation he had with Trevor. If only Trevor would give him the go-ahead to tell Logan what he found, but until he does, Philip had to keep up the charade.

"Since when do you tie my hands on digging up a story?" Logan scoffed.

"I'll let you know as soon as I hear something."

"All right. But I hope you find out something soon."

Philip could almost hear Logan's bloodhound tendencies howling and knew he would dig deeper. Time was running out for Trevor.

CHAPTER 39

SHORTLY BEFORE 3:00 p.m., Shana and Sarge arrived at the main gate at TR Tires in Conshohocken. A uniformed guard directed them to the employee entrance. They entered and the heavy metal door screeched. The potent scent of rubber spilled out. Tires filled the floor-to-ceiling shelves. A man stopped his forklift, and they asked for Nick Vega. He directed them to the office in the corner of the warehouse.

They approached glass doors with partially opened blinds. On the door were two names. Nick Vega, Plant Manager. Beneath his name, Adam Detweiler, Union Representative. As they opened the doors, a mousy thin short man with a long face, exited the first office.

Shana flashed her badge. "Nick Vega?"

"Yes. Won't you come in?"

"I'm Detective Doyle and this is Sergeant Ellis."

Vega directed them to two steel chairs with padded seats in front of a metal desk.

As Shana and Sarge sat, she said, "Do you know why we're here?"

The man made his way behind his desk. "Ah...Adam Detweiler's death?"

"We have questions about him and his wife's murders." She

pulled out her recorder. "Any problem with me taping this?"

Vega avoided eye contact. "Ah…no. That's fine. Anything I can do."

Shana pressed record. "How well did you know Adam?"

"We were pretty close. I met him at a Teamsters conference years ago. He represented RedChem as the union rep and I was there as the President of the Union Charter 600. We hit it off. Had the same views that bothered us about the unions."

"And his wife, Eileen?"

"I ah…never met her in person."

"How long have you worked here?" Sarge said.

"About two years. Adam knew I was a general manager at Knights Tires in New Jersey before I was with the union. My term as union president expired so when an opening came up here, Adam recommended me."

"Do you know of anyone who may have wanted to harm Adam or his wife?"

Vega crossed his arms over his chest and appeared to consider his response. "No. Why would I?"

"When did you see Adam last?"

"Not for almost a month." Vega moved his arms around on the desk as if trying to be more comfortable. "He was hardly here, with working on Madeline Richmond's campaign."

"Did you see him here on May 28th?" Shana said.

Vega moved papers on the side of his desk. "No…I wasn't here. The company closed early."

"Eileen Detweiler's time of death was the evening of May 28th? Where were you during that time?"

"Let me look at my calendar." Vega swiveled his chair to the credenza behind him, opened a worn tan leather briefcase with a heavy stain, and took out a Day-Timer.

Shana observed the briefcase and tilted her head at Sarge.

Vega's eyes wandered over the pages of his Day-Timer.

"Let's see. I had dinner with Mayor Gaffney on the 28th."

Sarge switched his gaze from the briefcase to Vega. "Are you two close?"

"Yes. We met years ago when I was with the union."

"Where did you have dinner with the mayor?"

"The Spotted Claw."

Sarge glared at Vega. "They recently had a fire in their kitchen. It's closed now. Who may have seen both of you that evening?"

"Only the people at the restaurant."

Sarge continued. "Adam Detweiler's time of death was between 2:00 and 3:00 in the afternoon of June 2nd. Where were you then?"

Vega scanned his Day-Timer again. "With the mayor then too. We had lunch at the Block and Clock."

"Any receipts?"

"No. The mayor paid."

"We understand RedChem researches tire improvements for TR Tires," Shana said. "Are they working on anything special for your company?"

"Not that I know of. Ah...why are you asking about RedChem?"

"We have information that Adam visited that company on May 17th. Do you know anything about that?"

Vega folded and unfolded his hands. "No."

Shana shifted her recorder to her other hand. "Who could we talk to at RedChem?"

"I don't know."

She remembered who Trevor mentioned, and the names she found in deciphering Adam's note. "What about Paul Edwards or Steve Heim?"

"Ah...I guess Paul Edwards."

Shana crossed her legs. "We heard you were in a meeting at TR Tires around the middle of May telling people to expect changes in the tires that would increase profits."

Vega stiffened. His high-pitched voice cracked. "I never said that."

"You didn't say the company would make a lot of money?"

"There was no meeting." Vega snapped.

"Mr. Vega," Sarge said. "Do you own a black limousine?"

"No. But I rent one. Why?"

"Someone sighted one bringing Adam's wife home early in the morning of May 18th."

"It couldn't have been mine. I don't use it much. I lease it from the Limo Rental Company. You can check it out."

"We will. Anything else you can tell us about Adam?"

"No."

Sarge stood, extended his hand, and thanked the man. Shana stopped the recorder and followed Sarge out of the office.

Once outside the warehouse, Sarge rubbed his buzz cut quickly and stopped. "The mayor is Vega's alibi on both deaths. Something fishy about those two."

Shana opened the car door. "Vega's not the only one that has a black limousine. The mayor has one as well and we should find out where his was on May 18th when Eileen was brought home."

"I still can't get in touch with the mayor."

"Should I call Betty? See if she has any idea why the mayor is avoiding you?"

Sarge shook his head. "Don't want to get her involved, just yet."

"Vega had a briefcase like the one Betty described Adam had brought into the mayor's office. Maybe it's the same one."

"If it is, how did it get in Vega's office?"

Shana shrugged. "That's the million-dollar question."

They got into the car and Sarge started the engine. "Doyle, what did you think about Vega's interview?"

"I feel he knows more. Seemed nervous when I asked him about RedChem. Did you see his body language when I mentioned Paul Edwards and Steve Heim? I'm eager to question the chemists on Wednesday. And how about the way he reacted when I asked if he saw Adam May 28th?"

"I saw. But if the company was closed and your daughter saw Adam going into the employee entrance, if Vega didn't see him, then who did Adam go to see?"

Sarge drove toward the security gate to leave the premises. "If what your daughter overheard is correct, then either this guy's lying about what he knows RedChem is working on or your friend Trevor Richmond is."

The gate rose, and Sarge turned onto the main road.

Shana rested her arm on the door. She hated that Trevor's name continued to pop up in the investigation. "But Trevor told me he hasn't been involved in the day-to-day operations at RedChem for some time."

"Doyle, you need to keep an open mind about your friend. I'll check out the Limo Rental Company. You contact Knights Tires. See if they'll tell you anything about Vega."

"Sarge, any more thought about who the mole is?"

"Not sure. But whoever it is, they're aware of your patterns and how you keep your notes on a disk."

Shana's suspicions that Fits might be the mole surfaced in her mind.

Later in homicide, Shana met Sarge in his office to update him on what she found out. "Knights Tires in New Jersey confirmed Vega worked there ten years ago and left to join the Union Charter 600. The company had little to say one way or the other about him. Nothing came up in the database on him. No record. Not even a driving ticket."

"I checked out Vega's limo. He's rented it for the past two years."

"None of this points to Vega being a suspect in the murders.

But my gut's telling me something underhanded is going on."

Back at her desk, Shana finished transcribing the interview with Vega. She pulled her notes disk from her inside jacket pocket, slid it into the computer, and typed updates to her existing list.

> **Mole:** *Who? Could it be Fits? He did know the case notes and my disk were locked in Sarge's desk.*
>
> **Briefcase:** *In Vega's office now. Claims it's his. Has a stain. If Adam had it on June 1st when he visited the mayor, how did Vega get it?*
>
> **RedChem**: *Vega confirmed Paul Edwards someone to talk to. Did Adam meet Edwards on May 17th?*
>
> **Limo:** *The mayor owns one and Vega rents his. Could one of them have brought Eileen home on May 18th?*
>
> **Break-in:** *Someone was after my notes disk. Why? Mystery man inquired about the apartment across from mine. Description matches who Ms. Gardner claims brought Eileen home on May 18th. Strange. He didn't exist per parents.*
>
> **Vega:** *Nervous when questioned about Adam and Eileen. Denies knowing anything about their deaths, specific research for TR Tires, or seeing Adam on May 28th. Suspicious, the mayor is Vega's alibi for the time of deaths of Eileen and Adam.*
>
> **Mayor:** *Check out Vega's alibi. Why is the mayor avoiding Sarge? Who owns the phone number the mayor called?*

She stopped typing and stared at her notes. Vega and the mayor were looking more suspicious than Trevor, and she was glad of it.

CHAPTER 40

June 7th, Monday

THE PHONE RANG. He closed the file on his desk and picked up the receiver.

"It's me, Nick. Detective Doyle and Sergeant Ellis were just here. I'm not sure I convinced them about Adam and his wife."

"Did you appear nervous like always?"

"Shut up," Nick said in his high-pitched voice. "I was cool."

Nick's squeak annoyed him. "Yeah, I bet."

"Hey, I never wanted this to happen to Adam. I liked him."

He rolled his eyes. "Stop being so sentimental."

"You better take care of me," Nick said. "I won't go to jail for this."

"Keep calm. This will all blow over."

"I don't think so. Doyle and her sergeant seemed to know a lot." Nick's voice rose. "And if they look into RedChem, they'll find out everything."

"You need to stop worrying. And don't call me here again."

"I'll call you anytime I like."

He slammed his fists on his desk. "Don't push your luck, Nick."

Nick cleared his throat. "All I'm saying is this is getting crazy. They probably think I had something to do with Adam and his wife's murders."

"Stop!" He leaned back in his high-back chair. "You told me you have a sample of the chemical and the original test results."

"Well. Not exactly."

He gritted his teeth. "What happened to them?"

"I had a minor disagreement with Adam when he was here on the 28th. He didn't have the results with him and when he left, we struggled and his briefcase dropped on the floor and opened. The vial with the chemical cracked and spilled in the briefcase and onto the floor."

"What do you expect *me* to do now?"

"Use your clout. Get those detectives off my back. The tires are going into production in two weeks. I'm not sure I can keep this together until then."

"You need to get a hold of yourself. You covered your tracks."

He slammed the receiver down annoyed that Nick had become a loose cannon. Those test results and the chemical sample would be the only proof of a coverup. He thought monitoring the case as it progressed would give him the information he needed, but his plan to expose everyone was failing, and he needed to find another way.

CHAPTER 41

THE FOLLOWING MORNING at the *Messenger*, Philip sat in his office and waited for his computer to boot up. He sipped the cup of coffee he'd gotten from the kitchen recalling last night and how another argument ensued with Ros. It wasn't only her twirling hair habit that returned, he had plenty to worry about with Ros's bottle of Valium almost empty. He hoped Jules and Shana could find out what's going on with her.

The screen flashed requesting his VPN password. He entered it and clicked on the Logan McIntyre folder, ready to read his draft on Senator Jenkins in the shared directory, but nothing was there.

Logan stood in the doorway. "Hey. Good morning."

"You're here early," Philip said. "Where's the draft of Jenkins's story? I thought you said you'd have it done last night."

"I worked on it at home and updated it in the shared directory. But when I logged into the VPN just now, the draft was gone."

Philip cocked his head forward. "What? How'd that happen?"

"Dylan, from IT, couldn't find it." Logan sighed. "He thinks it has something to do with the software he installed to prepare for the Y2K transition."

"Can you re-create your draft for the Sunday edition?"

"Probably." Logan pointed to his temple. "All up here, plus I have my notes at home."

"Great. Keep me posted, but to be on the safe side, I'll let Grant know there may be a delay on the profile stories."

Logan left and Philip took the penthouse key from his desk drawer. When he arrived on the fourteenth floor, the camera focused on him and the doors swung open. Grant motioned Philip to join him on the couch. As Philip sat, he told Grant what happened to Logan's draft on the senator.

"I hear things are going crazy with computers. Will it take him long to recreate it?"

"He said he could have it for Sunday's edition. By the way. When we interviewed Senator Jenkins, he told me to send you his regards."

Grant stared out at the skyline.

No response. Strange. "Did you hear me, Grant?"

"I heard you." Grant rested his arm on the back of the couch. "Isn't Madeline's campaign fundraiser coming up?"

"Yes. June 19th. Why?"

"Maybe we should wait until the Sunday after to print both profile stories. As you said before, anything can happen in a short time with politics."

Grant continued to talk, but Philip's mind drifted to Ros and their arguments, blocking out Grant's conversation.

"I'll talk to Dylan," Grant said as he stood.

"Oh…about what?"

"Weren't you listening, Philip? About the internet news he's going to manage. You all right? You seem a little preoccupied."

"I'm fine."

Grant made his way to his desk. "On another note, I wanted to ask you about Shana. I ran into her at PJ's the other day. She was with her daughters. I called her to ask her out, but it seems she's dating the chief medical examiner. Can you put in a good word for me?"

Philip stood and remembered Shana declined Grant's invitation. "If she's dating someone, I don't want to get in the middle of it."

"Hey, what are friends for?"

Philip always thought Grant could attract any woman, with his chiseled good looks. "Why don't you try to date someone else."

"I've always admired Shana. I like strong women."

Just like his wife. Philip's concern for Ros crept into his mind and didn't give him the capacity to tackle a conversation like this. Grant didn't like to lose, so no sense in trying to get him off the subject.

Philip took a deep breath. "I'll see what I can do. No promises. But leave her alone for now."

"Understood. Did you look into the senator's finances yet?"

That's the second time Grant asked him to do that. Philip had to hold back what Trevor and his friend at the IRS found until Trevor could make arrangements to pay back the funds. But Grant was known for turning over rocks to find the truth. Could he know about the IRS investigation? If he did, he would surely want a story written about it. He had to tell Grant something. "The senator is getting $8,000 a month deposited into his checking account in cash."

"Do you know where it came from?"

"Impossible to find the origin of cash."

"Interesting. Let me know when Logan's stories on Madeline and the senator are ready to go to print."

Back at his desk, Philip forced himself to focus on work and not Ros as he clicked open his TR file to recap his notes. He wished he could have asked Senator Jenkins more questions yesterday, but he couldn't take a chance of putting the IRS's investigation at risk or divulging too much to Logan while respecting Trevor's wishes. He typed one more item on the document in the TR folder. *Suspicious—Logan's draft on Senator Jenkins was deleted.*

CHAPTER 42

June 8th, Tuesday

OUTSIDE THE ROUNDHOUSE, Shana waited for Mac to go to their meeting with Oliver Pendelton at the University of Pennsylvania. The morning air was crisp and clean reminding her of the vacations, in her youth, she used to take with her parents up to the Pocono Mountains. Fond memories flooded her mind, but then as usual the case took hold and she thought about the reason for the visit today. She was skeptical Mac's friend could decipher the remaining piece of Adam's note but eager to find out.

Mac pulled up at 10:00 a.m. on the dot. They drove through heavy traffic down Race Street, which almost came to a standstill because of construction.

"How are you doing since the break-in?" Mac said.

"I'm okay. When Sarge placed the officer outside of my building, I thought it was overkill, but I'm glad he did it."

"Frank's always precautionary."

Shana turned to Mac. "Thanks for disguising your visit with the officer. No rumors or teasing surfaced."

Mac smiled. "I'm glad. I heard Russell is on desk duty."

"Russell sounds strange. I don't know anyone that calls Fits by his first name."

"I feel first names add a more personal touch with co-workers. Seems like you two aren't exactly the best of friends.

What happened between you two, anyway? Or is that none of my business?"

"I don't mind sharing." Shana decided to tell him about how Fits messed up on one of her cases instead of airing dirty laundry how she repeatedly rejected his requests for dates. "He was my first partner when I became a detective five years ago. After we'd been partners for about a year, Sarge allowed me to be the lead on a high-profile murder case. The secretary of the previous ADA."

"I read about the case in the Baltimore papers. Didn't some evidence almost get thrown out of court?"

"Yes. A silver cigarette lighter. Fits hadn't thought it relevant and picked it up without wearing gloves. He had a sticky bun before he arrived at the crime scene. You can probably guess where that went. Turned out the victim didn't smoke. Luckily an ex-girlfriend of the ADA came forward. We not only found a box full of identical silver cigarette lighters at the ADA's home, but an entire room with photos of women he had stalked over the years, with the most recent his murdered secretary."

Mac turned onto the Schuylkill Expressway and swerved when a car switched lanes in front of him almost cutting him off.

Shana grabbed the handle on the door. "Crazy driver. No wonder they call this road the Surekill."

"Hell of a name for it."

"Too many deaths on this road over the years. How do you know Oliver?"

"My wife and I met him at a forensic science convention in San Francisco about fifteen years ago."

"Faye went with you?" Shana felt she was on a first-name basis with Mac's deceased wife after he talked about her so much.

Mac took the off-ramp onto Walnut Street. "She wanted to see San Francisco, and she even sat in on Oliver's lecture on chemical compounds and their effect on human tissues."

Shana raised her eyebrows. "She sat through that?"

"Oliver's delivery intrigued her. He's charismatic. You'll see it when you meet him. Anyway, he and I hit it off right away. We've been friends ever since."

"Hopefully, he'll be able to help with Adam's note."

Mac smiled. "I bet he will."

Shana adjusted her seat belt over her jacket. "Do you stay in touch with him often?"

"Not as much as I'd like. His wife died five years before Faye and he told me it helped him get over his loss by getting involved with his work. After Faye died, he invited me to dinner several times. We'd discuss cases until well into the night. Helped me get my mind off the grief."

Mac became quiet. His face was void of expression. There it was again. The look when he talked about Faye. She shouldn't be jealous of a corpse and shook it off.

"He must be a great friend to you," she said.

"He is." Mac turned onto 34th Street and parked near the Chemistry Complex of the University of Pennsylvania. He hurried around to open the passenger side. She hid a slight grin and grabbed the manila file.

They entered the main entrance. Their footsteps echoed on the linoleum floors in the empty dimly lit halls. Mac opened the classroom door to room 444. The smell of burnt sulfur flew out, reminding Shana of a Bunsen burner in her college science class. A man with a well-groomed silver-gray ponytail that hung to the middle of his back sat on a wooden stool behind a black counter.

"Hey you old fox," Mac said.

The man turned and grinned as he stood. Deep wrinkles seemed to carve a map on the man's face. Even though the lines were deep, he still had handsome features.

"Hello, Mac. What's up now? I don't seem to hear from you unless you're working on a stubborn case."

"That's not true. We had dinner together last month."

The man raised one eyebrow. "A hot dog and a bottle of beer

at the corner bar wasn't my idea of dinner. Besides, if you recall, we talked about some chemical solutions found in a body's stomach. Not great dinner conversation."

They hugged and patted each other on the back.

"It's good to see you for any reason," the man said.

Mac released the hug. "I promise the next time I call; it will be to invite you to a good dinner with pleasant conversation."

"That's better." The man studied Shana. "Now, who is this?"

"This is Detective Shana Doyle."

He reached out and cupped his hand over hers. His skin was soft but dry. Not what she expected based on his weathered face.

"Pleased to meet you. I'm Oliver. Mac forgot his manners."

"Sorry about that," Mac said.

"I heard a lot about you." Shana released her hand and rubbed the chalk residue between her fingertips.

"Sorry. Blackboard chalk. So, you heard a lot about me?" Oliver faced Mac. "Is this more than business?"

Mac flushed. "Shana is working on a tough case. She deciphered part of a note but needs help on the rest. We think it might be related to a chemical."

"Tell me more."

Shana placed her file on the counter. "A female body was found in a dumpster and later her husband was killed. I discovered a cryptic note in the victim's home."

"Okay, Oliver. I told Shana all about your expertise in chemical compounds. You're the king." Mac whispered in her ear. "And he knows it."

"I heard that." Oliver sat on his wooden stool. "And don't forget it. Okay, enough compliments. What's going on?"

Shana opened the manilla file and spread a copy of the note, and the printed information on the chemists from RedChem on the countertop, explaining how she solved most of the puzzle.

She pointed to the bottom of the note. "I thought this might be an address, but after an internet search, there weren't any addresses like that in the city or the surrounding areas. Maybe it's an anagram or cryptogram like the chemists' names. Could be a clue to the two murders."

Oliver peered at the note. "If the beginning of this note resulted in two names of chemists, the address, as you call it, may relate to a chemical."

"Hopefully, you can find a solution," Mac said.

Shana told Oliver about how Mr. Roberts's insistence on identifying an odor was kept out of the news, and why she wanted a sample of the chemical.

"A smell test...from a trashman." Oliver chuckled. "That's a new one."

Shana smiled. "Mac said you were the best."

Oliver rose from the stool and winked at her. "The best, huh? I'm always a sucker for a beauty. All right. But I can't promise anything."

Shana gathered the papers and put them in her file. "Thank you, Oliver. Anything you can do I would appreciate."

"I'll call Mac if I find anything."

Mac headed for the door. "We need to go, old man. I'll be in touch."

Oliver gave Mac a bear hug and a gentle hug to Shana. On the way out of the room, she caught the sight of Oliver giving Mac a thumbs-up sign, which she suspected was his approval of her.

Mac turned to Shana as they walked down the hall. "I should explain why Oliver would only contact me with his findings."

"Don't worry. Sarge told me about how Oliver helps sometimes. Your secret's safe with me."

"Good. How about lunch?"

She thought about where she had to go next. "Raincheck. Can you take me back to headquarters? I have something I need to do."

CHAPTER 43

June 8th, Tuesday

WAS IT SMART meeting fits? Shana entered the Stage Deli later that afternoon, regretting turning down lunch with Mac for this. The aroma of the coffee, various scents of lunch meat, and fresh-baked donuts filled the air. Busy with several business types placing their specialty coffee and sandwich orders, it surprised her to find an empty table in the back.

Shana ordered a cappuccino while she waited for Fits. He sounded desperate when he called her this morning. She couldn't help but feel sorry for him and wondered what he wanted to tell her.

A girl served her coffee and Shana reached to her inside jacket pocket for her bi-fold wallet for payment. When she replaced the wallet, her fingers touched the plastic tampon applicator and brought to mind the embarrassing moment when she first became Fits's partner years ago.

Back then she had carried her personal items in the jacket side pockets. At her first homicide crime scene, she'd pulled out latex gloves, and a tampon fell on the ground near the victim. Fits retrieved it and discreetly handed it back to her. She recalled the panic when she returned to homicide and thought for sure there would be teasing. But nothing happened. That incident caused her to have pockets sewn inside all her on-the-job jackets.

Fits made his way through the crowd and pulled out a chair. "Hi, Doyle. I'm glad you agreed to see me. How are you doing? I mean after the break-in."

"I'm fine."

A middle-aged man walked over to the table. "Hey Russell, you going to be at the next Big Brothers meeting?"

"Sure. See you later," Fits said.

The man smiled and walked to the counter.

Shana stared at Fits. Maybe there's more to this guy than she thought. "Big Brothers?"

"Yeah."

"Why didn't I know this?"

"I don't like to brag."

"Brag!" Shana's eyes widened. "You can brag about your conquests, but not about something as important as you volunteering for Big Brothers?"

He lowered his head. "I should stop bragging about my ladies."

"You think? Not sure I should've agreed to meet you."

"I wouldn't blame you if you didn't. I've been a real idiot...lately."

She rolled her eyes. "Lately!"

"Okay, I deserve that. But I have something to tell you."

"This better be good." Shana raised the cup to her lips.

"It is, Shana."

She cocked her head and took a sip of coffee.

"Haven't called you that in years, have I?"

"No. What's this all about?"

Fits rested his arms on the table. "I have some information about the Detweiler case."

Shana crossed her arms. "What about it?"

"I was watching *Law and Order*—"

"Hold on, Fits." She unfolded her arms. "If you're going to tell me about a cop show, I'm out of here."

"No…No. Wait. That didn't come out right."

Shana scowled. "Get to the point."

"All right. But first I want to say I don't blame Sarge for putting me on desk duty. He gave me a simple task to investigate your neighbor after the break-in, and I messed up. After he gave me a good talking to yesterday, I was pissed at myself for screwing up again."

"You should tell Sarge this."

Fits leaned forward. "I wanted to talk to you first. I was hoping after you hear me out, you'd put in a good word for me."

"You're asking a lot." She glared at him. "We haven't exactly been pals lately."

He slumped in the chair. "I'm not opposed to begging."

She let a deep sigh. "I'll talk to Sarge if what you tell me is important. But no promises. It's up to him. What do you have?"

"I believe there's a mole in homicide."

Shana kept her emotions in check, knowing Sarge suspected the same thing.

She whispered, cautious of her surroundings. "What do you know?"

Fits lowered his voice. "When Ms. Gardner told us about the patrol car at the Detweiler house the day after Adam's death, I got to thinking."

"About what?" Shana pushed her cup aside and leaned forward resting her arms on the table. "I told you the motor pool said no cars were signed out, other than the normal ones. And you found out Perkasie Police didn't send anyone back to the house."

"But I got suspicious when Briggs called me at home last night and asked a lot of questions about the Detweiler case. At first, I thought Sarge would assign him to the case, but then he wanted to know how much you knew about Adam's involvement with RedChem. I thought it was an odd question. We hadn't investigated that company yet. So, while I was watching, the cop show—"

Shana held up a hand stop. "I'm going to leave if you don't get to the point."

"Sorry, but something was in the show about cops doing favors for other cops." He kept his voice low. "I have a friend in the motor pool who owed me a favor. He told me Briggs signed out a car on June 3rd between 8:00 and 9:00 the morning you and I went to Eileen and Adam's house the second time. My friend was told to keep it off the books."

"Briggs?" She widened her eyes. "Hard to believe. So, he must've been the one at the house? Why? What could he have been after? And who was he doing this for?"

"He must've made a mold of the key from the evidence locker. And now knowing he signed out a car, looks to me like he's into something."

"You should call Sarge."

"Can you talk to him first? I know it's a lot to ask. You probably figured out by now why I've been acting the way I have toward you after we ended our partnership years ago."

She smirked. "You mean because I rejected the many times you asked me out?" Although after Sarge told her about how Fits slipped before she was his partner, she wondered if that was the real reason for his arrogance. "This isn't my first rodeo dealing with men in the workplace. I heard what you were telling your buds about not working with a woman. I figured I'd be the better person and let it go."

"I'm sorry about that, Shana. Thanks for not contradicting."

"Forget it. I'll talk to Sarge. And don't call me Shana. It's freaking me out."

"Thanks…Doyle. I appreciate it. You won't be sorry."

She hoped she wouldn't.

CHAPTER 44

June 8th, Tuesday

SHANA'S HEART RACED thinking Fits might have found the mole and couldn't wait to tell Sarge. If it proved to be Briggs, it would clear her suspicion about Fits. But Briggs? He had a spotless reputation, second to Shana's.

Back in homicide she hurried to Sarge's office, closed the door, and sat. "I just met with Fits."

Sarge stopped sipping his ginger green concoction. "What are you doing talking to him?"

Shana relayed what Fits suspected about Briggs.

"Now this makes sense," Sarge said. "After I put Fits on desk duty, Briggs asked me if he could join the Detweiler investigation. He was insistent. I told him you and I would work the case. I thought his actions were strange and now that I think about it, he hung around Fits's desk too much."

"When Fits told me about Briggs, I tried to figure out why he'd go to the Detweiler house the day after Adam's death. If he is the mole, why would he jeopardize a brilliant career?"

"I heard his sister needed an operation on her spine and she wasn't insured. Something like that would make anyone do desperate things."

Shana rested back in the chair. "What could he be looking for? Maybe that briefcase? But it's now with Vega. If it's the same one. And how are we going to find out for sure if Briggs is the mole?"

"Need to think about it. I still can't get in touch with the mayor to ask him about what his secretary told you, and to corroborate Vega's alibi. Looks like I have to go to City Hall. Didn't you say the chemists will be in tomorrow at RedChem? Did you make an appointment?"

"No. I thought I would pay a surprise visit."

"Good idea."

"Sarge, I told Fits to talk to you. He genuinely sounded regretful about his mess-up. We wouldn't have known about Briggs if he hadn't put two and two together. Could you give him another chance?"

She couldn't believe those words came out of her mouth.

"Not sure if this is enough to get him in my good graces. But I'll call him and see how it goes."

"Might be a lot to ask, but he was really upset. He was like his old self when I first became his partner. Can you call him…now?"

"You changed your tune about him."

"Yes. I guess I did."

"Okay, I'll call him."

Back at her desk, she slipped in her notes disk and typed.

Now suspecting Briggs as the mole, it must be the mayor he's working for. Need proof. Mayor still avoiding Sarge. Why?

Shana saved the disk and put it in her inside jacket pocket when her phone rang.

"I heard from Oliver," Mac said. "He solved the last piece of the puzzle."

A jolt of adrenaline ran through her. "That was fast. When can we meet him? Now?"

"He said tomorrow."

"Damn!"

"I know. I have an appointment with the dean tomorrow, so

how about if I meet you at the university at 9:30 in the morning?"

"Dean? That's great. So, you took my suggestion?"

"Yes, and thanks. I'll see you tomorrow."

After the call, Shana found Sarge in his office and told him Oliver may have solved the rest of the note.

"I knew he would come through. Still nothing from the FBI. Guess our case hasn't risen to the top of their list."

"Were you able to talk to Fits?"

"Yes. And you were right. He did sound remorseful. Something I hadn't heard from him in years. I've agreed to give him another chance, under one condition. Suspecting Briggs is the mole is one thing, but we need to be sure. I asked Fits to see what he could find out from him. They were close at one point when they were partners a long time ago, so if Briggs is going to confide in someone, it would be Fits."

Shana's suspicious mind took hold. "You don't think they would be working together? Do you?"

"Fits isn't the best detective I have, but he always took pride in his profession. To answer your question, my gut is telling me he's not working with Briggs."

Shana smiled. "Your gut...got it." She hoped Sarge was right.

"Fits will meet you at RedChem tomorrow. I brought him up to date on everything so far."

"Including the mayor's interest in this case?"

"Yes. But he still doesn't know about Oliver. That's one thing Mac and I...and now you need to keep to ourselves."

Back at her desk, her cell pinged, and she answered.

"Ros agreed to meet us for breakfast on Thursday," Jules said. "It didn't seem like she wanted to, but I told her it was your idea and convinced her it would be good for us to get together. PJ's at 9:00? Please tell me you can make it."

"I'll be there. Thanks for arranging this."

"I still can't believe Ros is seeing Madame X again."

"It's crazy. I need to go. See you Thursday."

If after all this time, could Shana get back to spending more time with her friends and wean herself off her obsession? Finding out what's going on with Ros would be a good start.

CHAPTER 45

June 9th, Wednesday

THE NEXT MORNING, Shana arrived early at the university hoping to catch Oliver before Mac got there. Summer students scurried about, the girls dressed in cut-off jeans and tank tops, and the boys in long jeans and T-shirts. On her way to the Chemistry building, she smelled the fresh scent of dogwood trees that lined the pathway. A group of girls kicked a soccer ball on the open space under some shade trees.

When she reached room 444, Oliver's class was ending. Shana slipped in and sat at a desk in the last row.

After all the students left, Oliver walked to the back of the room and sat at the desk next to her. "Where's Mac?"

"I'm a little early."

"I guess you're eager to find out what I discovered." He raised an eyebrow. "Or is it something else you want?"

She gave him a playful smile. "I *am* excited about what you found."

"I may be old, but I'm not an old fool. You want to ask some questions about Mac. Am I right?"

She held her hands in the air. "I confess."

"What do you want to know?"

"It's about his wife, Faye."

"I wouldn't worry if I were you. Although Mac has been

back in the thick of things at his work, he hasn't had much of a personal life…until now. I see the way he looks at you."

Her mouth curled into a grin.

Oliver patted her hand. "There. I thought that would cheer you up. Mac is one of the kindest men I know and a dear friend. I can tell you have strong feelings for him. It shows. Rest easy. You need to follow your heart. It appears Mac is."

The classroom door opened and Mac entered. "What's this? I turn my back for a minute and you two are already solving the puzzle."

Shana stood. "I arrived a little early, and Oliver was telling me about his students."

"He loves teaching." Mac stepped closer to Shana, leaned over, and gave her a peck on the cheek. "I'm glad to see you."

Oliver stood. "Okay you two, I don't have much time until my next class."

They followed Oliver to the front of the classroom. He laid out papers on the lab table, picked up the copy of Adam's note, and moved to the blackboard. The chalk screeched when he wrote the address 790 Center Edge Pine Hollow Road.

"I focused on the number 790." He turned to Shana. "You mentioned when you deciphered the names of the chemists, the names were spelled backward, so I thought maybe your friend used the same technique. There's only one chemical with these letters and the number 790."

Mac moved closer to the blackboard. "Can you get to the bottom line?"

"Patience. Watch closely." He wrote CEPHR. "These are the first letters of the supposed street address." He then reversed it to create RHPEC followed by 790.

Mac stared at Oliver. "I know you mean well, but can you explain?"

Oliver put the chalk on the sill. "I'm sorry. I forget sometimes and ramble on. The RHPEC combined with the number is a liquid rubber chemical. It stands for Rubber Hybrid Polymer Elastones Compound. It's more commonly known as HPE 790."

Shana raised her arms and dropped them. "Which means what?"

"I don't know exactly. It's highly experimental. Hardly ever used. Too many mishaps in the development process."

Mac viewed the blackboard. "What kind of mishaps?"

"My research shows it pertains to adhesion."

Shana stepped closer to the chalkboard. "Adhesion?" As she examined the findings on the blackboard her mind went into rewind on the events from this past week. "Oliver, could this chemical be successfully used in automobile tires?"

"It has a threshold tolerance of 125 pounds. That means depending on the speed and the condition of the road, the compound possibly could break down and disintegrate causing a blowout."

She wondered if Adam had stumbled onto this and if it was the odor Mr. Roberts smelled. "Would this chemical have a strong odor?"

Oliver chuckled. "Strong odor is not the word. I'm told it's offensive. It could last a long time on hard surfaces, and it's thick. Like hair gel."

Shana turned to Oliver. "How long would the odor last, say on a body?"

"If you're thinking about your murder victim in the dumpster, not sure how it would react on skin."

"I need to get a sample."

Mac scratched the back of his neck. "You're thinking about the smell test, aren't you?"

Oliver raised his hand. "Hold on you two. Don't get ahead of yourself. It's hard to get because of its volatility."

"I bet RedChem has some," she said.

"If they have it, and are doing modifications. It could be dangerous."

Shana lowered her brow. "How dangerous?"

Oliver seemed to ponder his thoughts. "Well, by itself and if you were careful, you could handle it. But once mixed with another substance, I'm not sure what would happen."

She faced Oliver and then the blackboard. "This is great. You've given me a lot to go on. Thank you."

He bowed. "My pleasure."

Shana kissed Oliver on the cheek. "Thanks." She whispered in his ear. "For everything." As she pulled away, he winked.

Mac patted Oliver on the back. "See you soon, old man."

"I hope so."

Shana stood next to Mac in the hallway. "This is the first break in the case!"

Mac stared at her.

"What?"

"You're excited."

"You bet I am. Oh, I almost forgot. How did your meeting go with the dean?"

"They agreed to let me teach one night a week."

"That's wonderful." Shana glanced at her watch. "It's almost 10:30. I need to meet Fits at RedChem at noon."

"Fits?"

"Sarge gave him another chance. Hope he doesn't regret it."

"Frank wouldn't do that if he didn't think Fits would improve."

Knowing why Fits was put on desk duty in the first place, she only smiled.

"Shana, good luck questioning the chemists. Now with this information, you are one up on them. Someone may try to hide how dangerous this chemical is, so please be careful."

CHAPTER 46

June 9th, Wednesday

SHANA WAITED FOR FITS in the RedChem parking lot in Princeton, New Jersey. She finished the cheeseburger she picked up from McDonald's and called Sarge to update him on her and Mac's meeting with Oliver. Sarge sounded almost giddy. She suspected he would politely rub the FBI's nose in it, telling them we deciphered the note. After the call, she pulled out the tape recorder and dictated.

"*Note to myself: Oliver identified the chemical HPE 790 from Adam's note. Dangerous. What role does the chemical have in this case? Was Adam killed because he'd found out about the volatility of the chemical?*"

She stopped recording and her cell phone pinged. Annoyed it might be Fits telling her he'd be late, she flipped it open.

"Detective Doyle? It's Flora. Victoria Gardner's friend."

"What can I do for you?"

"You told me when you called about Victoria's visit, that if I thought of anything to let you know?"

"Yes."

"Victoria left a message yesterday on my answering machine to call her. I called several times and left messages, but she hasn't called me back. Something might be wrong."

Shana tried to console the woman. "I'm sure she's fine. Why don't you try her again later?"

"Please, Detective. I'm worried."

"Did you call 911?"

"No. I don't want to sound like an alarmist."

Shana switched the phone to her other ear and rolled her eyes. "Why don't you go see her yourself?"

"I don't have a car. Please, I'm worried. Can you check on her?"

Now she's a babysitter. Shana sighed. "Okay. I'm at an appointment. I'll visit her after I'm done."

Fits drove in and she met him as he pulled into a parking space next to her.

He stepped out of his car. "Doyle, thanks for talking to Sarge for me. You won't be sorry. I promise."

"Just don't let it explode in my face. Any ideas about talking to Briggs?"

"I figured I'd take him out for drinks."

"Good idea."

She told him about the deciphered note, careful to leave Oliver's name out of it as Sarge requested.

Fits squinted. "Say that chemical name again."

"HPE 790."

"How in the world did you figure that out?"

"Mac helped. Sarge said he brought you up to date on everything."

"Yeah, your interview with Nick Vega, his background, and the briefcase."

On their way to the front entrance, Fits said, "Do we have appointments with these two chemists?"

"No. Surprise visits. I called earlier. Both of them are in. I want to question Paul Edwards first. He's Steve Heim's boss."

The lobby of RedChem had a modern decor with floor-to-ceiling windows two stories high. They introduced themselves to the receptionist who sat behind a half-moon Corian counter. On the wall behind the desk hung a large silver metal logo sign.

"We're here to see Paul Edwards," Shana said.

After a few minutes, the receptionist hung up the phone. "Mr. Edwards will see you now. His office is on the eighth floor." She pointed. "Elevators around to the side."

They thanked the receptionist and entered the glass-walled elevator. While it climbed, Shana gazed at the lobby below. "Impressive."

Fits followed her gaze. "Yep. Didn't know chemical research could be so profitable."

The elevator doors opened, and they stepped onto a plush tan pile rug bordered in navy blue. Straight ahead were two smoked glass doors with raised black lettering, Research Department. The entrance looked like it would be a Wall Street firm in New York City.

Another receptionist directed them to the first door on the right. A well-built man with a combed-over hairstyle wearing a starched blue shirt sat behind his desk. Shana gave introductions, and they shook hands. She noted his manicured nails.

"Won't you two have a seat?" Edwards said.

Shana pulled her recorder from her jacket. "Mind if I tape this?"

"No problem."

She pressed record while they sat. "We're investigating Adam Detweiler and his wife's murders. We have information Adam met with someone here on May 17th? Was it you?"

"I didn't have any dealings with him." Edwards pulled his calendar close. "I had a meeting with my financial advisor on that date."

"We'll need contact information. Do you know who Adam might've met with?"

"No, I don't."

"Do you own or use a limousine?"

"No."

Shana watched his facial expression when she asked the next question. "Where were you on the evening of May 28th and between 2:00 and 3:00 June 2nd? Those were the time of deaths for Adam and his wife."

Edwards narrowed his eyes. "Am I a suspect?"

"Just routine," Fits said.

After examining his calendar again, Edwards said, "I was at a conference in Miami from May 27th until yesterday."

"Are you working on anything specific for TR Tires?" Shana said.

"Only normal research and development for better performing tires. Nothing out of the ordinary."

"Anything else you can tell us about Adam?"

"Didn't know him that well."

Shana stopped recording. "Okay. Then I guess we're done." She stood and handed Edwards her card.

He wrote on a sticky note. "Here's the number of my financial guys and the hotel where I stayed during the conference."

Fits followed Shana's lead, and they left.

While they headed for the elevator, Fits shook his head. "He wasn't helpful."

"Adam was here on May 17th, according to his parents. If it wasn't Edwards he met with, then perhaps he saw Steve Heim. We should meet Heim away from here. He might be freer with information if he isn't under the microscope of his boss. I'll call him." Shana handed Fits the sticky note. "You call Edwards's financial advisor and the hotel."

While standing in the parking lot, they made their calls. Fits ended his calls first and waited while Shana finished hers.

"The financial guy confirmed Edwards met with him on the 17th," Fits said, "He was there all day. And the hotel clerk confirmed Edwards checked in on May 27th and checked out yesterday afternoon."

Shana opened her car door. "Heim agreed to meet away from the office. He seemed eager to talk to us."

CHAPTER 47

AT THE ROUTE 206 DINER, about 25 miles from RedChem, Fits and Shana sat in a worn, red, imitation leather booth by the window and waited for Steve Heim. The smell of burnt bacon, stale coffee, and the aroma of what could be beef cooking on the grill, came from the kitchen. At 1:30 in the afternoon, only two other tables were occupied in the far corner.

"No wonder he suggested this place," Shana said. "How's things going with that young officer from Perkasie?"

"We broke up. She wanted a serious relationship and would probably want kids someday. I'm too old for that."

Shana hadn't known Fits to be serious about anyone he dated, and why would he start now?

A white Volkswagen Beetle pulled in and a middle-aged man with shaggy hair, wearing a pale blue plaid shirt, got out.

"This must be him," Shana said.

The man entered and walked over to the booth. "Detective Doyle?"

"Yes. Steve Heim?"

He nodded. After introductions, Fits stood and sat next to Shana. Heim slid into the booth across from them and a waitress took their order for iced tea and left.

Heim waited until the waitress was out of sight. "You said on the phone you have questions about Adam's death?"

"Yes." Shana pulled her recorder from her pocket. "Do you mind if I tape this?"

"I guess not."

She pressed record.

Heim lowered his brow. "Why did you want to meet me away from RedChem?"

Shana moved the recorder to the center of the table. "We questioned your boss, Paul Edwards, and didn't feel we were getting the straight scoop. Questioning you away from the office, we hoped, would make you more comfortable about sharing information. We wanted to question you and your boss earlier this week, but we had to wait until you were both back from your convention."

"Convention? I never attend those events. Wait...did he tell you that?"

"The receptionist told me you were both at a convention when I called Monday to make an appointment."

"Paul probably told the receptionist to say that...Now it makes sense. He must have suspected we would be questioned about Adam's death. Before I left to meet you, he came to my office and reminded me of the confidentiality agreement I signed when he hired me. He mentioned your visit. Told me to keep my mouth shut if you called."

"Shut about what?" Shana said.

Heim stared out the window. After a few seconds, he sighed and faced them. "The hell with the confidentiality agreement. Things are out of control. We were researching how to use an experimental chemical compound called HPE 790."

The same chemical Oliver uncovered.

"You said experimental?"

"Yes." Heim lowered his voice. "The life of automobile tires could be extended when the chemical was mixed with other materials in the production process. It worked at first in our prototypes, but then we found problems in the testing."

"What problems?"

Heim leaned forward still keeping his voice low. "There's a list of twenty-five items we normally test when introducing a new formula in the materials used for making tires. In my testing, using this chemical compound, statistics showed a thirty percent improvement extending the life of the tire under normal wear and tear."

Shana shrugged. "Is that acceptable?"

"Yes, but that thirty percent would only apply if the user traveled at speeds up to seventy miles per hour, which would meet the static stress test. The dynamic stress test failure rate was almost twice the norm when accelerating speed."

"Which means what?"

"Picture someone pulling your arm gently for about ten minutes. That would be static stress. But if someone jerked your arm, that would be dynamic stress. Think of dynamic stress in terms of picking up speed suddenly, like passing a car or stepping on the gas to enter an on-ramp. The dynamic stress failure proved tires would experience random disintegration."

Shana pulled the recorder close and paused it when the waitress served their iced teas. The waitress left and Shana pressed record.

Heim continued. "We found the chemical could be volatile when mixed with the other material in the tires and under the condition I mentioned. By itself, it's safe."

Shana poured a packet of sugar into her glass and stirred. "Why would your company want to take a risk like that?"

"Since the HPE 790 was experimental, the company purchased it for basically nothing. My job was to modify the formula so it would improve the dynamic stress test to acceptable levels. Paul told me TR Tires was having financial trouble and needed this new tire to increase profits. He said the increase in revenues, would be more than enough to offset any losses from lawsuits."

"Then he was expecting disasters?"

"I think so. I can't prove it, but I think Paul had some stake in this. The bonus structure for someone in his position would be substantial. If the formula in the tires is successful, it would mean huge profits for RedChem and TR Tires."

Shana leaned forward. "Were you able to eliminate the problem?"

"No. The dynamic stress failure rate was sporadic, but it existed. Another problem in using the chemical compound, it had an offensive odor when in contact with hard surfaces."

Everything Heim said so far confirms what Oliver had told her and Mac.

"Hard surfaces?" Shana said. "How would the chemical react, say on skin?"

"I have no idea. I always wore gloves when in contact with it. We found the chemical by itself had the offensive smell, but when mixed with the formula, the smell vanished."

Shana thought about what Mr. Roberts smelled and wondered if any substance found in the alley would have hidden the odor. "What would be in the formula that would eliminate the smell?"

"There are several rubber ingredients and other chemicals. There's no way of knowing what neutralizes the odor."

"Did you meet with Adam on May 17th?"

"Yes. How did you know?"

"We didn't until now. Why did you meet with him?"

"When I told Paul my concerns about the dynamic stress test, he told me it was no big deal. I believe Paul fudged the testing numbers presented to TR Tires. Adam and I became friends when we worked together at RedChem and I knew he would help me figure out what to do. I wanted someone else to be aware of the problem. Adam met me after work at a bar near here and I gave him a sample of the chemical in a vial along with my testing results." Heim lowered his head. "I can't believe I involved Adam in all this. If I hadn't, he might still be alive." He pushed his iced tea aside.

"Would Adam have told anyone?" Shana said.

"I don't know. He just said he would take care of it. Adam was a good guy. He wouldn't have allowed a dangerous product put on the market regardless of whether or not TR Tires had financial problems. My biggest concern is I believe Paul may have already approved the rubber formula using the HPE 790."

"Who would Paul notify?" Shana hoped it would not be Trevor.

"Nick Vega, the TR Plant manager is Paul's contact."

"Can you stop this?" Fits said.

Heim shook his head. "Paul Edwards has the final say."

Shana studied Heim. "Is there any way to get another sample of this chemical and the original testing results?"

"Not anymore. Paul keeps the samples, testing results, and formula under lock and key. I would suspect the only testing results he has, are the ones he modified. I checked my computer just before I left to meet you, and all my results and notes were gone."

The waitress called out from behind the counter. "Do you need refills?"

Shana shook her head and faced Heim. "Did Trevor Richmond know about the situation?"

"I don't think so. Nick Vega was our primary contact unless he told Mr. Richmond. If someone knew I told Adam, and now he's dead, then I could be in danger. I have a wife and two kids."

"Do you have somewhere safe to go until this is over?" Fits said.

"I have a buddy who has a cabin in the Poconos. I'm sure I can use that. I'll take vacation time."

"Keep your location a secret." Shana handed him her card. "Call when you get settled."

Shana and Fits waited a few minutes after Heim left. As they walked to their cars, Fits turned to Shana. "Heim confirmed the chemical you and Mac deciphered from the note."

"Yes. And I wonder what happened to the sample Adam received on the 17th and Heim's test results?"

"You need the chemical sample for Mr. Roberts…right?"

"Are you going to make fun of that now?"

"No. I shouldn't have made such a big deal about it before."

Now he's supportive. Seems like he learned his lesson after she vouched for him with Sarge. "You heard Heim's comment about how the odor could vanish. If it was the chemical on Eileen's hand and something in the alley neutralized it, then Mr. Roberts may be the one who can help find where Eileen was killed."

"Understood."

Shana lowered her brow. "If Steve's suspicions that Edwards may have a stack in this and Nick Vega is his primary contact, maybe Vega has something to lose if the tires don't go into production. We should question Vega again."

"Doyle, I know Trevor Richmond is your friend, but do you believe he knows nothing about this chemical problem. Both those companies are his. Why wouldn't he be in the loop? And if TR Tires is in financial trouble, your friend may want the tires put into production. It would be profitable for both of his companies."

Shana's stomach knotted. Could Trevor have known? She couldn't imagine he would put a dangerous product on the market. At least she hoped. But when there are money problems, people do strange things.

She pulled out her keys. "I have to go. I received a call earlier from Ms. Gardner's friend. She's worried about her. I promised I'd stop and check it out. Go back and talk to Sarge. See if he thinks we have enough probable cause for a search warrant for Edwards's office. If we can get a sample of the chemical and Mr. Roberts identifies it, then it may lead to the reason for Adam's murder. And perhaps Eileen's as well."

"Lots of ifs."

"Contact Vega. Schedule an appointment to question him again. I'll see you at the roundhouse later."

In the parking lot, Fits drove off, and Shana pulled her cell from her pocket. She called Ms. Gardner's number. No answer.

CHAPTER 48

June 9th, Wednesday

SHANA SWITCHED OUT the interview tape for her notes tape and left RedChem heading to Perkasie on Route 295. She dictated on the way.

"*Note to myself: Steve Heim confirmed RedChem is using HPE 790 for tire improvement, and it has a powerful odor. Chemical could be what Mr. Roberts smelled. Per Heim, the chemical in tires could cause accidents and Paul Edwards knew about the failed tests. Did Edwards falsify results and approve the chemical anyway? Edwards's alibi checks out for the time of the murders. Adam met Heim on May 17th. Where's the sample and Heim's test results he gave Adam? Did Nick Vega know about the formula problem? Does Vega or Edwards profit from the tires put into production? TR Tires in financial trouble? What does Trevor know?*"

At 4:15 p.m. she arrived in Perkasie and turned onto West Street. The late afternoon sunlight sprinkled through the branches of the full oak trees that canopied the street. The lawn at the vacant house on the right hosted weeds, and dandelions spread throughout. Ms. Gardner's lawn, plush deep green, neatly trimmed. The street seemed peaceful, not like last week when they found Adam's body.

Shana parked in front of Ms. Gardner's house and made her way to the front door. She could have kicked herself for agreeing to check on the woman and sure Ms. Gardner's friend let her imagination run away with her. The scent of freshly mowed lawn hung heavy in the air. She rang the doorbell, but no one answered. She rang again.

An elderly voice came from inside. "Who's there?"

"Ms. Gardner?"

"Yes, who are you?"

"It's me, Detective Doyle."

The sound of footsteps on the hardwood floor grew nearer to the front door. The voice inside asked again. "Who did you say was there?"

Shana yelled through the door. "Ms. Gardner, it's Detective Doyle. Your friend Flora called me. When you didn't answer your phone, she became concerned."

"Show your badge through the peephole."

Why did she ask for ID? Shana pulled her badge from her belt and displayed it. The locks clicked, and the door opened. An older woman with straggly gray hair, bundled in a blue terry cloth bathrobe stood in the doorway.

"Ah. Excuse me. I'm looking for Ms. Gardner."

The woman squinted. "What are you talking about? I'm Mrs. Gardner. And why are you calling me Ms. Gardner?"

Shana's eyes widened. "Can I come in? I'd like to talk to you."

"I'm not feeling well." She wiped her nose with a tissue. "I've been away on a trip. The first time I could get away I get sick and had to return early? Is this important?"

"Yes, it is. *Very* important."

CHAPTER 49

June 9ᵗʰ, Wednesday

AFTER SHANA RETURNED to homicide, she motioned for Fits to follow her into Sarge's office. Inside, she shut his door.

"Doyle, you look like you've seen a ghost," Sarge said.

"In a way, I did. You will not believe what happened. I just came from Victoria Gardner's house. I mean the *real* Victoria Gardner."

"What do you mean the real Victoria Gardner?"

"That original *Ms.* Gardner was a fake."

"What! You're kidding?"

"A fake?" Fits said.

"The real Mrs. Gardner just returned from a trip. I didn't think she would let me inside her house. After she showed me her license, and pictures of herself with her deceased husband, I realized she was telling the truth. Those picture frames weren't there before."

"Did she give you any idea who was posing as her?" Sarge said.

"No. My description didn't sound familiar to her. I think I scared her. She said she won a trip but didn't remember entering any contest. The notice came special delivery on May 30ᵗʰ when she got home from her volunteer work with her friend at the city library. She'd won an all-expense-paid trip to the Bahamas for three weeks, and she had to accept her prize immediately and leave the next morning. She couldn't remember the name of the company that sent her the tickets. Unfortunately, she threw away the envelope. I called her friend, Flora, and she didn't have any idea that someone else occupied her friend's house."

Sarge reached for his protein drink. "Who was the other Victoria Gardner, and how did she know so many details about the Detweilers?"

"The calendar in the kitchen had the woman's schedule. That's how the fake knew about the real Victoria's whereabouts. And her personal telephone book was in the kitchen drawer."

Fits said, "Did the real Victoria tell you anything about events that happened next door before she left on vacation?"

"She found out about Adam and Eileen when she got home. She did say she knew Eileen had gone missing several times before. According to her, it was nothing new, and she also knew about their financial problems. It's strange how the fake Victoria would have known that."

Fits continued. "And let's not forget the fake identified the mystery man. As well as the tip she gave us about the patrol car at Eileen and Adam's house, which led us to find out about Briggs."

Sarge rubbed his buzz and then stopped. "What older woman would pose as the neighbor, knowing there was a death next door unless she was being paid to be there to misdirect the investigation. Doyle, send forensics over to Mrs. Gardner's home to check for fingerprints. And get with the sketch artist on the woman who posed as her."

"Will do. Sarge, any luck with seeing the mayor?"

"No. I went over to City Hall this morning, and Betty told me he hasn't been in. He'd left her a message he would be out of town. Fits updated me on your visit to RedChem. Are you sure you can trust this Steve Heim? It sounds like he's a pawn, and he's trying to remove the blame from himself."

Shana shook her head. "I don't think so. He seemed genuinely shaken about Adam's death."

Fits faced Shana. "Doyle, what I don't understand is, if that cryptic note was meant for you, why wouldn't Adam just send you the information? Why would he tape it to the inside of his nightstand? He couldn't have known you would find it."

"Perhaps he didn't have time, or he was afraid for his life and wanted to hide it until later. I guess we'll never know."

"Sorry, Doyle." Fits cleared his throat. "I think we need to question Trevor Richmond again, especially after Heim said TR was in financial trouble."

"No need to apologize." She sucked in the fear her friend might be involved. "I'll get in touch with him and make arrangements. Sarge, what about a search warrant for Paul Edwards's office? I'd like to get a sample of that chemical for Mr. Roberts."

"Don't think so. With Heim's computer wiped clean and the original testing results missing, we don't have probable cause. Question Edwards again tomorrow. See what you can find out about the chemical now that we know he keeps it locked up. Fits, any luck with Briggs?"

"He's been quiet around me. I think he suspects something since he declined going out for drinks."

"I have an idea." Shana faced Sarge. "How would you feel about planting information with Briggs? We can have Fits tell him there's a link with the money in Adam's account to a prominent figure. I bet it goes back to the mayor."

"I despise thinking Briggs would resort to this level," Fits said. "He was a great partner."

"Hard to believe for me too," Sarge said. "But we have to be certain. Shana's suggestion might work."

Fits stood. "I'll talk to him later today."

"Okay," Sarge said. "Then we have a plan."

They agreed and left Sarge's office.

Back at her desk, Shana finished transcribing the interview of Paul Edwards, Steve Heim, and the real Victoria Gardner. She named the documents, according to who was interviewed, and saved them on the hard drive to the Murder Case folder 06021999. After she gave the tapes and hard copy to Sarge, she was packing up for the day when Logan called.

"Hey, Shana. I want to—"

"I don't have any update for you."

"That's not why I'm calling. I can't seem to get Adam out of my mind. You and I compared notes in the past on cases, can we do it on this one? Can I meet you at your apartment tonight?"

She thought about the officer guarding her apartment, but Logan's distant voice caused her to feel for her friend. "How about in an hour?"

Maybe Logan would have a lead for her.

CHAPTER 50

June 9th, Wednesday

WHILE WAITING IN HER APARTMENT for Logan, Shana sat at her desk, opened her laptop, and slid in her notes disk. She transcribed what she'd dictated to herself earlier and then typed new ones about Victoria Gardner.

Who sent the real Victoria Gardner the paid trip? Who posed as her and why?

She poured herself a glass of Chardonnay when the intercom buzzed. Within minutes, after Shana pressed the front door lock release, Logan walked in carrying a manila file. His eyes had dark circles under them and his sandy hair mussed, unlike his usual groomed appearance.

"You don't look so good." Shana closed the door.

"I told you I'm upset about Adam. Can't seem to get a good night's sleep."

Logan stepped in front of the wall mirror hanging near Shana's front door. He flattened the sides of his hair. "What's with the cop down the street? And you have a new security keypad outside." He glanced around. "Haven't been here in a while, but isn't this new furniture?"

"I may as well tell you. Someone broke into my apartment Saturday night while I was out, and my place was ransacked."

He turned abruptly. "Oh my God. Was anything taken?"

"No. Just vandalism. My sergeant posted the officer to monitor things. Haven't told my daughters or anyone else. Don't want to worry them. So don't tell Jules. Promise?"

"Okay." Logan sat on the new cream-colored sectional couch and dropped his file on the coffee table. "The cop gave me a funny look."

"He knows I expected a visitor." Shana rested her glass of wine on the coffee table. "Can I get you anything?"

"Sure. A beer."

She returned carrying an open bottle of beer and handed it to him.

He took a quick swig. "Did you get the new security system because of the break-in?"

"Yes." Shana didn't want to tell him it was installed the Friday *before* the break-in, fearing it would spur questions she wasn't prepared to answer.

She settled into her new oversized chair. "As a reminder, anything we discuss, keep to yourself. The murders are still under investigation."

"I know. We've always been successful with one of our brainstorming sessions. Maybe something I know will help you find out who killed Adam and Eileen."

"If we're going to share notes, then you should know Adam called me too."

"What! When? Why didn't you tell me when I told you about my call?"

"It was the day we found Eileen's body, and I wasn't sure how his call related to her death. I never spoke to him. He called twice but didn't leave a message or a number. Just told dispatch he would call me again."

"Oh my God, Shana. He was trying to tell us something. But what? Do you think Adam knew Eileen was dead when he called us?"

"I'm not sure. It ran through my mind, but Eileen's date of

death was May 28th and Adam didn't file the report until the 31st. If he knew she was dead, why didn't he say something to you when you talked to him on the 31st?"

"I wish I knew."

Shana picked up her glass of wine. "Tell me what you have so far."

Logan opened his file, pulled out several pieces of paper with handwritten notes. "I'm not sure how this relates to the murders, but Philip and I interviewed the senator on Monday for his *Messenger's* profile piece. He seemed off when I asked questions about Adam and Eileen."

"Do you think Senator Jenkins knows something about the murders?"

"Either that or he's hiding something else."

"Like what?" She took a sip of wine and placed the glass back on the coffee table.

He glanced at his notes. "For starters, my source told me he's getting $8,000 in cash deposited every month into his bank account. I tried to find out more in the interview, but he cut me off. If he's receiving cash deposits, I bet he's blackmailing someone, getting kickbacks, or into something illegal. His mansion's maintenance must cost him a fortune and he's in a lot of debt left from his deceased wife."

"You're speculating a lot without proof. But I agree with you, his mansion would need a lot of costly upkeep. I saw it in the *Philadelphia Magazine*."

Logan told Shana about the $100,000 paid to Trevor from Denver and Brown, and his suspicions after he couldn't find a lawsuit settlement in court records anywhere.

"You think Senator Jenkins had something to do with that money?" she said.

He tilted his head and his eyes wandered for a second.

She recognized that look. "You have a theory, don't you?"

"Yep. If those funds were from a lawsuit settlement, then why couldn't I find it in the records? Unless it wasn't supposed to be found, which would make it look like an illegal campaign contribution. Who else would want to discredit Madeline? With Adam working on Madeline's campaign, maybe he found information on the senator and was killed for it."

"That's a strong accusation. The senator has probably pissed off others in his career, and there were never any deaths surrounding him. And why was Eileen killed?"

"Maybe Adam told her what he found."

Logan's bloodhound instincts were usually spot on, but this time it seemed too far-fetched.

She shook her head. "I think you're stretching things."

"In the interview with Senator Jenkins, Philip asked him if he knew Trevor had worked for that law firm in the past. He said he didn't. I don't buy it for a second. That guy's running for his senate seat and would know everything about his opponent and her family. It's suspicious to have Trevor receive funds after Madeline announced entering the race."

Shana reached for her wine. "But what would planting money have to do with the deaths of Adam and Eileen?"

"There's a connection. I can feel it." Logan scanned his notes and looked at Shana. "I talked to Adam's parents today."

"Couldn't you have given them more time to grieve?"

"Adam's death has haunted me. Besides, they know me and I needed to find out whatever I could."

"How were they?"

"Seemed okay under the circumstances."

"What did they tell you?"

"They said they told me everything they'd told you. You found a sobriety chip. I can't believe Eileen finally went to AA. I wonder what happened to make her stop drinking?"

"I'm not sure we'll ever know."

Logan stared at his notes. "Do you know where she was May

16th and 17th? Atlantic City?"

Shana shrugged. "Not sure."

"Did you identify the limo that brought Eileen home on May 18th?"

"Not yet."

"Senator Jenkins has one?"

"So do a lot of other people."

"Do you think Eileen was in Atlantic City May 28th?"

"We're still looking into that. You didn't say anything to the parents about Adam's call to you on the 31st, did you?"

"No. I didn't think it would help them to know he reached out to me."

Logan flipped over the pages in his notepad. "What do you suppose was in the briefcase Eileen had with her on May 18th? Ironic, don't you think? Adam and Eileen's financial situation changed for the better after that day. Could there have been cash in that briefcase?"

Shana wanted to throw Logan off his scent. "We don't know for sure. But the parents said he got a bonus. No reason to not believe them."

"Did you find out anything about Adam's meeting at RedChem on May 17th?"

"We're still investigating." She glared at Logan. "And don't get any bright ideas to try to find out."

"Okay." Logan took his last sip of beer and placed the bottle on the coffee table. "How about the elephant in the room? RedChem and TR Tires are both owned by Trevor. But I can't believe Trevor would be involved. Can you?"

"No." But her suspicions about Trevor and TR Tires's financial problems surfaced in her mind.

"Think about it. Adam had worked for both of Trevor's companies as well as Madeline's campaign. Possibly money in a briefcase given to Eileen. Trevor received money after Madeline announced her campaign. Jenkins is getting $8,000 monthly in his account from an unknown source. There's a connection there somewhere."

It appeared Adam's parents didn't tell Logan about the miscarriages or he would've mentioned it.

Logan looked at his watch. "It's getting late. I need to go home."

Shana didn't want to get lost in Logan's conspiracy theories or reveal anything else about the case. Thankfully, he made the first move to leave.

He gathered up his notes. "Can we meet again? I have more questions."

"Who else knows this? Philip?"

"He only knows about the $100,000 paid to Trevor and the $8,000 in the senator's account, but not my interview with the parents."

"Good. Keep it to yourself. Remember, nothing gets reported until the case is solved. I'll call you when we can meet again."

Shana locked the two deadbolts after Logan left and sat at her desk. She opened her laptop, slid in her notes disk, clicked on the Word document in the Detweiler Folder, and typed.

$8,000 per month in cash paid to the senator. From whom? $100,000 perhaps a bogus lawsuit paid to Trevor through Denver and Brown. Logan suspects the senator is involved with those funds and maybe the murders. Again...what does Trevor know?

She caught sight of the *Philadelphia Magazine* under her mail and opened it to the layout of the senator's house. He was standing in front of his mansion and a black limousine was in the background. Her eyes drew her to the picture of his library. On the floor next to his desk—a tan, worn briefcase.

CHAPTER 51

June 10ᵗʰ, Thursday

SHANA PARKED AT PJ'S anticipating how breakfast would go with her girlfriends, after not being with them socially in months. She was about to get out of her car when her cell pinged and she flipped it open.

"Shana, you left a message," Trevor said. "You have more questions about Adam and Eileen?"

"Yes. Shouldn't take much time. Can we meet today?"

"Can't. Tied up with speaking engagements with Madeline."

"Trevor. It's important."

"How about Saturday late morning?"

After he resisted her requests to meet before then, she agreed to Saturday. As she ended the call, she wondered if the speaking engagements were real, or an excuse to avoid being questioned again.

Shana entered PJ's. Jules stood by the hostess station. Her chestnut hair cascaded below her shoulders. Shortly after, Ros entered. They exchanged hugs and as Shana released her hold, she noted Ros's puffy eyes and uncombed hair. Ros's curly hair was unruly at times, especially in the summer heat, but she always seemed to master keeping it under control. But today, it looked more disheveled than unruly.

The hostess escorted them to a secluded corner of the

restaurant, and a waitress took their coffee order as they all sat. Ros twirled the hair on the top of her head and quickly stopped. The same thing she did at the funeral.

"When I was making plans for us to meet today," Jules said. "I thought about our weekly chick-chats we used to have years ago. Remember that? We used to talk about everything."

Shana nodded. "Yes. It was fun catching up every week."

"I miss that. Do you think we could do that again? Just us girls."

"That would be almost impossible," Ros said. "We all have busy lives now."

Ros turned to Shana. "I'm glad you finally agreed to meet us. It's been a long time."

Shana was sure Ros wouldn't feel that way if she knew the real reason for this breakfast.

Ros pulled a white envelope from her purse. "I found these photos in my closet when I was getting ready. They're from our high school days and some from our weddings."

The last thing Shana wanted to do was reminisce about her wedding.

"Let's see," Jules said. "Oh, I should have brought some too."

Ros held up a photo. "This one is my wedding. Look at those hats."

Jules laughed. "Yikes. We all had those big-brimmed hats for the bridesmaids at our weddings."

"Yeah, Shana," Ros said. "You were the first one to make us wear those."

"Sorry girls."

Ros bowed her head. "Oh, I'm sorry, Shana. Shouldn't have brought up your wedding."

"It's okay. It was a long time ago."

The waitress served their coffees, and they all ordered the veggie omelet special and passed around more photos. Ros's face seemed to light up talking about old times. Shana observed Ros staring at the photos as if she physically returned to those days.

"Look at this picture." Ros handed it to Shana. "It's us on the beach in Wildwood the summer after high school."

Shana stared at it and smiled. "I'll never forget that weekend. On the way home, we stopped at the Route 50 Bar to watch the moon landing. The bartender let us stay, and we were only eighteen."

Jules laughed. "Everything's fine in '69."

"And do you remember after we left the bar?" Shana chuckled, "Madeline drove around the Jersey circle down a one-way street?"

Ros laughed so hard, she wheezed. "She was crazy in those days."

"I still can't believe Madeline's into politics," Shana said. "She'll have to be punctual if she's elected. Not like the half-hour lead time we used to give her back then when we would go out."

"I almost forgot about that." Jules leafed through the photos and picked one up. Her face saddened. "Oh…this is Eileen with us in high school." She put the photo on the table. "We all started as friends. Not sure what happened after she married Adam. They kinda stayed to themselves."

Knowing about the miscarriages, Shana certainly could understand how they stayed away with everyone else having children.

Jules faced Ros. "You were the only one who stayed in touch with Eileen. How did she seem to you?"

Ros quickly gathered up the photos. "I don't want to talk about them. Too depressing."

Shana observed Ros zoning in and out all through breakfast. After they finished their meals, Ros sipped her coffee and rested her hands next to the cup. "I looked in the mirror this morning and this middle-aged woman stared back at me. Where did that eighteen-year-old go?" Her eyes watered. "Did you guys ever feel like that?"

"I know what you mean," Shana said. "Some young rookies call me ma'am. You're not upset about age, are you Ros? All those health drinks you concoct from your medical journal probably stop you aging."

Jules snickered. But no reaction from Ros, who just stared into the coffee cup.

Ros mumbled as she reached the top of her head and twirled her hair. "Madame X helps."

"You aren't seeing her again, are you?" Jules said.

"I don't want to talk about it."

"She's after your money," Shana said.

Ros raised her voice and stopped twirling her hair. "I said, I don't want to talk about it."

Shana feared Ros would leave, and it was a good time to change the subject. "On a good note, I'm dating someone."

"Really?" Ros continued to stare into her coffee cup.

"His name's Mac. He's the chief medical examiner."

"Ugh!" Jules said. "What are your conversations like at dinner?"

Shana grinned. It was the same comment her daughter Kim said. "We talk about what other couples talk about." She expected a smart remark from Ros about Mac's profession, but it never came.

"So how long has this been going on?" Jules sneered.

"We've only had one date." She recalled how tender Mac was after the break-in. "But I have a good feeling about this." Shana saw the disapproval expression on Jules's face. "Okay, Jules let me have it."

"Events like this should be shared. This proves you need to let go of whatever you're dealing with and see us more often."

The last thing Shana needed was a lecture. She felt bad enough avoiding them. "I've told you time and time again, when

I became a detective, my time would be limited."

"Yes, but since your parents died, we haven't seen much of you at all," Jules said. "Are you all right?"

"As I said at the funeral Saturday, I'm fine." No way would she reveal the truth.

Jules applied a dark rosy lipstick that complemented her olive complexion. "Well, I wish it were different. Anyway, I hope this guy works out for you. I've said this before, but please try to make our next dinner."

"I'll try," Shana said knowing it was unlikely until she could get her obsession, diving into her murder cases, under control.

"You hardly touched your meal, Ros," Jules said. "Are you okay?"

Ros placed her napkin on the table. "Just not hungry."

The waitress dropped off the check. They all put their credit cards on top and asked to split the bill.

Shana remembered the promise to Philip, stole a glance at Jules, and faced Ros. "Okay Ros, what's going on with you?"

Ros knocked over the glass of water. She dabbed the tablecloth with her napkin. "What do you mean?"

"Don't avoid the question. Jules and I saw you twirl your hair at the funeral, and you did it throughout breakfast."

"I'm fine. Kelsey's schedule is hectic. So...when are we getting together again?"

"Ros, don't change the subject."

"No honestly. I'm fine."

Shana touched Ros's arm. "We're your friends. We can help whatever it is."

"Friends?" Ros glared at Shana. "Then why haven't you been around us? I wouldn't call that a friend."

Shana's heart almost stopped. It was a harsh comment, but true. "I'm sorry. I don't know what to say."

"Oh, forget it." Ros turned away. "I'm a little on edge. I'll be fine when the production of *Annie* is over."

But Shana couldn't forget Ros's comment or the icy stare.

They signed their checks and Jules checked her watch. "Crap. It's almost 10:30. I told the vet I'd be back by now."

Shana stood. "I need to go back to work too."

They hugged each other and said their goodbyes.

On the way to her car, Shana waved to Ros and Jules as they all drove their separate ways. Within minutes her cell pinged, and she answered.

"Don't know what you're going to tell Philip," Jules said. "Do you buy the Kelsey excuse?"

"No. Something's going on, and Philip will have to find out on his own."

Driving back to the roundhouse, Shana thought how Ros's comment about their friendship cut to the core. Oh, how she wished she never went down this slippery slope of obsessing over her cases. She realized, she had to change, but how?

CHAPTER 52

June 10th, Thursday

BACK IN HOMICIDE, Shana motioned for Fits to follow her into Sarge's office. Keeping Logan's identity a secret, she updated them on what he'd told her last night, and what she saw in the *Philadelphia Magazine*.

"The briefcase keeps popping up," Sarge said. "I'll schedule a meeting with the senator. Doyle, not sure your source's speculation about $100,000 being a phony campaign contribution is valid. Or if it has anything to do with the murders of Adam and Eileen."

"What about the $8,000 deposited each month in the senator's account?" Shana said. "We should check it out."

"We can't get a warrant just based on what your source told you."

"The senator has a black limo, which adds to the list of people that could've brought Eileen home on the 18th."

"More questions for the senator. Forensics called. They checked the Gardner woman's house. The only prints were of the real Victoria Gardner."

"I figured that," Shana said. "Whoever posed as her, wouldn't be stupid enough to leave any prints."

Sarge turned to Fits. "Where are we in questioning Vega and Edwards again?"

"The receptionist at RedChem told me Edwards is away on business. Convenient. Edwards's home phone number is unlisted, and I tried to get it from his company, but they wouldn't give it to me. And Vega. The receptionist said he was out sick, although I did leave a voice message for him on his office phone. I found his home phone number and had to leave a voice message there too. I'll keep checking back."

Sarge faced Shana. "Doyle, what about Trevor Richmond?"

"I scheduled a meeting with him this Saturday. He couldn't meet until then because of commitments relating to his wife's campaign."

"Sounds like he's avoiding you," Fits said.

She had to agree as well and shrugged.

Sarge leaned forward. "Between the mayor avoiding me and Vega and Edwards suddenly out of reach, it makes them all look suspicious." He turned to Shana. "And so does your friend, Trevor."

Shana's stomach churned as she and Fits left Sarge's office. Oh, how she hoped Trevor wasn't involved.

Back at her desk, she slid her notes disk into the computer. After an intense hour review of her notes with no clear path to a killer, she stood to stretch her legs. A cup of coffee would help. She returned from the kitchen and her phone rang. It was Mac.

Shana whispered knowing Fits was close by. "Glad you called. I needed a break."

"From what?"

"Paperwork."

"Do you want to meet me at the Block and Clock tonight?"

"Just what the doctor ordered."

Mac chuckled. "Great. See you at 8:00?"

"Perfect."

Shana took a sip of the strong cold black coffee and spit it back into the cup. The burner must have been off. She grasped the mouse and moved it swiftly over the pad trying to wake up the computer. Her notes document was no longer on the screen. She rapidly clicked in the folder Murder Case 06021999 on her hard drive, hoping she'd saved it there, but all the documents from the interviews were also gone.

She peered over the cubicle at Fits. "Did you notice anyone suspicious around our computers lately?"

"No. Why?"

"I was reviewing my notes before I went for coffee and when I returned, all the documents related to the Detweiler case were deleted on the hard drive and my disk."

His head flinched back. "That's crazy! You better call IT."

She placed the call and within minutes Dylan Holden arrived. His glasses slid down his nose and he pushed them back as he sat. He typed in code that looked like hieroglyphics and clicked repeatedly with the mouse. The screen flashed back and forth between folders.

"Any luck?" Fits talked over the cubicle.

Shana shook her head. "Not yet."

"Want any coffee?"

"No more for me. Thanks."

Fits headed for the kitchen.

Dylan removed his glasses and pinched the top of his nose. "I don't know what happened, but I can't retrieve your documents. Something on your disk must've corrupted your computer."

"Isn't there some type of virus protection or a backup system?"

"It should have worked." Dylan put his glasses back on. "With the Y2K approaching and the software we installed to prepare for it, we've had complaints of corrupted backups. Sorry. I'll report this."

"Can't you look into this now?"

"I'm…ah just a consultant. I'll make sure the right people

are notified. He apologized and rushed off."

Shana stared at her blank screen, subconsciously hoping the documents would re-appear.

The smell of coffee circled as Fits returned carrying a cup. "Made a fresh pot if you want any."

"I'll pass."

"Was Dylan able to find your documents?"

She slouched in her chair. "No."

"How the hell can that happen?"

"Beats me. Dylan said it's the Y2K thing. I need to tell Sarge."

In his office, Shana told him what happened. "Dylan said he thought my disk corrupted my computer. But that doesn't make any sense when the only documents deleted were on the Detweiler case. We checked the copy of my notes disk in your drawer before, but let's check it again."

Sarge unlocked his desk drawer. He slipped her disk into his computer. She watched over his shoulder as he clicked on the folder named Detweiler Case. All her note documents were still there.

Shana stepped away. "If opening a copy of my disk on your computer worked fine, then my computer has some type of virus on it." She turned to the filing cabinet. "We should check my interview tapes again."

Sarge unlocked the cabinet and Shana inspected every tape. All of them were intact.

Shana lowered her brow. "If Briggs had a hand in this somehow, why delete the interview case notes on my computer? I could easily re-create them. He knows my process and that you keep my tape recordings locked up. And if he was the one that broke into your desk, and has a copy of my disk up to the time of the break-in, why delete all my notes."

"Sounds like someone is trying to disrupt the investigation." Sarge ejected the disk.

Shana picked up the recordings. "I want to re-create the

interview case notes."

"I don't think that's necessary, since we have the hard copies. But I know how you like to refer to everything on your computer in one place. How long will this take?"

"Don't know. If there's a virus on my computer, there's a risk they would be deleted again. Can I use yours?"

Sarge picked up his plastic thermos filled with his green shake. "Sure. I'll go to the gym. Save the interview notes on a disk and once we get your computer squared away, you can upload it."

"I'll need to update my notes disk on events after the break-in."

"All right, but with suspecting someone broke into your apartment to get your disk, and now it was wiped clean, I want a copy when you're finished."

It took Shana most of the afternoon into the early evening to finish transcribing the interview tapes and update her notes disk. She thought hearing all the interviews again would spur something in the direction of a prime suspect, but no luck. Sarge returned. He locked up a copy of her notes disk and the interview disk.

On the way to meet Mac, she couldn't help but wonder if the deletion of her documents meant someone else was interested in this case, besides the mayor.

CHAPTER 53

June 10th, Thursday

TREVOR SAT BEHIND his desk in his office chewing a few Tums. The pain in his upper stomach hadn't subsided since the middle of May and now with Shana wanting to ask more questions about Adam and Eileen, it had gotten worse. Why did he panic when Shana called? Telling her about speaking engagements must have sounded suspicious, but he had to form his thoughts. He needed to put his concerns about Shana's visit to the side, for now, knowing what he had to do. The light on the phone line went out.

A few seconds later, Madeline stood in his doorway. "Where's Iris?"

Having the office to themselves was best. "I told her to take the rest of the day off."

"Why would you do that? I have so much work to do."

He sighed. "I have to tell you something."

"You look beat, Trevor. Are you okay?" Madeline stepped in. "What's the matter? You're pale. I thought you were going to the doctor." She stared at him with a straight face. "Why do you look so serious? You're scaring me."

"We have a problem."

She threw him a quizzical look. "What problem?"

"You know the $100,000 Denver and Brown gave me as part of my fee for a past lawsuit settlement."

"Yes. Thank God we received those funds in time to start my advertising campaign."

He blew out a deep breath.

Madeline sat on the edge of one of the barrel chairs. Her brows drew together. "Oh…you know I hate bad news. What's wrong?"

"I found out there was no lawsuit settlement."

She jerked her head back. "No lawsuit settlement! What do you mean?"

"The funds can be traced back to Senator Jenkins?"

"Jenkins?"

"It may be a plant to look like an illegal campaign contribution."

She bolted from the chair. "What!" She paced the room. "How can this be happening?"

"Damn it, Maddie! Please, sit down! Let me explain."

"This is terrible." She eased into the chair.

Trevor told her what Walter Brown had found, careful not to mention Philip and Logan were the ones who suspected the problem.

Madeline looked upward and shook her head. "Things were going so smoothly." Her nostrils flared. "So, this is how the senator wants to play."

"I recommend returning the money. If you're elected, you can call for a full investigation."

She bent over holding her head in her hands. "We've spent most of it on advertising."

He stepped from behind his desk with a box of tissues. "Look at me Maddie."

Slowly she raised her head, eyes full of tears. He handed her a tissue. "We're going to get through this. If my figures are correct, the next fundraiser should net us enough to pay back the money and still have funds to continue with the campaign."

"I hope so." She blotted her eyes. "I'm thrown by your old law firm's involvement."

"Still looking into that."

"Trevor, I wanted to make a difference. You remember what my father went through before he died, trying to make ends meet after the unions got into his business." She slouched in the chair. "His problems are why I entered the race, to minimize the impact the unions have on small businesses."

"I know Maddie."

She strolled to the window and stared out. "I guess this is what real politics is like, isn't it?"

"I'm afraid so. Are you up for it?"

She bowed her head to the street below then slowly turned. "The way I see it, we're fortunate we have friends who informed you of this. So, yes. I'm ready."

CHAPTER 54

June 10th, Thursday

LATER THAT AFTERNOON, the burning in Trevor's stomach had calmed somewhat after he had told Madeline about the bogus lawsuit settlement. But the stress kicked in again at the thought of how they'd return the funds. He opened his file on their campaign finances and reviewed the figures for the upcoming fundraiser when the phone rang.

"Trevor Richmond, here."

"Mr. Richmond, I'd like to meet you about an important matter?"

"Who is this?"

"Betty Leonard, Mayor Gaffney's secretary."

"What is this about?"

"I can't talk on the phone. Please meet me. It's important."

Cautious of the mysterious phone call he'd received last month with a tip on the senator, he took a deep breath. "How do I know you are who you say you are?"

"This may convince you. I met you in City Hall about a month ago. I bumped into you and spilled my coffee on your suit."

"I remember." He thought for a moment. "There's a small bar in Manayunk called the People's Pub. Say around 6:00 tonight?"

She agreed and Trevor gave her directions. He would have to leave now to beat the rush hour traffic.

On his way out, he peeked in Madeline's office. She was typing on her keyboard. "Working on your speech?"

She raised her head. "Yes, but I keep getting side-tracked thinking about those funds. I want to get this resolved as soon as possible before this gets out."

Trevor tried to reassure her. "When the fundraiser is over, we'll get this off our backs."

She looked at her computer screen as she spoke. "Where you off to?"

"I have a meeting at the law offices. I'll see you at home."

"Okay see you then." She gave him a quick nod and returned to clicking the keyboard.

It amazed him how she could focus, even after what he'd told her.

Within the hour, Trevor turned on the road to the People's Pub and parked two blocks away cautious not to fall into another trap. How could he have been so stupid before? At least this time he picked a public place.

When he entered, the scent of beer and pickled eggs hung heavy. He occupied a corner table near the front of the bar with an unobstructed view of the outside.

The bartender called over. "Yo! Want a drink, buddy?"

"A scotch neat."

The bartender poured the drink and set it on the bar. "You want it, come and get it."

Nothing's changed since he used to meet his buddies here after softball games back in his twenties. He paid for the drink and returned to the table.

A woman with short hair wearing a black suit entered and approached. He recognized her.

"Thank you for meeting me, Mr. Richmond."

The bartender yelled over. "Ma'am you want anything?"

"No thank you." The woman sat holding her purse tight in her lap.

"What's this all about?" Trevor said.

"Please, Mr. Richmond, I'm trying to make things right, I guess. I'm here to give you what I found."

She pulled out a white letter-size envelope from her purse, placed it on the table, and slid it toward him. "These are for you."

He took the envelope and pulled photos out flipping them over one by one. His pulse quickened. Pain flared in his upper stomach. His greatest fear had come true…he and Eileen in bed together half-dressed.

A smaller envelope inside the white one contained the negatives. Trevor placed the photos and the negatives back in the envelope and put it on the table. He took a large gulp of scotch, hoping to settle his stomach, but it only made it worse.

"I'll leave you now," she said. "To the best of my knowledge, these are the originals with the negatives."

Trevor cocked his head back. "Why are you giving these to me?"

"You can do what you think is best. I'm not after anything."

"No one is this honest. Where did you get these?"

"I am honest, and I can't tell you where I got them."

"These were taken without Eileen Detweiler's or my knowledge." He scoffed. "I could construe this as extortion."

She arched her back. "Extortion!" Her voice stammered. "I don't know who took them. I'll be in more trouble than you realize if these photos are discovered missing."

He sensed her uneasiness. Could it be true she didn't want anything? Could she be putting herself in danger, to do the right thing?

"Betty. I'm truly thankful."

"I've been working at City Hall for a long time and have seen and heard all kinds of things. I saw my chance to do something that might make up for all the other times I did nothing."

When Trevor arrived back at his office, Madeline had already gone home. Now that he saw all the photos, and how obvious some of them were staged, he would tell Madeline tonight. He sat at his desk and opened the white envelope, counting the number of negatives. When he counted the printed photos, accounting for the one he had in the safe, his stomach tightened.

One printed photo was missing.

CHAPTER 55

June 10ᵗʰ, Thursday

SHANA ARRIVED A LITTLE after 8:00 p.m. at the Block and Clock to meet Mac. The place was packed. The smell of hot roast beef sandwiches, their specialty, made her mouth water. She edged her way through the crowd where Mac sat at the bar. He stood and gave her his seat.

She perched herself onto the stool. "Busy, isn't it?"

As he broke away from a tender kiss on her lips, he stared at her. His mouth formed a small grin.

"Why are you looking at me like that?...Do I have something on my face?"

"I'm just glad to see you." He smiled and rested his arm on the bar.

She nudged her shoulder against his chest. "Glad to see you too."

The moment faded when the bartender asked if she wanted a drink.

"Oh yes, I'll have a Merlot." She faced Mac. "Do we have long to wait for a table?" She grabbed a hand full of peanuts, plopped them into her mouth and chewed.

Mac took a sip of beer. "The hostess said about fifteen minutes, but according to the bartender, the wait is more like thirty minutes."

"I don't mind. I enjoy sitting here with you." The bartender brought her drink, and she lifted it to make a toast. "It's my turn. Here's to an evening with a special man."

Mac lightly clinked his glass against hers, and she returned the gesture. She couldn't believe how comfortable she'd become around him. Her concern about getting involved with him all but vanished. She gazed into her glass. All the voices on the interview tapes were still fresh in her mind and questions about the case swept over her.

"Always thinking, aren't you Shana?"

She tilted her head toward him. "Sorry?"

"I can almost see the wheels turning in your brain."

"You are so in tune with my thoughts." She chuckled. "Maybe we were the same person in a previous life."

Mac pressed a finger to his lips. "I wonder who we were?"

"Very funny. I'm serious. About our thoughts I mean."

"I believe you are." He took a sip of his beer. "How's the case?"

She told him about the files deleted from her computer.

"How'd that happen?"

"Don't know. It's suspected to be a Y2K thing, but it's strange only the Detweiler notes were affected."

She lowered her voice and told him about her visit to RedChem and her meeting with Steve Heim and Paul Edwards.

"At least Steve Heim confirmed the chemical Oliver uncovered from Adam's note. Sounds like they're trying to hide their research. Or at least Paul Edwards is."

Shana swiveled the stool and rested her arm on the bar. "Another thing. After what Oliver told us, I have a feeling that chemical was on Eileen's body. How and why is a mystery? I wish we could get a sample for Mr. Roberts to confirm."

"Me too."

Her voice still low, she told him about her visit to the real Victoria Gardner.

"That's strange. Why would someone be posing as the

neighbor?"

"Not sure. What I am sure about is the fake Victoria Gardner knew a lot about the Detweilers that was confidential and gave us misinformation. I need to find out why."

Mac's cell pinged. He checked the number. "I have to take this call." He moved to the side of the restaurant near the windows. Within minutes, he returned. "I need to go, Shana. A bus accident on the Schuylkill."

"The Surekill takes more victims. Sorry to see you go, but I understand."

"To be on the safe side, we're pulling in all the pathologists from the surrounding counties." He put cash on the bar. "I'll call you later."

He kissed her on the cheek and left. She took a sip of her wine and thought about breakfast this morning with Ros and Jules. She felt bad about failing Philip, not being able to get Ros to open up. He sounded so disappointed when she told him earlier. The comment Ros made questioning her friendship rushed in her thoughts. How could Shana, after all this time, make her friends understand? It wasn't too late to visit Ros and Philip. Maybe it was time to explain why she had distanced herself from them.

She left her half glass of wine on the bar and slid down from the stool. Senator Jenkins and Mayor Gaffney were standing by the side exit. The mayor was doing all the talking and pulled on the senator's arm, jerking him back. Shana headed to the front of the bar to make a call.

"Sarge, the mayor is here at the Block and Clock, arguing with the senator."

"So he's not out of town. Go talk to him. Tell him I need to see him."

Shana sifted through the crowd back to the side entrance. The senator and the mayor had left.

CHAPTER 56

June 10th, Thursday

TONIGHT, PHILIP was determined to find out why Ros's nervous habit had returned. Now that he knew Ros didn't open up to Shana or Jules, his concern something else was going on nagged at him? It couldn't be any sickness in the family. Ros would have the medical journal out on the kitchen counter at her fingertips. He hadn't seen that book in almost a month. Philip entered his house through the garage and climbed the stairs to the kitchen.

The odor of oregano, garlic, and tomatoes cooking met his nostrils. Not pasta again. Ros stirred a large pot on the stove.

"Where's Kelsey?" Philip said.

"She went to the shore with my aunt for about a week."

"That girl has more vacation than we do. Ros, you need to sit down and tell me what's going on. And no more arguing. I need the truth."

She turned off the stovetop and paused for a moment. "I'm fine."

"Please, Ros. Come here."

She slowly took a seat and raised her arm to twirl her hair.

"Your nervous habit is worse." Philip gently took her hand to stop her. "And why are you taking so much Valium? And seeing Madame X? You have my stomach in knots. I don't want to fight, just tell me what's going on."

Tears swam in her eyes. He couldn't remember the last time she'd cried.

"Ros. Please, tell me."

She blinked to clear her eyes and tears trickled down her cheek. Philip pulled a napkin from the lazy susan and handed it to her. "You're scaring me. Is something going on with the kids…you?"

Taking a deep breath, she slowly exhaled and wiped the tears away. "No. It's nothing like that."

Philip was losing his patience. "Damn it! Tell me…please."

"All right. But I need you to be calm. Do you remember the Friday before Memorial Day, I said I was visiting a new voice coach for Kelsey?"

"Vaguely."

"That's not what I was doing."

"What do you mean? Where did you go?"

She blew out a slow breath. "I called your office, and they told me you'd gone to TR Tires. After Kelsey went to the shore with my aunt for Memorial Day weekend, I wanted to surprise you. Go to dinner." She released a deep sigh. "I didn't see your car, but I went in any way. Where were you?"

"I went to interview Adam for a background on the unions, but he called at the last minute and canceled. I went back to work. I didn't know you called for me." Philip folded his hand on hers. "What is this all about?"

Her eyes welled. "I…saw Eileen Detweiler."

Nausea swept over him.

She wiped the tears from her cheeks with the napkin. "Eileen was leaning against a pole in the middle of the warehouse. When she saw me, she let go of the pole and weaved back and forth toward me. She was drunk."

He swallowed hard. "What are you saying?"

"After I told her I was looking for you, she rambled on about how she could steal you away from me."

"That's ridiculous."

Ros drew a breath and raised her voice. "Don't you think I know that?"

Her reaction frightened him. He gently touched her arm and calmed his voice. "Tell me what happened."

"I didn't mean to...I mean I couldn't stop her."

He wrapped his arms around her and held her close as she cried into his chest, scared of what she was going to say next. He tenderly lifted her head in his hands and gazed into her eyes. "It's okay. Tell me."

She slowly pulled away. "Eileen pushed me, telling me I thought I was better than her. I pushed her back, and she...hit her head against the pole. She fell to the floor. She didn't move. I tried to wake her, but then I saw...blood on the concrete. Oh my God, Philip. What have I done?" She sobbed into her hands.

He hugged her tightly as his stomach soured. "Was she...still alive?"

Ros raised her head. Tears filled her eyes. She wheezed and gasped for air. "I...don't... know."

CHAPTER 57

June 10th, Thursday

SHANA TOOK HER LAST BITE of a fish sandwich from McDonald's on her way to Ros and Philip's house, regretting she didn't have dinner with Mac. After she made a call to Sarge telling him she could not get to the mayor before he left the Block and Clock, she pulled her recorder out and dictated.

"Note to myself: Why were the senator and mayor arguing at the Block and Clock? Why would the mayor tell Betty he was out of town?"

She arrived at her friends' house just before 9:30 p.m. and knocked on the side door. It swung open. Philip stared at Shana. His posture slumped. The whites of his eyes were like roadmaps of blood.

"Philip, you look awful. Is everything okay? Where's Ros?

He let out a deep breath, ran his fingers through his hair, and pushed both sides behind his ears. His voice but a mere whisper as he stepped aside. "She's in the kitchen."

Shana followed him through the family room. The TV was on but no sound. They climbed the steps to the kitchen. Ros sat at the table twirling her mussed curly hair on the top of her head. She stopped and looked at Shana, revealing puffy red-rimmed eyes. Philip nodded toward a medicine bottle on the kitchen counter.

"Would you like some coffee," Ros said in a robot-like fashion.

"That's okay, Ros," Philip said. "I'll get it for her. You need to rest." Philip helped her upstairs.

Shana picked up the medicine bottle—Valium.

When Philip returned to the kitchen, she held the bottle at him. "What's going on?"

He sank into a chair at the table. "She's better this way."

Shana took a seat next to him. "What do you mean? Did you find out why the nervous habit returned?"

He rested his head in his hands.

"Philip. What is it? Is she sick? Tell me, please!"

"Nothing like that." He raised his head at Shana. His face became lifeless. "We need your help. It's about Eileen." Philip's eyes watered. "Ros had nothing to do with the murder. I'm sure of it."

Her chest tightened. "What do you mean nothing to do with the murder?"

Ros entered the kitchen.

Philip hurried to her side. "Hon. Go back upstairs to bed. I'll handle this."

"I'm still a little foggy…but I need to tell Shana."

Philip guided Ros to the table.

Shana's gaze shifted between the two as they sat. "You guys need to tell me what's going on."

Ros told Shana why she was at the warehouse and repeated what she'd told Philip earlier. She went limp in the chair. "There. It's out in the open now."

Shana tried to process what she'd heard. "Why didn't you come to me. I'm your best friend."

Ros dabbed her eyes with a napkin. "You haven't exactly been readily available."

If there was ever a time to regret avoiding her friends, this was it.

"I wanted to tell you and Jules at breakfast. But I lost my nerve. And when Madame X told me to beware of a woman with a gun. I panicked."

"Oh, Ros. That woman is not your friend. I am."

"I should have told you." Her eyes filled with tears.

Shana softened her voice. "Are you up to answer some questions?"

Ros nodded.

"When was the exact date and time you were at the TR Tire warehouse?"

"The Friday before Memorial Day, around dinner time maybe a little after 6:00. The gate was open. No one was at the gatehouse."

"When did you leave?"

"I wasn't there long. Maybe ten minutes or so."

"If you left Eileen on the floor, do you have any idea who may have moved her?"

"Whoa!" Philip raised his hand. "Wait a minute. You sound like you're cross-examining her."

"I'm sorry. Instincts from my job, but I have to know the details if I'm going to help."

Ros patted Philip's hand. "It's okay. I'm fine. I need to talk about this. No, I don't have any idea who moved her. But I heard some men talking in the corner office. I believe there were two."

A visual of the corner offices ran through Shana's mind from her visit to see Vega.

Shana faced Ros. "Could one of the voices you heard have been Adam's?"

"I would have known his voice. It wasn't him."

"Did Eileen say why she was there?"

"She said she came to meet Adam, but I didn't see him."

The timeline flashed in Shana's mind. Eileen didn't go to Atlantic City on the 28th.

Philip looked at Shana. "I told Ros, I was supposed to meet Adam there that afternoon, but he called while I was on my way. He said something came up. So, I went back to work."

"Why were you going to meet him?"

"To corroborate information about the unions. Those corner offices belong to Nick Vega and Adam. If Ros said one wasn't Adam, then one of them could have been Vega."

Shana recalled how Vega was nervous when asked if he saw Adam on the 28th. Could his reaction have been because he was at the warehouse on that date and he did see Eileen?

Ros's lip quivered. "I wish I would have checked to see if she was still alive." Her voice trembled. "But the voices in the office stopped, and I was so scared I ran out of there. The next thing I knew, the police found her in the dumpster. I thought for sure I'd killed her and those men got rid of the body." She lowered her head. "This is a nightmare."

Philip stood, hugged Ros from behind, and stroked her back. "I'm sure Shana will get to the bottom of this."

Ros slowly faced Shana. "Could I have been responsible for Eileen's death?"

"I believe someone found the incident convenient. Did anyone see you?"

"No, I don't think so."

"Did you see any cars?"

"There were a few, but one caught my eye. It was red. I didn't think about it at the time, but it was parked on an angle taking up two spaces."

Eileen did drive herself to the warehouse. But where is her car now?

"Do you remember anything else?" Shana said. "Anything the men were saying? Please Ros, think."

She hesitated. "Wait. I remember something. I heard them say the word chemical more than once. And there was an odd odor near where Eileen fell. I thought it was from the tires, but it wasn't a rubber odor. Rather repulsive."

The sound blared from the TV in the family room. "The mute must have stopped." Philip made his way downstairs.

Ros bolted from the chair. "Wait!" She rushed after him.

Shana followed. A news station occupied the screen.

"That's one of the voices I heard that night," Ros said.

They all stared at the TV. Mayor Gaffney was endorsing Senator Jenkins who stood in the background. They'd seemed at odds at the Block and Clock tonight, just before this broadcast and now they acted like best buddies.

"Are you sure it was the mayor you heard?" Shana said.

Ros stared at the screen. "I'm positive."

Philip turned off the TV and guided Ros to the couch. "I'll walk Shana out?"

Shana placed her hand on Ros's shoulder. "I'll find out what happened. I promise."

Outside Philip stopped Shana in the driveway. "I bet the other voice talking to the mayor was Vega. I don't trust him."

"Why do you say that?"

"I remember him from years ago when he was with the Union Charter 600 that supported the workers in the *Messenger's* printing factory. He tried to insist some machinery was defective and needed repairs. I think he was lying. Grant worked something out with him. Saved a lot of money for the paper."

"When was this situation with Grant?"

"It was two years ago this month. I remember because it was a month before Grant's wife died. I couldn't believe he was able to handle that situation while his wife was on her death bed."

Shana blew out a heavy sigh. "Philip, I have to ask you where you and Ros were between the hours of 2:00 and 3:00 the afternoon of June 2nd when Adam was killed?"

He jolted back. "What the hell? You're treating us as suspects for Adam's murder?"

"If I'm going to help, I need to know everything. No surprises."

"I get it." He lowered his head. "Sorry." His bloodshot eyes stared at her. "The 2nd was the day before the *Messenger* printed the story on Adam and Eileen. I was in a meeting with accounting that started at lunch and wasn't over until the end of the day."

"And Ros?"

"Oh, I remember. She called me during my meeting. She was at rehearsals all day with Kelsey for *Annie*. I don't want Ros to go through any more questioning. She's fragile enough. Please, Shana. I'm asking a lot, but can you look into this privately?"

"You don't know what you're asking, Philip. Keeping this from my Sergeant would jeopardize my career."

"But you saw her condition. I don't know what would happen if she's arrested."

Shana closed her eyes and then glared at Philip. The destruction of her career flashed in her mind, not to mention a jail term for obstruction of justice. The guilt of not being around Ros helping her through this took hold, and how could she resist helping her best friend?

"Shana? Please?"

"Let me see what I can do. No promises."

CHAPTER 58

June 10th, Thursday

THE CODE OF ETHICS ran through Shana's mind as she drove away from Philip and Ros's house. Digesting everything she heard this evening and seeing Ros in a vulnerable state, left an acid taste in her mouth. Her stomach knotted knowing she couldn't keep Ros's confession from Sarge as much as Philip's plea haunted her. She flipped her cell and punched in Sarge's number. After a few rings, it went to voice mail. She ended the call without leaving a message. Relieved he didn't answer, she could now figure out her next steps. She pulled out her recorder from her jacket pocket and dictated.

"Note to myself: Ros saw Eileen at TR Tires on May 28th and pushed her. If Eileen was dead when Ros left, how did Eileen's body get in that condition? Ros arrived at around 6:00 and left shortly after. Eileen said she was there to meet Adam. If Adam changed his plans and wasn't going to meet Eileen, who did he meet? Why was the mayor at TR and perhaps Nick Vega? Ros heard the word chemical and smelled a foul odor near Eileen. Could it be the HPE 790? Vega's inspection at the Messenger on June 1997. Grant settled it. How? Philip doesn't trust Vega."

After Shana pulled in a favor and met with a judge friend to get a search warrant for the warehouse, she called Mac and he agreed to meet her at TR Tires. If any evidence existed to prove Ros's innocence, Mac would find it. She knew the protocol to have her partner with her, but after how Fits acted about questioning Trevor and dealing with another friend's issues, she didn't feel comfortable with him.

She arrived at the main gate a little before midnight. The elderly night watchman squinted to see her badge, and search warrant.

"I need to get approval," the man said. "Wait until I make a call."

"You're hindering a murder investigation," Shana scolded.

"Whoa. Wait a minute. Okay…I guess it's all right. I'll meet you up there with a key."

The gate swung open.

"I'm expecting the chief medical examiner." She studied the guard. "Were you on duty the night of May 28th?

"That was the start of Memorial Day weekend. The factory closed early."

"Would the gate be open that night for any reason?"

He grabbed a key and exited the booth. "Not unless someone left it open."

Shana drove to the entrance Ros described, the same one she and Sarge entered to question Vega.

The watchman arrived and unlocked the door. "I should stay here with you, but I need to admit your medical examiner. Let me know when you want me to lock up."

Shana waited for Mac in the shadowed parking lot under the dim light hanging over the employee entrance. Clouds hovered over the full moon, giving it a mystical look. Time to pray she would find something to clear Ros.

Within a few minutes, Mac arrived.

"How was the bus accident?" she said.

"Not as bad as it could have been. Two deaths."

He grabbed his satchel from the back seat and followed Shana into the warehouse.

"Mac, thanks for meeting me."

"I'm glad to help."

She spotted the pole that Ros mentioned and pointed Mac in its direction. "That's the spot. Look for anything and everything."

Envisioning the events Ros described, Shana, made her way to the corner offices. Since Ros had recognized the mayor's voice, Shana felt confident Vega must have been the other voice. After trying the door finding it locked, she peeked through the cracks of the blinds in the windowed walls into Vega's office. A dim light from the desk shone on the credenza. The briefcase was gone. Mac called out for her.

She hurried toward him. "What is it?"

"Faint bleach smell. On the pole and the floor."

"That means someone must have cleaned up the blood."

Mac paced a five-foot radius around the pole and stopped. He put on his reading glasses and bent down. "Shana, look at this. It's a stain on the concrete."

She joined him to examine the floor. Mac knelt, pulled a knife from his satchel, and scraped a small area in the middle of it.

His head jerked back. "Wow. Smells terrible."

"Could that be the chemical?"

"Oliver and your chemist said the odor would last longer on hard surfaces. My scraping must have stirred it up."

Shana stared at the floor and glanced back to the pole. "Mr. Roberts said he smelled something on Eileen's hand when it fell out of the dumpster. She must've touched it after my friend pushed her. Can you get a sample?"

"I'll do what I can. Luckily it doesn't look like bleach was used to clean this up." Mac placed some scrapings into a small glass jar.

The urgency to clear Ros overpowered her. "It's late, but maybe Mr. Roberts will be available for a smell test."

CHAPTER 59

AT NEARLY 1:30 a.m. Shana unlocked the front door to the coroner's office for Mr. Roberts.

"Thanks for coming down here so late," she said.

"Sounded like it was urgent, so I obliged."

The elevator doors slid open onto the coroner's floor and Shana escorted Mr. Roberts to the lab down the hall where Mac waited with samples.

As they entered, Shana motioned for Mr. Roberts to have a seat and turned to Mac. "Are you ready?"

"Yes. Thanks for agreeing to meet us, Mr. Roberts."

"Glad to help."

Mac placed Petri dishes on a cart. "I'm going to lift the lid on each one. Let me know when you recognize anything."

Mr. Roberts sniffed in and out rapidly several times. "Okay. I'm ready. Needed to clear out the nostrils. Let's see if my smeller is working tonight."

On another day, Shana might have found this amusing. But with her best friend's future at stake, she wasn't in the mood.

Mac wheeled the cart to Mr. Roberts's side and barely lifted the lid off the first dish when Mr. Roberts held his hand up. "Stop!"

Shana stepped closer. Her excitement waned when Mr.

Roberts said, "That's dead worms. Not the odor on the body."

"He's right," Mac said.

Disappointed, she stepped back and waited for the next sample.

Mr. Roberts smiled. "See? Told ya. I'm known as the nose."

"It appears, your smeller is working just fine." Mac reached for the next sample.

Mr. Roberts sniffed repeatedly around the remaining Petri dishes and pointed to one. Mac removed the lid and Mr. Roberts's eyes blinked as he jerked away. "This is it."

Mac nodded as his nostrils flared. He replaced the lid. "The smell must've gotten stronger in the closed Petri dish."

"Are you sure, Mr. Roberts?" Shana said.

"You bet, I'm sure. My smeller hasn't failed me yet."

Shana's excitement returned. "Thank you. You helped. More than you know."

After taking Mr. Roberts to the lobby, Shana returned to the lab.

As she entered Mac said, "When are you going to tell Frank about tonight?"

"I'm exhausted. I'll tell Sarge when I go to homicide."

"Shana. You are going to tell him…right? You can't let your friendship cloud your judgment."

A flash of her career coming to an abrupt halt, if she didn't. "Of course, I'll tell him."

Shana left Mac to document the samples and headed for home. On her way, she pulled her recorder out and dictated:

"Note to myself: Found the substance with the odor in the warehouse. Mr. Roberts's identified it as what he smelled on Eileen's body. It must be the chemical HPE 790. Briefcase gone from Vega's office. Need to question the mayor and Vega again."

She stopped recording and almost wanted to throw up thinking about Ros's fragile state after the confession. If only she had stayed in touch with her friends, maybe Ros wouldn't have had to deal with this terrible burden for as long as she did. Believing Nick Vega was the other voice Ros heard talking to the mayor, they would be the only ones to prove Eileen was still alive when Ros left. But would they confirm that, if they had a hand in killing her?

Identifying the odor wouldn't explain why Eileen's body was moved, or if she was still alive when Ros left. But at least now Shana had a lead wherever it took her.

CHAPTER 60

June 11th, Friday

IN THE ELEVATOR ON the way to homicide the next morning, Shana yawned, drained from lack of sleep worrying about Ros. She'd stayed up most of the night updating and reviewing her notes disk, hoping it would reveal something to steer suspicion away from Ros, but it only pointed out how complicated the case had become.

Her pulse raced knowing she had to face Sarge and tell him everything that transpired last night. How would he take her blunder of not following protocol? She couldn't remember the last time she felt this nervous. Telling her ex-husband she wanted a divorce came to mind, fearing he would jump into a rage.

Mac's voice tugged on her conscience. She hated to think he doubted if she would tell Sarge. Who was she kidding? She doubted herself too.

She stepped off the elevator and headed to her desk. Odd, the lights were out in Sarge's office. He must be at the gym. She had a reprieve, but only until he returned.

"Hey, Doyle. You look like hell," Fits said.

"Thanks for the compliment." She yawned. "Not much sleep last night."

"IT set up a new computer for you this morning. They told me you can upload your documents whenever you want."

"Thanks." Shana sat.

"I planted the information with Briggs last night."

"How'd he react?"

"He didn't flinch. But that could've been to throw me off."

Fits's phone pinged, and he answered it. "Okay. We'll be there."

He relayed the call to Shana. "They found a dead woman at The Royale Hotel and suspect murder."

Last night still fresh in her mind, it was the last thing she needed, another murder to investigate.

"Fits, I'm beat."

"Sorry, Doyle. We're the only ones here."

Within about twenty minutes, they pulled up in front of the hotel. The Royale was the exclusive place in Philadelphia for prominent people to stay and had an impeccable record of keeping their guest's actions private. Nothing unlawful ever happened there, let alone a murder.

Several patrol cars and the coroner's van were already on the scene. Reporters flashed cameras and shouted questions as the officer pushed them back. News vans arrived in front. A crowd formed in the hotel lobby. Shana and Fits headed through the crowd and flashed their badges. An officer let them pass and told them the body was on the 8th floor, room 821.

On the way to the elevator, Shana heard her name and turned. "Logan. How did you get past the police?"

"You have to ask? So, what's going on here?"

"Don't know yet."

"I'll wait."

"Of course you will."

While in the elevator, Shana cupped her hand over her mouth and yawned.

"You going to be able to stay awake for this?" Fits said.

She ignored his comment. The elevator doors slid open. Shana and Fits entered room 821 and showed their badges to a young female officer standing guard. The forensic team was dusting for fingerprints.

"I'm glad you're here, detectives." The young officer stood at attention and opened her notebook.

Shana thought for sure Fits would try his charm on the woman, but he didn't. Maybe he did change.

The officer continued. "The maid found the body approximately at 9:30 this morning. She's in the next room, waiting to be questioned. She contacted the manager at 9:45 and he called 911."

Shana inwardly chuckled, listening to the rookie recite details by the book. So like Shana when she first earned her badge.

"We arrived on the scene at 10:05." The officer flipped pages in her notepad. "The coroner and forensic team arrived at 10:15. Her name, per the ID in her purse, is Natalie Portsmith. She didn't have a license, only a Screen Actors Guild card."

"Thank you," Shana said. "Any security cameras in the hotel?"

"Only the lobby, according to the desk clerk."

"Where's the body?"

The officer pointed toward the corner of the room where a young woman wearing a coroner's jumpsuit stood. Shana and Fits approached. Behind the couch lay the victim on her stomach with a towel wrapped around her neck. Her head turned away to the side, stringy gray hair covered her face.

Shana turned to the coroner. "Any preliminary findings?"

"She was strangled. I would say she's been dead for approximately twelve hours. I'll know more after the autopsy."

The female officer stepped over. "The manager is here."

"Why don't you question the maid," Shana said to Fits. "I'll talk to the manager."

Fits entered the next room.

The manager told Shana most of what she already knew, except that the woman paid cash for the room. She thanked him for his time and stopped her recorder. Shana joined Fits, informing him of what the manager told her.

"The maid verified what we already know," Fits said.

"We have a bunch of nothing."

"Yep. Sounds like it."

The coroner called from across the room. "Detectives, we're ready to remove the body. Do you want to take another look?"

Shana made her way to the body, now on the stretcher, and peered into the victim's face in the unzipped body bag. Her jaw dropped. "Oh my God!"

"Doyle, what is it?" Fits turned toward the body. "I can't believe it. It's the fake Ms. Gardner. I guess you don't have to worry about a hit on the sketch."

CHAPTER 61

June 11th, Friday

AFTER SHANA AND FITS witnessed the autopsy on Natalie Portsmith, they visited the address on the Screen Actors Guild card, which turned out to be a vacant lot. They returned to the roundhouse, and the acid rose from Shana's stomach knowing she had to face Sarge and tell him about Ros's confession. She rehearsed in her mind what she would say.

When the elevator doors slid open on the homicide floor, Fits's raised voice got her attention. "Hey! Doyle. Did you hear me?"

She stepped out. "Sorry...what did you say?"

Fits followed her. "I said, I'll contact the Screen Actors Guild."

"Okay."

When they reached their cubicles, Shana noticed Sarge's unlit office. "He's still not in." She looked at her watch. "It's almost 3:30."

"Wonder where he is?"

After Shana transcribed the hotel manager's interview and details about the actress's murder, she stepped away from her desk into the hallway and called Mac.

"I thought I would see you at the morgue earlier," she said.

"I was in the middle of an autopsy. Why were you here?"

"Remember I told you about a woman posed as Eileen and Adam's neighbor? Well Fits and I witnessed her autopsy?"

"What? Another twist to the case."

"She was found in The Royale Hotel. I'm sure you'll see the report, but that's not why I called. I wanted to talk to you about last night. I didn't like the way it ended. I mean your question if I was going to tell Sarge about Ros's confession."

"Your nerves were on edge. I wanted to make sure you were keeping perspective on your job and would tell Frank."

She looked down at the floor. "I can't lie to you. I thought about not telling Sarge how Ros pushed Eileen."

"Only you know what to do. Frank will be there soon."

"How do you know?"

"He will tell you. I need to go. Another autopsy. Talk to you later."

When she turned the corner to go back to her desk, she bumped into Fits.

He stared at her for a moment. How long had he been there?

"Sarge is back," he said. "Autopsy report was just delivered."

They entered Sarge's office and sat in front of his desk.

Shana spoke up. "Fits and I investigated a murder at The Royale, and the victim was the woman posing as Eileen and Adam's next-door neighbor."

"What! Damn! Another death related to this case? If anyone other than you two were on the scene, we might've never known the connection."

Shana nodded and told Sarge the victim's name and the information from the scene.

"Forensics called a little while ago," Fits said. "No prints in the hotel room, except the victim and the maid."

"Any security cameras?" Sarge said.

"Only in the lobby," Shana said. "We saw the woman check-in at 8:15 Thursday night. Unfortunately, the camera was positioned primarily on the front desk, so anyone could've made their way to the room without being seen."

"Not much to go on. Did you find out anything about this Natalie Portsmith?"

"I called the Screen Actors Guild," Fits said. "The victim had no acting gigs for almost three years. They didn't have any other address for her other than the bogus one on her guild card."

Sarge rubbed his buzz then stopped. "If she was unemployed for that long, she may have needed the money. Someone must've paid her very well to pose as the neighbor. How else would an out-of-work actress afford to stay in a five-star hotel? What about her autopsy?"

Fits handed Sarge the autopsy report.

Shana leaned forward. "She was strangled from behind with a hotel towel. There was a bruise in the middle of her back. Autopsy suspected it could have been an imprint of a knee holding her down. Fibers under her nails and in her throat matched the hotel carpet. Time of death was between 9:00 and 11:00 last night."

"Doyle, close the door," Sarge said.

She did as he asked.

"I have something to tell you both. Since the mayor hasn't been returning my calls, I went to his home earlier…and found him dead."

Shana slowly sat back. Her concern for Ros overshadowed any feelings of remorse she might have had for the mayor. Now with the mayor dead if Nick Vega was the other voice that night, then he would be the only one left to prove Ros's innocence. Competing thoughts circled. Philip's plea to handle this privately and Mac's voice telling her to keep her perspective.

"What happened Sarge?" Fits said.

"His housekeeper showed up the same time I did. We found him in his den sitting in his recliner. I just witnessed the autopsy. It was a heart attack. We need to keep this quiet until the commissioner holds a press conference."

"But we were at the morgue," Shana said. "We didn't see you."

"Since it was the mayor, Mac had the autopsy secluded from others."

"Anything else come up in the autopsy?"

"They found blood on the mayor's shirt, which wasn't his. No bodily fluids were on the chair. We suspect that's not where he died. Per Mac, the preliminary time of death was sometime between 10:00 and 11:00 last night. Probably closer to 11:00 since Mayor Gaffney was endorsing Senator Jenkins on live TV at 10:00. The mayor's housekeeper said he wasn't home last night when she stopped by at 10:30 to pick up his laundry. There were what appeared to be wheel marks on the carpet in his den, which she doesn't remember seeing when she was there."

"Wheel marks?" Shana lowered her brow. "The mayor was like a big whale. If he died elsewhere, someone had to have something to get him into his house."

Sarge nodded. "That's exactly what I was thinking."

"Whoever brought him home would risk being seen," Fits said.

"Not according to what the housekeeper told me. The mayor always left the back door open for her. Anyone could have brought him in that way. Someone knew the mayor's habits. I have an appointment with the senator tomorrow afternoon. We'll see what he knows since he must've been the last person to see the mayor alive."

Fits scratched his head. "With the mayor dead, Sarge, how are we going to confirm Briggs is the mole?"

"I've been thinking about that. The commissioner will announce the mayor's death at 7:00 tonight. I'll have a meeting, with the staff before then. When I make the announcement, Fits, you stand near Briggs. Let's see how he reacts."

"Will do." Fits snuck a glance at Shana. "Sarge, I have

something to say."

Shana held her breath, certain Fits overheard her call with Mac.

"Wait," Shana interrupted. "I have to tell you what happened last night."

She told them the conversation with Ros, her timeline on May 28th, what she found at the warehouse, and Mr. Roberts's identification of the odor.

"Sarge, I tried to get in touch with you on your cell late last night, but it went straight to voice mail."

"My cell was off." Sarge glared at Shana. "But that doesn't excuse the fact you should've called Fits. You jeopardized the investigation by going to the warehouse without a partner. A defense attorney could poke holes in the case because Ros Anderson is your friend. Anything you found could've been compromised."

"But Mac was with me."

"I don't care if the Pope was with you. You know better than that."

She slouched in the chair. "I'm sorry. It won't happen again."

"Just make sure Mac documents everything properly. Why did you take him?"

Shana sat back. "Because Ros said she smelled something offensive near Eileen. After she told me she overheard the word chemical from the men in the corner office, I wondered if it was the chemical Mac helped identify."

"I'll deal with him later." Sarge huffed.

"One thing's for sure," Fits said to Shana. "You were right about Mr. Roberts."

Shana stood. "After Ros identified Mayor Gaffney's voice as one of the men at the warehouse, and the proximity of the office, I believe she also heard Nick Vega as the other man. My friend

Ros saw Eileen at the warehouse around 6:00 and wasn't there long. If my friend's push killed her, then what happened to Eileen between May 28th and June 2nd when we found her? How did her body get so disfigured?"

Sarge faced Shana. "Doyle if your timeline is correct with who came and went at TR Tires the night of the 28th, then with the mayor dead, Vega may be the only one who knows what happened to Eileen."

"I realize that. With the senator and the mayor arguing at the Block and Clock last night, I bet those two, along with Vega, knew about the problem with the tire formula. And maybe about the murders."

"We need proof."

"I have a question," Fits said. "If Eileen went to the warehouse to meet Adam, and he called her at home to tell her plans changed, then when Adam didn't find Eileen at home, wouldn't he have gone to the warehouse?"

Shana said, "Perhaps she found the divorce papers and if Adam saw the half bottle of whiskey, he probably assumed she had gone straight to Atlantic City as she typically did. Maybe Adam went back to the warehouse. We'll never know."

"Fits, what did you want to say before?" Sarge said.

"Briggs didn't have any reaction before when I told him we suspected the money in Adam's account was from a prominent figure. I was thinking it may have sunk in by now and with the announcement of the mayor's death, he may be ready to talk."

Sarge nodded. "Maybe you're right. What about Vega?"

"Still can't get in touch with him," Fits said. "He hasn't been at work and they don't know when he'll be back. No answer at his home."

"We need him down here for more questioning. Go to his home. If he's not there, get a BOLO out on him. Fits what about Edwards?"

"RedChem won't give me a straight answer. Only that he's

on a leave of absence. I'm thinking he's long gone. But I'll put a BOLO out on him, anyway."

Sarge leaned back and stared at Shana. "You should bring in your friend. You can't ignore a confession. Friend or no friend, we have murders to solve."

Shana took in a deep breath. "Sarge, my gut is telling me with the murder of the actress, Natalie Portsmith, there must be something else going on. I believe it was convenient that someone found Eileen at TR Tires and finished her off. Ros and her husband have alibis for the time of Adam's murder. I checked it out. Can you give me some time before we have to bring my friend in? She's in such a state. I'm concerned about her."

Fits stood. "Sarge, something may turn up over the weekend. Give us time to find Vega and Edwards and question the senator."

"And we're questioning Trevor again tomorrow," Shana said.

Sarge tilted his head toward Shana. "I shouldn't do this, after what you pulled." He tightened his lips. "I'll give you until Monday. If nothing surfaces, your friend Ros needs to be brought in."

"Thanks...Sarge. I appreciate it."

Sarge unlocked his filing cabinet and handed Shana the disk with the transcribed interviews she'd re-created. "Before you upload this onto your new computer, check with IT to make sure their backup is working."

While walking back to their cubicles, Shana stopped short and faced Fits. "Thanks for supporting me in getting more time to clear my friend."

"No problem." He whispered. "You did the right thing, Doyle."

"You overheard my conversation with Mac, didn't you?"

"Yeah. But I wasn't going to say anything. I'll see you later.

Going to Vega's house."

Had their relationship turned the corner. Could she now trust him to have her back?

CHAPTER 62

June 11th, Friday

IT WAS NOW TIME for Sarge to announce Mayor Gaffney's death. Fits had returned to homicide, unable to find Vega, he'd put a BOLO out on him. The detectives and a few officers gathered in the board room. Shana overheard conversations speculating the meeting's purpose. Anything from pay cuts to layoffs. She stood by the door directly across from Fits, who'd lodged himself on the deep windowsill. Briggs stood next to him leaning against the wall. Fits gave Shana a nod.

Sarge took his place at the head of the room, made the announcement, and told the group the commissioner will hold a press conference tonight at 7:00. You could almost hear a pin drop. Shana wasn't sure what that meant. The mayor never supported the police, so no love lost there. While the crowd thinned out, Briggs pushed his way through and exited the room. Shana and Fits met Sarge by the door.

"Fits, how did Briggs react?" Sarge said. "He left in a hurry."

"His face flushed. Seemed nervous, tapping his leg. I asked if he wanted to go for drinks, and he said no and rushed out. I'll go see him at his home. See what I can find out."

"Okay. When I told the commissioner about the mayor's obsession with the Detweiler case and our suspicions about Briggs, he wants us to wait until tomorrow to inspect the mayor's office. Keep the news from suspecting anything other than a natural death. Saturday is an off day at City Hall, so I'll meet you both there tomorrow morning at 7:00."

After the commissioner's press conference, Shana received a call from Logan and agreed to see him at her apartment to continue comparing notes. Eager to hear what else Logan may have found out, she left the roundhouse and headed for home.

On the way to the front entrance of her building, she almost waved to the patrol car no longer there. Shana had convinced Sarge with the mayor's death and now monitoring Briggs, plus her new security code, she didn't feel the protection was necessary.

Once in her apartment, she carried a glass of wine into her bedroom and set it on the nightstand. She reached for lounging pants from the hook in her closet and eyed her parents' accident file hanging over the top shelf. She reached for it and hesitated, remembering her promise to her shrink to stop reviewing their deaths. Philip's voice sounded over the intercom and diverted her attention. She viewed her watch. Logan would be here soon. She grabbed her wine and placed it on the coffee table on her way to the door.

Within minutes, she unlocked the two deadbolts and Philip brushed by her.

"The mayor's dead." Philip's voice cracked. "He held the key to confirming Eileen was still alive when Ros left TR Tires."

She closed the door.

He eased onto the sectional couch and lowered his head. "How are we going to prove it now?"

She settled next to him. The worry lines that formed around his puffy eyes concerned her, and she dreaded what she was about to tell him. She took a large gulp of wine for liquid courage. "I had to tell my Sergeant about Ros."

He slumped into the couch. "Oh my God! Now she'll be arrested."

"If I didn't tell him and he found out I knew, it would be my badge." She wanted to give him some hope. "I got him to agree to hold off bringing her in until Monday."

His blood-shot eyes stared back at her. "It's Friday night. That only gives you two days."

Now with the chemical identified, she felt confident it may be a lead. She made an effort to comfort Philip. "Anything can happen in an investigation in two days."

He closed his eyes and dropped his head. "How can this be happening?" He slowly raised his head and stared at Shana. "With the mayor dead and if it was Vega in that office, then he's the only one who could clear Ros. Did you question him?"

Concerned how Philip would act, Shana kept Vega's disappearance from him. "We're still looking into it. Philip, I have to put my detective hat on. There could be a possibility that—"

"Don't say it. Ros didn't kill Eileen." He rubbed his thighs in quick succession. "This is a nightmare." He raised his head to the ceiling. "I guess if we hadn't told you last night—"

"But you did. Besides Ros couldn't have gone on too much longer wondering if she had killed Eileen."

The buzzer rang. Logan's voice came through the intercom. Philip faced Shana. "Logan's here?"

"We've been comparing notes."

"If this can help clear Ros, I want to take part, but please don't mention her confession. I'm glad Logan's here. It's time I tell both of you something I found out."

CHAPTER 63

SUNDOWN APPROACHED. He stared out the window at the red and orange striped sky. Red skies at night, sailors delight. Red skies in the morning, sailors take warning. A red sky is a good sign. His phone rang.

"It's Nick. Shit! Did you hear the commissioner? Now with the mayor dead, it makes me look even more suspicious. He was my alibi for the time of Adam's and his wife's murders."

"You better calm down. You heard the press conference. They found the mayor in his home. Heart attack. They have nothing on you."

Nick's high-pitched voice pierced into the phone. "What if they find something in the mayor's office?"

He gritted his teeth. "Then take care of it."

"How am I supposed to do that?"

"You figure it out."

"Detective Fits has been trying to get in touch with me. I've been avoiding him, but I can't keep this up."

"So what if they question you again?" He blew out his frustration. "The mayor's dead. It's a full-proof alibi."

"But there are too many loose ends. I'm thinking about getting out of town."

If Nick left, then his plan would fall apart. "You can't leave.

If you do, it'll make you look guilty. Lie low."

"All right. But don't forget, I know a lot. It would be in your best interest to back me up."

"Don't threaten me."

"I'm not," Nick's voice rose. "It's just a fact."

After the call with Nick, he thought about all the documents he viewed on the computers. Having them deleted was a risk, but he was sure things would work out in his favor. Nick was more trouble than he was worth. Time to make a call.

CHAPTER 64

LOGAN ENTERED SHANA'S apartment. "How about it?" he said. "The mayor died at home watching TV. Heart attack." He spotted Philip. "What are you doing here?"

Shana camouflaged her comment from their last meeting where she told Logan to keep things from Philip. "The more brainpower on the case to find the killer, the better."

Logan shrugged and plopped on the couch next to Philip. "Okay, if you say so." He glanced at Shana and nodded his head toward Philip. "Does he know?"

Philip looked at Shana. "Know what?"

Shana didn't want to discuss the break-in with everything else that was going on, but now she didn't have any choice and told Philip.

"Didn't you notice the new furniture?" Logan said.

Philip glanced around. "Oh. Sorry. Haven't been here in a while. I didn't notice."

Shana knew Philip wouldn't have noticed if the apartment had black walls, with his mind on proving Ros's innocence.

Logan faced Shana. "What happened at the Royale Hotel? The manager told me the murdered woman was an actress, Natalie Portsmith. He said she paid cash for the room. Care to make a statement?"

"How did you find that out?"

"Twenty bucks goes a long way."

"No comment, until we notify the next of kin. Either of you want a beer?"

Logan raised a finger and Philip declined. She returned with an open bottle, handed it to Logan, and sat in the oversized chair.

She looked at Logan. "You wanted to meet again. Did you find out anything else related to the murders?"

"Sorry. All dead ends. I thought maybe you found out something."

"I don't have any additional information for you."

She picked up her wine glass from the coffee table and focused on the two of them. "Everything we discuss stays in this room unless what you tell me can help the case."

Logan and Shana told Philip what they discussed at their last meeting, including the parent's interview and the call Adam made to Shana. Going over everything again left a sour taste in Shana's mouth knowing she was no closer to solving the murders and clearing Ros. She could feel Philip's disappointment.

"Thanks for bringing me up to date," Philip said. "There is something I need to add."

Philip told Logan and Shana what Trevor found out from Walter Brown, the junior law partner at Trevor's old firm.

Shana picked up her wine glass. "Logan, your theory about a plant as an illegal contribution could be true." She took a sip.

"I knew the senator would be involved." Logan faced Philip. "Why didn't you tell me you spoke to Trevor."

"Because Trevor asked me not to. After he told me you contacted Denver and Brown, against my advice, by the way, I finally convinced him to let me tell you. But I promised we wouldn't report on this. Not yet. Trevor needs time to find a way to pay the funds back."

"I know he's our friend," Logan said. "But this would've

been a great story to reveal how Senator Jenkins will go to any lengths to get re-elected. What about your contact at the IRS?"

"I spoke with him as well." Philip turned to Shana. "I hope you will be discreet about how you handle this information I'm about to tell you."

"If it has to do with solving these murders, I can't make any promises."

Philip stared at the floor for a few seconds. "All right. My guy said they found suspicious small periodic withdrawals from the state funds over the last year, with no trace of the expenditures. The amounts kept it under the radar until they noticed a withdrawal of $25,000 on May 17th. That's when they suspected the senator of embezzling state funds."

Logan turned to Shana. "That's the day Adam visited RedChem, and the day before Adam's parents said Eileen was brought home in the limo. Do you think it's a coincidence?"

"Nothing seems to be a coincidence in this case."

"Did you ever find out who Adam met at RedChem on the 17th?" Logan said.

Shana couldn't mention Steve Heim's name without revealing all the other information Steve told her and Fits. "No. Not yet. Philip, what about the $100,000 paid to Denver and Brown last year? Was there any evidence it came from state funds?"

"No. But the IRS confirmed an account exists at Fork Bank in California, in the senator's name, which was opened in November 1998 with $100,500 cash. They couldn't find any other accounts anywhere for the senator, that would explain where that cash came from. Within days after the account was opened, a check was drawn to Denver and Brown for $100,000."

"That confirms what Trevor found out," Logan said. "Let's not forget the senator is getting $8,000 in cash from someone."

"The IRS confirmed the $8,000 too. But they don't know the origin of those funds."

"Wait a minute." Shana rested her glass on the coffee table. "With no other means of substantial income, besides his salary and the monthly deposits from someone, if the senator's embezzling state funds, then it's obvious he's in financial trouble."

"The senator's wife did leave him in debt," Logan said. "Plus, the maintenance on his mansion."

Shana nodded. "Exactly. So where did he get $100,000 to open an account in California to pay Denver and Brown? And why California? If the senator intended those funds to look like an illegal campaign contribution, why didn't he have this information released to the press somehow? What is he waiting for? Something doesn't add up. And what do those funds have to do with Eileen's and Adam's murders?"

"Not sure what it has to do with the murders," Philip said. "But the election is over a year away and Senator Jenkins may be waiting for the right time to release the information on the funds paid to Trevor."

Logan raised his arms. "What a story this would make. Damn, I hate my hands are tied. I knew following the money trail would lead to something. We should question the senator again."

Shana faced Logan. "Hold on, bloodhound. I need to take it from here with the senator."

"We all need to be careful how we handle this information from the IRS," Philip said. "If a story breaks too soon, it could ruin their investigation." He stared at Logan. "Did you hear me?"

"Yes, I get it. Hands off."

"This is all good information," Shana said. "But we need to tie that money to the murders."

Logan picked up his bottle of beer. "There's got to be a connection with Jenkins and the murders." He took a swig of beer and some trickled out the corners of his mouth. He wiped it away with the palm of his hand. "All this would've made my story on the senator fantastic."

"You know you can't add this to your story," Philip said.

"I know. I'll only re-create what was deleted."

Shana stiffened. "What did you say?"

"There was a computer glitch and my draft on the senator was deleted Tuesday from the *Messenger's* shared directory. Our IT consultant guy, Dylan said—"

"Dylan? Is his last name Holden?"

"Yes."

"You're kidding me! He consults for us too. Did he tell you it was a Y2K thing?"

"Yes. He did. Why?"

"The same thing happened to me at headquarters yesterday. All documents related to the Detweiler case were deleted from my computer."

Shana looked at her watch, flipped open her cell, and called IT at headquarters. Within minutes she confirmed Dylan had quit this morning. She relayed the information to Philip and Logan. "Philip, is there anyone at the *Messenger* you can check with this late about Dylan?"

"It's worth a try." Philip pulled his cell and punched in the number. Within a few minutes, Philip confirmed Dylan gave notice yesterday.

"I just remembered," Shana said. "The day Eileen's body was found, I bumped into Dylan leaving the homicide area. He said he ran diagnostics on my computer. Maybe he planted something then. Come to think of it, he seemed nervous when I asked him to find out why my documents were deleted."

Shana glanced over at Philip. He was staring at the floor as if lost in his thoughts. She knew his mind must be focused on clearing Ros.

"I bet Senator Jenkins put Dylan up to it," Logan said.

She shrugged. "Why? What would his motive be?"

Logan faced Philip. "What do you think?"

Philip raised his head. "Oh…I'm not sure."

"Here's what I think. If the senator planted those funds to Trevor, maybe he hired Dylan to plant something on our computers to monitor our information."

"But why delete the documents?" Shana said. "It seems we both could re-create them."

Logan shook his head. "It's strange." He took a sip of beer.

"My Sargeant is questioning the senator tomorrow. Logan, is there anything else I should know?"

"Besides asking about Dylan, see what you can find out about the $8,000 each month in his account. Philip, what do you think? Anything else?"

"Just be careful not to mention the IRS."

Logan checked his watch. "That's it for tonight. I need to get home. Jules and I are trying to decide on another dog."

"She told me at the funeral you were looking," Shana said. "What are you leaning toward?"

"An English Setter. They make good hunting dogs. Gotta go. Remember, I get the exclusive on this." Logan said his goodbyes and left the apartment.

Philip stood. "I'm glad I stayed. I'm not sure our brainstorming helped find evidence to clear Ros. But with what the parents told you and Logan and what I found out from the IRS, I'm even more convinced something else is going on and Ros may have been caught in the middle of it."

Shana walked him to the door. "I'm thinking back to Vega. Can you ask your IRS contact to check on his finances? I mean dig deep?"

"So, you do suspect Vega."

"Perhaps." She opened the door. "Can you reach your contact tonight? With only the weekend to clear Ros before she's brought into homicide, time is of the essence."

Philip let out a heavy sigh. "You don't have to remind me.

I'll call on my way home." Philip rubbed his neck. "Something has been bothering me." He stared at the floor. "Oh, never mind."

"Philip, if you know something, you need to tell me."

"Just a feeling about someone. I can't say until I check something out first."

CHAPTER 65

SHANA LOCKED THE TWO deadbolts after Logan and Philip left. Re-connecting with lifelong friends felt good, even if it meant discussing a murder case. She got angry at herself, allowing her transference diagnosis to consume her and distancing herself from friends. Maybe it was time to go back to the shrink.

She sat at her desk and transcribed her previous note recordings, and updated what she found out tonight. Before she had a chance to review them, her cell pinged a call from Betty.

"Shana, I'm visiting my sister in Florida and saw the news about Mayor Gaffney's heart attack. I can't tell you how many times I tried to get him to take better care of himself."

"I saw his eating habits first hand. Everything okay?"

"Yes. But now with the mayor gone...I need to tell you something I found."

"About Adam's visit to the mayor on June 1st?"

"No. It's not that."

A long silence fell on the other end.

"Betty, are you there?"

"Oh, I hate telling you this...Last Saturday, when I met you in Manayunk, I mentioned something else I didn't like about Mayor Gaffney."

"I remember."

"Earlier that day I was putting some papers in the mayor's safe and I saw a stack of photos with a rubber band around them. I couldn't help but look and right away recognized…Mr. Richmond."

"What were the photos of?"

Betty cleared her throat. "He was with Eileen Detweiler…in compromising positions. They were in bed together."

Shana's stomach tightened, fearing for Trevor. This could be a motive for Eileen's murder.

"Why didn't you tell me about the photos before?"

"I really didn't think they had anything to do with the murders. I was just concerned that the mayor was into something underhanded and he could have made Mr. Richmond's life hell. I couldn't let that happen."

"What did you do with them?"

"I gave the photos and the negatives to Mr. Richmond last night before my flight. He seemed relieved and I don't blame him. I left to visit my sister because I wasn't sure what the mayor would do if he found them missing. He would know it was me who took them."

"Was there any information why they were taken?"

"There was a piece of paper under the stack with a date on it of May 18th. I removed it before I gave the photos to Mr. Richmond."

The date ran through Shana's mind like a bolt of lightning. That must be where Eileen was the night of the 17th before she was brought home in that limo. Finding out about the safe that may contain evidence to clear Ros became foremost in her mind. "Tell me about the safe."

"It's behind the framed painting above his credenza. The mayor had a hidden drawer installed inside his safe. That's where the photos were. I was the only one who knew about it."

Betty gave Shana the combination and the instructions on

how to find the hidden drawer. "If you have to talk to Mr. Richmond, and I'm sure you will. Please let him know I was hesitant about telling you."

After ending the call with Betty and recalling the information Logan and Philip shared this evening, Shana sat back and digested what she learned. Her mind jumped into the case, running over all the events and speculations. What was she missing? Was there something on her disk that could clear Ros? She slid the mouse to wake up the computer screen and reviewed her notes, cutting and pasting to create a new list.

Mole: Briggs. Was he at the house the day after Adam was found? What was he after? Working for the mayor? He's missing.

Briefcase: Does it belong to the Senator? Eileen had it, Adam had it, Mayor had it, Vega had it. Same briefcase? No longer in Vega's office. Where is it now? When did the stain occur? Is the stain significant?

Cryptic Note: Oliver completed deciphering the note. Chemical HPE 790. Offensive odor. Dangerous.

Chemical: Used by RedChem to prolong the life of tires for TR. Has a powerful odor. If used could cause accidents. Scrapings found at TR Tires were identified by Mr. Roberts as the odor he smelled on Eileen's body. Could it be the HPE 790?

RedChem: Steve Heim claims Paul Edwards falsified testing results. Steve saw Adam on May 17th and gave him a chemical sample and accurate test results. Where are they now? Edwards told Steve TR Tires was in financial trouble. Could Trevor know about the chemical problem?

Victoria Gardner: Real Victoria Gardner won a trip, by unknown. Unemployed actress Natalie Portsmith played the role. Who killed her and why?

Adam's death: Was he killed because he knew about the

chemical problem in the tires? Who killed him? Cateline saw Adam at TR Tires on May 28th at around 5:00. Adam left a message for Eileen at 5:05—change of plans. Did he meet with Vega? Why? Source of $50,000 deposit?

Eileen's death: *Photos were taken May 18th. Where? Ros pushed Eileen on May 28th at TR Tires. Doesn't prove Ros killed her. Ros arrived at around 6:00 and left shortly after. Eileen said she was meeting Adam. He wasn't there. What happened to Eileen after May 28th?*

Mystery man: *The tall, bald, muscular man with a glass eye. Who is he? Why is he involved?*

Computer Virus: *Why were the documents on the Detweiler case deleted and my notes disk wiped clean? Senator's draft deleted from Logan's computer. Dylan's a consultant for the Messenger and Headquarters. Did he plant something? He's gone from both places. Was Briggs behind this or someone else?*

Break-in: *Was it the mystery man who broke into my apartment? Why? Could the break-in have anything to do with the files deleted from my and Logan's computer?*

Photos: *Betty found photos of Eileen and Trevor in the mayor's safe. Date attached to them, May 18th. Gave them to Trevor with the negatives. Were the photos what Eileen wanted to tell Madeline at the fundraiser?*

She reviewed all her notes since the beginning of the case. Convinced of Ros's innocence, desperate to identify the murderer, she made a list of potential suspects.

Senator: *IRS investigating him for embezzlement. The record shows May 17th he withdrew $25,000 from state funds. What was that money for? Senator has an account in California. No evidence where the funds came from to open the account. IRS confirmed $100,000 was sent to Trevor's old firm from the* *senator's California account. Senator getting $8,000 a month. From whom? Would he do anything to protect his career? He has a limo.*

Vega: *Did he know about the chemical problem in the tires? How would he benefit? Potential suspicious inspection at the Messenger in June 1997. Was Vega at the warehouse on May 28th when Ros was there. Claims the mayor is his alibi for Eileen's and Adam's murders. Did Vega meet with Adam on the 28th? Vega claims the briefcase is his. He has a limo. Vega missing.*

Mayor: *Dead doesn't mean he's innocent. Can't corroborate Vega's alibi. What did the mayor know? Where did he die? At odds with the senator at the Block and Clock Thursday night before the mayor's time of death. Adam visited the mayor June 1st with a briefcase and left it. Adam withdrew $25,000 on that date. Who did the mayor call on the private number? Photos found in the mayor's safe. He had a limo. What was the mayor doing at TR Tires on May 28th? Did he see Eileen at the warehouse that night? Did the mayor know about the chemical defect?*

Paul Edwards: *Knew about failed test results. Falsified results sent to TR Tires? Vega his contact. Would he receive a large bonus? He has an alibi for the time of the murders. But, still complicit with the chemical problem. He's missing.*

Regrettably, she continued to type another suspect.

Trevor: *Were the photos taken of him and Eileen on May 18th the reason he was so nervous when questioned about Eileen, or was it something else? Did Adam tell Trevor about the chemical problem? Did Trevor want the tires put into production to get TR out of financial trouble?*

Shana stopped and sat back to re-read her writing. Her stomach churned suspecting Trevor of murder. Thinking of Ros, could one friend replace another as a prime suspect?

CHAPTER 66

June 12th, Saturday

ON THE WAY TO CITY HALL the next morning, Shana's thoughts from last night continued to circle in her mind. Worrying about Ros and how Trevor became more of a suspect, had deprived her of another night's sleep. Thinking about clearing two friends made her nauseous. She could never believe either of them capable of murder. If Eileen was dead after Ros pushed her, it must've been an accident. There must be a logical explanation to clear them both. Shana was determined to find out more when she and Fits question Trevor later. Hopefully, he would reveal something to convince them of his innocence, which would remove one of her friends from suspicion.

She parked behind City Hall and got out of her car. Fits had already arrived and directed the driver to hook up the mayor's limo to the tow truck.

Shana pulled Fits aside to avoid yelling over the roar of the truck's lift. "You almost done here?"

"Yeah."

Sarge approached them. "Fits, did you see Briggs last night?"

"He wasn't home, so I stopped by this morning. I woke up the building superintendent and he let me in. The place was empty, which tells me Briggs must've been planning to leave town. He couldn't have moved that quickly after the announcement of the mayor's death. The super said Briggs didn't leave a forwarding address."

"Let's get a BOLO out on him."

"Briggs will know how to avoid being found. But it's worth a try."

The tow truck motor stopped.

"I figured out what probably happened to my computer," Shana said.

Not divulging her meeting with Logan and Philip, she told them about Logan's story on the senator deleted from his computer at the *Messenger* and that Dylan Holden was their IT consultant as well.

"More documents deleted?" Sarge said.

"Yes, and I have confirmation Dylan quit at headquarters and the *Messenger*."

"Fits, put a BOLO out on him too."

Keeping Philip's name secret, Shana told them the IRS is investigating the senator for embezzling state funds, the details of withdrawals, and the account in California opened last year. "My source found out the $100,000 paid to Trevor through his old firm did come from the senator's California account at Fork Bank."

"Why would the senator have an account in California?" Fits said. "Is there any evidence?"

"He said it exists. We need to find out if the senator is involved with the murders. If he planted the funds with the law firm, he could've had Dylan plant software on the computers."

"A lot to question the senator about," Sarge said.

"We can't mention the IRS," Shana said. "It would jeopardize their investigation."

She thought about the photos and how the suspicions mounted toward Trevor. She couldn't keep this information from Sarge, not after she pissed him off about how she handled Ros's confession. "There's something else."

She took a deep breath and told them about the photos Betty found, and the date of May 18th on the piece of paper attached to them.

"This certainly makes Trevor Richmond look guilty," Sarge said. "We should bring him in for questioning."

"Trust me, Sarge. If Trevor doesn't have a solid explanation, we'll bring him in."

Fits's cell interrupted the conversation. "Great," he said into his cell. "Take him down to headquarters. I'll be there shortly."

Shana turned to Fits. "Vega?"

"Yep. Local police picked him up at the airport."

"Keep Vega in holding until we can question him," Sarge said.

The driver motioned they were ready to leave. Fits drove away following the tow truck. Shana and Sarge retrieved Mayor Gaffney's office key from the guard and within minutes they were in the mayor's office snapping on gloves. They stood in front of the portrait of George Washington above the credenza.

"Seems strange to have such a prominent figure hanging in this man's office, don't you think?" Shana said.

Sarge raised his eyebrows. "I'm surprised a self-portrait isn't hanging there."

She chuckled and felt around the sides of the painting where she found a small latch on the left side, as Betty had described. The picture moved easily to the right and revealed a wall safe. She turned the dial to the designated numbers that Betty had given her. The safe opened, and she placed the contents on the mayor's desk. She pressed the right side of the safe wall. A shallow drawer flipped open at the bottom revealing a large brown envelope. Inside were two white letter-size envelopes and a plastic bag containing a computer disk.

Sarge waved the plastic bag at Shana. "I bet this is a copy of your notes disk from my desk."

He opened the first white envelope and unfolded papers.

Shana leaned over his shoulder. "It's a copy of our case notes."

Sarge opened the other envelope and pulled out a bank receipt of a deposit showing $25,000 made on May 17th. Attached to it was a three-by-five card, with Raymond Gaffney engraved in the corner. He read it out loud. "*Received $25,000 cash from Curt Jenkins on May 17th.*"

"The senator? That's the amount my source told me was a recent withdrawal from state funds on that date."

After going through everything in the office, there was nothing to show what the mayor was doing at TR Tires on the 28th.

Sarge stood. "Let's finish up." He went to close the safe and felt around the picture frame. "There's a nick on the side of the painting. Looks like someone may have tried to break into the safe. Question the guard to see if anyone has been snooping around."

Minutes later, Shana returned. "The guard told me a phone repairman came yesterday right around the time of the mayor's death announcement. He told the guard there was a problem reported. When I asked the guard if he could describe the man, guess what he said?"

"Don't tell me...a big bald guy?

"Yep. He was tall, bald, and muscular."

"That guy keeps popping up. Anything about a glass eye?"

"The guard said the man wore tinted glasses."

Sarge placed the documents from the safe in a large, plastic, evidence bag.

Shana glanced at her watch. "It's almost 11:00. Fits and I are meeting Trevor at his office."

"After your interview get Fits to check out the mayor's bank. I'm to meet the senator at 1:00. I'd like you with me."

"Okay, I'll meet you at his house. Should Fits check out the

KAREN REDMAN | 300

senator's bank too?"

"Let's see what transpires in our interview with him. Just remember, what I said. Bring Trevor down to the roundhouse if he can't provide evidence of his innocence."

They locked up and left. On the way to her car, Shana pulled her recorder and dictated.

"*Note to myself: Mayor received $25,000 on May 17th supposedly from Senator Jenkins. Could it be the same $25,000 the IRS found withdrawn from state funds? What was it for and why give it to the mayor? Did the mystery man try to break into the mayor's safe? Copy of what looks like my disk and the case notes in the mayor's safe. Must be Briggs who gave them to the mayor?*"

She hesitated and continued. "*Nothing found relating to May 28th that would clear Ros.*"

Shana stopped the recording when she received a call.

"Detective Doyle. It's Steve Heim."

"Everything all right?"

"With me, yes. But I contacted my assistant to tell her I wasn't coming in for a while, and she told me they sent the prototype tires to TR this morning to be installed on Trevor Richmond's BMW."

"Who made the request?"

"Mr. Richmond. He must've been told the test results passed. You need to stop this. I tried to call his office but there wasn't any answer. I don't have another number."

"I'll take care of it."

She quickly punched in Trevor's cell number. No answer. She tried his office, no answer there either. He's supposed to meet her at his office, why wasn't he answering? She tried Madeline's cell. No answer. Shana's stomach knotted. She needed to find him. He could be driving a death trap.

CHAPTER 67

June 12th, Saturday

THE TIRES SCREECHED and her car sirens blared as Shana drove off out of City Hall's parking lot. Only ten minutes away, she called Trevor's office again. Still no answer. She double-parked in front of the MIC building and rushed inside. When the elevator arrived on Trevor's office floor, she dashed to his door and tried to open it, but it was locked. She banged on the door. "Trevor! You in there?"

The outer door opened. Trevor stood there holding his portable phone to his ear. He cupped his hand over the receiver. "I'm on with the marketing firm. What's going on?"

Her pulse quickened. "Hang up!"

He did as she asked. "What's wrong?"

She rushed in and frantically told him everything Steve Heim had relayed to her about the chemical defect, Adam's involvement, and the danger with the prototype tires.

"Oh my God, Shana. I had no idea. Madeline's at the factory getting the tires put on my car."

He punched in numbers on the portable phone as they entered his office. Within seconds he ended the call. "No answer. It went straight to her voice mail." He entered more numbers and shortly ended that call. "Damn it." He sat behind his desk and slammed the phone down. "Weekend voice message at TR Tires.

Shana, I can't believe this is happening." His hands brushed the sides of his face. "If Maddie takes her regular route back to the office, she'll use the Schuylkill. If she speeds up...you know what that could mean."

"We'll find her." Shana phoned Fits.

"I'm on my way," he said.

"Never mind. Get an APB out on Trevor Richmond's car."

She quickly rattled off what was going on. Trevor wrote the license plate number, and Shana told Fits.

"Hang tight, Doyle. I'll call you when we know something."

She closed her cell. "Fits is going to find her. Don't worry."

Trevor's face contorted. He massaged his upper stomach and pulled the Tums bottle from the drawer. He popped two in his mouth.

"Are you okay? You in pain?"

"It's nothing. When Nick Vega told me RedChem came up with a way to extend the life of a tire, I was thrilled it would get TR Tires out of the red. But if I had known about the problem, I never would've let these tires go into production. Nick told me the new tire formula passed all the tests with acceptable levels. As I typically do with a new tire, I requested the prototypes be put on my car." Trevor leaned his head back. "I can't believe I put Maddie in danger." He grabbed the phone again and pressed in numbers. "Still no answer. Where the hell is she?"

"Trevor, I have something I need to ask you. It's not perfect timing, but I had a conversation last night with Betty Leonard, Mayor Gaffney's secretary."

He let out a heavy sigh. "She told you about the photos, didn't she?"

"Yes. She found them in the mayor's safe."

"So, it was the mayor. I suspected as much. Could this day get any worse?" He rose from his chair, turned to the oil painting hanging behind his desk, and opened his safe. His hand shook as he handed a letter-size white envelope to Shana. "Please, take it. Now you'll understand why I acted the way I did when you questioned me about Eileen's death before. And why I tried to delay you questioning me again. I had to figure out how to tell you and how much to tell you. I already told Maddie about these the night after Betty gave them to me. Before you look inside, please understand I was set up."

Shana opened the envelope and peeked at the first few photos. "I don't need to see anything else. Why didn't you destroy these?"

"Some photos make it clear I was unconscious. If anyone else had copies, they may be selective about what they release. I was waiting to hear from the blackmailer."

"Blackmailer?"

Trevor continued as he rubbed his stomach. "After I received one photo in the mail toward the end of May, a call came telling me to wait for instructions, but I never heard from him again. When Adam called me the day of his death, I thought he wanted to meet me about the photo. I wondered if he received one too. But after what you told me about the tires, maybe his call was about the tire problem."

"Could you recognize the blackmailer's voice?"

"No. It was raspy, seemed disguised. Now that the mayor's dead, I'm not sure if I have all the photos. Betty told me these were the only ones, and I have the negatives, but…" He exhaled hard. "There's one printed photo missing. Maybe she held one back for herself."

"I don't think she'd do that. I've known her for years. She's a very caring person. Why else would she give you the photos and the negatives? And she was concerned about betraying your confidence."

"Then where is the last photo? What if someone else is taking over the blackmail and there are other photos? Where is Maddie?" Trevor called her again. "Still no answer. Shana, can you check with your detective?"

"I assure you Fits will call as soon as he finds her."

Shana needed to keep Trevor talking about the photos, hoping he would reveal something, anything to set her mind at ease he wasn't involved with the deaths of Eileen or Adam. "When were the photos taken?"

"I got to the hotel close to midnight of the 17th and the pictures must have been taken after I got there. I woke up alone the next morning."

Shana thought about the paper attached to the photos Betty found. "So, they were taken May 18th. What hotel?"

"The Centen in Northeast Philly."

"Why in the world would you go there? The owner of that place is notorious for avoiding the law. It's known for drug trafficking."

"I received a phone call tip from a muffled voice that if I went to this hotel, I would find evidence to discredit the senator. I don't know why I went. I should have known better."

"How did you explain that to Madeline?"

"I didn't. I told her I had business in town and stayed overnight."

Shana hated what she was about to say. "I had to tell my sergeant about this. May 18th is a significant date in the investigation. I'm going to need to keep the photos."

Trevor lowered his head. "I understand. But is there any way to keep them private?"

"I can't promise, but I'll try. After Steve Heim told us Paul Edwards mentioned TR Tires had financial problems, you became a suspect."

"What?" Trevor sat forward. "I can't believe you thought I would have killed Eileen or Adam. Maddie and I had solid alibis."

"After the photos surfaced, it wasn't looking good. Tell me more about the night the pictures were taken. Do you remember anything at all?"

Trevor closed his eyes appearing to visualize the scene. "I've been trying to piece this all together since it happened." He looked at Shana. "When I got to the room, I caught a glimpse of a man in the mirror before he knocked me out. He was taller than me and bald. I remember his face was shiny. As if he was perspiring."

Her eyebrows rose. "Could you recognize him again?"

"I don't think so. Things happened so fast."

"Did you ever connect with Eileen about that night?"

"I tried at our fundraiser last month. The one where Maddie told you what Eileen said in the ladies' lounge."

"Yes. I remember."

"I attempted to talk to her, later that evening. I mentioned that night, but she was too drunk and I couldn't get anything out of her."

"So, you think Eileen wanted to tell Madeline about the photos?"

"I think she tried, but the booze must have clouded her memory." Trevor looked at his desk clock. "What's taking so long? Why haven't you gotten a call?"

Before Shana could tell Trevor to be calm, her cell pinged. She flipped it open and hesitated to put it on speaker in case the news wasn't good.

Trevor stared at Shana. He held his breath.

"We found her," Fits said. "She's okay."

Shana cupped the cell. "She's safe."

Trevor exhaled. "Thank God." He leaned forward. "Where is she?"

Back on her cell. "Fits, where did you find her?"

"At the Plymouth Meeting Mall. She was in Macy's."

Shana chuckled. "I'll see you back at the roundhouse."

"What was so funny?" Trevor's eyes widened. "What did your detective say?"

"I didn't mean to laugh, but you can appreciate this. She was shopping at Macy's."

Trevor slouched back. His face relaxed. "Never thought I'd be glad she went shopping. Thank you, Shana, for telling me about the tire problem and finding Maddie before anything disastrous happened. TR has indeed been having problems with sales, but I would never put Maddie's life or anyone else's in danger. You need to believe me, neither Maddie nor I had anything to do with Eileen's or Adam's murders."

"I realize that now. There's too much evidence pointing elsewhere."

"Shana, you said Steve Heim gave Adam a sample of the chemical and the accurate test results. So, where are they?"

She shrugged. "We don't know. And with Steve's computer wiped clean, I don't know how you'll get the accurate results. Not sure if Nick Vega knew the extent of the problem, but Paul Edwards certainly did."

"Well, I don't need the results to fire Paul Edwards. I'll make sure he doesn't work anywhere again and I'm stopping the production of those tires immediately."

"We can't locate Edwards. Something tells me you don't need to worry about firing him."

Trevor rested his arms on his desk. "Do you think someone killed Adam because he knew about the problem?"

"Strong possibility."

Trevor stood and turned to the open safe. "Before you leave, I have something for you." He pulled out a manilla envelope and handed it to Shana. Printed in the top left corner, Denver and Brown, Esq. "I told Maddie about this and I think it's time you should know as well."

CHAPTER 68

June 12th, Saturday

ON THE WAY TO MEET Sarge at the senator's house, Shana's mind swam with all she'd learned from Trevor. She pulled out her recorder.

"*Note to myself: Trevor didn't know about the chemical problem in the tires. Photos of Eileen and Trevor. Mayor blackmailer? One photo is missing. The man at the hotel taking pictures early morning on May 18th fits the description of the mystery man. Trevor provided proof of $100,000 that Denver and Brown received from the senator's account in California. Trevor should be removed from the suspect list.*"

Shana pulled in front of Senator Jenkin's house a little before 1:00 p.m. and passed a black limousine parked in front of the five-car garage. She greeted Sarge and told him what had transpired earlier and the additional information she received from Trevor regarding Denver and Brown.

"I'm sure now Trevor didn't kill anyone," she said.

"Doyle, his company was in financial trouble, and producing those tires would have solved that."

"He wouldn't have put his wife in danger if he knew. And he didn't have to give me the photos. He could have destroyed them and then it would be Betty's word against his. It appears Trevor and Eileen were pawns in a blackmail scheme that seems to have fallen apart. Besides, Trevor told Madeline about the photos and the bogus lawsuit settlement, so there would be no reason for him to kill Eileen or Adam."

"Perhaps you're right. Let's see what the senator knows."

"Don't forget. We need to be careful with the information from the IRS investigation."

"Understood. Forensics rushed through the fingerprint analysis on what we found in the mayor's safe. The mayor's prints, and a partial from Briggs, were on the disk. Prints were inconclusive on the hard copies of the case notes."

"At least now we know for sure Briggs is the mole."

Shana's cell pinged. She turned to Sarge. "I need to take this."

She stepped away and answered the call. "Philip, tell me you have something."

"I heard from my IRS friend about Vega. He's going through a divorce. His bank account is frozen. Only about $2,000 in there and he's behind on his mortgage."

"I thought there would be something, anything to help clear Ros. Sorry to say sounds like a dead end."

"I was hoping too. Still don't trust Vega. Shana, please let me know whatever you find out…no matter what?"

Philip's anxiety echoed in her mind as she approached Sarge and told him what her call was about.

"You thought your source would reveal something suspicious about Vega's finances?"

"I hoped something would show up why Vega was in cahoots with the mayor."

"Maybe we'll get something out of the senator."

They headed toward the front door. Sarge peered at the building. "Nice mansion. Like something from a college campus in Cambridge, England. I wonder how many square feet this is. Seven thousand?"

"At least ten, according to the *Philadelphia Magazine* article."

The butler let them in and requested they wait in the foyer.

A large floral arrangement of red and white tulips centered the octagon dark oak table near the front door. While waiting for the butler to announce them, Shana and Sarge admired the oil paintings. The butler returned and led them to the opened double doors by the foot of the winding staircase. As they entered Shana noted the huge library and the large mahogany desk with hand-carved elephant feet. The senator stood and reached out his hand while holding a golden liquid in a short glass in the other.

"Thank you for agreeing to meet with us." Sarge released his handshake.

"Always glad to help law enforcement." The senator motioned toward the round table in front of the bay window that matched his desk. "Let's sit over there. It's more comfortable."

Sarge cleared his throat as they all took seats. "Senator, I know you and Mayor Gaffney were close. I'm sorry for your loss."

"Thank you. I'll miss Raymond."

Shana suspected that comment was for their benefit. She was sure they weren't as close as everyone thought, recalling their argument at the Block and Clock.

The senator took a sip of his drink and placed it on the table. "Would you care for anything?" He pointed to his glass. "It's single malt scotch."

"We're fine," Sarge said. "We have some questions for you."

Shana pulled the recorder from her pocket. "Do you mind if I tape this?"

He massaged his protruded belly in a clockwise motion and stopped. "Go right ahead."

A slight glimmer caught Shana's eye when his diamond cufflinks glistened from the sun shining in the windows. She pressed record. "We're investigating the murders of Adam and

Eileen Detweiler."

"Like I told the reporters from the *Messenger*, I know Adam worked with Madeline Richmond's campaign, but I don't know anything about his or his wife's murder." The senator cocked his head. "I hope I'm not a suspect."

"It's routine," Sarge said. "Do you know where your limousine was on May 18th?"

"Why are you asking about my limo?"

"There was a report of a black limousine that brought Eileen Detweiler home that morning."

The senator adjusted his cuff links and gazed at Sarge. "I have to check my calendar."

As the senator rose, Shana said, "Do you know a computer consultant by the name of Dylan Holden?"

"No. Should I?" He carried his drink to his desk, set it on the corner, and took the lid off a brass cigarette case. "Do you mind if I smoke?"

"I do," Shana said.

"All right." He closed the lid.

The senator sat behind his desk, and Shana and Sarge moved from the table to the chairs in front of the desk.

"Can you check your calendar for May 18th?" Shana said.

He opened his Day-Timer and stared at it for a few seconds. "I didn't use the limo on that date. I was home all day."

"For the record, regarding the murders of Eileen and Adam Detweiler, where were you on the evening of May 28th and on June 2nd between the hours of 2:00 and 3:00 in the afternoon."

He swiftly flipped the pages in his Day-Timer almost ripping them. "Can't believe you think I had anything to do with their deaths." He stopped and his eyes wandered over the pages. "Nothing entered on those dates which means I was home. Check with my butler."

"Do you own a tan briefcase, a little worn?" Shana said.

"Yes. I had a briefcase like that when I first entered politics. I lost it…Wait. Why are you asking me about it?"

"Eileen had a similar one with her when she was brought home in the limo on May 18th."

"Why would you think it was mine?"

"It fits the description of the briefcase I saw in the photos of your house in the *Philadelphia Magazine*."

"Ah…yes." An air of pride oozed from his voice. "That was an excellent piece on me, wasn't it?"

She forced a smile. "Do you have an account at the Fork Bank in California?"

His eyes narrowed. "Why would I have an account out there?"

Shana leaned on the arm of the chair. "We found evidence there's an account in your name at that bank. And $100,000 was withdrawn and sent to a law firm in Ottsville, Denver and Brown. Then the firm gave that same amount to Trevor Richmond, which was right after his wife announced she was running opposing you. Care to comment?"

The senator didn't flinch. "You've been given false information."

Shana sat straight. "Are you telling us you know nothing about the $100,000 given to Trevor filtered through his old firm?"

"That's what I'm saying."

"Let's move on," Sarge said. "We found a note in the mayor's safe in which he received $25,000 in cash from you. What was that for?"

The senator stared at them as if searching for his next words.

"Are you going to answer me, Senator?"

The senator broke his silence and hammered his fist on his desk. His face reddened. "Those bastards!"

"Who?" Shana said.

"Nick Vega…and Mayor Gaffney. I'm being framed."

"Framed for what?"

"They asked me for money for some type of scheme they were working on."

Shana pointed her tape recorder toward him. "What scheme?"

"They didn't tell me and I didn't want to know."

"Why would they ask you for money?" Sarge said.

The senator cleared his throat. "Ah…they said they had a full-proof scheme that would guarantee my re-election. I didn't buy it. So, I declined to give them anything."

"When was this?"

"I can't remember. Sometime in May, I think."

"Was it May 17th?"

"Sounds about right."

Sarge raised a brow. "That's the date on the note in the mayor's safe with your name on it."

The senator glared at him. "I bet when I didn't give them the money, they tried to implicate me. What I do know is the mayor told me he met Nick at his office at TR Tires on the Friday before Memorial Day. Something about a tire problem. They heard some commotion in the warehouse and found Eileen Detweiler lying on the floor."

Shana got an adrenaline rush, thinking about clearing Ros. "That would be May 28th. Did the mayor tell you what happened to her?"

"No, but he claimed he was shocked when he heard the Detweiler woman was found dead in a dumpster."

Her excitement faded. "Convenient, now with the mayor dead, he can't corroborate."

The senator glared at her. "I'm telling you the truth."

"Why didn't you tell us this before?"

"Because it had nothing to do with me."

"Are you saying Nick Vega and Mayor Gaffney had

something to do with Eileen's murder?" Sarge said.

"Maybe. I think they were concerned about what she overheard."

"And what was that?" Shana said.

"The mayor didn't tell me."

Disappointed she couldn't get any more information about that night, Shana turned to Sarge, and he continued the questioning.

"A woman, by the name of Natalie Portsmith, was murdered at The Royale Hotel in center city Thursday night. She posed as the Detweilers' neighbor. Her time of death was between 9:00 and 11:00. Your live TV broadcast with Mayor Gaffney was that night at 10:00, which shows you have an alibi, but do you know anything about her?"

"Posed as a neighbor?" The senator shrugged. "I don't know anything about her."

"One more thing, Senator, if you don't mind," Sarge said. "We learned you're receiving $8,000 in cash each month. Can you tell us where that's coming from?"

"I'll tell you the same thing I told the reporters from the *Messenger*. It's none of your business." He picked up his drink and took a sip. "I think we're done here." He pressed the button on a small box next to his phone.

The butler appeared in seconds. Shana stopped recording.

The senator stood holding his drink and turned to the butler. "Show them out."

Shana walked to the door, and the senator tripped over the leg of the desk. The glass flew out of his hand and spread the contents in Shana's hair, down her white blouse and jacket.

"Let me get you something to wipe that off," the butler said.

"Never mind." Shana brushed it off with her hand. "I'll go home and change."

The butler escorted them to the foyer. "Detective, let me get you a cloth. It's no trouble."

Within minutes he returned with a small damp towel. Shana asked the butler the whereabouts of the senator on all the dates in question.

"To the best of my knowledge, the mayor has only been out of the house on a couple of dates these past months. May 10th, when he met with his accountant, and this past Thursday night June 10th when he appeared in an ad on TV with Mayor Gaffney."

She wiped what she could from her blouse and jacket, and handed the towel back. Shana thanked him and she and Sarge left.

After they were outside, Shana continued to brush the liquid from her blouse. "Strange the senator has been almost housebound for the last month or so. He seemed pretty adamant about not knowing anything about the murders. And he didn't move a muscle when I mentioned the account in California and the funds paid to Denver and Brown."

"I noticed that too. I don't buy his claim the mayor and Vega were framing him. Maybe the senator's the one framing them. And with the mayor dead, who knows what's true."

"I hope the part is true what he claims the mayor told him about Eileen at TR Tires on the 28th and that Vega was there. What did you think about his suspicions Vega and the mayor were involved with Eileen's death?"

"We can't go on his say so." Sarge rubbed his buzz and stopped. "After what you told me about the state funds and what we found in the mayor's safe, I believe the senator did give $25,000 to the mayor. And with the proof Trevor gave you about Denver and Brown, we need to look into this more before we formally accuse the senator."

Her stomach churned remembering Sarge's deadline to find out something to clear Ros by Monday. "Now can we get a warrant for the senator's accounts? It's Saturday afternoon. The bank is still open. If we don't get more information now, we'll have to wait until…Monday."

Sarge stared at her. "I know I imposed the deadline. I'll call in a favor and get a warrant, and get Fits to check out the senator's accounts."

"Thanks."

"While Fits is at it, I'll have him obtain a warrant to pick up Vega's limo. I'll include the office; if the briefcase is there someplace. Meet him down at the roundhouse and go with him. We'll question Vega after we get that done."

She glanced down at her blouse. "Tell Fits to pick me up at my apartment. I need to change."

"Doyle. Not so secretive about your sources now?"

"I knew you would figure that out. But let's keep that between us."

"I hope those *Messenger* reporters are sharing information with you and not the other way around."

"Of course."

Shana retrieved the photos and the Denver and Brown envelope from her car and gave them to Sarge before she left. As she drove around the circular driveway, the black limousine parked in front of the garage earlier was now gone.

CHAPTER 69

June 12th, Saturday

ON HER WAY HOME, Shana pulled out her recorder and dictated all that she learned from the senator's interview.

"Note to myself: According to the senator, Vega was at TR Tires with the mayor on the 28th. What happened to Eileen that night? What did the senator know about the tire problem? Senator denies the California account and giving $25,000 to the mayor. Sensitive when asked about income. Senator implicating Vega and the mayor in a scheme. Could it be the photos of Trevor and Eileen? Senator claims to know nothing about the Detweiler murders, the actress Natalie Portsmith or Dylan Holden."

After entering the security code to her apartment building, she climbed the three flights of stairs and unlocked the deadbolts. She threw the scotch-stained jacket on the arm of the couch. In her bedroom, she dropped her badge and holstered gun on the bed, and headed into the bathroom to freshen up. The scotch had left her hair sticky. She turned on the shower and left the bathroom for a clean set of clothes. As she passed her bedroom doorway, she peered out and saw the front door wide open. Her pulse raced. She'd forgotten to lock the deadbolts.

A glance on the bed showed her holster was empty. She dashed into the bathroom and retrieved her emergency Glock 43 from the linen closet. With the Glock in hand, she crept toward the bedroom doorway and peeked around the corner. No one was in sight.

"Who's there?" she shouted.

She slowly stepped out of the bedroom, pointing her Glock. Someone kicked her hand, and she dropped it. A tall, bald man, stood pointing her 9mm at her. His muscles bulged under his tight black T-shirt. The man picked up her Glock and stuck it in his belt. His left eye looked away from her. This must be the glass-eyed guy they'd been looking for. Sweat dripped down the sides of his face.

"Who are you?" Shana said.

The man's voice was deep. "I was in the next room when you and your sergeant were at the senator's house."

"So, you work for Senator Jenkins?"

"His driver."

"Or should I say…his henchman?"

"Shut up!" He held the barrel of the 9mm close to her face.

She backed away and hid her fear. "How did you get into my building?"

He smirked and wiped the sweat from his forehead with the back of his hand. "You should be more careful when you enter your new door code. Binoculars work wonders."

"You broke into my apartment last week, didn't you?...Why?"

His icy stare went through her like a knife.

"No more talking!" he said.

She ignored his demand. "What do you plan to do?"

He laughed. "You're going to write a suicide note," he boasted. "I heard the Detweilers are your friends. You're distraught because you can't solve their murders." He motioned the nozzle of the gun toward her desk.

"No one will believe I'd kill myself."

She had to distract him. Get him off guard. It would be difficult to overpower his strength. But if she did nothing, she'd be dead for sure. She kicked the coffee table hard, and it jammed into his shin. He fell backward onto the couch. She dove on top of him. They struggled with both of their hands on the gun. She bit his hand, and he dropped the gun on the floor next to the couch. She felt a crack on her jaw and tasted blood as she fell.

He pulled her Glock from his belt and aimed. She kicked the gun from his hand and it flew to the other side of the room. He lunged, and they fell to the floor. His hands gripped tight around her throat and his fruity breath blew over her face. She tried to pull his clammy hands away, but she couldn't get a good hold. She jabbed her thumb into the side of his neck and pressed as hard as she could. His veins bulged. It didn't phase him. Gasping for air she stretched with her arm for something—anything to hit him. Her fingers touched her jacket on the floor and she fumbled to retrieve the tampon hard-plastic applicator from the inside pocket. Blood rushed to her head. This couldn't be how she died. She took one last stretch, clutched the applicator tight, and jammed it into his good eye.

"You bitch." He released his hold on her neck and cupped his hand over his right eye. He panted and coughed.

The intercom by her door buzzed. "Doyle, it's Fits."

She staggered to the door. The man grabbed her waist and pulled her down. She tried to crawl away, but he dragged her by the ankles toward him. With full force, she raised her leg and jammed her foot into his face. He let go and cupped his nose.

She heard banging on the front entrance. Fits's frantic voice came over the intercom. "Doyle! Open up!"

She crawled to the door, inched up the wall, and dove to hit the front door lock release. Her voice strained. "Fits! Help!"

The man grabbed her and sealed his hand over her mouth. She bit it. He yanked his hand away. She spit the copper and salt taste from her mouth.

Fits rushed into the apartment, pointing his gun. "Stop! Or I'll shoot!"

The man backed off and raised his hands. Fits grabbed his arms, pulled them behind his back, and snapped on handcuffs while quoting his Miranda rights.

"Doyle. You all right?" Fits said.

She stumbled to her feet and massaged her neck rubbing away the dampness from the man's perspired hands. She coughed and cleared her throat. "I'm fine. Let's get him…locked up." She picked up the two guns.

Fits struggled to keep the man under control as he jerked his body forcing himself toward Shana.

The man glared at Shana taking in several deep breaths. "I should have shot you when…I had the chance."

Fits escorted the man to the door and discreetly picked up the tampon and handed it to Shana. They exchanged a glance. She knew he remembered the embarrassing moment years ago.

CHAPTER 70

LATER IN SARGE'S OFFICE, Shana sat holding an ice pack to the side of her face. She could still feel that man's hands around her neck. She massaged it and swallowed hard. If Fits hadn't arrived when he did…she shuttered to think what may have happened.

"You okay?" Sarge said.

"Yes." She pulled the ice pack away.

"Doesn't look too bad."

"I don't understand this guy. He was in the next room at the senator's house and heard both of us. Why attack me?"

"We'll find out when we question him."

Fits entered carrying a bottle of water and handed it to Shana. He placed his hand on her shoulder. "You all right?"

She nodded. "That bastard was strong. I thought this was my time to die."

"You're too stubborn to die. Besides, who would be my partner?"

Shana smiled. "Thanks for arriving when you did. I don't know how much longer I could have hung on."

"Don't underestimate yourself," Sarge said.

Fits sat. "The attacker's name is Dirk Yates. He's being processed."

Shana unscrewed the bottle of water, took a drink, and

swallowed slowly feeling the coolness coat her throat. "This Yates guy fits the description of our mystery man. Sarge, did you look at the photos of Trevor and Eileen?"

"Yes."

Trevor's plea echoed in her mind requesting to keep the photos private. "They're pretty nasty. Can we keep these under the radar?"

"Not sure that's going to be possible."

Fits turned to Shana. "After Sarge updated me on the senator's interview and what you found out from Trevor, I contacted Denver and Brown before I went to your apartment. It appears the senior partner, Karl Denver, has gone missing. I talked to Walter Brown, and he confirmed the information Trevor gave you. He said Trevor called and told him to cooperate, which he wouldn't have done if he had something to hide."

Now that Fits defended her friend, Shana regretted not calling him Thursday night to go to the warehouse.

Sarge faced Fits. "Make sure Vega and Yates are away from each other in holding. Funny feeling about those two."

"Will do. When they picked up Vega, he had the briefcase with him. It contained over $12,000 in cash and an invoice where he purchased his plane ticket yesterday from a travel agent in West Chester. And there was something else." He handed Sarge a plastic bag containing a piece of paper with a string of numbers written on it. "Fingerprints were inconclusive on this."

Sarge inspected it. "Can't be a phone number. Too many digits."

"Let me see it." Shana stared at it for several seconds. "Fifteen digits. Something about this looks familiar."

Fits pulled out his notepad. "I contacted the senator's and the mayor's banks. I'll start with the mayor." He viewed his notes. "The mayor deposited $25,000 on May 17th into a savings account he hasn't touched since it was opened in June 1997 with

$75,000."

"The $25,000 ties in with the note from the senator in the mayor's safe," Shana said.

"That's what I figured. Then later on May 17th, the mayor withdrew $50,000 in large bills from that account."

Shana lowered her brow. "Why would the mayor deposit $25,000 and then withdrawal $50,000 from the same account?"

"Maybe to show a paper trail," Sarge said.

"Here's the interesting thing," Fits said. "The manager told me the mayor put the cash in a tan briefcase."

"Briefcase again?"

"Too much of a coincidence." Shana took another sip of water. "It must be the same briefcase Eileen had with her on May 18th. Based on the time frame of the mayor's withdrawal, that $50,000 could have been a payoff for Eileen's participation in the photos of her and Trevor." She caressed the side of her face. "We can't forget that we suspect the briefcase originally belonged to the senator. Maybe he was involved with those photos?"

Fits continued. "There was another cash deposit into the mayor's same account of $12,500 on June 4th."

"Wonder what that was for?" Shana said.

Fits flipped pages. "Now onto the senator. I checked his local bank account. Doyle, your source was right. The senator is getting $8,000 each month deposited in cash. Going back over the year, the manager said the senator never had anything close to $25,000 in that account."

"That confirms what else my source told me. The senator must have gotten the $25,000 on May 17th from state funds."

"What about his account in California?" Sarge said.

Fits faced Shana. "The information Trevor gave you panned out. The account does exist in the senator's name. I found out the check for the $100,000 was mailed from Fork Bank in California to the attention of Karl Denver at Trevor's old firm.

And the address on the Fork Bank account is a P. O. Box, which makes the senator look even more suspicious."

"We should check his whereabouts when the account was opened," Sarge said.

"I'm way ahead of you. I called the senator's secretary, and she was very obliging. She told me he was at a conference in San Diego the first week in November last year, which coincides with the date of the deposit in Fork Bank. And I did a little more digging. That bank is only an hour's drive from San Diego."

Shana sat forward. "Then the senator could've easily opened an account there. My source said the IRS did a thorough check and didn't find $100,000 withdrawn from state funds. So where did the senator get that money to open the account?"

"Good work Fits," Sarge said. "I'm headed to get a warrant for the senator's limo and I'll question him again when I serve it. Fits, take an officer with you and get Vega's limo towed down here.

Although shaken from the attack, Shana insisted she wanted to accompany Sarge to the senator's house, clearing her friend Ros as her priority.

"You sure you're up to this, Doyle?" Fits said.

"I want to go back there. He knows more about the murders. I can feel it."

"Okay," Sarge said. "I'm not going to argue with you. Fits, see what you can dig up on Yates when you get back from getting Vega's limo."

Fits agreed and left the office.

Shana took another sip of water. "I want to transcribe the senator's interview. Maybe there's something we missed asking him before."

Sarge glanced at his watch. "It's almost 6:00. You review your notes, and I'll get the warrant. Why don't I meet you at the senator's around 7:30?"

Back at her desk, she completed the transcription of the

senator's interview and saved the document on the hard drive in the Murder Case 06021999 folder that she'd re-created. Nothing jumped out at her that were unanswered questions, except his finances, which she was sure the senator wouldn't divulge where he was getting his money.

She slid in her disk, transcribed her recent notes to herself, and reviewed her suspect list, hoping it would spur something to clear Ros. She removed Trevor and there were no changes to Paul Edwards from what she had before. She added Dirk Yates.

Dirk Yates: Senator's driver. Wanted to kill me. Why? Could he be who broke into my apartment? Why? He fits the description of the man reported on several occasions. 1) before the break-in, he inquired across the street from me; 2) what Trevor recollected the night the pictures were taken of him and Eileen; 3) who the guard at City Hall remembered. Why did the actress mention him as bringing Eileen home on May 18th? How would the actress know about him? What does he know about the murders?

Questions circled about her remaining suspects.

Senator: What else did the mayor tell the senator about the night of May 28th at the warehouse? An account does exist in California in the senator's name. What does the $100,000 paid to Trevor from that account have to do with the murders? Was the scheme the senator said Vega and the mayor were in on, the photos? Did the senator know about it? The briefcase Eileen brought home on May 18th fits the description of the senator's.
Vega: He was at TR Tires on May 28th, per the senator. Vega must know what happened to Eileen that night. Did Adam confront Vega about the defect in the tires? Was Vega involved with the photo blackmail? What was the over $12,000 from

and the fifteen digits on the paper found in the briefcase?
Mayor: *Where did the mayor get $75,000 back in June 1997? Is that related to the case? Did the senator give the mayor $25,000 on May 17th? Was the note in the mayor's safe a plant? What is the $12,500 deposit on June 4th? Was the mayor blackmailing Trevor regarding the photos? Was the $50,000 withdrawn on May 17th a payoff to Eileen?*

She saved her disk, slipped it into her inside jacket pocket, and left the roundhouse to meet Sarge.

CHAPTER 71

SHANA ARRIVED at the senator's house right before dusk and greeted Sarge who was waiting, leaning on his car. The house was dark. No lights on anywhere.

She got out of her car and approached Sarge. "Are you sure he's expecting us?"

"Yes. I talked to the butler."

At the door, Shana pressed the button on the dragon's head. The outside light flashed on and the large carved door opened, but the butler blocked their entry. "I don't think Senator Jenkins is up to seeing you now."

"What are you talking about?" Shana said. "We were here earlier, and he was fine."

"The doctor came after you left." The butler stiffened. "He's been under a lot of strain."

Sarge held up the search warrant to the butler. "We have to serve the senator a warrant for his limo we have downtown."

"What's it doing there?" The butler sighed. "Don't tell me. Dirk did something?"

"What do you mean?" Shana said.

The butler stepped aside allowing them to enter. "My loyalty is to the senator. I hate how Dirk has manipulated him."

"In what way?"

A tulip petal fell from the arrangement on the table, and the butler picked it up. "For instance, you heard the news report that Mayor Gaffney died at his home. Well, he didn't." The butler put the petal in the trashcan. "He was here Thursday night around 11:00 after the telecast where he endorsed Senator Jenkins."

"What happened?"

"I heard raised voices and then the senator buzzed me for a glass of water for the mayor. When I went into the drawing room, the senator's mouth was bleeding and the mayor was on the floor gasping for breath clutching his chest. He died here."

Shana recalled the blood found on the mayor's shirt, which must've belonged to the senator.

"Do you know why they were arguing?" Sarge said.

The butler shook his head. "Later I saw Dirk and the senator struggle to put the mayor's body in the limousine's trunk. I bet it was Dirk's idea to move the mayor and not call the police."

"Why didn't you come forward?"

"And lose my job? No thank you."

"What else do you know about Dirk Yates?"

"He started here about a couple of years ago. Before that, he was in the Army. That's all I know about him. Dirk made some comments recently that made me uncomfortable. He referred to Senator Jenkins as his cash cow."

"We need to see Senator Jenkins." Shana headed toward the drawing room doors.

The butler rushed in front of her. "Wait…please be kind. Once you see him—"

A gunshot pierced the air.

They ran to the drawing room. Sarge kicked open the locked doors. The senator lay head-down on his desk, in a pool of blood. A bullet hole in his right temple. A gun clenched in his right hand and a letter in his left.

Sarge felt his neck for a pulse. "He's dead."

The butler raised his hand to his forehead and crossed his

chest. "Father, Son, and the Holy Ghost.

Sarge slipped on gloves from his side jacket pocket and gently unfolded the senator's fingers to release the letter. "It's a letter from the IRS. The senator is being audited."

Staring at his lifeless body, Shana's only thought was of Ros and clearing her name wondering where to go from here.

"Please, don't leave the premises," Shana said to the butler. "We may have some questions for you."

Shana and Sarge searched the entire drawing room and found nothing to implicate the senator in the murders. Even though it was clear this was a suicide, with no note they had to handle it as a suspicious death. Soon the forensic team and Mac arrived.

As Mac entered the house, he eyed Shana's face and stopped close to her. "What happened to you?"

She touched the side of her face and told him about the attack.

"Are you alright? Should you be here?" He looked closer at her neck. "Nasty bruise. Did you see a doctor?"

His voice showed the same concern as he did the night after her break-in. Knowing he cared filled her heart.

"Seriously. I'm fine." She pointed to the open double doors near the foot of the stairs. "You better get in there."

With Dirk Yates now a person of interest, the butler directed Shana and Sarge to Yates's room at the back of the house. A sad legacy of a man's life. One nightstand, a dresser, and a twin bed with a plain white partially soiled spread. No photo frames, no pictures on the wall, and no other personal items. They searched the entire room and found nothing related to the case.

Sarge flipped open his cell. "I'll call Fits. We need to question Vega and Yates tonight."

After a preliminary search of the house, Shana and Sarge questioned the butler again and discovered nothing new from what he had said before.

Mac met them in the foyer. "Frank. We're finished. Another high-profile death. It's late. Let's do the autopsy in the morning."

Everyone had left and Shana drove through the open iron gate leaving the senator's house. Her mind flashed the events of the evening. The Monday deadline Sarge gave her to clear Ros was a little over twenty-four hours away. Now with the senator and the mayor dead, questioning Yates and Vega had become crucial to clearing Ros. But would they reveal who is behind the murders of Eileen, Adam, and the actress? Could there be a connection between the three?

CHAPTER 72

June 12th, Saturday

SARGE AND SHANA ARRIVED back in homicide close to 11:00 p.m. Fits met them in Sarge's office and they discussed the senator's suicide, their search of the house, and what the butler told them.

"Shit!" Fits said. "How many other deaths are going to be related to the Detweiler case?"

Shana shook her head. "Good question. They seem to be dropping like flies."

"Forensics is examining the limos from the mayor, senator, and Vega, along with the briefcase."

"Let's talk to Dirk Yates first," Sarge said. "Vega's been here since this morning. He seems the nervous type. By the time we get to him, he'll be ripe for the picking. Fits, did you find out anything on Yates?"

"Nothing. No record."

"The butler said Yates was in the army."

"Army? I have a buddy that owes me a favor. I'll see what I can find out."

Shana turned to Sarge. "When Yates was at my apartment, he seemed protective of the senator. If we tell him about the senator's suicide, he might be more receptive to providing information."

"Let's see how it goes. The senator's death could be a wild card for us. Fits, make sure everyone in holding keeps the senator's suicide quiet from our two guests."

Within a half-hour, Fits escorted Yates into the interrogation room and directed him to sit across from Shana and Sarge, while Fits stood in the corner. Yates's face revealed a swollen eye and blood-stained nose.

"Look at this." Yates sneered at Shana and pointed to his face. "This is police brutality."

"Not if it's self-defense."

She focused on his injuries recalling his strength and how her neck jab didn't cause him to flinch. There he sat, a well-built figure of a man, his muscles bulging. And there she was, a woman half his size, and she brought him to his knees with nothing more than a tampon plastic applicator.

"What did you stick me with?" he said.

"Secret weapon."

Fits cleared his throat.

Shana recorded the date, time, and those present.

Yates leaned his chair back on its hind legs. His face glistened with perspiration. To the point it made Shana feel uncomfortable for him.

"I'll be out of here soon," he said with an air of confidence.

"You're being charged with attempted murder," Sarge said.

He grabbed the edge of the table with his cuffed hands and rocked the chair back and forth. "I'm not worried. I have contacts."

Shana wondered if his one phone call was to the senator before he killed himself. "Why did you try to kill me?"

"I'm not talking."

She threw questions his way, hoping to spur a reaction. "What do you know about the murders of Eileen and Adam Detweiler?"

"I'm not saying anything. I'm telling you I won't be here

much longer."

"Did you break into my apartment on Saturday, June 5th?"

He released his hands from the table, leaving damp handprints. The chair dropped. "I don't know how many times I need to say this. I'm. Not. Talking." He stared at the corner of the room.

"This is no use," Sarge said. "Let's take him back to holding and bring up our other guest."

Yates widened his eyes at Sarge. "What do you mean other guest?"

"Not to worry. You don't want to cooperate. We'll find out information another way."

"You don't have anyone else. You're bluffing."

Fits pulled on Yates's arm and forced him to stand. "Let's go."

Yates jolted forward and glared at Shana. "Bitch!"

"You better watch it." Fits shoved Yates through the doorway.

Shana shivered and shook it off. "That glass eye gives me the creeps."

"You okay, Doyle?"

"I'm good? Let's question Nick Vega."

It wasn't long before Fits had dropped Vega off in the interrogation room and went to forensics. Vega sat across from Shana and Sarge and folded his arms on his chest. "I'm not saying anything until my attorney gets here."

The door opened. A heavy-set man, wearing a tailored suit much too tight for his frame, entered and sat next to Vega. "What charges do you have against my client?"

"No charges yet," Shana said. "We have questions about a murder that occurred on May 28th. We traced the body to TR Tires in Conshohocken, where your client works."

"I don't know anything about that," Vega said and turned

to his attorney. "Ask them why they have my briefcase?"

"Strange you call it your briefcase. We saw that same one in a photo in the *Philadelphia Magazine* at Senator Jenkins's house."

"That doesn't mean it's the same one."

"Why are you so concerned about the briefcase? Could it be the cash inside?" Shana pulled a plastic bag from her side pocket, containing the paper that had the fifteen-digit numbers. She held it up so Vega and his attorney could see it. "Or is it this?"

Vega shifted. "If it was in that briefcase, it must've been in there when I found it."

"You found it?"

The attorney raised his hand to speak.

"Don't worry," Sarge said. "We have a search warrant for the briefcase and Mr. Vega's limousine."

"Not sure what you'll find in my limo." Vega sneered. "It's a rental."

"We need to check it for clues as to the murder of Eileen Detweiler. Something may lead to her whereabouts on May 18th and May 28th."

The pitch of Vega's voice rose. "I told you I know nothing about her murder."

"We heard you before. But your alibi was the mayor who can't corroborate. Why were you traveling to the Bahamas with a one-way ticket?"

"Don't say another word." His attorney touched Vega's arm and faced Sarge. "I need a moment in private with my client."

Shana followed Sarge from the room. The door closed.

"He's nervous as hell," Shana said.

"Yes, but will he be nervous enough to tell us about the murders?"

CHAPTER 73

ABOUT A HALF-HOUR LATER, a knock came from within the interrogation room. Sarge and Shana entered and sat across from Vega and his attorney.

Vega's attorney folder his arms on the table. "This is off the record. If you like what you hear, we want a deal."

"That'll be up to the DA's office," Sarge said. "And it depends on what your client has to say."

The attorney turned to Vega. "Tell them."

"It all started when Adam called me on May 17th. He claimed to have found out a chemical compound RedChem used in the formula for a new tire developed for TR Tires could be dangerous."

"Why did Adam contact you?" Shana said.

"He knew I was in charge of the production. I told him the test results I received from Paul Edwards at RedChem showed within the normal range. Adam claimed they were tampered with and he had proof. He gave me two weeks to make arrangements to pull the tires from production or he'd tell Trevor Richmond. I needed some help to sift through this, so I called Mayor Gaffney."

"Why would you call *him* about a tire problem?"

"We did favors for each other. He knew how to get out of tough jams. And I needed my bonus."

Shana scowled. "Are you telling me after Adam warned you of a potential problem with the tires, you would still let it go into production to get your bonus?"

"Hey!" Vega blurted. "How would I know if Adam was telling me the truth? I contacted Edwards again, and he assured me his results were accurate."

"What did you and the mayor do?"

"The mayor wanted to know about Adam and his wife. I told him how Adam had confided in me about his wife's drinking and gambling problems and how that racked up a lot of debt. That gave the mayor the idea to arrange compromising pictures taken of Trevor Richmond and Eileen Detweiler for blackmail. As he put it, killing two birds with one stone. Keeping Adam quiet about the tire problem, and it would discredit Trevor, which would get his wife to drop out of the race."

This must've been what they told the senator would cinch his re-election.

"Discrediting Trevor would benefit the senator," she said. "What about the mayor?"

"The mayor supports the senator."

Shana rested her arms on the table. "Who else knew about this scheme?"

Vega shifted in his seat. "The mayor told me Dirk Yates took the pictures. He's Senator Jenkins's driver, and he'd do anything for money."

"When and where were the pictures taken?"

"I don't know. That was all up to the mayor and Yates. All I know is the mayor came up with $50,000 to payoff Eileen."

That not only confirmed what the withdrawal was the mayor did on May 17th, but the $50,000 Adam deposited was what Eileen brought home in the briefcase, and was a payoff.

"Why so much?" Shana said.

"I think he wanted to make sure Eileen would go through with it."

Thinking of clearing Ros, Shana jumped to the night Ros pushed Eileen. "What about May 28th?"

"Adam came to see me earlier that night to check on my progress about stopping the tire production. He had a sample of the chemical and was going to show it to Trevor."

"What time did you see Adam?"

"I think around 5:00. He accused me of blackmail. Said he received a photo that day of his wife in bed with Trevor Richmond. I denied it, of course, but Adam didn't believe me. I knew the mayor must have sent it to Adam. He stormed out, and I ran after him. We struggled. I grabbed his briefcase, and it opened. When it fell, the vial cracked and spilled in the briefcase and onto the warehouse floor."

Shana mentally confirmed what Mr. Roberts identified was the HPE 790. It was clear now why Adam was so protective of his briefcase when Cateline knocked it out of his hand. "Was it the same briefcase you had in your office when we questioned you before?"

He didn't answer.

She stared at Vega. "How did you end up with that briefcase?"

"Adam ah...left it."

Remembering what Betty told her, how could Adam have left it with Vega on the 28th when Betty saw it with Adam on June 1st? "Convenient, the sample was destroyed."

"You fought with Adam?" Sarge said. "That gives you a motive for his murder."

"Hey, wait a minute." Vega's voice rose. "It was just an argument. I didn't kill him. After he left, I called him and pleaded for him to give me a couple more days and he agreed. If there were other test results, I needed to find them, so I called the mayor again. He said he would take care of it, but he never did."

Shana glared at him. "If you felt confident Edwards told you the truth about the results, why did you want to find what Adam had?"

"I…ah, needed to be sure."

"When we questioned you before," Sarge said, "you told us you were out to dinner with Mayor Gaffney on the 28th."

"I'm telling you the truth now."

Sarge sat back. "If you were so innocent, why were you traveling to the Bahamas?"

"When I found out Trevor requested to have the new tires installed on his BMW, I panicked. If what Adam said was true and Paul Edwards was lying, I didn't want to stick around."

"You're lucky," Shana said. "We found Trevor's car before any damage was done. We know Eileen Detweiler was at the warehouse the night of May 28th. Did you see her?"

"The mayor came to my office after Adam left and we were discussing the chemical problem and how to handle it. We argued about the photo blackmail. I told the mayor he shouldn't have sent the photo to Adam. Then later, we heard some commotion in the warehouse. We went to see what it was and saw a woman lying on the floor by a pole. It was Adam's wife. I recognized her from the picture on Adam's desk."

"What time was this?"

"After 6:00 I guess. Her head was bleeding. When she came to—"

"Say that again." Shana's heart jumped.

"When she came to, we could tell she was drunk. She rambled on. Said she overheard us talking about the chemical and the testing results and threatened to tell Adam."

Excitement ran through Shana. This proved Ros's push hadn't killed Eileen.

Vega continued. "The mayor panicked. He punched her a couple of times and knocked her out."

Shana remembered the bruise on the mayor's hand when she and Sarge met with him.

"The mayor. Such a wimp. He ran out, leaving me to handle the mess. So, I made a call."

"Who did you call?" Sarge said.

Vega rested back. "I need to speak with my attorney in private again. I'm not saying another word until I get a deal in writing."

Sarge looked at his watch. "It's after midnight. I'll contact the DA in the morning."

Vega faced his attorney. "Hey, I don't want to stay here."

"Calm down," his attorney said. "We'll clear this up in the morning."

The attorney left and an officer took Vega back to holding.

In the hallway, Shana faced Sarge. "Did you hear Vega? Eileen was alive after the mayor left. That means my friend would not have been responsible for her death."

"I heard. I will admit your friend appears to have been at the wrong place at the wrong time. But Vega told us that off the record. You should wait until we have everything on tape."

"You're right. What do you think about Vega calling the mayor to help find the test results Adam had?"

"Sounds to me like he knew the tires would be defective and didn't care."

"That's exactly what I'm thinking."

Fits hurried down the hall. "Forensics analyzed the prints on the briefcase. There were several, but the only ones they could identify were Adam Detweiler, Nick Vega, and Mayor Gaffney."

"The mayor?" Shana said. "Betty saw Adam bring a stained briefcase into the mayor's office on June 1st and he left it. That confirms Vega is lying about Adam leaving the briefcase with him on May 28th."

Sarge said, "If he's lying about that, what else is he lying about? Fits, did forensics analyze the stain."

"They're still working on it."

"Why don't both of you go home. I'll witness the senator's autopsy first thing in the morning. Get some sleep. We'll finalize the Vega deal and talk to Yates in the morning."

"I'll leave after I update my notes disk," Shana said.

Sarge smiled. "Dedication."

Fits left. Shana sat at her desk and slid in her disk. As she transcribed her notes from the Senator's suicide, she filled in the gaps in the timeline.

Adam confronted Vega about the chemical problem with the tires on May 17th. Vega called the mayor for help. The mayor came up with the idea for a blackmail scheme, photos of Eileen and Trevor. Yates took pictures the early morning of the 18th. $50,000 was a payoff to Eileen. Adam met with Vega on May 28th around 5:00, showed him a sample of the chemical, they fought. The sample vial broke. Ros arrived at TR a little after 6:00 and left shortly after. Then the Mayor hit Eileen and left. Vega claims no knowledge of falsified testing results. Don't buy it. Who did Vega call?

She stopped typing and packed up to leave for home. How could she rest with her best friend's fate hanging on the testimony of two men? One who would rather get a bonus than save lives and another who almost killed her?

CHAPTER 74

June 13th, Sunday

SHANA SAT SLUMPED at her desk the next morning, exhausted from lack of sleep. Anxiety plagued her to get the deal done with Vega and question Dirk Yates. Mac called.

"Just checking on you," he said. "Were you able to get any sleep last night?"

"Not much. We questioned Dirk Yates and Nick Vega until after midnight. Although I have some good news. Nick Vega confirmed Eileen was alive after Ros left."

"That is good news. Did Frank show you the autopsy report on Senator Jenkins?

"I haven't seen him yet. Care to share?"

"Tox report will take some time, but according to the medical records his doctor sent over, the senator has a long history of taking Diazepam. Taking that drug for an extended time could cause depression."

"That might explain his suicide."

Shana told him Vega confessed how the chemical vial spilled.

"Makes sense now," he said. "We finished testing the briefcase and found traces on the inside latch of what was on the floor at TR Tires. It confirms it was the chemical, HPE 790."

"Great. What about the three limos?"

"Vega's rental had a smorgasbord of forensic evidence, but nothing related to the case. The mayor's limo was clean. However, the senator's limo is another matter. We matched the particulates found under Eileen's nails to the trunk carpet and found traces of standard carpet cleaner. Whoever tried to clean it didn't do a good job. We also found hair follicles, matched to Eileen. There was something else in the trunk, but hard to pinpoint. Have to do more testing."

Sergeant Ellis and Assistant DA Harry Foreman walked off the elevator.

"Mac. I have to go. Let me know what you find."

Harry was who Shana had hoped would turn up. His six-foot-five frame, deep voice, and tailor-made suits gave him an air of confidence that intimidated his opponents.

She followed the men into Sarge's office. "Mac called. He gave me the condensed version of the senator's autopsy."

"I was just telling Harry about it and what forensics found in the limos."

"Sarge, where's Fits?"

"He's looking into something on Dirk Yates. Bring Harry up to date on what we have so far."

After she relayed the case details, Harry said. "This is a new one. A smell test?"

"Strange but true," Shana said. "And since Mr. Roberts verified the odor on Eileen, we were able to trace her steps to TR Tires in Conshohocken. It confirms what Vega has been saying."

"By the way," Sarge said. "Neither one of these guys know the senator killed himself."

A little while later, Shana, Harry, and Sarge sat in the interrogation room with Vega and his attorney. Vega had a slight beard growth on his thin, long face. The bags under his eyes and his wrinkled white dress shirt showed he had a sleepless night. Harry told Vega's attorney that the DA would agree to accessory to murder in the second degree if Vega's testimony would lead to arrests. Shana pressed record and dictated the time, date, and those present. Vega repeated what he told them late last night.

Shana's anxiety flared, wanting to get Vega to confirm on tape that Eileen was alive when Ros left the warehouse. "All right, Mr. Vega. Let's get back to the night of May 28th and how you found Eileen Detweiler."

"As I said before, the mayor and I found Adam's wife passed out on the warehouse floor. When she came to, she ranted about what she'd heard us talking about and threatened to tell Adam. She was drunk. That's when the mayor panicked and knocked her out."

"What time did he leave?"

"Around 6:30."

Shana inwardly sighed relief, now it was on tape. "You said you called someone. Who?"

"After the mayor left, I ah…called Dirk Yates. He arrived around 7:30. Adam's wife woke up. I saw Dirk punch her and knock her out. He wanted to beat her again, but I stopped him. I think he enjoyed hitting her. Scary dude. It appeared the blackmail scheme wouldn't work on Adam, so holding the wife would be a way to stop him from telling Trevor about the chemical. Dirk said he would take care of things and hold her someplace."

"Hold her? Or kidnap her?" Sarge said.

"Hold her!" Vega's voice rose an octave. "At least that's what Dirk was supposed to do. We thought she was unconscious, but when we put her into the trunk, she moaned. Dirk drove away and the next thing I knew, she was found dead in a dumpster."

Sarge leaned forward. "What about Adam Detweiler's murder?"

"Hated what happened to him. The mayor directed Dirk to go to Adam's house and threaten him with his wife's life to keep quiet about the chemical. I didn't know anything about it until after. When I heard you found Adam in his garage, I knew Dirk must have killed him."

"But you don't know for sure he killed Adam," Shana said.

"I'm telling you, I bet he did."

Vega's attorney spoke up. "For the record, my client had nothing to do with the murder of Adam or Eileen Detweiler."

Harry faced Vega. "Continue."

"I worried if the original test results existed, they would be in his house someplace."

"So, you knew the test results Edwards told you about had been tampered with?" Shana said.

"No, but I couldn't take the chance. I contacted the mayor, and he said he would take care of it this time for sure. Later I found out the mayor had one of your guys on his payroll and sent him to the house, but he couldn't find anything."

Shana knew now it was Briggs, and he was after the test results, not the briefcase.

"Forensics found Adam's fingerprints, yours, and the mayor's on the briefcase," Sarge said. "How did the mayor's get there?"

"You were right," Vega said. "The briefcase isn't mine. The mayor gave it to me."

"Wait," Shana said. "Adam had it, the mayor had it and then the mayor gave it to you? Why?"

"The mayor came to my office with the briefcase after they found Adam dead. He told me he had put up half of the $50,000 to payoff Eileen and he blackmailed Adam with the pictures to get back his portion. The mayor is…oh…was a greedy bastard."

Her mind flashed to the $25,000 withdrawal on June 1st from Adam's account and what Betty told her of Adam's visit to the mayor on that same day. "You said the mayor put up half of the $50,000. Who put up the other half?"

"I…ah…don't know."

"Did it come from the senator?"

Vega sat erect. "I said, I don't know. The mayor told me he wanted to hide the briefcase because his secretary saw it in his office when Adam visited. He agreed to give me half the money he received from Adam if I held onto the briefcase. That bastard probably wanted to plant the briefcase on *me*."

It was clear now that the $12,500 deposited in the mayor's account on June 4th was half of the $25,000 the mayor received from Adam.

"When you were picked up, there was over $12,000 in the briefcase," Sarge said. "That was from the mayor?"

"Yes. Except for what I used for my plane ticket. Didn't want it traced to my bank account. I'm going through a divorce and my wife would want a piece of it."

Shana pulled the plastic bag containing the paper with the fifteen digits on it. "Can you tell us what the numbers on this piece of paper mean?"

Vega eyed his attorney and then faced Shana. "That paper was in the briefcase when the mayor gave it to me."

"You're saying the paper belonged to the mayor?"

"I guess so."

"Let's move on," Shana said. "There was a woman, Natalie Portsmith, who posed as the Detweilers' neighbor. She was found murdered at The Royale Hotel. Do you know anything about that? Her time of death was between 9:00 and 11:00 Thursday night. Where were you during that time?"

Vega shrugged. "I have no idea what you're talking about. I was visiting a friend in West Chester that night. I bought my plane ticket and stayed with him until my flight. You can check."

"We found the invoice in the briefcase, but we'll contact your friend."

Vega's attorney handed her a note. "This is his friend's

information. My client is done. Do we have a deal?"

"With the mayor dead, we can't corroborate any of this," Sarge said.

"I'm telling you the truth." Vega's voice rose.

Sarge paused for a moment. "If your alibi pans out with your friend in West Chester, then looks like we may have a deal." Sarge gave Harry the nod.

Shana turned the recorder off.

"I'll have the papers drawn up," Harry said on his way out.

Vega's attorney followed, and an officer took Vega back to holding.

Now outside the interrogation room, Shana faced Sarge. "Dirk Yates bubbled to the top of the suspect list."

"Perhaps, but just because Vega suspects Yates of murder doesn't mean it's so. We don't have any proof. It's almost noon. Let's interview Yates after lunch. The longer he stays in holding, the better our chances are of him talking."

Shana flipped open her cell. "I'm going to call my friend Ros and tell her the good news." She left and found a secluded spot to make the call. Philip answered after a couple of rings. When she told him Ros was cleared, he wept into the phone.

"I don't know how to thank you," he finally said. "Ros took a Valium last night to help her sleep. I'll tell her when she wakes up."

"Philip, I need a favor. I have what I believe may be an off-shore bank account number. Can you contact your friend at the IRS for me?"

"Sure. Does this have to do with the case?"

"Yes. I'll send you the number."

"I'll call him right away."

Back at her desk, Shana slid in her notes disk and typed.

Vega suspects Yates is responsible for Adam's and Eileen's deaths. Only Vega's testimony. No proof. The $25,000 Adam *withdrew on June 1st was given to the mayor. Mayor split it with Vega. $12,500 deposit June 4th in mayor's account. Who put up the other half of the $50,000? Someone on the mayor's payroll—Briggs. Could the fifteen digits be an off-shore account? Philip to find out.*

Shana entered Sarge's office after the luncheon shop down the street delivered pizza. "I got a confirmation from Vega's friend. Alibi checks out."

Sarge spread the food on his desk.

Fits walked in and handed a manila file to Shana. "Here's some information I gathered on Yates. Interesting past."

She perused the file. "This *is* interesting. Where did you get all this information about Yates in the service?"

"My buddy now works at the Pentagon." Fits picked up a slice of pizza.

"Fits, you never cease to amaze me," she said. "Let's see what Yates has to say."

CHAPTER 75

June 13th, Sunday

AFTER LUNCH FITS escorted Yates into the interrogation room. A peculiar body odor drifted in the air from Yates's damp black T-shirt. His cuffed hands clanged on the table as Fits shoved him into the chair opposite Sarge and Shana. Fits backed off and leaned against the wall.

After a night in holding, Yates's shadow of a beard surrounded his jawline. His nose had swollen and his right eye had turned darker shades of black and blue from Shana's fight with him at her apartment.

Shana pressed the recorder in the middle of the table, dictated the usual, and faced Yates.

"Attempted murder would get you a stiff sentence," she said. "Especially against a law officer, but you could reduce it if you tell us what you know about the murders of Eileen and Adam Detweiler."

He coughed. "I don't know anything about them."

"I have a nice file on you." She opened it. "Says here no family. So, who do you think would come to get you out?"

He avoided eye contact.

Shana took notice of his age in his file. Even though Yates's hands were around her throat, she hadn't focused on his looks until now. His shaven, bald head showed stubbles that hinted at a receding hairline. His grayish tinted skin, sunken cheeks, and deep crow's feet around his eyes made him look older than his thirty-eight years.

"According to your records," Shana said. "You enlisted in the Army at nineteen and had some run-ins with the MP's. Your anger must have gotten the best of you with your BCD in 1997. That's a bad conduct discharge, isn't it? Says here no jail time. How did you manage that?"

He slammed his body forward. "Where did you get those records? They're supposed to be sealed."

Shana viewed the file. "Attempted murder of a fellow serviceman, that's pretty serious. I see a pattern here."

"It was self-defense," Yates's nostril flared. "A trumped-up charge. My lieutenant didn't like me."

"Are we supposed to feel sorry for you?" Sarge said.

He smirked. "Yeah, you should."

Sarge glared at him. "Is that how you lost your eye? In a self-defense situation?"

"It's none of your business how I lost it." He winced as he repositioned his body.

Shana flipped the pages. "Let's see…you were a dental technician in the army, which would make you familiar with anatomy, wouldn't it? Our victim, Eileen Detweiler had her teeth cleanly extracted and a fatal injection of alcohol. You see where I'm going with this, Mr. Yates?"

He gritted his teeth. "You have nothing on me."

"Don't be too sure," Sarge said. "We have testimony pointing to you as the last person to see Eileen Detweiler alive at TR Tires on May 28th. And we heard you were involved with a blackmail scheme taking pictures of her and Trevor Richmond."

Yates sneered. "Who told you that?"

"Nick Vega," Shana said.

He slammed his fists, and the handcuffs cracked against the

table. He leaned forward and flinched. "That weasel. I'll show him. If he thinks he can get away with anything, he's got another thing coming."

"We cut him a deal. He told us a lot about you."

"You can't listen to him...I know what's really going on."

"Are you saying you want a deal too?"

"I don't care about that." He coughed uncontrollably. After catching his breath, he said, "Just don't give Vega one until you hear what I have to say." He cleared his throat. "I know plenty, and it will pale in comparison to an attempted murder charge."

Sarge stood and headed for the door. Surprised with his action Shana paused the recording, grabbed Yates's file, and she and Fits followed.

Outside in the hallway, Sarge's nostrils flared as he exhaled. "This man's a disgrace. I ran into guys like that in the army. Always a chip on their shoulder. As much as I hate to admit it, if he is telling the truth about knowing more, Nick Vega's deal may be a mistake."

The ADA, Harry Foreman walked toward them in casual clothes, carrying a file. It was the first time she could remember him without his briefcase and not wearing his freshly pressed suit.

"Frank, they told me you were here," Harry said. "I have the papers for Nick Vega."

"Is it too late?"

"What do you mean?"

"We've been talking with Dirk Yates, the senator's driver. He's pretty confident he has information to incriminate Vega."

"Sarge, strange Yates didn't want a deal," Shana said.

"Yeah. I picked up on that too."

"We need to find out what he knows before I give Vega's attorney the papers," Harry said.

Shana faced Sarge. "I bet the note we found in the mayor's office safe with the senator's name has something to do with this photo blackmail scheme. Let's tell Yates the senator is dead. Who knows what else he'll tell us?"

Sarge hesitated for a second. "Okay. I'll give you the nod when I think it's time to bring it up."

Back in the interrogation room, they took their seats.

Yates's face and head looked clammy, moist. He wheezed. "Who's this guy?"

Harry introduced himself. "Are you all right?"

"I'm fine. Let's get on with this."

Shana pushed the record button and dictated the usual.

Harry faced Yates. "I hear you have information about Nick Vega."

Yates cocked his head. "You bet I do."

"Let's hear what you have to say if there's a deal to be had."

"As I said before, I don't care about a deal for me." Yates took a deep breath and blew out slowly. "Just don't give one to Vega."

"You don't look so good," Shana said.

"I said I'm fine."

"If you say so. Forensics found evidence in the senator's limo trunk that matches Eileen Detweiler's body."

"You're bluffing." Yates shrugged. "Couldn't be."

"Is that because you tried to clean it up?"

He huffed.

"For the record. The ADA has seen your file."

Yates took several quick breaths. His cuffed hands trembled. "Is it hot in here? I need some water." He licked his lips.

Sarge gave Shana the nod.

"Mr. Yates. We're sorry to tell you Senator Jenkins committed suicide last night."

Yates jumped up. His chair fell backward. "You're lying!" He picked up the chair with his cuffed hands and slammed it against the wall. His face contorted. With his black and blue eye and his perspired reddened face, he looked like something from a horror movie.

Harry stumbled to the far corner.

Fits stood in the way. "Knock it off."

Sarge, Shana, and Fits pushed Yates against the wall and tried to restrain him. He overpowered them, swung his cuffed hands wildly, and hit Sarge in the face. Sarge flew back and grabbed his nose. An officer sped in and together with Shana and Fits controlled Yates.

Sarge cupped his nose. "Get him out of here."

Fits and the officer grabbed Yates's arm and pulled him out of the room.

Yates yelled out as he left. "I know everyone's dirty secrets. You need to listen to me." The door shut and his voice faded.

"Damn it." Sarge pinched his nose. Blood dripped onto his white-uniformed shirt. "I think this is broken."

Shana stepped over to help him. "Not just your nose, the side of your face is cut. Looks deep. You better go to the hospital."

Sarge pressed his hand hard against his face. "Let Yates stew in holding. Doyle, you're in charge. Question him again later after he cools off. We can't lose momentum on this. Harry, what about the deal with Nick Vega?"

"My deal was that Vega's testimony would lead to an arrest regarding the murders. I need to hear more from Dirk Yates. I'll hold off on the deal for now. Let's get you to the hospital."

CHAPTER 76

A LITTLE OVER AN HOUR had passed since they returned Yates to holding and Sarge left for the hospital. Shana slipped her notes disk into the computer and updated it under Yates's name.

BCD from the army. Attempted murder of fellow serviceman. No jail time. He was a dental technician in the army. Likely person to inject booze into Eileen and extract her teeth. He doesn't want Vega to get a deal but isn't interested in one for himself. Why? He blew up when he found out about the senator's suicide. How protective was Yates of his boss? Yates seems ill. Per Vega, Yates was only supposed to hold Eileen and was involved in the photo blackmail scheme. Did Yates kill Eileen and Adam?

She sat back staring at the computer screen then doodled, Natalie Portsmith, on a yellow pad and circled it several times.

Fits leaned over the cubical wall and viewed her scribblings. "Do you think Yates killed her?"

"During the time of her murder, the mayor was on TV with the senator and Vega was in West Chester. Yates would be the logical one. Did you notice he seemed to have trouble breathing?"

"Yes. And he's sweating a lot."

"Why don't you call your friend at the Pentagon. See what you can find out about his medical history."

"I'll call him at home."

Shana heard her name from across the room. Mr. Detweiler made his way to her cubicle.

"Sir, what are you doing here? Is everything okay?"

He pulled a white envelope from his jacket pocket. His sigh softly deflated. "We were going through Adam's safe deposit box and found this." He handed it to her. A sadness consumed his face. "I thought it would be important with RedChem's letterhead, so I wanted to get this to you."

She opened the envelope and unfolded the paper. Steve Heim's name was at the top of the page. It didn't take a rocket scientist to read the report and know this was Steve's original test results. Several line items had the word failed in bold letters.

"Thank you, Mr. Detweiler." She stood and extended her hand. "This is important."

He offered a grim smile and left homicide.

Fits leaned over the cubicle wall. "What did Adam's father give you?"

"The original test results from Steve Heim. Now we have proof those tires should've never been approved to go into production. Vega claims Adam never showed him the test results. I find that strange. Need to question Vega again."

"I talked to my buddy at the Pentagon about Yates's medical history and told him the urgency of the matter. He said he would contact his weekend staff and see what he could find out." Fits's phone rang, and he answered it. "Really? All right. Bring him up." Fits ended the call and talked over the cubicle wall to Shana. "You're not going to believe this. Yates says he's ready to talk."

She raised her head upward. "What the hell. Let's hear what he has to say."

On their way to the interrogation room, Shana turned to Fits. "We should turn off our cells. I don't want any interruptions."

About fifteen minutes later, an officer escorted Yates into

the room. This time his hands cuffed behind his back. The officer prompted Yates to sit across from Shana while Fits stood behind him. His T-shirt, almost completely drenched, gave off a foul odor.

Shana stared at the man who almost killed her. His strength seemed to escape him as his arms shook making his body twitch in the chair. "Are you ready to talk?"

"This better not be a waste of time," Fits said.

"It's important, believe me." Yates shifted uncomfortably. "Can't you uncuff me?"

Shana rested her folded arms on the table. "Cuffs stay. Since you know Senator Jenkins is dead, there's no one to protect you."

He jammed his body forward against the table and sneered at her. "I could just…"

Fits grabbed Yates's damp shoulder and yanked him back. "Cool it, buddy." Fits cringed and wiped his hand on his pants.

"Take him back to holding," Shana said. "He doesn't know anything."

"No wait!" he said. "I'll talk."

She pressed record and dictated the usual. "Go ahead."

"You were right. Eileen Detweiler was in the senator's limo trunk. I was supposed to take her somewhere for a while. Just until Vega could resolve a tire problem involving a chemical. Seems she overheard some things between the mayor and Vega at TR Tires on May 28th."

"What time did you get to the warehouse?"

"I think around 7:30 or so."

Confirms what Vega said.

"Where did you take her?"

"To the Centen, the same place I took racy pictures of Eileen Detweiler and Trevor Richmond."

"We'll get back to the picture business after you tell us what happened to Eileen on the 28th."

"When I went to get her out of the senator's limo trunk, I knew she recognized me from taking those pictures. Then I started thinking. If she told her husband about the chemical, then she would tell him about the pictures. I'd take the fall for the blackmail scheme. I had to kill her."

"What did you do with her car?"

"Vega had her keys. I made a call and had a buddy dump it in a junkyard."

"How did you murder her?"

"She was already drunk. I used a needle to finish her."

The injection Mac found. "Needle?"

"Ah…I had one for my insulin. I'm a diabetic."

That explained the traces of insulin Mac found by the needle mark on Eileen.

He took slow deep breaths. "I'm feeling a little faint."

Shana leaned forward. "Are you sure you can continue?"

"I need to. Anyway, she passed out, and I shot her up with vodka. It would've only been a matter of time until she was dead." Yates shifted his cuffed hands behind his back. His arms twitched again. "Can you take these things off?"

"No. Why shoot her up with alcohol?"

"I had a cousin who was an alcoholic and Eileen had those same symptoms. She would've built up a tolerance. The only thing that would take her over the top, would be an injection."

"Why did you strip her?"

"There was an awful smell on her. I was afraid she'd picked up something in the warehouse that could tie her to being there."

Shana rested her arms on the table. "So why pull her teeth, cut her nails, and burn her fingerprints?"

"Hiding her identify would give me time to get an alibi."

Yates licked his lips. "Hey, can I get some water?" He tried to catch his breath.

"We'll take a break." Shana paused the recording and turned to the officer. "Keep an eye on him."

Fits followed Shana outside the interrogation room. She pulled her cell from her pocket and turned it back on. No messages. She thought she would've heard from Philip by now.

"What's going on?" Fits said. "You waiting for a call?"

"My source, with the IRS contact. That number on the piece of paper may be an account number to an off-shore bank."

"How did you figure that?"

"Do you remember that murder case when we were first partners? The investment banker who embezzled funds? He had an account off-shore in the Bahamas and it had fifteen digits."

"Oh yeah. That's right."

"I need to make a call."

She stepped away to call Philip. It went straight to voice mail. She made her way back to Fits who spoke on his cell.

"I owe you," Fits said into his phone and hung up.

He faced Shana. "That was my friend at the Pentagon."

"What did he find out?"

"Yates didn't get jail time regarding his bad conduct discharge because he's dying."

Her eyes widened. "Dying?"

"Yeah. At the time of the discharge two years ago, doctors gave him one year to live. He was diagnosed with advanced diabetes and his liver and kidneys were compromised. According to the records, Yates's eye got infected after that fight with the serviceman and it had to be removed. When they did tests for surgery, they found his illness."

"That explains why he didn't want a deal." Even though this man almost killed her, Shana felt somewhat worried for the man. "Get him some water."

While Shana waited for Fits, she called Mac. "How's the analysis going? Anything else in the senator's limo?"

"Just got finished. Forensics found traces of the mayor's bodily fluids in the trunk."

"That confirms what the senator's butler told us about the mayor being moved after he died."

"We also found a fragment of the chemical on the rim of the spare tire."

"Must've been from Eileen's hand. Yates confessed he used a needle to inject Eileen. He said he's a diabetic."

"That explains the insulin on the injection site on Eileen."

"Mac, what can you tell me about advanced diabetes? Could it be fatal?"

"Yes, if it isn't treated properly. It will affect all the organs, especially the kidneys and liver. Why are you asking?"

"Because we just learned Dirk Yates has it and was given a year to live two years ago. He's been perspiring, breathing heavily, his body has the shakes. And when he attacked me at my apartment, there was a fruity odor on his breath. Sounds strange, but it almost smelled like nail polish remover."

"That would be the acetone from his kidneys. Sounds like he may be in the final stages."

She ended the call with a new found urgency to get Yates to tell them all he knew.

CHAPTER 77

June 13th, Sunday

AFTER FITS RETURNED WITH a bottle of water for Yates, Shana relayed Mac's findings and the additional information about Yates's illness. She instructed Fits to have paramedics on standby, and he made the call. They turned off their cells and entered the interrogation room. Fits took a seat next to Shana and placed the bottle on the table.

Yates stared at Fits. "Hey. Can't you take off the cuffs for this?"

Shana motioned to the officer who uncapped the bottle and brought it close to Yates's lips. Water dribbled out the sides of his mouth.

She pressed record. "We learned about your advanced diabetes."

"How did you find that out?"

"Not important."

"Then you know I don't have long. I need to get through this. I can't let Vega get away with anything."

Knowing that Yates's condition could change at any moment, Shana continued. "What about the photo blackmail scheme? Who was behind that and why?"

"The mayor, Vega, and…the senator."

"So, the senator was involved?"

"It was all their idea. Those three have been in each other's pockets for years."

"We heard from Vega the reasons behind why he and Mayor Gaffney were in on this."

"What did he tell you?"

Shana repeated what Vega told them last night.

"Can't believe Vega told you the truth, except for one thing."

"What's that?"

"The mayor didn't get involved because he supports the senator. He went along because the senator knew he took bribes from the union over the years."

"What about Senator Jenkins?" Shana said.

"His ego couldn't take it that the Richmond woman was beating him in the polls. He wanted in on the scheme to discredit her husband, believing it would cause his wife to withdrawal from the race."

"How did you persuade Eileen to pose for those pictures?"

Yates coughed and paused before continuing. "Vega told me about her gambling and drinking problem. I met up with her at Harrah's in Atlantic City and became her drinking buddy. She confided in me about their debt. When I told her, she could earn enough to pay off their debt and have more leftover if she did me a favor, she agreed. I was to offer her $50,000."

Shana rested her arms on the table. "Who gave you the money?"

"Half came from the mayor. Senator Jenkins came up with the other half he got from state funds."

"Did Eileen know what was going on?"

"Not until I took her to the hotel."

A sadness clutched Shana's heart, knowing Eileen had no idea what she'd gotten herself into. "When did this happen?"

"I took Eileen to the hotel the night of May 17th. She was already loaded, so I gave her a bottle of vodka and waited until Trevor Richmond arrived."

"How did you lure him there?" Shana knew from Trevor, but she wanted to hear it from Yates for the record.

"I called him and told him he'd find a tip about the senator at that hotel. That his wife could use it to help her campaign. When Richmond arrived, I knocked him out. Eileen kept waking up, so I just gave her some more booze. After I took the pictures, I dropped Eileen off in front of her house around 4:00 in the morning with the senator's briefcase full of cash. The senator was real pissed I left his briefcase with her. I left Richmond to fend for himself."

"When we questioned the senator, he said he lost his briefcase."

"I overheard his conversation. He wasn't going to admit what happened to it."

"Why did you attack me at my apartment?"

"The senator knew your reputation and you would dig deeper. When you and your sergeant left after questioning him, he was afraid you'd find out about his involvement with the photo blackmail scheme and taking $25,000 from state funds to pay off Eileen. I didn't want to lose my meal ticket, so I decided I would take care of you to protect him."

Shana crossed her arms on the table. "Did the senator order you to kill me?"

"No. I called him to get me bailed out and told him what I'd done at your apartment. He was mad. When you told me the senator killed himself...I lost it." He cleared his throat. "My attempt to kill you must have driven him over the edge. I'm really sad about that." Yates lowered his head and coughed. "He was good to me when I got out of the army. I couldn't get a job with my BCD and he hired me."

Yates's entire head and face dripped with perspiration and trickled into the corners of his eyes.

"Forensics found the mayor's bodily fluids in the senator's

trunk," Fits said.

"Hey, I didn't kill him," Yates blurted. "He had a heart attack at the senator's house after the broadcast."

"What time was that?"

"Around 11:00."

"We understand they argued that night," Shana said. "What about?"

Yates blinked the sweat away. "The mayor was the one who held the pictures of Eileen and Richmond. Senator Jenkins was fearful the mayor had information that would incriminate him and Vega about the photo blackmail. They fought, and the mayor took a poke at the senator. That's when the mayor had a heart attack."

"Why didn't you call 911?" Fits said.

"The mayor was dead, and the senator didn't want the publicity. So, I took the mayor to his home and planted him in his recliner to look like he died there."

"Wheel marks were found on the carpet in the mayor's den," Shana said.

Yates sneered. "I had to use an old wheelchair the senator had in his garage to get that fat slob into his house."

Shana sat back. "Did you know anything about an actress who was killed at The Royale Hotel in the city? She posed as the Detweilers' next-door neighbor."

"Don't know about her."

If Yates was at the senator's house at the time of the actress's murder, and all the other suspect's whereabouts were explained, then who killed her?

Shana continued, anxious for Yates to fill in the gaps to the case before he became too ill to go on. "You fit the description posing as a telephone repairman at the mayor's office the day they found him dead."

His breathing became shallow. "Vega and the senator wanted me to get those pictures from the mayor's safe and anything else the mayor had on them. But I didn't find anything."

She thought about the secret drawer. "What about Adam Detweiler?"

"Vega told me to threaten him with his wife's death, to keep him quiet about the tire problem. There were testing results that showed the formula was dangerous. Vega thought they were in the house. He suspected I already killed the wife and threatened to expose me, so I had to try to find it."

Shana shook her head. "Vega said the mayor told you to keep an eye on Adam."

"Of course, he did." Yates took several rapid breaths. "The mayor's dead. What do you expect? The mayor also called me. He must have known Vega told me to go to Adam's house. The picture blackmail scheme fell apart, and he wanted me to find the photo he sent to Adam."

"You did things for the mayor?"

"Hey, anyone who'd pay me." He coughed for several seconds. "Can I have more water?"

Shana motioned to the guard and waited until Yates took a gulp. "What happened to Adam on June 2nd?"

"I parked across the street in the back of the school, which was closed. I listened with my audio detector. Adam had called Richmond earlier that day. They didn't connect, but I suspected Adam already knew something happened to his wife and would reveal the information about the danger with the new tires. That would unravel everything, so I took matters into my own hands."

Yates let out a hacking cough, almost unable to stop.

"I think you need medical attention," Shana said.

He took in a breath. "I told you...I need to get through this."

Shana reluctantly agreed, but looked at Fits and nodded toward the door, knowing the paramedics were standing by. "Continue. What happened to Adam?"

Yates took a deep breath and coughed. "When I snuck in the

back door, I heard the water running upstairs. Adam was getting into the shower. I attacked him, we struggled, and he hit his head on the tub. He was barely conscious. I filled the bathtub so I could find out what I needed to know."

"So, you tortured him."

"Adam graciously told me he kept the photo in his nightstand."

That explained the position of Adam's nightstand when she searched the house after his death.

"What did you do next?" Shana said.

"Unfortunately, Adam didn't make it before I could find out where the test results were kept. I dressed him and put his body in the car in the garage, started the engine, and left."

"You had to know the autopsy would find the water in Adam's lungs," Fits said.

"Who knew you guys would show up. I saw the divorce papers in the nightstand drawer. I thought the local cops would think he committed suicide, especially if his wife's death was made public."

"Where is the photo now?" Shana said.

"It's taped on the back of the third oil painting of the French countryside going up the stairs in the senator's house. It was my insurance."

Yates took a breath in and slowly exhaled. He bent forward and let out a hacking cough that lasted for several seconds. "I need more water."

Shana motioned to the officer again who unscrewed the bottle and held it to Yates's mouth. When Yates took a sip tinted red water slipped out of the corner of his mouth onto the table. He noticed it and licked his lips.

"You need a doctor," Shana said.

"No." He coughed. "I'm fine. Let's go on."

"Okay…you told me at my apartment you had binoculars watching me enter my new code. I know now, based on the description we were given, you also watched me from a vacant apartment across from mine before you broke into my apartment."

He took rapid breaths.

"I was told you kept a disk with your personal notes on cases." He panted. "The mayor wanted me to find it. He was afraid you uncovered the photo blackmail scheme. As you know I didn't get it. Later I found out the mayor got it another way."

Shana snuck a glance at Fits. He nodded. She knew he thought of Briggs too.

Yates's face dripped with sweat. He swirled his tongue licking his lips. "Give me some more water."

Shana motioned to the officer. Yates's body shook hard. When the officer turned the bottle to Yates's mouth, water dribbled from the corners in bright red.

"You need to go to the hospital," Shana said.

"No. I don't have much time. There's someone else behind this." Yates slumped over. He struggled to catch his breath. "It's the same person Vega called on May 28th to take care of Eileen."

"He said he called you."

"Not true." His chest expanded and contracted with each heavy breath. "I was supposed to kill Vega...and I was going to handle it after I took care of you." In between breaths, he said. "I should have killed him first."

Shana shouted. "Fits, get the paramedics in here." She faced Yates. "Who is this other person?"

The paramedics entered, rushed to Yates, and tried to slip on an oxygen mask. He jerked his head away. With a final inhale, he passed out and dropped to the floor.

Shana motioned the officer to remove the handcuffs. She and Fits stood to the side while paramedics placed on the oxygen mask.

Yates's eyes opened a crack and motioned for Shana to come

close. She squatted next to him. He moved the mask away and wheezed for breath. With a faint whimper, he muttered...ask Vega. He let out a heavy exhale and his body fell limp.

The paramedic felt for a pulse. "It's faint. We need to get him to the hospital."

CHAPTER 78

June 13th, Sunday

SHANA AND FITS STOOD outside the interrogation room while the paramedics wheeled Yates out. She turned on her phone to check for messages. Philip left a voice mail. She played it.

I heard from my friend at the IRS. He said the account number belongs to an off-shore account in the Bahamas. I have more information. Meet me at the Messenger at 7:00 this evening. Check your email first.

She glanced at her watch. Almost 6:00. She pressed re-dial. It went straight to Philip's voice mail.

At this point, she didn't care if Fits knew her sources and relayed Philip's message. "I need to get to my desk."

Fits followed her, and she logged onto her computer. She clicked on her email from Philip. No message, just an attachment. Fits peered over her shoulder as she opened it.

"It looks like a transaction report from the off-shore account," Shana said. "The name on the account is Nicholas Vega and not the mayor's account like Vega led us to believe."

The original balance showed a deposit of $150,000 made two years ago, on June 20th, 1997. Shana quickly slid her notes disk into the computer and scrolled down her document to notes from Philip and Logan's brainstorming session.

Vega's inspection at the Messenger on June 1997. Grant settled it. How? Philip doesn't trust Vega.

"June 1997," she said. "I knew it."

"What's with the date?"

"Philip told me Grant settled a dispute with Vega during that time."

"Grant Harriman? He's the owner of the *Messenger*. You think he's involved in the murders?"

"If Grant was paying off Vega, how much more did he know or was involved with?" She flipped open her cell and tried Philip. No answer. She left him a message to wait for her. "Let's get Vega back up here. Now!"

Minutes later Fits escorted Vega to another interrogation room and directed him to sit across from Shana.

"Why am I here?" Vega cuffed hands clanked on the table. "I have a deal."

"It's not final yet," Shana said.

"What do you mean?"

She kept Yates's condition from him. "The ADA is holding your deal, because of information Dirk Yates provided about you."

"Whatever he said, he's lying," Vega said in his high-pitched voice.

"Yates told us you were involved in the murders. More than you let on. That piece of paper with the fifteen digits from the briefcase wasn't Mayor Gaffney's. It was your off-shore account in the Bahamas. If you want your deal finalized, you better tell us what else you may have kept from us."

Vega slumped in his chair.

"I mean it," Shana said.

"All right! I blackmailed Grant about a defect in the factory that didn't exist. When I told the mayor and the senator, they wanted a piece of the action and they also blackmailed Grant."

Shana thought back to the time frame of the factory blackmail. That must have been where the mayor got that

$75,000 in June 1997. "Why the off-shore account?"

"I was trying to keep it from my wife. Our marriage was on the rocks, and I expected we'd get a divorce. If she knew about the money, I would have to give her half. I just wanted to leave and sit on a beach somewhere."

Her rush to get Vega to talk made her pulse quicken. "According to Yates, you were the one who asked him to keep an eye on Adam on June 2nd and threaten him with his wife's life to keep the chemical secret. It wasn't Mayor Gaffney as you stated."

Vega rested his cuffed hands on his lap.

Shana continued. "And he claims you knew Eileen was dead when you asked him to do that."

"I suspected Yates killed Eileen, but I didn't know for sure. I called his bluff and then he confessed."

"Yates said you wanted him to find the test results from Adam."

Vega rested back. "I wanted the results so I could destroy them, just in case there were any disasters with the tires."

"You knew about the chemical defect?"

"Yes, but I didn't kill anyone."

"Another thing," Shana continued. "You knew where the money came from to pay off Eileen for those photos, didn't you? You were just as heavily involved in that blackmail scheme as the mayor and the senator."

Vega lowered his head. "I'm screwed."

"Looks like it," Fits said.

"We have the testing results Steve Heim conducted," Shana said. "There were several failed items on that report. You're damn lucky those tires were not put into production or you would have several counts of reckless endangerment added to your sentence. Yates said you were not the one who called him to take care of Eileen on the 28th. So, who did you call?"

"Grant Harriman. He's the one who called Yates."

"Why did you call him?" Fits said.

"I wanted to get Eileen out of TR Tires that night and Grant knew all kinds of people to take care of things. He wanted to know why I needed to hold her someplace, so I had to tell him about the tire problem. Then Yates arrived. What about my deal?"

Shana slanted her head. "You lied in your original interview and knew Yates killed Adam and Eileen. You're an accessory after the fact and you obstructed justice. No deal for you. What else is Grant involved with?"

"I don't know." Vega's voice squealed. "I swear."

Shana turned to Fits. "Get him out of here."

Fits called an officer to take Vega back to holding. She tried again to call Philip. Still no answer. Her stomach burned. "Fits, we need to get to the *Messenger.*"

CHAPTER 79

SHANA AND FITS RUSHED into the empty lobby of the *Messenger* building. She leaned over the front desk and called out. "Anyone here?"

Within a few seconds, a man in a security uniform stepped out from the office behind the desk. "Hey. What's going on?"

They flashed their badges.

"Did you see Philip Anderson here?" Shana said.

"Yes. He went up to see Mr. Harriman about a half-hour ago. I'll check his feed to see if they're still there."

"Feed?"

"Yeah. Mr. Harriman installed a security camera outside his office."

Shana tapped her hand on the counter while the guard viewed his screen.

The guard tilted his head. "That's strange. His camera feed is turned off."

She turned to Fits. "We need to get up there."

"Should I call Mr. Harriman?" the guard said.

"No!" Shana shouted. "What floor is he on?"

"The fourteenth. But you can't get there without a key."

Fits stepped to the counter. "If you have a key, you better hand it over."

The guard flinched and opened the drawer to his right. He pulled out a large ring with a square key. Fits snatched the key from the guard's hand.

"I'm not sure about this," the guard said. "Mr. Harriman doesn't like surprises. I need to call him."

"Don't call him!" Shana snapped. "You'll hinder a police investigation."

She and Fits ran to the elevator. Fits knocked over the out-of-order sign in front of the other elevator. Shana punched the up button repeatedly. The doors opened. Fits turned the key and pressed for the fourteenth floor. As the doors closed, the guard picked up the phone.

"Son-of-a-bitch," Shana said. "I bet he's calling Grant." She threw out her arm to stop the doors from closing and yelled out. "Put the phone down! Or face arrest for obstructing justice."

The guard hung up as the doors closed. Shana watched the digital numbers at the top of the elevator door rise, 2 ...3...4... "Shit, this will take forever."

She stared at the numbers, wondering why Philip would approach Grant on his own if that's who he suspected. Her heart pounded as she tapped the side of her leg. "Oh my God. Hurry." 9...10...11.

When they arrived on the fourteenth floor, the doors opened. Grant was dragging Philip's lifeless body toward the open elevator shaft. He dropped Philp, pointed his gun, and fired. Fits fell.

Shana aimed, but Grant fired again and shot Shana's gun from her hand. She grabbed her hand with her other. "Grant, you don't need to do this." She turned and saw Fits down. Blood soaked his shirt. "I need to tend to him."

"Stay still." He pointed the gun.

She cried out. "What did you do to Philip?"

"Never mind about him. I gather since you're here, you figured out everything?"

"We know all about how Vega, Mayor Gaffney, and Senator Jenkins were blackmailing you."

Grant's eyes were cold. He tightened his grip around the handle of the gun. "Those three were a thorn in my side, always contacting me for direction."

Shana turned around and saw Fits lying still, eyes closed. A large pool of blood had formed around his body. "Please let me check on my partner."

"He's gone."

She feared he was right. Praying she wouldn't be next, she continued hoping to keep Grant talking until she could find a way to overpower him.

"Dirk Yates confessed to the murders of Eileen and Adam Detweiler," she said. "And Vega told us he contacted you to get Yates to help take care of Eileen on May 28th."

Grant scoffed. "When Vega told me Eileen overheard him and Mayor Gaffney talking about a chemical defect in the tires and that Adam knew, I figured this was my chance to get something on them and stop the blackmail. Yates was supposed to hold Eileen someplace as a threat to Adam until the tires went into production. At least that's what Vega told me."

"Grant, why don't you give me the gun. We can talk this out."

He shook his head. "I didn't know Yates would kill Eileen. I swear. He called me after he did it. Said Eileen recognized him from some photo blackmail scheme and told me the details. Then he wanted me to give him an alibi."

Shana repositioned her hand and winced. "We know about the photos and who was involved. What about the actress, Natalie Portsmith, posing as Eileen and Adam's neighbor?"

"After you found Eileen's body, Yates told me Vega wanted him to watch Adam and make sure he didn't tell Trevor Richmond about the chemical defect. I was afraid something would happen to Adam, so I sent the neighbor on a vacation and hired Natalie to play the role to keep an eye on him. Unfortunately, Yates got to Adam before I had a chance to warn him."

"Warn him?"

"I didn't want anyone killed. After Adam was found, I instructed Natalie to steer your investigation toward the senator, by identifying Yates as the man who brought Eileen home in a limo. I hoped you would uncover the senator's involvement in the photo blackmail scheme. Knowing the senator, he would then implicate Vega and the mayor and then all my problems would be solved."

"Grant, one thing you didn't count on. Adam's parents were there when the limo brought Eileen home and they didn't see anyone get out, except Eileen."

Shana moaned and held her hand upright. "Did you kill the actress?"

"I had to. She wanted more money to keep her mouth shut. I lost it. I couldn't take another person bleeding me dry." His hand holding the gun twitched. "We're done here." He hesitated. "I'm sorry, Shana." He raised his arm and aimed.

She squeezed her eyes shut, taking a deep breath, thinking of her daughters and Mac. A shot rang out. She flinched and flipped her eyes open. Grant stared at her and dropped his gun. His hand clutched over his heart. Blood seeped between his fingers and he fell back into the open elevator. Within seconds a muffled thump echoed from the bottom of the shaft. She turned. Fits lay on his side, eyes shut, holding his stomach with one hand, blood everywhere. Gun in the other.

Shana knelt next to him. "Oh my God. Fits." She flipped open her cell with her good hand and pressed the speed dial for dispatch. "Officer down at the *Messenger* building, fourteenth floor." She dropped her phone and pressed both hands on his wound as she groaned in pain. "Help is on the way. You need to hang on."

He opened his eyes slowly and whispered. "Did I get him?"

"Yes. You did. Don't talk." She struggled to help him lay on his back with her good hand and painfully ripped off her jacket. Pressing it hard against his wound, she brought his hand to hold the jacket. "Can you hold this? I need to check on Philip."

Fits nodded.

She turned her attention to Philip fearing the worst. She knelt at his side and tried to prop him up, as she checked for wounds. The back of his head was bleeding. Her bloody hands felt for a pulse, leaving his neck smeared in red. "Philip. Philip. Can you hear me?"

He stirred and slowly opened his eyes. "Shana...it was Grant...He's—"

"I know."

CHAPTER 80

June 13th, Sunday

PARAMEDICS ARRIVED and rushed Fits out on a gurney while others tended to Shana's wounded hand and Philip's injuries. Within less than a half-hour, the fourteenth floor was like an anthill with the forensic team and other officers milling about.

Mac stepped off the elevator and rushed to her side. "Are you all right?"

She felt warm inside knowing he had concerns for her safety. She cradled her hand. "Other than this. I'm fine."

"You need to go to the hospital. From the looks of the blood-stained bandage, you'll probably need stitches."

"Seriously, Mac. I've had worse. Did you talk to the paramedics about Fits?"

"Yes. Saw them downstairs. It's pretty bad. What happened?"

Shana rattled off the events of the evening.

"Oh my God, Shana, you could have been killed."

"It's not the first time. And probably won't be the last." She glanced at the door into Grant's office. "I'm going to question Philip now. I promise after I'm finished, we'll both go to the hospital."

He tenderly touched her shoulder. "I have to go down and help Jonesy with the body. See you at the hospital."

She entered Grant's office where Philip sat on the circular couch.

"How you feeling?" Shana eased down beside him.

"I'm fine, I guess." He gazed out over the city. The lit buildings brightened the dark sky. "Funny. Grant said this view helped him keep his perspective on things. I don't think it helped."

She switched her gaze from the skyline to Philip. "You had a close call. Was it Grant you had in mind when you mentioned you suspected someone at our brainstorming session?"

"Actually no. It was the senator. But I didn't get a chance to do more investigating because of Ros's situation."

"Did you get my message to wait in the lobby?"

"Yes, but after I saw the transaction report from the off-shore account, I suspected Grant may have paid Vega off and I wanted to give him a chance to explain. I owed him that much. We've been friends for over twenty-five years. Besides, I was going to see him anyway to resign."

"Resign?"

"After you called and told me Ros was cleared, I took stock of my life and realized I needed to spend more time with my family."

Shana told Philip all that Yates and Vega confessed.

"So, the defect didn't exist." Philip gritted his teeth. "I knew I didn't trust Vega for a reason. It sounds like Eileen was in the wrong place at the wrong time, just like Ros was."

She continued and told Philip what Grant confessed while Philip was unconscious.

"He told me about the blackmailers as well." Philip reached the back of his bandaged head and moaned.

"You up for questions?" Shana said.

He nodded.

She pulled out her tape recorder and pressed record. "What did Grant tell you before we arrived?"

"Most of it you already know. But it was Grant who set up the account in California in the senator's name. He wanted to frame the senator and get the blackmail to stop. Grant thought an account out of state would look suspicious. So, he hired someone to pose as the senator and had it opened while the senator was at a conference in San Diego."

"Clever. Did he say how he got Denver and Brown to cooperate in the scheme?"

Philip massaged the back of his neck. "Damn my head hurts."

"Maybe we should do this later."

"No, I'm okay. Grant had information on the senior partner, that he tampered with evidence in an old case."

"Why was Grant after the senator? The mayor and Vega were also blackmailing him."

"Grant told me Vega, and the mayor accepted a lump sum as a blackmail payment, but the senator wanted his payoff monthly. Grant said it would never end. He also had Dylan install software on your computer to monitor progress on all the players in the case."

"So, Dylan did install software on my computer the day Eileen was found. How would Grant know to monitor the case? And what about Logan's deleted story?"

"Grant knew Logan and I keep detailed notes on stories in our shared directory. He got Dylan to give him access to our files to find out what he could on the senator. He stumbled on Logan's notes suspecting the body in the dumpster was Eileen. Grant knew Dylan also worked at police headquarters, so he got the idea to keep track of the case notes, hoping it would lead to the senator."

"Then he had Dylan delete the files? Why?"

"He wanted to delay the investigation to give us more time

to discover the money given to Trevor was a plant to hurt Madeline's campaign. Dylan wanted that internet job so bad, he did anything Grant wanted."

"I wonder where's Dylan now?"

"According to Grant, he gave Dylan enough money to last for a while and he left town."

She noticed her bandage had turned red and propped up her arm. "If Grant only confided in you about Vega's blackmail on the factory defect, all of this probably wouldn't have happened."

"You're probably right." He let out a deep breath. "Looking back, I should have suspected something was wrong with Grant. He wanted the paper to endorse Madeline, which we never do. Then he insisted I look into Senator Jenkins's finances, more than once. I also remember how Grant appeared annoyed when I told him the senator sent his regards. Now I know why." Philip shook his head. "I still can't believe my friend was so desperate that he resorted to murdering the actress."

"Sad when anyone resorts to murder. Anything else?"

"That's all I have. I'm feeling a little dizzy."

Shana stopped the recording. "Let's get you to the hospital."

"Grant liked you, Shana."

"Somehow that's not comforting."

A paramedic entered. He positioned the wheelchair next to Philip and turned to Shana. "Do you need one?"

"No. I'm good."

When they exited the building, the large *Messenger* sign flickered and illuminated the sidewalk. Patrol car's flashers spun. All the local news reporters were everywhere pushing microphones into everyone's face, anyone that would give them any information. Shana followed officers as they escorted the paramedic wheeling Philip through the crowd, shielding them from reporters. The paramedics helped Philip and Shana into the back of the ambulance. Logan approached. An officer rushed over to direct him to leave.

Shana nodded. "He can stay."

"What the hell happened here?" Logan said.

"I'll tell you at the hospital," Philip said. "Meet me there."

Other reporters with camera crews circled like vultures as Jonesy and Mac wheeled the gurney holding the full body bag out the front entrance and slid it into the coroner's van. Officers scurried over and directed the reporters to back away. The ambulance doors closed and drove off sirens blaring, taking Shana and Philip to the hospital.

Later after Shana contacted her daughters and her brother, fearing they would see her on the news, she rested on an emergency room bed waiting to be released. Her cell phone pinged. She struggled to flip it open with her good hand.

Sarge's nasal voice came over the phone. "Doyle. You all right?"

"Yes. Twenty stitches, but I'm okay. How about you?"

"Ten stitches on the side of my face. I'm home. Broken nose. They packed my nostrils up to my brain. I got an update from the lieutenant. How did you figure it out?"

Shana gave him the condensed version of how the information led to Grant.

"Good job. Looking forward to reading your report. Any word on Fits yet?"

"Not yet. I'll call when I know something."

"What about Yates?"

"He didn't make it. Passed away on the way to the hospital."

Mac entered and Shana ended the call. He reached for her good hand and held it tight. "You scared me, Shana. I'm so glad you're okay."

"How's Fits?"

Mac smiled. "He's going to be okay. Out of surgery. The bullet missed all his organs. Lucky guy."

She struggled to speak. "Thank, God. When I saw him lying

there with blood everywhere, I thought I'd lost him. Strange. He can pluck my nerves, but when it came down to it, he had my back."

Jules, Madeline, and Ros entered.

"What are you guys doing here," Shana said.

Ros stepped closer to the bed. "After Philip called me. I called Jules and Madeline."

Mac winked at Shana. "I'll come back."

Shana wouldn't let go of his hand. "I want you to meet my friends. Everyone, this is Mac."

Almost in unison, they responded. "Glad to meet you."

He returned the greeting and kissed Shana on the forehead. "I'll see you later."

"Mac, can you call Sarge and update him on Fits?"

"Sure." The door closed behind him.

"Good looking," Ros said.

Jules stood at the foot of the bed. "Looks like he's into you,"

Madeline grabbed Shana's good hand, "How are you, darling?"

Shana repositioned her injured hand. "I'm good."

Ros pulled up a chair and sat. "Philip told me what happened."

"How is he?" Shana said.

"A slight concussion, but the doctor said he'll be fine. He needed some stitches."

"Logan's with him," Jules said. "Getting a statement for a story, of course."

Shana smiled slightly. "Of course he is."

"I'm so glad you're okay," Madeline said. "I told Jules and Ros everything that's been going on with Trevor and his companies."

Ros teared up. "And I told them about the night I saw Eileen. Shana, I don't know how to thank you for clearing my name."

"I'm just glad it's over."

Jules stared at Ros and Madeline and then at Shana. "We have a bone to pick with you."

Shana raised her good hand. "Don't give me a lecture? Before you say anything, I'm sorry I haven't been around you guys that much."

"That's not what I was going to say," Jules said. "No lecture, just that we're your friends and will always be there for you."

Shana confessed what she had been doing since her parent's death and her shrink's transference neurosis diagnosis. "I'm going to go back to the psychiatrist. I guess I wasn't using my better judgment by ignoring you guys."

"There's a flaw in your judgment," Jules said. "You don't need to use *any* judgment with us. We're like your sisters. Can't get much closer than that. Family to the end."

CHAPTER 81

June 19th, Saturday

A WEEK LATER, Shana stood in front of the convention room at the Adam's Mark Hotel on City Line Avenue, waiting for her friends to arrive for Madeline's fundraiser. She stared at Madeline's poster for the event and chuckled knowing shopping may have saved her life. Thoughts about Adam's and Eileen's case flashed in her mind like a movie on fast forward. After all the evidence and confessions, even if she'd gotten Adam's calls in time, she knew now there was nothing she could have done to prevent his death. Yates would have gotten to him, anyway.

Her thoughts were broken, when Logan and Jules arrived. They hugged and complimented each other on their formal attire.

Logan adjusted his cummerbund under his tuxedo jacket and scoped the area. "Where's your date?"

"He'll be here soon." Shana adjusted the white glove covering her bandaged hand.

Logan smirked. "Is he going to show?"

Shana glared at Logan. "Yes. You'll see."

"Stop it, Logan," Jules said. "Oh, look. Ros and Philip are here." Her jaw dropped. "I don't believe it. Philip cut his hair."

Shana turned. "I can't believe it either."

"I lost the bet." Logan went to greet them.

"Bet?" Shana gave a quizzical stare.

Jules shook her head. "Oh, never mind. Something at the office. Ros looks happy. Glad things are back to normal."

"Me too." Shana stepped toward Philip. "Like the haircut."

Philip started to push the hair behind his ears then stopped. "I miss it. But with my new position as chief editor, I needed to look more professional."

"Congrats on the promotion," Shana said. "Is it true? Grant left the paper to you?"

"Weird but true. I have a lot of things to take care of, starting with making sure the factory is safe. We can't have any repercussions from the union."

Ros grabbed Philip's hand. "You'll get it worked out."

Shana faced Logan. "Anything in the wind for you to take Philip's job?"

"It was offered, but I'm still mulling it over. I enjoy being in the field. Not sure management is for me."

"I know what you mean," Philip said. "I miss it sometimes too, but you would be an excellent managing editor."

"Logan, your exclusive was well written," Shana said. "You wrote a nice tribute to Eileen and Adam. The money trail from Trevor's old firm and the photo blackmail made it clear Trevor was a political victim. Based on the polls, it doesn't look like that breaking news about Trevor hurt Madeline's campaign."

"Not sure who's going to run against Madeline yet. But with my story, I'm thinking she'll have the public on her side." He leaned and whispered to Shana. "Thanks for the exclusive."

"You're welcome. Wish you hadn't put in there about my expertise in deciphering cryptograms. I like to keep my hobby private."

He gave her a smug grin. "It made the story more mysterious, which my readers love about me."

Shana rolled her eyes. "So humble. You'd better behave when you meet Mac."

"I'll be extra nice." Logan winked.

Shana motioned for them to go in. "I'll see you after Mac arrives."

She stood in the back of the large room. The brass chandeliers provided a warm glow on each table. The silverware and crystal glasses sparkled, giving an air of sophistication. There must've been two hundred tables. This evening would gather a nice sum of campaign funds, surely more than enough to pay back the funds to Denver and Brown.

Shana scanned the table where her friends were sitting. The thought of being around them more often brought a smile to her face. She caught Mac out of the corner of her eye and turned. How handsome he looked in his black tux. Her heart fluttered. She inched close to him, brushing her body against his. He reached for her good hand and gently gave her a peck on the lips. She smiled.

He whispered. "You look great. How's your hand?"

She whispered back. "Stitches out on Monday."

"Can you introduce me to Trevor afterward? Oliver has some ideas on how to perfect the chemical compound."

The acting mayor stepped to the podium.

Shana raised a finger to her mouth. "Shush." She whispered. "I'll make sure you get to talk to him when this is over."

After Madeline was introduced, the crowd cheered. Shana grabbed Mac's hand, and they dashed to their table. The applause subsided. Madeline brought up the news story at the beginning of her speech. A standing ovation and a thunderous round of applause erupted. She choked up and reached for Trevor's hand. While the crowd sat, Madeline dove right into her campaign promises. At the end, she brought up her support for the Child Abuse Foundation. Madeline and Shana exchanged smiles. Shana joined the crowd in their vigorous applause, clapping her good hand on her other wrist as she blinked the tears away thinking about the abused eight-year-old girl she couldn't protect.

It was nearly 9:00 p.m. when the fundraiser ended, and the crowd thinned out.

Shana grabbed Mac's hand and together with all her friends, they made their way to Madeline and Trevor who were greeting people by the stage. She introduced Mac to Trevor. While they talked, Madeline pulled Shana aside.

"Darling, can you imagine." Madeline tilted her head slightly at Shana. "I received about a dozen phone calls asking me to support the Child Abuse Foundation."

"Really?" Shana gave her a sheepish grin.

"I wanted you to know I was planning on supporting them. Trevor and I both feel it's a worthy foundation."

"Thanks, Madeline. Your support will make all the difference."

"Shana, when you told us about Eileen's miscarriages, we wished Adam would have told us. Maybe there was something we could've done."

"We all feel that way."

Madeline gave Shana a tight hug. "I have to go and rub elbows with the politicians."

That was something Shana thought she'd never hear coming from Madeline's mouth. They joined Mac and Trevor.

"Everything okay?" Shana said.

Trevor nodded. "More than okay. Those original test results will give Mac's friend Oliver information to help fix the chemical reaction in the tires."

"You going to press charges against Paul Edwards?"

"No. I decided, there's enough publicity already going on with the money trail from the account in California that Grant set up. Besides, I got the word out. It will be a cold day in hell before Paul gets another job in this industry wherever he is."

Madeline wrapped her arm through Trevor's. "Come on

honey, we need to socialize with the acting mayor."

Moments later while Shana and her friends headed toward the hotel lounge for drinks, Logan turned to Mac. "Was your hair that white before you met Shana?"

There it was. Shana had to laugh as did everyone else, including Mac. How she missed this.

"I can tell you are true to your reputation," Mac said.

Logan smirked. "I couldn't resist. If I didn't make a smart remark, everyone would think I was sick. Didn't want to disappoint."

"Well, Logan," Jules said. "Can you try to disappoint just once?"

CHAPTER 82

Five months later
November 28th, Sunday

SHANA FUMBLED TO GRAB the ringing cell phone from her nightstand. She opened one eye to glance at the digital clock— 5:20 a.m. Trying not to move from her comfortable position under the covers, she pulled the phone to her ear and answered the call.

Ros sobbed on the other end.

Shana blinked to clear the sleep from her eyes. "Ros. What's wrong?"

"I can't believe it." Her voice cracked. "They found my cousin Anthony dead late last night…and the police are saying it was suicide."

Shana propped herself on one elbow. "Oh my God, I'm so sorry."

"I'm telling you my cousin didn't commit suicide." Her voice changed to strong, defiant. "I spoke with him the other night. He was so happy about taking his wife to Hawaii for a long-awaited honeymoon. You know him. No way he'd kill himself."

She thought back to when she first met Ros's cousin. Handsome, jet-black hair, green eyes, like something out of a Ralph Lauren photo shoot.

"Ros, calm down. I haven't seen him in years, so I wouldn't

know about his mental state."

"I need you to investigate this...*please*."

"Where did it happen?"

"In a sleazy motel in Philadelphia. Don't know the name. Not his style."

"If it's in the city limits, I can check it out when I get to headquarters. I'll call you as soon as I know anything."

"Thank you. I knew I could count on you."

Shana placed the phone back on the nightstand and slid under the warm covers, pulling them to her neck. She closed her eyes, wondering how she would handle this inquiry with Sarge. As if he didn't have enough of her friends in the Detweiler case. She felt a tug on the comforter as Mac caressed her naked body. She twitched when his whiskers tickled her shoulder with a gentle kiss.

He pulled away slowly, keeping his arm under her neck. "Is everything all right?"

She stared at the ceiling. "Don't think so. That was Ros. She's so upset. They found her cousin dead, and the police are calling it a suicide. She doesn't believe it."

"What are you going to do?"

"No sense going back to sleep now. I'll get dressed and go to headquarters. See what's going on."

"Who said anything about sleep?" Mac turned and brought her body close to his. He crept his kisses down her neck and whispered in her ear. "Are you sure you have to leave now?"

Shana smiled.

Note from Shana:

This Detweiler case was a difficult one for me. Not only because it involved longtime friends, but my investigation became more complicated with each passing day. Certainly, a case I'll never forget.

To bring you up to date, Nick Vega never got his deal and is serving a 25-year sentence. His legal fees ate up all the funds in his offshore account. Paul Edwards is nowhere to be found. Rumor has it Dylan Holden set up an IT self-help company in Aruba. Detective Briggs committed suicide. His life insurance policy covered his sister's back operation. And Steve Heim is now the head of the research department at RedChem.

I hope following my investigation helped unleash the sleuth in you. If you enjoyed reading about my recent case, please consider leaving a review on Amazon.com. Don't forget to access Karen Redman's website (karenredmanauthor.com) to sign up for her newsletter to be notified when my next case, involving another cryptic message, will be in print.

Shana

Shana Doyle
Detective, Homicide Division
Philadelphia Police Department

ACKNOWLEDGMENTS

For the many people who have supported me through my journey, thank you from the bottom of my heart.

To Thomas P. Lynch, Susan Lynch, Cathy Solomon, and Tom McMonagle, for taking the time to provide feedback that convinced me I was on the right track.

To Lisa Wroble, your early coaching gave me the willpower to continue.

To DiAnn Mills, for helping me become a better writer. Your insight and encouragement have meant the world to me and gave me the strength to bring my book to a conclusion.

To my longtime friends, whose personalities helped shape the characters in this book.

Last, but not least. A special thank you to Jim.

ABOUT THE AUTHOR

Karen Redman grew up outside the city of Philadelphia in the beautiful area of Montgomery County. She has enjoyed the many perks the city has to offer, thus the backdrop for her novel *Flawed Judgment*. Karen has been writing stories for twenty years and recently completed her first novel.

An avid reader of murder mysteries, she enjoyed putting pen to paper to deliver a mystery that will delight your senses and *unleash the sleuth in you.* She's retired and lives in Florida with her husband of thirty-plus years. When she's not writing, she enjoys playing golf and spending time with her large family, and friends.

Visit her online at karenredmanauthor.com to check out her social media links, and to view book club discussion questions. She would love to hear from you.

ABOUT THE SERIES

The first in the Shana Doyle Mysteries series is set in circa 1999, City of Philadelphia.

Shana Doyle, left a successful career to join law enforcement late in life and is the first and only female detective in the city's homicide division. She's earned top detective status due to her analytical process and expertise in deciphering cryptic messages and clues.

Shana's a strong independent woman with a bad marriage thirteen years behind her and two grown daughters on their own. She deals with an arrogant partner, her close group of friends of thirty years that always seem to have issues, a new romance, and an unresolved personal tragedy that gnaws at her.

Join Shana in her next murder investigation and learn how she unravels the case while dealing with overwhelming challenges in her life.

Made in the USA
Columbia, SC
15 February 2022

55967402R00238